BY CAROL GOODMAN

THE SONNET LOVER

THE SONNET LOVER

A NOVEL

CAROL GOODMAN

BALLANTINE BOOKS 🏛 NEW YORK

Copyright © 2007 by Carol Goodman

Published in the United States by Ballantine Books, an imprint of The Random House
Publishing Group, a division of Random House, Inc., New York.

BALLANTINE and colophon are registered trademarks of Random House, Inc.

ISBN 978-0-345-47957-0

Library of Congress Cataloging-in-Publication Data
Goodman, Carol.
The sonnet lover / Carol Goodman.
p.   cm.
ISBN-13: 978-0-345-47957-0 (acid-free paper)
1. Women college teachers—Fiction.   2. Florence (Italy)—Fiction.   3. Shakespeare, William,
1564–1616. Sonnets—Fiction.   I. Title.

PS3607.O566S67 2007
813'.6—dc22   2006036111

Printed in the United States of America on acid-free paper

www.ballantinebooks.com

9 8 7 6 5 4 3 2 1

First Edition

Book design by Carol Malcolm Russo

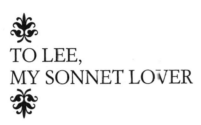

TO LEE,
MY SONNET LOVER

ACKNOWLEDGMENTS

I'd like to thank my editor, Linda Marrow, for her always insightful editing and my agent, Loretta Barrett, for her encouragement and support. Thanks, also, to all those at Ballantine whose hard work and belief in me made it possible for me to write this book: Gina Centrello, Libby McGuire, Kim Hovey, Brian McLendon, Gene Mydlowski, Lisa Barnes, Dana Isaacson, and Daniel Mallory. Thanks, too, to Nick Mullendore and Gabriel David at Loretta Barrett Books.

I'm grateful to my circle of first readers: Barbara Barak, Laurie Bower, Connie Crawford, Gary Feinberg, Emily Frank, Marge Goodman, Lauren Lipton, Beth Lurie, Andrea Massar, Wendy Gold Rossi, Scott Silverman, and Sondra Browning Witt. Special thanks to Beth Lurie, Director of the Beth Lurie Language Institute, who gave invaluable assistance in providing and correcting Italian phrases in the book—and for teaching me how to order a cup of coffee in Italy! Thanks, too, to Andrew Cotto for consultation on Italian food and wine, and Bennett Nayer for research assistance.

Most of all, this book couldn't have been written without the poetic talent and vision of my husband, Lee Slonimsky. All of the sonnets attributed to Ginevra de Laura in this book were written by Lee. I couldn't have written a book about poetry without his poems; I couldn't have written a book about love without his love.

THE SONNET LOVER

CHAPTER ONE

T HE MOST THANKLESS JOB ON THE PLANET MAY WELL BE TEACHING RE-naissance love poetry to a group of hormone-dazed adolescents on a beautiful spring day. I had saved up against just such a day, through the deep snows of February, the sleets of March, and April's endless deluge, one of the most popular and accessible of Shakespeare's sonnets, but I might as well have been reciting the Dow Jones Industrial Average for all the impact the Bard's words were having on the class. Even Robin Weiss, my best student, was more interested in the sunbathers and Frisbee players cavorting five stories below us in Washington Square Park than in answering my last question.

"I'm sorry," he says, his eyes still on the sun-splashed scene outside the window. "Could you repeat the question?"

"I asked what you thought of Shakespeare's promise to his beloved to immortalize him through art."

"Hmph." Robin begins by ejecting a disdainful breath of air. "I think of it the way I think of most lovers' promises, that he 'speaks an infinite deal of nothing.' "

A chorus of sighs from the girls in the back row greets Robin's pronouncement. Had they all had their hearts broken recently? I wonder. Perhaps by Robin himself? Weren't they a little young to be giving up on love? But then I remember that this is exactly the age that feels love's disappointment the most keenly, the age when one might forswear love, never guessing there might come a day when one is forsworn by love.

"So you don't think that art provides immortality?" I ask, unwilling to let Robin hide behind the world-weary pose he's worn, along with a vintage Versace tweed jacket lined in yellow silk, since returning from the fall semester in Florence. I still remembered the fervor he'd had in Freshman Comp. He was going to be a playwright because, he said, to have your words spoken on the stage after your death meant you'd never truly be dead. I knew he'd switched his ambition to filmmaker since then and had spent his time in Italy making a film that the whole campus was talking about. In fact, tonight it was to be shown at the Hudson College Invitational Film Show, where it was expected to win first prize. Was Robin already jaded by success?

Turning from the sun toward me, though, his face looks not so much jaded as *bruised.* His pale blue eyes are dilated and bloodshot, his full lips are chapped and swollen, and his delicate skin is chafed and raw. His sandy brown hair looks as wild as the signature Medusa heads on the buttons of his jacket. I'm used to my students looking haggard around finals time, but Robin looks as if he'd spent the last week weeping. I would happily let him off the hook—especially since I can tell by the shuffling of books and shouldering of backpacks and by my watch, which lies on the desk in front of me, that the class's hour is drawing to an end—but Robin chooses to answer my question with a question. Or rather, two questions.

"If you lost someone you loved, would reading something about him—or by him—lessen the loss one iota? Wouldn't you trade all the poems and all the plays in all the world for just five minutes with him again?"

"Well," I begin, intending to deal with Robin's questions as I usually deal with difficult—or in this case, unanswerable—questions in class: by turning it back to the student. Maybe even assigning it as an essay topic. But Robin is looking at me as though he really expects an answer. As if he'd been offered this Faustian bargain last night at the Cedar Tavern and there's a sinister-looking man in a dark overcoat waiting in the hall for his answer. All of literature for five minutes with your lost beloved? Even the class's incipient rustling, which should have swept us all out of here like a late November rainstorm cleaning out the dead leaves, has been stilled by Robin's urgency.

"Five minutes?" I ask. As if I could bargain. Get in on the deal.

Robin nods, the ghost of a smile curving his chapped lips, reminding me of someone else whose lips used to curve in that same Cupid's bow.

"Sure," I say, blushing at the memory of that other mouth, "who wouldn't?"

There's another class in the same room after ours, so there's no lingering. In the hall I answer a few of my students' questions about the final and the term paper and explain, riding the elevator down to the lobby, that my regular office hours are suspended today because of the film show and reception tonight. When the elevator reaches the ground floor the students quickly disperse, and I'm surprised to see Robin, who had bolted out of the class after I answered his question, still in the lobby. It's been a while since he's waited for me after class. I'm even more surprised to see him in conversation with a young man who might have sprung from my Faustian fantasy of ten minutes ago—right down to the black sheepherding overcoat and sinister expression. The boy turns his face to the light and I'm startled both by how handsome he is—his finely modeled features like a white marble bust of a Greek god framed by blue-black ringlets—and by something *familiar* about him. No doubt he's a drama major whom I've seen in a student play. He certainly seems to have a flair for the dramatic as he replies angrily to something Robin says, shakes his fine head of hair, and then sweeps out of the lobby, the tails of his coat floating behind him.

For a moment Robin looks as if he were considering following him, but then he sees me. "I know you don't have office hours, Dr. Asher," he says, "but could I walk with you a minute?"

"As long as you don't ask any more soul-searching questions," I say, preceding Robin through the revolving doors. Although it's late in the afternoon, the light is so bright that I have to fish in my bag for sunglasses. When I've gotten them on, I see by Robin's downcast expression that he's taken my remark seriously.

"Oh, no, you *do* have another soul-searching question. Well, ask away, but try to remember that I'm old, Robin, and such urgent questions of love are a little less urgent these days."

"You're hardly old—" he begins, but I wave my hands in the air to stop him. God, had I been fishing for a compliment? Had I—even worse—been flirting?

"Actually, that's what I wanted to ask you ab-bout," Robin says, stuttering a little on the last word. I haven't heard Robin stutter since first semester freshman year, when he started taking voice and acting classes. It must be the film show tonight that has him so nervous. "You're . . . what . . . in your mid-thirties?"

"Thereabouts," I say, thinking, *Close enough.* No need to tell him that at thirty-nine I'm at the bitter end of my thirties. "Why?"

"Because you were at La Civetta when you were in college and I wondered if some of the same teachers were there. I'm going back there this summer and I'm trying to decide what classes to take."

We've reached Graham Hall, the nineteenth-century brownstone that houses the comp lit department and my office. The building is named for Hudson College's most famous alumnus, Cyril Graham, who donated his New York townhouse to the college, along with the use of his villa in Tuscany, La Civetta, four decades ago. There's a plaque with Cyril's profile etched in bronze beside the front door, and as I turn to answer Robin's question (making it clear, I hope, that he shouldn't follow me up to my office), I can almost feel the old man's hawklike eyes boring into my back.

"Well, let's see," I say, pretending that the year I spent at La Civetta twenty years ago is such a distant and minor episode that I have to ransack my memory in order to recall its dramatis personae. "The old man himself was there, of course," I say, cocking a thumb over my shoulder at the plaque, "teaching that class . . . what did he call it?"

"The Aesthetics of Place," Robin says, smiling.

"My God, is he still at it? Does he still go on about the Mitford sisters and the Duchess of Windsor?"

Robin smiles and looks a little more relaxed. "He manages to imply he went to Oxford with both Oscar Wilde *and* Evelyn Waugh—a chronological impossibility—and was simultaneously lunching with Fellini on the Via Veneto while making silk screens with Warhol at the Factory—a geographical impossibility."

I laugh, relieved to see that Robin's stutter has disappeared again. The remarks about Cyril Graham sound like a set speech. Even his pose—one hand grasping the lapel of his vintage jacket so that the sun glances off its gold Medusa-head buttons—looks rehearsed. I suspect that Robin, like many a stutterer before him, has learned that his delivery is improved by rehearsal. "I have to admit that I enjoyed that class. It was such shameless gossip and a rest after declining Latin nouns with Harriet Milhouse and memorizing Renaissance architectural terms with Professore DelVecchio."

"I think they've retired," Robin says, "but I would have thought the class you'd mention first would have been the one on the sonnet—"

"Oh, but the professor who taught that class was a graduate student," I say, perhaps a little too quickly—as if I'd had my excuse for not mentioning him ready. "He went back to Rome the next year to finish his degree."

"Bruno Brunelli, right? He's back. His wife, Claudia, took over the job of hospitality coordinator from Bruno's mother, Benedetta, only in Claudia's case it's really a misnomer—"

"Oh, really? I didn't know." I hold up my wrist to check the time but my watch isn't there. "Damn," I say, "I must have left my watch in class." I always take my watch off in class and lay it on the desk so that I can keep track of where I am in my lecture without having to look at my wrist. I've never left it behind, though. Had Robin's question rattled me that badly?

"I'll run back for it," Robin offers gallantly. "Will you be at the film show?"

"Of course, Robin, I wouldn't miss your opening night, but please don't bother—"

"Then I'll give it to you there," he says, brushing away my objections, "and we can talk some more? There's something really important I have to discuss with you."

"If I can get through your flock of admirers after your film is shown, I'll be happy to talk to you." The shadow that had been over him in class is back—or perhaps it's just that the spring light is fading from the sky, leaving us both in the shade of the brownstone.

"I might need rescuing from an angry mob instead. The film isn't going to be what everyone expects."

"That's just opening-night jitters, Robin. I'm sure it'll be great."

"But even so, will you?"

"Will I what? Rescue you?"

Robin lays his fingertips on my wrist—in just the place laid bare by my missing watch—and I shiver at his touch. The spring day's promise of summer has faded to chill evening. I start to laugh at the absurdity of Robin's request, but when I see the look in his eyes I don't.

"Of course," I tell him, "I'll do my best."

I carry the chill of Robin's touch up three sweeping flights of the main staircase and one back-stairs flight to the garret (formerly a maid's room) under the eaves that's been my office for the six years I've taught at Hudson College. Mark Abrams, the college president, has offered to relocate me to the new faculty building on Mercer, where I'd have elevator service, high-speed Internet access, and German coffee machines perking finely ground Colombian coffee all day long. But I prefer my little garret with its egg-and-dart moldings and nonworking fireplace. Besides, I have my coffee at Cafe Lucrezia on MacDougal, which has two working fireplaces and makes the best cappuccino this side of the Atlantic.

I wish, though, as I open the door, that I'd run in for a cup on the way here, because the office, with its blinds closed all day against the spring sunshine, feels cold. An unaccountable sadness stirs in me—as if I'd missed something by closing out that light from my dusty bookshelves and faded green upholstered Morris chair—and pulls me across to the window to open the blinds before turning on the desk lamp.

The Graham brownstone is on the west side of the park and the sun has already passed over its roof, but I can still see the last of the light reflected on the old townhouses that line the north side of the park, turning the sooty New York bricks to a rich Florentine ochre. I close my eyes to preserve that Mediterranean color for one moment longer and feel, where I'd felt chill before, the warmth of an embrace spreading across my back.

"You've got to stop letting yourself in," I say, turning into Mark's arms. "I'm going to scream one of these days and the secretaries in comp lit will come running."

"We'd just have to explain that you were reacting to departmental budget cuts. You wouldn't be the only one screaming about that."

I'm about to register my concurrence with my colleagues but Mark kisses me, pressing the length of his body against mine so tightly that I feel the wide ledge of the window cutting into the small of my back. I ease myself onto the ledge, pulling away from his kiss.

"I wish all my faculty were so easily persuaded to see the necessity of cutting back," he says.

"I certainly hope you don't use the same persuasive techniques on them," I say, leaning lightly onto the cold windowpane behind me. I imagine that one day I'll lean back a little too hard and the two of us will crash through the glass and hurtle to the pavement below, where we will land, limbs entwined, below the amused bronze gaze of Cyril Graham. This is where we made love the first time, three years ago, after a faculty party, and even though I live only two blocks away and Mark's apartment is only a short subway ride uptown, we've made love here many times since then. It's the risk, I think, of someone discovering us that still draws us here. Mark had thought then that we should keep our affair secret—at least until I made tenure. At first I'd been suspicious that he wanted to keep the relationship secret only because he didn't intend to stay in it, but he's been (as far as I can tell) a faithful lover for three years. Only lately, as my tenure review looms near, have I found myself wondering whether half the pleasure in our affair comes from that enforced secrecy, and half the pleasure in making love here from feeling that cold glass barrier, hard but fragile, always at my back.

Mark brushes the hem of my dress halfway up my thigh, but I catch his hand. "Don't you have a speech to give in, like . . . ten minutes?"

He makes a face but quickly smooths my dress back over my leg—a little too compliantly, I think.

"Is this what you're wearing to the reception?" he asks, taking a step back to observe my outfit—and also to give me room to get down from the window seat.

"That's the plan," I say, moving past him toward my desk. I slip out of the jacket I wore to class and slide the silk scarf from around my neck to reveal a sleeveless black cocktail dress that I found in a vintage clothing store on Horatio Street last week. Then I sit down at my desk and turn to the mirror I keep propped up on the bookcase between the collected *canzoniere* of Petrarch and Helen Vendler's book on Shakespeare's sonnets. Mark sits on the windowsill and lights a cigarette—another vice he saves for my company alone even though I've managed to quit—while I let my hair down and start to brush it.

"You should wear it down," he says when I start to coil it back into a twist. "The color is so pretty—like a Botticelli madonna." He smiles at his own compliment, proud, I think, that he's recalled my favorite painter.

"Why this sudden concern for my appearance?" I ask, leaning a little closer to the mirror to see whether he's right—whether the color is still more gold than silver. It is, but only just. I still look fairly young (*mid-thirties,* Robin had said) but for the tiny lines at the corners of my eyes and the light silvering around my temples. "It's just the student film show."

"Some of Cyril Graham's Hollywood cronies are coming and they're sure to report back to him. It wouldn't hurt to make a good impression."

"That will be good for Robin Weiss," I say, ignoring the idea that anyone from Hollywood would be interested for two seconds in a forty-ish English professor, "to have his film seen by people in the industry."

"I'm pretty sure that's why they're here. Graham told them the film was done on the grounds of the villa and he expected from what he saw of the filming that it would be quite interesting—and there's even talk of a major film being made at La Civetta based on a screenplay Robin's written."

I frown into the mirror—instantly aging my face several years—remembering what Robin had said. *The film isn't going to be what everyone expects.* "Well, I hope it's not too much pressure on Robin," I say. "He looked ragged in class today."

"Don't you think that you're perhaps too emotionally involved with your students?" Mark asks.

I angle my mirror so that I can see Mark's expression—or rather, more important, to see whether he's watching *my* expression. To see whether what he's really concerned about is my emotional involvement with *this* particular student. Three years ago, when Mark and I first found our way back to my office after that faculty party, Mark had expressed his professional concern that I'd become overly familiar with Robin Weiss. I'd been seen having coffee with him at Cafe Lucrezia and he spent a lot of time in my office.

"I wouldn't worry," Mark had said then as we climbed the back stairs to my office, "except that it would be natural for a boy to have a crush on a such a beautiful woman."

The compliment had taken me by surprise. Not because I didn't think a man could find me beautiful, but because Mark Abrams had struck me as too serious a man to bother with compliments. I knew he was very ambitious for the college, that he planned to transform Hudson College into a premier liberal arts institution. Like a lot of my colleagues, I had not always been happy about how he was going about achieving that goal—deferring money from more traditional academic departments to the more high-profile film department, for instance. I had become so used to thinking of him as an adversary in departmental meetings that I hadn't considered him as a prospective suitor.

When I had let myself into the office I crossed to the window ledge, where I sat down and lit a cigarette (I still smoked then). Instead of reminding me of the no-smoking rule, he crossed the room and, letting his hand rest on mine for a moment, took the cigarette out of my hand and raised it to his lips.

"Maybe," I said, watching him inhale. His lips were a trifle thin— no Cupid's bow—but he had a strong jaw and the kind of clean-cut features that aged well. An undeniably handsome man. "But would it be natural for a woman my age to be interested in a boy?"

He didn't answer. I'm sure he thought it was a rhetorical question and that the way I pronounced *boy* was meant as a disparaging comparison with the charms of an older man. He tossed the cigarette out the window and kissed me, pushing me onto the windowsill until I felt the cold glass at my back. He never asked me about Robin Weiss again, but I've often wondered whether it's ever occurred to him that I never answered *his* question, that I merely turned it back on him the way I did with my students.

He doesn't appear to be thinking about that now as he stands at the window, one hand in his trouser pocket rumpling the line of his good gray wool suit, one hand still holding the cigarette, which has nearly burned down to the filter. He's looking out over the park, toward the NYU buildings on the east side, their violet flags glowing in the late spring sunshine. He looks like a general surveying a neighboring kingdom and planning his attack. He doesn't appear to notice that I haven't answered his latest question, either. He flicks his cigarette out the window and comes up behind me, resting his hands on my shoulders. "You need a vacation," he says, massaging the tight muscles.

I glance at my own reflection in the mirror to gauge my expression. The last time Mark and I discussed the summer, we decided (or rather, Mark suggested and I agreed) that we should spend it apart. After all, my tenure review was coming up in September. Why risk anything now? Had he changed his mind? Did I want him to have changed his mind?

"I'm taking one," I tell him as I apply a coat of mascara to my eye-lashes. "Six weeks at the cabin in Woodstock, where I plan to finish the sonnet book."

"That's not a vacation," he says, "that's hard labor."

"Surely you're not discouraging a faculty member from publica-tion, President Abrams," I say teasingly.

But Mark doesn't laugh. "Actually, I have a better place for you to work, a place a little closer to the birthplace of the sonnet . . ."

"Sicily?" I ask. "If you mean the court where Giacomo da Lentini was employed—"

"I meant Italy in general," he says, sounding impatient, "and La Civetta in particular. Graham says he's got some very important sixteenth-century manuscripts—"

"Cyril Graham is a crank, Mark, you know that. He's spent the last twenty years dangling the promise of 'very important' manuscripts in front of half a dozen different academic institutions to raise interest in that moldering old villa of his so that he'd be sure to spend his twilight years surrounded by eager young scholars."

"That moldering old villa, as you call it, has been estimated to be worth nearly a billion dollars," Mark says, "and crank or not, Graham is on the verge of bequeathing it to Hudson College . . . unless he changes his mind and chooses another institution. There's a rumor he's been talking to one of the SUNYs—"

"Ah," I say, swiveling in my chair to face Mark. "Cyril's playing coy with his will again. I thought all the papers had been signed—"

"Some complications have come up and it looks like I'll have to spend the summer—along with one of our lawyers—at La Civetta."

"Poor baby," I say, pursing my lips. "Most of the professors are fighting tooth and nail to spend the summer there. I hear Frieda Main-bocher in women's studies had a fit when she learned Lydia Belquist in classics was going to teach the Women in Italian History class this sum-mer."

"I solved that by making them co-teach the class," Mark says. "So that's who I'll have for company over there if you don't come: Lydia, Frieda, and the drama department. I thought that if you could work on your book there we'd get to spend some time together, but if you'd rather be alone . . ." The look of hurt on Mark's face makes me instantly regret teasing him. Clearly he wants us to spend the summer together, and I would, too—just not at La Civetta.

"I don't think I'd be any help with Graham," I say. "He wasn't happy with me when I left."

"Really? He speaks quite fondly of you. He said he's been reading your sonnets in *The Lyric* and was quite impressed."

"Oh, please," I say swiveling back to the mirror to put on my lipstick—and to hide the blush of pleasure the compliment has caused. "Cyril hasn't read anything but *Debrett's Peerage* and *Town & Country* in decades."

"Then someone must have shown them to him," Mark says, rubbing my shoulders again. His right hand drifts from my shoulder down the front of my dress, but I'm finding it hard to focus because I'm replaying the professors Robin Weiss said were in residence at La Civetta. There's only one whom I can imagine subscribing to *The Lyric*.

"No," I say, laying my hand over his before it reaches my breast, "I'm afraid you'll just have to make do with Lydia and Frieda. I can't possibly go."

CHAPTER TWO

ARK LEAVES BEFORE ME, TAKING THE BACK STAIRS TO AVOID ANY LINGER-ing secretaries in comp lit. We've joked that those stairs have probably accommodated any number of Graham men after clandestine visits to the maids—but we don't joke tonight. He's not happy that I haven't agreed to his idea of going to La Civetta. He must have thought I'd be happy to spend the summer with him. And I would be if he had chosen anyplace else. Unfortunately, I can't explain that to him.

I exchange the flats I wore for teaching for a pair of high-heeled sling backs and the conservative suit jacket I wore earlier for a cashmere wrap. I take the main staircase down, three grand curving flights that always make me feel as if I'm a heroine in a nineteenth-century novel. Tonight I feel like Lily Bart in *The House of Mirth* when she finally decides to accept Sim Rosedale's offer of marriage only to discover that the offer's been downgraded to mistress. I feel, in other words, as if all the compromises I thought of as desperate measures have turned out to be made to no avail.

Half the park is already in shadow as I cut across it, but when I reach the center I find a patch of sun warming the statue of Garibaldi just past the fountain and decide to sit there for a moment on its base to collect my thoughts before going to the film show. There are more comfortable benches close by, but I've always been fond of the statue—a reminder of the neighborhood's Italian community. Besides, the granite, having soaked up the day's sun, feels comfortingly warm. Leaning against it, I remember that when the statue was moved in 1970 a glass vessel was discovered in the base containing newspaper clippings about Garibaldi and the dedication of the statue. Another thing I like about the statue. It reminds me that hidden messages may be embedded in impervious stone.

I wonder how many of the students gathered in the dry basin of the central fountain even know who Garibaldi was. The girls, who had unpacked their thrift store summer dresses for the first time this year, are shivering now under denim jackets and college sweatshirts, many of them in NYU's violet, but quite a few in Hudson College's blue and gold. Hudson's not entirely a newcomer to the neighborhood. The Graham brownstone has housed a small portion of the college since the sixties, when the college opened as an alternative liberal arts college. Along with the New School, the School of Visual Arts, Pace, and Baruch, it's carved out a small niche for itself in the downtown landscape dominated by NYU, often taking the overflow of artistically minded students drawn to the city. Then, five years ago, the college received a large donation from Cyril Graham to start a film program and a promise that at his death Graham's Tuscan villa, along with its valuable art and rare manuscript collection, would be given to the college as a center for film and the performing arts.

Such an influx of wealth into a small academic institution was bound to create friction as well as opportunities. I myself have wondered what place a specialist in the Renaissance sonnet would have at

Hudson among the glittering new cast of film directors and acting teachers who had swept into the school. I also couldn't help noticing that the type of student drawn to Hudson College was changing. I had more drama majors than English majors these days, more actors than scholars, and more would-be screenwriters than would-be poets.

Of course, college-age kids are dramatic to begin with, but it has seemed to me lately that there's an element of performance in everything this latest crop does. Right now my eye is drawn to a girl with long frizzy hair streaked with bright raspberry dye who is balancing on the rim of the fountain as if it were a circus tightrope while she narrates a story to a group of admirers crouched below her. She's dressed in the standard navel-baring jeans, but hers ride so low that I can make out her bare hip bones. When a particularly expansive gesture offsets her balance, several boys are there to steady her. I notice that one of the boys is Robin and that the girl manages to time her fall so that she lands, shrieking, in his lap.

I find myself smiling at her exuberance and then sighing. Perhaps I'm concerned about the direction Hudson is moving in because it seems to be moving *away* from me, because I'm beginning to feel old when I look at my students. Maybe I'm just jealous. I glance once more at Robin and his pink-haired girlfriend and resolve to enjoy the sight instead of resenting it, but then I notice that I'm not the only one watching them—and this observer is definitely *not* watching them with a friendly eye. He's leaning against a fence on the far side of the fountain, his long dark coat merging with the late afternoon shadows. It's the same boy I saw talking with Robin earlier. Again I think he seems familiar and yet surely I'd remember that Greek profile and that full, mobile mouth (shaped now into a pained grimace) if I'd seen him before. As he pushes himself off the gate and walks toward Robin I feel a sudden urge to move forward to intercept him before he reaches the fountain, but it's the pink-haired girl who jumps up and places herself in between Robin and the stranger.

"What are you doing here, Orlando?" I hear her ask.

"I am here to talk to Robin, Zoe," he answers in an accent that might be Italian or Spanish, "about something he's stolen from me."

I can see from here—without realizing it I've left Garibaldi and moved closer to the fountain, drawn by the scene being played out by the three young people—that Robin's face has turned as pink as his friend Zoe's hair, but when he opens his mouth to answer the charge, he's not able to get past the first syllable.

"Th-th-th-," he sputters.

Zoe reaches her arm behind her to stop Robin from coming closer and answers for him. "You're just jealous, Orlando." Turning to Robin, she adds, "Ignore him; no one will believe him for a second. Come on, the film show's about to start and you're the star."

Robin and Zoe turn and start walking toward the auditorium on the south side of the park, leaving the boy—*Orlando,* I think, *what a perfect name for him!*—staring spitefully at their backs. They look like such a perfect image of young love—moving through a drift of petals fallen from the park's Bradford pear trees—that I can't blame him for feeling jealous. I feel a pang myself, watching Robin stop and stoop to the ground, scoop up a handful of petals, and toss them at his companion, who playfully careens into him, clutching his jacket for balance. Orlando pauses on the same spot and kneels to the ground as if he wanted to absorb that moment, but then as I pass by him he stands up, slipping a few petals into his pocket, and calls to me.

"Scusa," he says, his accent now clearly recognizable as Italian, "you are the *professoressa* of Robin?"

"Yes," I tell him, trying not to smile at his name for me. Leave it to the Italians to make a dry academic title sound like the honorific of nobility. "I work here at Hudson. Are you a student here?" As we approach the south side of the park I'm looking around for a police officer or campus security guard. There's something unnerving in this boy's manner that has set my nerves tingling.

"No, I go to university in Florence. I met Robin there at the American school at La Civetta, where my father teaches. I think you may know him, my father, Bruno Brunelli?"

I stop three feet from the sidewalk and turn to face him, searching for the resemblance to Bruno in his face, but while this boy looks like a statue of a Greek god, I'd always thought his father's profile was a little craggier—more like that of a Roman senator. No, the reason Orlando looks familiar is because he looks like his mother. "Yes, of course," I say, "I took your father's class on the Renaissance sonnet when he was still a graduate student. He was a wonderful teacher . . . and a wonderful poet. Does he still write?"

Orlando laughs and his face is transformed from the mask of anger he'd assumed a few minutes ago while watching Robin and Zoe to something so much softer that I wonder whether I'd imagined the previous look. But then his father was also very good at assuming a mask. "Not so much anymore. My father always says, oh, how do you say it in English? *Non vale la pena?*"

"Not worth the pain," I translate. Yes, I remember Bruno using that expression, but I had never imagined him using it about poetry. "And how is your mother?" I ask. "I heard she was the hospitality coordinator at the villa." A *misnomer*, Robin had said, but of course I don't repeat that.

"Yes, she took over the job when my grandmother died."

"I was sorry to hear about your grandmother. It's hard to imagine La Civetta without her." This is true. Benedetta Brunelli, Bruno's mother, had no academic standing, but she had come to La Civetta during the war when she was a young girl, first as Lady Graham's private secretary and then, when the villa was turned into a school, as the hospitality coordinator. She'd managed everything, including the vegetable gardens, where she grew the tomatoes and herbs for the kitchen, and the olive groves, which still produced the villa's cooking oil. I remember that her hands—she would often give you a little pat on the face, cooing *"Que facia bella!"*—felt like satin, softened by years of pressing olive oil. She had made the villa feel like a home. It's hard to imagine Claudia in her place.

"*Sì,*" Orlando answers, his expression turning dark again, "she was the real mistress of La Civetta, but like most Americans Cyril Graham takes what he wants and never thinks to share. Like Robin. All the time I work on the film with him and I never guess what he is doing . . . that he is stealing . . .”

"Are you accusing Robin of plagiarism?"

Orlando shakes his head, making his dark ringlets tremble, and furrows his brow. “Plagiarism?” he says, pronouncing the word with difficulty. “I am not sure what this means. Does it mean to steal?”

"Well, it means to steal someone else's words."

"*Sì, sì,* he's stolen words and told lies. Someone must help me . . .” Orlando's voice is agitated again. I look around for help and see with relief that Mark is standing at the entrance to the auditorium, just across the street.

"The president of the college is right over there," I say, putting my hand on Orlando's arm to steer him across the street. “If you have any concerns about the eligibility of Robin Weiss's entry in the film show, he's the man to talk to.”

I'm relieved to see that Mark has caught sight of me, but then I see his face darken as he notices my companion. I've only wanted to make him aware of a potential disturbance to the show, but I'd forgotten how jealous Mark can get. It's flattering in a way, but right now I just want Mark to know that this boy isn't some lovestruck student of mine—he's potential trouble.

"President Abrams," I say as Mark makes his way toward us, “I think you should have a word with this young man. He has some concerns about one of the films.” I extend my arm to usher Orlando forward, and as soon as he's in front of me, I mouth the word “trouble” to Mark. Mark responds with an almost imperceptible nod, but it's enough for me to see he's taken my meaning and will handle it. The face he turns to Orlando is calm and concerned, but firm. It's one of the things I admire most about Mark—his ability to take charge and get things done. I'm confident that he won't let a hot-tempered student disrupt the film show—especially with dignitaries present.

As I leave Mark talking to Orlando and find my way to the reserved faculty seating near the front of the auditorium, I feel a pang of concern—not for Orlando, but for Robin. What if Orlando's accusation of plagiarism has some merit? Sinking into my seat, I realize that it wouldn't be the first time.

Robin had taken an Intro to Shakespeare class with me his freshman year. He was one of my best students, always lingering after class with a question about that day's reading. The questions were astute and revealed reading beyond what was assigned. Unlike some of my students who were fascinated by the so-called authorship question (which, I always went to great pains to explain, I didn't consider a question at all), Robin was fascinated by whom Shakespeare was writing *to*—he wanted to know the identity of the young man and the Dark Lady of the Sonnets. He'd written a brilliant term paper on the possibility that Shakespeare had written the sonnets to one of the boy actors in his acting troupe. It was a little too brilliant. One of the phrases in particular echoed in my head with a nagging familiarity: "Of all the motives of dramatic curiosity used by our great playwrights, there is none more subtle or more fascinating than the ambiguity of the sexes." I submitted it to ithenticate.com—the Web site I used to check student work I suspected of plagiarism—and discovered its source. It had been written by Oscar Wilde in 1899. In fact, Wilde had written a small book (published posthumously in 1921) called *The Portrait of Mr. W.H.,* in which I found the crux of Robin's theories about the sonnets.

When I called Robin into my office and confronted him with the plagiarism, he burst into tears. He'd meant to credit Wilde for the theory and of course for the quote. Hadn't I gotten the bibliography attached to the paper? I told him I hadn't and that I had to give him an F for the paper. In addition, if I ever found any cause to suspect him of plagiarism again, I'd have to report him to the dean's office.

Although I told him I couldn't give him credit for it, Robin rewrote his paper. He did good work throughout the rest of the class, and even with the one F he managed to get a B-minus for the term. Most surprisingly, he kept taking classes with me and kept lingering after class. He'd never given me any reason to suspect him of plagiarism since, and I liked to think that he had learned his lesson. Now I wasn't so sure.

Worse, I couldn't help thinking that by not reporting Robin's first in-fraction I might have given him the idea that he could get away with pla-giarism. Had I been swayed by how much I liked him? And by how much he obviously liked me? I certainly didn't relish telling Mark about the Oscar Wilde paper, which I'd have to do if Orlando's claims turn out to have merit.

When the lights dim I realize how tired I am. I close my eyes to rest them for a moment and only half listen to Mark's opening remarks. I know the spiel well enough. How Hudson's film program has grown since Cyril Graham's generous donation, the many Hudson graduates whose films have won prizes at film festivals around the world, the growing prestige of the internship at La Civetta, which many of tonight's filmmakers will be taking advantage of this summer . . . all this glamour casting a reflected glory onto the college in general. I've heard it all before—it's practically all Mark talks about these days—and the reflected glory is beginning to look a bit tarnished to me.

Five years ago a student like Robin with his passionate love of Shakespeare and Renaissance poetry might have chosen to go on to graduate study in English or comparative literature—or maybe an MFA program in playwriting. But instead the new film program has pro-pelled Robin into a filmmaking career that I can't help but fear—remembering how ragged and tense he looked in class today—is too much for a boy of his age. Perhaps it is even the kind of intense pressure that might compel a boy like Robin to embellish his film with someone else's words.

As the first film begins, another thought makes me queasy. What if this is what Robin wanted to talk to me about earlier today? Maybe he'd wanted to confess that he'd "borrowed" part of the script to his film and that was why he was worried about how people were going to react to it. He'd asked me to come to his rescue. But what on earth could I do for him? And what would Mark think if I came to Robin's defense?

I try to concentrate on watching the films, willing my heart to beat slower, willing the voices in my head to quiet. I let the montages of dis-connected (at least they seem disconnected to me) images and loud music roll over me until I feel a little numb. I can barely feel my heart beating at all. But then the second-to-last entry is filmed with a hand-held camera that's so shaky, I begin to feel nauseous. I close my eyes until I can tell by the applause that it's time for Robin's film. When I open them, my heart begins to race again.

It's as if I've been transported to the garden at La Civetta at the height of summer. The scene is so lush, so green, that when I breathe in I'm surprised the air doesn't smell of lemons. The avenue the camera moves down is lined with lemon trees, each one in its own huge terra-cotta pot. A slim girl steps out from behind one of the pots and, as the camera hovers just over her right shoulder, she opens an old leather-bound book and turns past its marbled endpapers to a page marked with a yellow ribbon. As she begins walking down the avenue of lemon trees, her head bowed to the book as though she were reading, we hear a voice reciting Shakespeare's sonnet 18.

> *Shall I compare thee to a summer day?*
> *Thou art more lovely and more temperate.*

The camera hovers over the girl's shoulder, so close that strands of her golden hair stray across the lens, but the angle allows us only to glimpse her profile. The breeze that blows her hair also stirs the climbing rose vines that cling to the arbor arching over the avenue. The camera follows a trail of loose petals as they float down to the tiled walk and drift beside the girl's feet.

> *Rough winds do shake the darling buds of May,*
> *And summer's lease hath all too short a date;*

The girl stops and shades her eyes against the sun for the next line:

> *Sometime too hot the eye of heaven shines,*

And then a shadow moves across her face while the narrator reads:

And often is his gold complexion dimmed;

The choreography of poem and image would be hokey if the girl weren't so mysteriously beautiful and the voice so strangely sad. It's Robin's voice, I realize as the girl pauses at the end of the lemon avenue to look out at a view of the Tuscan countryside and the orange-tiled roofs of Florence in the distance.

And every fair from fair sometime declines,
By chance or nature's changing course untrimmed.
But thy eternal summer shall not fade
Nor lose possession of that fair thou ow'st,

It's the same poem we read in class today, but while most of my students could barely be bothered to listen to it, this audience seems to be held in thrall as the girl turns from the sunlit lemon avenue to a shady path between clipped yew hedges.

Nor shall Death brag thou wand'rest in his shade,
When in eternal lines to time thou grow'st;

At the end of the yew walk is a marble tomb, surmounted by a statue of a reclining woman, her face veiled. As Robin reads the concluding couplet of sonnet 18 we see the same lines inscribed in the marble:

So long as men can breathe or eyes can see,
So long lives this, and this gives life to thee.

The tomb and the statue are from the late Renaissance, but the lines were added in the early twentieth century by Cyril Graham's father, Sir Lionel, who was so taken by Shakespeare that he peopled his gardens with statues of Shakespearian characters and adorned every available inch of bare marble with lines from the plays and sonnets. The tomb stands, I remember, just outside the lower entrance to the *teatrino,* the green theater, so I'm not surprised when we follow the girl into the semicircular grove framed by topiary clipped to look like side wings and footlights. The green stage is peopled by statues modeled after Shakespeare's leading ladies. The girl strolls by Miranda, Ophelia, and Juliet, and then comes to pause in front of the last statue. This one is of a boy, or rather, I realize, it's supposed to be Rosalind from *As You Like It* dressed as a boy. But when the girl leans forward and kisses the statue, it becomes a real boy—one I recognize as Orlando. As she embraces him, I recognize her as well—she's the girl from the park, Zoe, wearing a blond wig. The embrace is so realistic that I begin to wonder whether *this* is what all the fuss was about in the park—a teenage love triangle that's gone sour. Maybe the real theft Orlando was upset about was of this girl—not a piece of writing after all.

The long embrace is broken by a noise that we don't hear but sense in the couple's guilty expressions. While the girl locks behind her, the boy snatches the book from her hand and flees the *teatrino,* disappearing into the shrubbery. We see the girl's face for one moment, her features contorted with grief; then she plunges into the hedges to follow him.

The camera follows the girl crashing through dense woods. The garden has become a wasteland of overgrown thicket and toppled and broken statuary. It takes me a few minutes to recognize—or even notice—the sonnet Robin's reciting now: number 35, which begins "No more be grieved at that which thou hast done"—Shakespeare's note of forgiveness for his beloved's betrayal. The poem's images of corruption—cankerous roses and mud-stained fountains—are mirrored in the landscape through which the girl wanders. The rose petals that drifted by her feet in the first scene appear again, but now they stain the tiled walk like splotches of dried blood. Her face is scratched by thorny bushes and her clothes are stained with mud by the time she comes out of the wilderness and sees the dark-haired boy sitting on the rim of a ruined fountain with another woman, their heads bent over the Moroccan-bound book, laughing at what's written there. We can see from Zoe's ravaged expression that her degradation is complete. When the couple leaves the fountain, they leave behind the book, which Zoe picks up.

She turns away and begins walking up a wide, bare avenue, which I recognize as the lemon avenue of the first scene—only now the lemon trees are gone and the rose arbor, which had been flowering in the first scene, is bare. In the course of the short film, spring has become fall, afternoon has become evening. We see the sun setting over the Tuscan hills as the girl pauses outside a stucco building, the last light seeping into its rich ochre paint. I recognize the building as the *limonaia,* the lemon house, where the potted lemon trees are kept in the winter. The girl presses her face against the glass and we can see her breath crystallize on the cold pane. Inside, the lemons glow like jewels against the glossy green leaves. The lemon trees, beyond the glass, are like a mirage of summer, more a memory than something real. The camera stays on her face as we hear the last poem.

It's not one I recognize, which is unlikely considering I wrote my dissertation on Shakespeare's sonnets. I realize after a moment that although the language, the rhythm, the structure, even the turn of mind, are undoubtedly Shakespearian, the poem could not be by Shakespeare. After all, Shakespeare never wrote a sonnet about a lemon house.

> *The way the* limonaia *wombs these trees,*
> *Within its sun-veined skin of fragile glass*
> *To be reborn amidst spring's gentle breeze,*
> *I'll give to thee, whose face art can't surpass.*
> *For how thy memory has lingered on—*
> *In spite of cruelest winter's drear and howl—*
> *By inner mirror seen; I've dwelled upon,*
> *I must confess, my treachery most foul.*
> *But then!—I spy such lemons hanging bright,*
> *And delicately sheathed with glass to show,*
> *How prosperous our love might be despite*

Betrayal, wombed against entombing snow.
When love feeds on a fruit as bold as wine
I once again can conjure thy love mine.

There's something heartbreaking about the poem. The lost love trapped behind the glass, the sense of summer giving way to cold winter. Or perhaps it's just my own associations with the *limonaia* that have brought tears to my eyes.

CHAPTER THREE

HEN THE SCREEN GOES DARK, THERE'S A LONG MOMENT OF SILENCE. THEN the applause begins, slowly at first, but building to a steady roar. It's all Mark can do to silence the crowd long enough to announce *The Lemon House* (I must still have had my eyes closed when the title played) by Robin Weiss as the winner of the Hudson College Invitational Film Show. The applause becomes thunderous. As Robin appears on the stage, I feel a sob catch in my throat at the sight of him. He looks so frail and ghostly pale caught in the spotlight.

There's clearly no way I'll be able to get through this crowd to congratulate Robin, so I beat a hasty retreat to the reception, where I'll have less competition. I show my invitation and faculty ID to the security guard stationed in front of the elevators and ride ten floors up to the penthouse suite.

I realize I'm a little *too* early when I get off the elevator, but at least there's no line at the bar. Plus, I recognize the bartender as a former student.

"A Greek Goddess, Dr. Asher?" he asks me as I approach.

I look behind me as if expecting a white-robed Athena to appear from behind one of the potted trees in the corners.

"It's the party's signature cocktail," he tells me, pouring a drop of orange liqueur into a glass flute. "A hint of Grand Marnier, Cointreau, and"—popping the cork on a bottle of Moët & Chandon—"champagne."

When the fizz settles, he hands me a drink the pale orange color of Tuscan stucco. I take an experimental sip and nod my head appreciatively. "Nice, Jake," I say, pulling his name out of an invisible roster in my head. "Are you graduating this year?"

"I graduated last year," he tells me, lining up a dozen champagne flutes and carefully measuring a few drops of Grand Marnier in each one. "I'm bartending until I can get an acting job. I heard there's going to be a lot of film people here tonight."

The elevator opens and a flood of laughter and perfume wafts into the room. I see Jake looking over my shoulder appraisingly at the crowd. "Well, I'll leave you to it, then," I say. "Good luck."

I walk away from the newcomers toward the wall of north-facing windows overlooking the park. It's a gorgeous view, one of my favorites in the city, especially at this time of day, when the sky is the cobalt blue of twilight. Across the park, the Washington Square Arch, recently cleaned and restored, gleams white, and the lights of Fifth Avenue seem to spring out of it like a luminescent river that casts shimmering droplets along its banks. Something in how the lights look tonight, distant beyond the cold glass, reminds me of the lemons in the *limonaia* in the last scene of Robin's film. I find myself pressing my face against the glass just as Zoe had.

"You shouldn't stand so close to the glass," a voice says from close behind me. "It could break and you'd fall to your death."

I turn, wincing at the image of my broken body—the second I've entertained today—and force my face into a smile to greet Mara Silver-man, wife of Gene Silverman, the head of the film department.

"Hello, Mara." I tilt my head to receive a kiss on the cheek. "Actu-ally I'd just end up on the balcony, but thanks for the warning."

The balcony, which runs along three sides of the building, has a Plexiglas railing so as not to obstruct the view. There are two metal doors to it, one each at the east and west corners of the room, but they've been locked tonight because of an incident at a party last year when a distraught sophomore tried to climb over the railing and was saved from ending her life only by one of her friends, who hung on to her feet until security arrived.

Mara's cheek—colder even than the glass—grazes mine, and then she pulls back as if stung by the contact. Or maybe she's just afraid of getting lipstick on the collar of her buttercup yellow Chanel suit. As usual, she's overdressed for the event. She looks as if she's dressed for a country club dinner or a formal bar mitzvah instead of a film show in downtown Manhattan. What's painful is knowing how much time and money she probably spent picking out the outfit and having it altered to perfectly conform to her size-four figure, then having her shoulder-length black hair touched up to hide the gray, blown, and set, her nails manicured, and even her feet, which are hidden in tasteful Ferragamo pumps, pumiced and pedicured. I know because I once made the mis-take of accepting an invitation to a "girls' day out" with Mara, and this is what we did.

"Is Gene here?" I ask, looking hopefully around for her husband.

"He's still downstairs with all those Hollywood people." Mara shudders and takes a sip of her sparkling water. Mara never drinks. "But I felt claustrophobic so I came up here. Can we move away from these windows? I don't like heights. Didn't one of those suicides hap-pen here?"

"No, that was at the NYU library." I follow Mara a safe distance from the windows. "They've had to glass in the atrium at Bobst. They should make these railings higher, too. That's why the doors are locked."

A waiter with a tray of miniature quiches approaches us, but Mara waves him away as if he were a homeless person begging for money. No, that's not fair. Mara would give money to the homeless person way before she'd allow dairy to pass her lips. "So far, though, Hudson's been relatively lucky in that department—" I begin.

"Imagine not knowing your child was in that much trouble. I bet they're mostly children of divorce."

I've heard Mara's views on divorce before. On our girls' day out she talked of little else. She told me she "didn't believe in it," as if divorce were a figment of the popular imagination like Santa Claus or the Easter Bunny.

"What if you knew your husband was cheating?" I'd asked, knowing full well that Gene was infamous for sleeping with his students.

"Men," Mara had said, crossing her legs and nearly kicking the pedicurist in the head. "What can you expect from them? They think with their penises. The trick," she said in a stage whisper that only the women under the hair dryers would miss, "is to never let on that you know."

I had stopped feeling sorry for her, but it was too late. By then I was the only professor or faculty wife who had spent any time with her and so she always latched on to me at college functions. I resign myself to spending the next quarter hour with Mara and ask after her son, Ned. She treats me to a rundown of Ned's college application procedure, which sounds as if Mara herself had been the one actually applying. After she has recited his application essay to Cornell verbatim, I remark that it's a shame he hadn't wanted to go to Hudson, as he would have been eligible for tuition reimbursement.

"Yes, well, he was interested in the acting program, but I helped him to see how impractical *that* was. He has to make a living, after all, and he always did so well in science, so he agreed to be premed if he could do the theater program in Italy this summer. Besides, I didn't think Hudson would be right for Ned," she says, and then adds, in a throaty whisper, *"Too many gays."* Mara's eyes dart nervously around the room, as if on the lookout for homosexual predators. But again I realize I'm being unfair to Mara. She's not exactly a homophobe—she loves her gay hairdresser, for instance, and *La Cage aux Folles* is her favorite musical—she's just a little overprotective when it comes to her Ned.

I follow her gaze around the room, which is filling now with men in crisp suits and women in summery cocktail dresses. The lights have been dimmed to show off the glittering skyline beyond the windows. Votive candles in blue and gold glass bowls are scattered about the room, echoing the lights of the city. The room feels more like a garden party than an academic reception on the tenth floor of a Manhattan building. I see Robin and the girl Zoe talking to Mara's husband, at the center of a cluster of men in white suits. As no self-respecting New Yorker would wear a white suit before Memorial Day, I conclude that these must be Cyril Graham's friends from Hollywood. Robin himself is wearing the Versace tweed over a white T-shirt and faded jeans, but he looks every bit as sartorial as the Hollywood clique—and he doesn't look a bit like he needs saving.

"There's Robin Weiss, the one whose film won first prize," I tell Mara. "He's talking to Gene."

Mara wheels around and scans the room to find her husband. When she does, she undergoes a sea change, not so much in her expression (she's had far too much Botox for her face to give away anything) as in her posture. Her shoulders hunch up to her ears and she wraps her bony arms over her flat chest as if defending herself from an attack. I look back to see what's brought on this bout of anxiety and notice that Zoe's standing very close to Gene, one slim bare hip cocked against his leg. Poor Mara. She must be afraid that Gene's found another conquest.

On our girls' day out Mara had devoted a good half hour to extolling Gene's good looks. He'd been the handsomest boy at Tufts, she'd assured me; all the girls were after him. She'd even shown me a picture she carried in her wallet of the two of them at their senior prom. "Yes, quite handsome," I'd said, trying not to inject too much enthusiasm lest Mara decide that I, too, was after her husband. The truth was that I'd never found Gene's type—wispy blond hair cut in a seventies shag framing a babyish face and grazing footballer's shoulders—that attractive. And two decades had done nothing to improve his looks, which have gotten softer rather than sharper. He still wore his hair longish—often pushed back by sunglasses on the top of his head even at an evening event like tonight's—and his face had gotten pudgy around the eyes and jawline. His shoulders still strained the expensive Tommy Hilfiger jacket he wore over black jeans, but much of that muscle had turned to flab. He still managed to attract enough student admirers to keep Mara on her guard, though. Clearly she now thinks that Zoe is a threat.

Just when I'm feeling sorry for her again, she points across the room to a cluster near the east door to the balcony. "Who's that lovely young woman President Abrams is with?"

I turn and see Mark talking to a slim blond woman in a tailored dove gray suit. "I think she's the new lawyer working on the Graham bequest," I say, my voice neutral. I can guess what Mara's up to. On our girls' day out I'd stupidly confessed that Mark and I were involved. Now she must think that if she has to feel jealous of her husband, she would like company. I swallow the last sip of my champagne cocktail, making a silent promise to myself *not* to get sucked into Mara's games again, and hold up the empty glass between us. "Can I get you something from the bar?"

"No," she says, "I can't mix alcohol with the medication I'm on."

Her eyes are darting back and forth nervously. In addition to her fear of heights and flying, Mara admitted to me at the salon that she's an agoraphobe—clearly panicked to be left alone in the growing crowd.

"I think I'll get some air." She edges away from me toward the door on the west side of the balcony.

"President Abrams has ordered the doors to be locked . . ." I begin, but Mara has already summoned a security guard (the one posted, in fact, to keep people off the balcony) to open the door for her. It doesn't take long for the guard to yield to the incipient hysteria in Mara's voice. She slips out onto the balcony, keeping her back pressed up against the window and staying as far as she can from the railing. The folds of her

yellow knit suit creased against the glass make her look like a rare butterfly specimen splayed between sheets of wax paper—caught between
her warring fears of the crowd inside and the sheer drop from the balcony.

When I turn from her, I feel curiously flattened and exposed as
well, as if my motives for putting up with Mara Silverman were as transparent as the glass itself. "Just because you slept with a married professor once upon a time doesn't mean you have to make up for all the
wronged faculty wives of the world," my friend and colleague Chihiro
Arita has told me. I wish Chihiro were here tonight, but she'd opted to
take her twelve-year-old niece to an anime film instead. "Give me
katana swordplay over faculty politics any day," she'd e-mailed me last
night when I asked whether she was coming.

I look for Robin and see he's still in his crowd of admirers, but
when he sees me he waves for me to come over. As I approach the
group, though, one of the white suits peels away—like a petal falling off
a chrysanthemum. I'm so pleased with the image that I'm reaching into
my purse for pen and paper when I realize that the man is headed
straight for me.

"Dr. Asher, isn't it?" he asks, thrusting forward his hand.

"Yes," I admit, submitting my hand to his firm grip. Everything
about this man looks firm, in fact, from his flat stomach and well-
developed chest muscles under a close-fitting black T-shirt and gleaming white cotton jacket to his tanned bare skull. "I'm sorry," I ask, when
he releases my hand, "have we met?"

"Leo Balthasar," he says, as if I'm supposed to recognize the name.
He draws a business card from the breast pocket of his jacket. *Leo
Balthasar,* I read, *Producer, Lemon House Films.*

"I'm sorry," I say, "I don't get to the movies much."

He throws back his head and laughs as if I'd said something very
witty. The top of his skull shines in the yellow candlelight. Without
turning his head, he reaches out to intercept a passing waiter's tray of
champagne flutes and procures us each one of the orange-tinted cock-
tails.

"Have you had one of these Goddesses, yet? Cyril Graham claims to have invented it on a cruise with Jackie Onassis in the Greek isles."

"Ah, so you're a friend of Cyril's . . ."

"That's who told me about you. He said you were the one to get on board the sonnet project. Said no one had a better feel for Shakespeare's sonnets."

"That's hardly true," I say, sipping my champagne. "There's Helen Vendler, for instance—"

"You," Leo Balthasar says, leaning in closer and holding his glass of champagne up to my face like an orange exclamation point, "are the one Cyril Graham wants on the project."

"And what project is that?" I ask, trying not to appear as clueless as I feel.

"The Shakespeare project. A film based on the sonnets of Shakespeare. The whole Dark Lady–slash–beloved boy–slash–famous poet triangle. It's your boy's idea." Balthasar looks over his shoulder toward Robin Weiss. *My boy?*

"Robin's my student," I say, instantly hating how prim I sound. A Miss Jean Brodie in the making. "Do you mean the film we just saw? *The Lemon House?*"

Leo Balthasar laughs his full-bodied laugh again, which seems to require leaning his head far enough back to draw in air from the upper reaches of the ceiling. "What we saw tonight was a sweet student effort, but what I'm interested in is a script Robin Weiss sent me two weeks ago. I don't usually pay attention to student work, but this project has potential—and backing. Cyril Graham has interested some of his rich friends in making the film at La Civetta. Picture *Shakespeare in Love,* only steamier. And set in Italy, of course."

"Italy? There's no proof Shakespeare ever went to Italy."

"There's no proof he didn't, eh?" he asks, winking at me. "According to Robin, there's a legend at La Civetta about a woman poet who lived there in the sixteenth century who some people believe was Shakespeare's Dark Lady."

"He must mean Ginevra de Laura," I say, finishing my Greek God-

dess in an unwisely large swallow and looking around for an exit strat-
egy. In a minute he'll be telling me that Shakespeare didn't write the
sonnets. "I've heard of her. She was the mistress of Lorenzo Barbagianni, the villa's owner, and said to be a great poet, only all her poems
were lost, so that's really just speculation. I've never heard this rumor
about her being the Dark Lady, though."

"But, see, at least you know who she was," Balthasar says, waving
his glass in the air. "That's why we want to get you aboard as a writer on
the script. With your credentials—"

"There are plenty of academics with better," I tell him.

"But none," he says, clicking his half-full champagne glass against
my empty one, "who also writes sonnets. You see, we want the poet's
sensibility, not one of these dry-as-dust academics'. Of course, the
money will be a little better than what your average academic publisher
pays." He leans in even closer so that I can smell the sweet orange
liqueur on his breath and mentions a figure that's roughly ten times
larger than the advance I'd gotten from the university press that's publishing my book on the Renaissance sonnet.

"And that's just for six weeks' work this summer," he says rocking
back on his heels. "All expenses paid, of course, and first-class airfare."

"Airfare?"

"To Italy. I'm doing the preliminary location scout in July and then,
if everything checks out and we've got a script, we'd start shooting at La
Civetta in August."

It's the second time today I've been invited to La Civetta, and although I have no intention of accepting this offer either, I suddenly
have the uneasy feeling that, like a hero in a fairy tale enduring some
test of will, I will find the third time the offer is made the hardest to
resist.

"Thank you, but no thank you," I say, putting my empty glass on a
table and holding my hand out to shake his. He takes my hand, but instead of delivering the firm shake he'd greeted me with, he pulls me in
closer to him.

"You've got my card," he says. He makes it sound almost like a
threat. Like I'd taken something that belonged to him. "We'll be in

touch." Then he lets me go and turns away. I see him go out the door to the west side of the balcony, which—once breached by Mara—has now filled with cigarette smokers. I turn back to look for Robin. The nucleus of white-suited men has acquired an outer ring of film students in their uniform of black jeans and black T-shirts. Robin, at the center of this circle, is beginning to look a little wilted. If the movie people around him are anything like Leo Balthasar, I'm surprised there's any air left to breathe in the room. When he sees me he throws me a desperate look. I see him mouth the words "save me." A bit dramatic, I think, reminding myself that Robin is one of the drama crowd now—a group well known for their histrionics. I'm worried, too, that Robin has been talking about me to these film people. What impression must he have given for Leo Balthasar to refer to him as "my boy"? But still, I can't leave without at least congratulating him.

As I head toward Robin, I tell myself that once I've fulfilled my promise I can go home. I pick up another Greek Goddess on my way and pause to listen to the comments of some nearby partygoers. I overhear two young men condemning Robin's film as overly sentimental and a girl with lime green hair earnestly explaining to three other girls, who, like this girl and Zoe, have dyed their hair in various fruit shades (tangerine, pink grapefruit, kiwi), why the winning film wasn't by a woman. "It's a boy's club at Graham's villa," she complains. "They get all the best equipment and first pick of the prime locations. And the best rooms. The girls were all stuck in an old convent with bars on the windows and no ventilation. It was like an oven."

I'm tempted to stop and commiserate with the girl—I've been in the "little villa," as the old convent is called—but I intercept another desperate look from Robin and I'm afraid that if I don't get to him soon he might begin calling my name aloud. As I get closer to Robin, the comments I overhear grow more favorable, but there's still an edge of resentment to many of them. Near the center, a skinny boy in torn jeans, cowboy boots, and an Invader Zim T-shirt asks Robin whether he didn't feel as if his film was derivative. "I mean, the words weren't your own, man. You were just quoting some dead white guy."

"Finding images to evoke Shakespeare's sonnets is no easy feat," I say, feeling I've arrived just in time to speak up for Shakespeare as well as Robin. Of course, it's only Robin who can reward me with those bow-shaped lips curving into a smile. "I thought the film was lovely," I say, raising my glass to Robin. "Worthy of the Bard."

A few people join me in the toast, including Gene Silverman, who calls out, "Here, here," and claps Robin on the back. His hand slides off Robin's shoulder and somehow manages to find its way onto Zoe's arm. He's probably just drunk, but I find myself wondering whether there's anything to Mara's suspicions. I take a long sip of champagne to drown out the thought, and as I'm lowering my glass, Leo Balthasar, returned from the balcony, turns to me.

"And what did you think of the last sonnet, Dr. Asher? Worthy of the Bard, as well?"

"It's hard to judge on a single hearing, but I found the last sonnet"— I pause and stare past Balthasar's amused smile to the windows as if looking for the right word in the lights streaming along Fifth Avenue, but really I'm remembering again that final image of the lemon trees be-hind glass—"moving. The comparison between the lemon trees surviv-ing the winter and the endurance of a betrayed love was . . ." I stop because I see Orlando Brunelli entering the room. How in the world did he get in? I'd thought for sure that Mark would alert the security guards to his presence. "Um, very nicely developed. The rhymes were exact and the iambic pentameter consistent," I finish lamely, glancing around the room to locate Mark. Orlando has spotted Robin and Zoe and is walking straight toward us. "Although I'd have to see it in print to make a more considered evaluation."

"But could it have been written by an Elizabethan poet?" Balthasar asks. "By Shakespeare's Dark Lady, perhaps?"

I laugh. "I don't see any reason to think so. The poet seems to be offering his or her beloved the gift of a *limonaia*—which is sort of an Italian greenhouse for lemons. And if we take the *limonaia* as a synecdoche—"

"Oh, I know what that is," Zoe calls out. "It's when a part of some-thing stands for the whole thing, right?"

"Very good. So here the *limonaia* might stand for the whole villa. In which case, the poet intends to make a gift of the entire villa to the beloved. If Shakespeare had inherited an Italian villa, I think we would have heard about it." A few people laugh and I'm glad to have diffused the situation with a joke. Glad, too, to see that Mark has managed to intercept Orlando and is talking to him now—until I see Robin's expression. His pretty lips are curving downward and he looks stricken—just as he had when I'd accused him of plagiarism. And yet in this case I'm not saying that I don't believe he wrote the poem. In fact, I suddenly realize that the opposite is probably true, that Robin wrote the last poem of the film and is claiming that it's a poem he found. In our little talk about plagiarism, the focus was all on taking credit for someone else's writing, *not* pretending something you wrote was written by someone else. Is that what Robin's up to—presenting his own poems as the lost poems of Shakespeare's Dark Lady?

"Did you write the poem?" I ask Robin gently. "I'd like to see a copy of it."

Robin stares at me for a moment, his eyes glassy, his skin an unhealthy color. He takes a step toward me and stumbles. I reach forward to catch him and he presses something into my hand. "Here it is," Robin says, beginning to stutter, "w-w-watch."

The envelope he presses into my hand is thick and lumpy. I realize it must be my watch that he went to fetch for me. I start to thank him but then he leans his face against mine. For one terrible moment, I think he's going to kiss me, but then he only whispers, "I need to talk to you alone."

"Well, tomorrow's Saturday," I say, slipping the envelope into my purse. I feel somehow ashamed of the transaction, as if Robin were passing drugs to me. "But if it's really important I could meet you in my office."

" 'Tomorrow,' " Robin says, rearing back on his heels, his eyes full of disappointment, " 'and tomorrow, and tomorrow / Creeps in this petty pace from day to day.' " His speech is no longer stuttering, now that he's reciting Shakespeare's words. When he turns away from me, he sees Orlando. He suddenly looks as if he's going to be ill. Orlando tries to approach Robin, but Mark has a hold of his arm.

"*Lascia me,*" he says, wrenching his arm out of Mark's grip. "I only came to get what belongs to me. The last poem in the film . . . he stole it—"

"I-I-I-," Robin stutters.

"Any accusations of plagiarism will be taken into due consideration," Mark tells Orlando in a loud, firm voice, "but this is not the time and place for it."

The word "plagiarism" echoes around the room as it's taken up by students and faculty. There'd been a messy plagiarism scandal last year that had resulted in a student's expulsion. Robin looks at me and I imagine he's afraid that I'll bring up the incident of the Oscar Wilde paper. "Dr. Asher," he says, "I swear—"

"President Abrams is right," I say. "This isn't the time or the place, Robin. Maybe you should get some air—"

"That sounds like an excellent idea," Gene Silverman says, putting one arm around Robin's shoulder and the other around Zoe's and steering them both toward the balcony door. Leo Balthasar follows them, taking a cigar out of his pocket. As they pass me I hear the Hollywood producer ask Gene, "Are you sure there's not a problem with the script?" I expect Mark to tell them that the balcony's off-limits, but he's got his hand clasped firmly onto Orlando's arm and is trying to steer him toward the elevators. I notice that Orlando winces and I feel an unexpected pang of sympathy for him. I consider following them to make sure Mark isn't being too rough on the boy, but then decide against it. All I need now is for Mark to think I'm trying to defend Bruno's son. There have been enough jealous scenes for one night.

Turning back toward the balcony, I see I'm wrong. Mara has worked her way around to this side of the balcony and found her husband with his arm around the nubile young Zoe. Since the doors are closed I can't hear what she's saying, but from her expression I can guess. Even from here I can see that her lips are white with rage. She's backed Zoe, and Robin with her, against the edge of the balcony, where they both cower under her assault. The scene has its comical elements—Leo Balthasar, puffing on his cigar in the corner of the balcony, seems to find it amusing—but I'm uncomfortable with the students' proximity to the railing.

I look around to find Mark and see he's waiting at the elevator with Orlando and the blond lawyer. As Mark leans closer to hear something she's saying, Orlando suddenly bolts away from them. He crosses the room in surprisingly few long-legged strides, his black leather coat billowing out behind him and brushing against my leg as he passes me and opens the door to the balcony.

"Shit," I hear Mark say, close on his heels. I follow them to the balcony door, but it swings shut behind Mark and before I can open it the guard suddenly appears and blocks my way. "*Now* you're keeping people off the balcony?" I ask incredulously.

"President Abrams said—" he begins, but I push by him and struggle with the heavy door. When it swings open I feel a warm gust of air on my face and hear the sound of someone screaming. It's Mara, I see, who's turned away from the balcony, clutching Gene as if she's afraid the wind will sweep her away. Leo Balthasar is pulling Zoe away from the railing where Mark and Orlando are standing, looking down at the street below. Only when Mark steps back, one arm still around Orlando's chest, do I really take in the fact that Robin is gone.

CHAPTER
FOUR

THE SCREAMS, HIGH-PITCHED AND ODDLY REGULAR, ALMOST LIKE CHANTING, infect the room with hysteria. A dozen or so people rush by me onto the balcony. I stay where I am: frozen. It still feels like I'm separated from what's happening by a wall of glass and that if I stay very still, there will be an opportunity to undo what's happened, and the last five minutes can be rewound and erased.

It is not, I realize now, as if anything can be done for Robin. The crowd that rushes past me out onto the balcony might hope that there's a ledge on the other side of the balcony railing or a protrusion in the building that could have caught him in his descent. That he'll pop up from behind the railing smiling—the whole thing a joke, a staged finale to his film. But I am sure there's nothing on the other side of the railing but a sheer drop to the pavement. I don't have to see the expressions on the faces of the people who look over the edge, or hear the sirens already moving toward us, to confirm what I know has happened to Robin.

I search the knot of people clustered around the balcony door for Mark, but it's Orlando who breaks through the crowd. I reach out a hand to stop him, but when he turns to me and I see his eyes—distended and bloodshot like a panicked horse's—I let go of him. He says something in Italian—I'm almost sure it's *"Mi dispiace"*—I'm sorry—and then he runs for the stairs. I turn, looking for Mark again, and see Zoe struggling to make her way into the room with Leo Balthasar close behind her, whispering something in her ear. I don't know how she can hear anything with those screams, which seem to be getting louder—but then I see that's only because their source is approaching me. It's Mara, crumpled up against her husband's side, weeping mascara-stained tears into his sport jacket and emitting those awful shrieks, as desperate in their repetition as those of an animal being slaughtered. Gene sees me and heads in my direction. I look around for some escape, but Gene corners me.

"Can you take her to the ladies' room and get her some water?" he asks, gingerly easing Mara off his arm. "President Abrams needs me to call the police." And then, lowering his voice, "See if she's got anything in her purse to calm her down."

"Okay." I put my arm over Mara's bony shoulders, still wishing I could find Mark. I don't know what I expect from him, but since he was closest to Robin when he fell I feel like I won't be able to process what's happened until I talk to him. Clearly, though, someone has to attend to Mara. She's stopped screaming, but now she's babbling something over and over again. When I lean closer I make out the words "It wasn't my fault."

"Of course not," Gene says, "he was a very troubled boy. Now, go with Rose and clean up your face. I have to talk to the police." He takes a handkerchief out of his jacket pocket—to wipe away tears, I think, but then he uses it to mop up the mascara stain on his jacket, making a face at the black mess that comes off. Over Mara's shoulder he mouths, "She's hysterical. I can't have her talking to the police like this." Then he pockets the black-stained handkerchief and puts as much distance as he can between himself and his wife.

Great, I think, leading Mara to the faculty women's lounge, where I know there's a couch, *he fucks his students, but then he can't be bothered to take care of his hysterical wife.*

I get Mara into the women's lounge and lock the door behind us. I sit her down on the couch, but when I stand up she starts to shriek again.

"Okay, okay, I'm just going to get you some water and paper towels. I'll be right back."

I go to the nearest sink and turn on the cold water. It's then that I realize that I'm still clutching the half-full champagne flute. I spill the remains of the drink down the basin so I can use the glass for Mara, but the smell of the orange liqueur is too much for me. I feel my stomach heave and barely have time to rush into a stall before throwing up. Fortunately, it doesn't take long to empty the contents of my stomach— three Greek Goddesses, a mini quiche, and the cup of yogurt I ate for lunch today. When I'm done I rinse my mouth and the champagne glass at the sink and then fill the glass with water, which I bring, with some wet paper towels, back to the couch, where Mara has collapsed into a pale yellow puddle. She's lying on her side, her stockinged legs pulled up to her chest in a fetal position. I sit down next to her on the couch and cover her forehead with the wet paper towels. Then I put the glass down on the floor so that I can look through her purse. The toes of Mara's high-heeled pumps, I notice, are neatly aligned. Even hysterical, Mara is obsessively neat.

Her purse, though, is a mess: tissues and dollar bills and Post-it notes wadded together, an uncapped tube of clear lip gloss leaking onto the silk lining and coating a collection of loose pills. I sort out a little pile of white circles and white ovals in the palm of my hand. Mara reaches over and plucks a white circle out of my hand.

"Valium," she says, dry swallowing the pill, and then, when I reach down to get the water for her, she takes one of the ovals and swallows that, too.

"Are you sure—?"

"It's just my Xanax," she says, sipping from the champagne glass. Then she lies back down and closes her eyes.

I wad up the rest of the pills in the old Kleenex and stash them in my purse so I don't have to worry about Mara taking more. Then I pat Mara's face with the wet paper towels, wiping clean the mascara. She makes a sort of cooing noise while I stroke her face and, to my surprise and embarrassment, she adjusts herself so that her cheek rests on my leg, her damp mascara seeping into my, thankfully, black dress.

"It must have been awful," I say soothingly. "I couldn't really see what happened—"

"It *was* awful," Mara confides. "I thought Gene had finally given up his little flings. All he's talked about this year is that boy. Robin this and Robin that. Robin was going to give him a producer credit on his movie and Robin was going to be his ticket back to Hollywood. I thought for once I didn't have to worry." Mara emits a laugh that turns into a mucusy cough and then a rattling sob.

"But, Mara," I say, shaking pills out of the wadded tissues in my purse to hand her, "I really don't think that Gene and Zoe—"

"And then that other boy—the dark-haired one—came outside and had the nerve to yell at me!"

"Orlando. I'm sure he wasn't yelling at you. He was angry at Robin about stealing something in the film. What was he saying?"

"I have no idea. I don't speak Italian. And then Gene pulled me away, and so I couldn't see what was happening. . . . I heard Robin say something that sounded like what my Portuguese maid says when I ask where something is—not that I ever accuse her of stealing . . ." She makes another sound that I think is a sob, but then, bending closer, I realize she's snoring. She's fallen heavily asleep. I wait another few minutes until I'm sure that she's really out, and then carefully ease her off my leg, sliding my folded shawl under her head.

When I open the door, I find Gene leaning against the wall opposite the ladies' room, smoking a cigarette in flagrant violation of the no-smoking law. "How is she?" he asks, dropping the cigarette to the floor and grinding it out with the heel of his dark boot. Cowboy boots, I notice. Lord, how old does he think he is?

"She's very upset, of course. She said she didn't see anything, but—"

"No, thank God I pulled her away before Robin fell—"

"So he fell?"

Gene looks startled by the question. "I—I'm not really sure . . . I was busy with Mara. You saw how hysterical she was . . . How many pills did she take, by the way?"

"One Xanax and one Valium."

"And the rest of the pills?"

"I put them in my purse," I say, holding up my beaded evening purse for him to see.

"Good idea. She gets confused sometimes about how many she's taken when she's upset."

"Yeah, well—" I try to walk past Gene, but he reaches out and grabs my arm.

"I want to thank you, Rose. You've always been a good friend to Mara. You're the only faculty member that gives her the time of day. It means a lot to her."

I instantly feel like scum for all the ungenerous thoughts I've had about Mara, and then I feel angry. Who is Gene Silverman to make *me* feel like scum? "The rest of the faculty are embarrassed around her," I say, pulling my arm away from Gene, "because they know how you treat her."

Gene bows his head, giving me a good view of his gray roots and his bald spot. A pathetic aging hipster, I think; you could almost feel sorry for him. "Yeah, I know," he says, sadly scuffing his cowboy boots against one another, for all the world like a ten-year-old who's been caught playing hooky. "I've been a real bastard, but you know, I've really been better this year." He looks up and smiles sheepishly. "I've been so busy working with Robin on his project, I haven't even looked at another woman. I mean, Robin had such amazing talent. You know how it is? When you encounter a student who makes you remember why you loved your subject in the first place, his promise . . ." Gene's voice cracks and his eyes fill with tears. In spite of what I know, I can't help feeling sorry for him, for what seems like his genuine grief over Robin's lost promise. But then he takes a deep, ragged breath and finishes: "He promised I was going to get a producer credit on the film," and I turn away to leave him to his drugged and sleeping wife.

The reception room has been transformed from a garden party to something that looks more like a disaster relief shelter. The silver trays of champagne flutes have been replaced by coffee urns and Styrofoam cups. The lights are on full blaze and the curtains to the balcony have been drawn, as if the view would be upsetting to the survivors huddled in small groups clutching their hot drinks.

There's a terrible vacancy in this room because of the one person who's gone. I remember something that a friend told me after she gave birth to her first child attended by a midwife in her own house. "Someone new was in the room who hadn't come in through the door." Scanning these faces now, I realize I'm still looking for the one who left without going through the door.

Then I notice Mark talking to a uniformed police officer and a sobbing girl. It takes me a moment to recognize Robin's friend Zoe, so transformed is she since I first saw her this afternoon, laughing and flirting in Washington Square Park.

"No, I didn't really see what happened," she's saying as I approach the group. "When Orlando came out onto the balcony, Mr. Balthasar pulled me away. I think he was afraid Orlando was going to hurt me, but really it was Robin who he was jealous of—"

"Orlando Brunelli," Mark says, ducking his head and rubbing the back of his neck. With his hair falling into his eyes and the tails of his shirt coming untucked, he looks twenty years younger than his forty-five years, but when he lifts his head I see that his eyes look old and haunted. Poor Mark. I know he blames himself for what happened. I come close enough to him so that I can surreptitiously slide my hand onto his arm without anyone seeing. I'm startled to feel that he's trembling. "He was fighting with Robin earlier in the evening," Mark continues telling the officer. "He accused Robin of stealing part of the script for his film, which won first prize tonight. I had assured him we would look into the matter tomorrow, but then he managed to get away from me and run onto the balcony. I only managed to catch up with him and hold him back on the balcony."

"But that's not right. Robin wouldn't have stolen someone else's work, would he, Dr. Asher?" Zoe asks, turning unexpectedly to me. I'm startled that she even knows my name. "He was in a lot of your classes, right? He was always saying that you were his favorite teacher. He worshipped writers. He'd never steal from someone else, right?"

"Is that right, Dr. Asher?" the police officer asks me. "Had this student ever been accused of plagiarism before?"

"Well, actually, there was one other incident . . ."

Mark tilts his head and blinks at me. "I wasn't aware of any other incidents with this student," he says, his voice icily formal. I wince at his tone but then remind myself that he's in shock. Still, I'm hurt when he shifts his weight so I'm no longer able to touch his arm.

"It was his first infraction so I didn't think it was necessary to make a formal complaint," I say. "He was so upset, and he promised it would never happen again. As Miss—" I stumble, looking to Zoe, realizing I don't know her last name.

"Demarchis," she says.

"As Miss Demarchis just said, Robin was very sensitive. I think any accusation of plagiarism in the film would have been very upsetting to him, especially now. He looked very stressed today in class—"

"Yes, I think the picture's coming together," Mark says, shifting his gaze from me to the police officer. "The boy had a history of plagiarism, he was under a lot of stress because of finals and the film show, then Orlando Brunelli shows up and accuses him of stealing the screenplay for his film . . . He felt his only way out was suicide."

"Suicide?" Zoe asks, her eyes widening. "But I thought he just fell . . ."

"But you said you didn't see what happened," the officer says. "Are you changing your statement, Miss Demarchis?"

Zoe shakes her head, "No, I mean . . . I didn't see, I just assumed it was an accident or that Orlando pushed him."

"No, I'm afraid it wasn't an accident, and I was holding back Orlando. Robin looked straight at both of us, and then he pushed himself off the balcony." Mark covers his eyes with his hand and shudders. "If I'd only known that the boy was suicidal . . ."

"I don't believe it!" Zoe Demarchis cries, her voice verging on hysteria. With her pink hair and bloodshot eyes, she looks like a crazed rabbit. Mark tilts his chin up and as if by magic Frieda Mainbocher, the women's studies professor, appears out of nowhere. I certainly hadn't noticed Frieda here earlier. In her dowdy denim jumper and orthopedic Mary Janes she doesn't look like she's dressed for a party. I imagine she sensed the crisis brewing from her apartment on Thompson Street and showed up just in time to whisk Zoe off to the Women's Counseling Center.

When they're gone I turn back to Mark. "Orlando looked wild when he ran onto the balcony. Are you sure he didn't push Robin?"

Mark shakes his head. "I know it's difficult to accept when a young person we've been close to—whom we think we've helped—gives up on himself," Marks says, slowly and deliberately. I feel myself blanche under his gaze. He's afraid, I realize, that I'll blame myself for Robin's death. The idea that I may have been partly to blame effectively silences me.

"There's going to be a lot of denial surrounding this boy's death," Mark continues, turning to the police officer. "Everyone expected so much from him." *The film isn't going to be what everyone expects,* Robin had said. Had Robin been that frightened of disappointing people that he'd chosen to kill himself? Had I been one of the people he'd been afraid of disappointing?

"You say he won first prize in the contest tonight," the police officer says, shaking his head. "It seems a strange time to kill himself."

"Sometimes success can be the worst kind of pressure," Mark says.

I glance at Mark, surprised that he would voice this sentiment. Mark is one of the most ambitious and driven men I've ever met. He wouldn't be a college president at forty-five if he weren't. "And many people were jealous."

"Like this Orlando fellow, right?" the officer asks. "Did he tell you what he wanted, President Abrams?"

"There was apparently some dispute about credit for the film. Mr. Brunelli seemed to think he deserved credit as a collaborator on the film, but of course he wasn't a Hudson student, and only works by Hudson students can be entered in the film contest."

"Everybody wants a producer credit." The remark comes from Leo Balthasar, who has come up behind me. He's taken off his white jacket, and his immaculate black T-shirt has come untucked from his trousers. He looks a little yellow under his tan.

"Is that what the two young men were arguing about on the balcony?" the officer asks.

Balthasar nods, but he's looking at Mark and not the police officer as he answers. "Yes, that seemed to be what the argument was about. Robin was pretty drunk and was very upset at this other boy's attack—"

"Attack?" the police officer asks, looking up from his notebook. "Did you see Orlando Brunelli push Robin?"

Leo Balthasar glances at Mark and then back at the police officer. "Excuse me. I meant *verbal attack*. From where I was, it looked like Robin jumped. But you were closer to him and Orlando, President Abrams. Is that what happened?"

Mark nods, his jaw so clenched that his lips look white. "I'm afraid so."

"And what about you, Dr. Asher? Where were you when Mr. Weiss jumped?"

"I tried to follow President Abrams out onto the balcony, but the guard stopped me. I couldn't see what was happening because I was behind the door . . . Maybe if I had been able to talk to Robin . . ." My voice falters and Mark takes a step toward me, putting a protective arm around my shoulders. I sink into him, relieved that he's not angry with me for not telling him about the earlier plagiarism incident with Robin.

"I think we all feel that we somehow failed this troubled boy," Mark says. And then, looking at the police officer, he adds, "Dr. Asher takes her responsibility to her students very seriously. I've often had to chide her for being too emotionally involved. This is particularly hard on her. If you don't have any further questions, we really should let her get home."

The officer closes his notebook and says he's done for now anyway. Mark gives my shoulder a squeeze and then takes his arm away to shake the officer's hand. As they walk toward the elevators together, I turn to Leo Balthasar. "What exactly was Orlando saying to Robin?" I ask, but before he can answer, Balthasar reaches into his trouser pocket to retrieve a vibrating cell phone and, glancing at the caller ID screen, says to me, "I've got to take this," and turns his back on me.

I wait until Mark's seen the police officer onto the elevator to approach him to explain the plagiarism incident, but before I can reach Mark, the young blond lawyer appears with Gene Silverman, who's helping a heavily sedated Mara to the elevator. She leaves Gene and Mara at the elevator door and then comes to stand very close to Mark, cups her hand over his ear, and whispers something. Mark nods and then she joins the Silvermans. By the time I've reached him, they've already disappeared into the elevator.

"You look exhausted," I say. "You should go home."

He shakes his head. "I'm going to work in my office tonight. I've got press releases and e-mails to write. I'm calling an emergency faculty meeting for ten a.m., so you'd better get home and get some sleep yourself."

"But tomorrow's Saturday," I say, remembering that I'd offered to meet Robin in my office. I'd thought I was acting generously—I hardly ever offer Saturday office hours—but now I realize that "until tomorrow" had been too long for him to wait. I should have offered to talk to him right then and there.

Mark shakes his head. "By Monday the story will be all over the campus. I don't want our teachers going into their classes unprepared. I'll e-mail the faculty myself. I'm sure they'll see the importance of taking a little time out of their weekends for this."

"Mark, I want to explain about the incident with Robin, the reason I didn't tell you—"

"It's not important, Rose, although I wish you'd shared the information with me before—" He stops, seeing how devastated I look. "It really wasn't your fault. I should have gotten that Brunelli boy out of here sooner."

"You couldn't have known how badly Robin would take his accusations—" I stop, alarmed by a flickering of doubt in Mark's eyes. "Mark, are you sure Orlando didn't push Robin? You would have told the police if he had, wouldn't you?"

Mark shakes his head. "No, Rose, I'm sorry. I know it's hard to face the fact that Robin killed himself, but that's what happened. But I do think that Orlando shares *part* of the responsibility for Robin Weiss's death." The way he emphasizes the word "part" makes it clear to me who he thinks shares the other part of the blame for Robin's suicide. If I'd reported the first plagiarism case . . . if I'd referred Robin to the counseling center . . . ?

I open my mouth to say something—what I'm not sure—to apologize? to explain why I didn't tell anyone about the plagiarized paper?—but the elevator door opens and the slim blond lawyer steps out.

"Are you going down, Dr. Asher?" she asks. "Shall I hold the door for you?"

I look at Mark. He nods and gives my shoulder a squeeze as he guides me through the doors. Then, before I can turn around, the doors are closed again and I'm alone in the elevator. The first time I've been alone all night. The downward motion of the elevator pushes the acid in my stomach up into my throat and I'm afraid I'm going to throw up again. Or start crying hysterically.

The bright lights of the lobby feel like a dousing of cold water. I navigate the polished marble floor as if it were an ice-skating rink and give the security guard a nod so brittle I feel like my head might fall off. I step outside and see the yellow police tape cordoning off the pavement on the east side of the building, but I keep moving. Across the street the park lies deserted and white under the streetlights, the ground covered with white pear blossoms, which drift across the street—carrying my gaze with them—and over the dark-stained sidewalk where Robin fell. I close my eyes and see Robin walking through that drift of petals and scooping up a handful to toss at Zoe Demarchis.

The memory of that gesture mixed with the sight of his blood on the pavement is too much for me. I double over as if I've been hit in the stomach. I manage not to fall only by grabbing the edge of a bench and half falling onto it. I take deep breaths until the pain in my stomach subsides, staring off into the distance at the white arch across the park, which shivers and shakes in my vision. After a few minutes the shape of the arch comes into focus and my breathing begins to even out. It's then that I notice the white figure in the center of the basin. It's as if the park has grown another statue. Nothing near as gallant as Garibaldi wielding his sword, this one seems to be a personification of grief. A beautiful young man, his skin gleaming like old marble in the lamplight, sits with his knees drawn to his chest, his head resting on his knees. I can tell from the dark curls that it's Orlando.

I look for a police officer on the street, but there are only the yellow crime scene tapes, flapping in the freshening breeze. I wonder whether I should go back inside to find a security guard or approach Orlando on my own, but when I turn back I see I've already wasted too much time. The figure in the fountain is gone. It's as if he's melted into the dry basin.

CHAPTER
FIVE

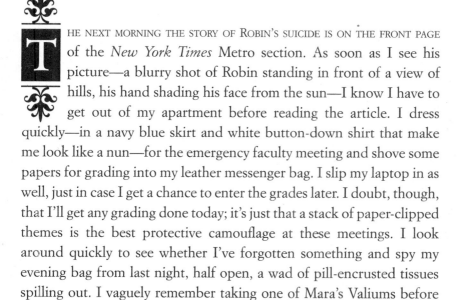 HE NEXT MORNING THE STORY OF ROBIN'S SUICIDE IS ON THE FRONT PAGE
of the *New York Times* Metro section. As soon as I see his
picture—a blurry shot of Robin standing in front of a view of
hills, his hand shading his face from the sun—I know I have to
get out of my apartment before reading the article. I dress
quickly—in a navy blue skirt and white button-down shirt that make
me look like a nun—for the emergency faculty meeting and shove some
papers for grading into my leather messenger bag. I slip my laptop in as
well, just in case I get a chance to enter the grades later. I doubt, though,
that I'll get any grading done today; it's just that a stack of paper-clipped
themes is the best protective camouflage at these meetings. I look
around quickly to see whether I've forgotten something and spy my
evening bag from last night, half open, a wad of pill-encrusted tissues
spilling out. I vaguely remember taking one of Mara's Valiums before

going to bed last night, which might explain the clotted sensation in my brain and the feeling I have that my normally comfortable—beloved, even—apartment feels like a prison this morning.

Though small (the only bedroom is really more of a sleeping alcove, the kitchen a compact galley off the living room), the apartment's been a haven to me since I returned from Italy and found that my aunt Rosalind, whose death had brought me home, had put my name on the rent-controlled lease. It meant I didn't have to move back in with my mother on Long Island even though I was going to have to stay in New York. Since Roz was gone, there was no one else to take my mother to doctor's appointments, to the hospital, to chemo. Most of those appointments, though, were in the city (my mother had never gotten over the prejudice of a native New Yorker who believes the *best* doctors and hospitals are in the city), so I could ride the train out to get her and then take her where she needed to go. I could stay overnight on the island when she needed me, but as she grew sicker and spent more and more time in the hospital, I was conveniently nearby. I was even grateful for the apartment's smallness and the building's lack of an elevator. It meant my mother couldn't move in.

And so, through the last years of my mother's life—and the decade of my twenties—I was able to go to NYU (not the University of Bologna or Cambridge as I had hoped) and get my doctorate in comparative literature. It wasn't the life I had envisioned when I left for Italy in my junior year of college—the life of writing and travel and romance that had seemed to open up briefly like a sunlit view of the Tuscan hills—but it would have been churlish of me to complain. It wasn't me who was dying; it was my mother, of lung cancer, which she blamed (as she blamed most everything) on my father, who had smoked a pack of Lucky Strikes a day before walking out on her when I was twelve and moving to Los Angeles with a twenty-five-year-old secretary to "start a new life." The fact that my father had quit smoking and was in perfect health, jogging five miles a day on the beach in Ventura, was only one item on my mother's list of life's unfairnesses—a litany that she would recite to every doctor, nurse, lab technician, and fellow patient we encountered. I swore to myself that I would not become the sort of person who complained of "missed opportunities."

Instead I counted my blessings, Aunt Roz's apartment being on the top of the list. It wasn't just that it was rent-controlled and convenient to NYU—and then Hudson, when I was hired there—it was that in leaving it to me, my aunt Rosalind bequeathed to me a piece of the life that she had led. A talented artist, she had moved to the city from Brooklyn over my grandparents' objections and taken classes at the Art Students League. She'd supported herself as an illustrator for women's fashion magazines, but in the summer she and two other women artists had banded together to rent a farmhouse in upstate New York, where they painted and swam naked in the backyard creek and made love to artists and folk musicians from the nearby artists' colony Byrdcliffe.

When I came back from Italy, I brought with me a watercolor—a view of the Tuscan hills from La Civetta—and a few pieces of Deruta pottery whose colors reminded me of Italy. And my books, of course. Otherwise the apartment is much as I found it. The walls are covered by oils and watercolors, sketches and woodcuts of the world my aunt lived in. Views of the Catskill Mountains from the farmhouse, shaded wood trails, nude figures bathing in the Esopus River, tiny botanical studies of flowers and ferns. Many are by my aunt's roommates and friends, but my favorites are the small domestic still lifes that my aunt painted. A china cup and a glassful of wildflowers beside a window looking out onto a windswept meadow, a woman's hand parting a lace curtain to reveal a snowy orchard, a Morris chair, its green upholstery cracked and scarred, the sun soaking into a rich red shawl tossed over the chair's back, its colors echoed in the autumn foliage glimpsed through a window behind the chair. Each scene seems invested with a kind of contemplative joy. There's peace—but also a hint of wildness in the outer landscape. The paintings expand the horizon of my tiny apartment, providing windows into distant landscapes and other rooms.

And so I've never felt cramped here until this morning when I looked at the picture of Robin standing in front of the same view that's in my little Italian watercolor. It's the view from the stone arch at the end of the lemon walk. I remember standing there one day, looking out at the hills of the Valdarno for so long that I felt that the landscape was imprinted on my heart. When Bruno had found me there I told him that I felt a part of myself would always be there. He had smiled and touched my hair and said, "I hope you'll leave more than your ghost here." This morning when I saw the picture of Robin standing beneath the same arch, I suddenly felt that I had left my *real self* behind at La Civetta and that the person here in my aunt's apartment is the ghost, an empty shell. It's that emptiness I feel now pressing on the walls of my apartment. I take down my raincoat from the hook by the door, grab an umbrella (I can see the rain misting the windowpanes), and close the door on all those places.

Fortunately, another blessing in my life is Cafe Lucrezia, which is a block north of my apartment on MacDougal Street and owned by one of my aunt's old friends. Camille is there this morning, seated at a green marble table by the window, peering through tiny gold-framed glasses at an adding machine and a stack of receipts. The minute she sees me, she takes off her glasses and opens her arms.

"*Cara* Rosa," she croons, pressing me into her crinkled silk blouse, "I read about that poor boy this morning. Wasn't he that pretty boy who used to come in here with you?"

I nod, blushing at Camille's description of Robin. But then, Camille calls half the young men in New York "pretty boys," and she usually has one or two dancing attendance on her. I lean into her embrace, breathing in the lilac scent she wears, and kiss her cheek. Her skin feels thin and papery, and I can see, as I pull back from the kiss, the fine lines around her eyes—but they're the only sign of her fifty-something years. Her figure, clearly visible in pencil-thin jeans and her clingy blouse, is still girlish, and her masses of tightly kinked hair are tinted the same shade of Titian red-gold she wore when my aunt first brought me here during my freshman year of college and got me a job waiting tables.

"Francesco," she calls to the dark-haired young man behind the espresso bar, "*due machiati, per favore.*"

As I sit down at Camille's table, I steal a quick glance at the boy, who looks like he comes from one of the outlying suburbs and not Italy. Chances are his name is Frank. Camille always rechristens the help with Italian names (when I worked here I was "Rosa") and blithely throws out orders in that language whether they know it or not. They either catch on quickly or are replaced by a seemingly endless supply of Giannis, Tommasos, and Marcos.

"Why ever would a sweet young thing like that take his own life?" Camille asks, her curls trembling as she shakes her head.

"I don't know. Someone accused him of plagiarizing a part of his film."

"Pshaw!" Camille says, pursing her mouth. "What kind of reason is that?"

I shrug and Camille narrows her eyes. "Are you sure he did kill himself?"

"I wasn't on the balcony when it happened . . ." My voice falters and I close my eyes to calm myself, but the image I see is of Orlando's wild eyes as he fled the room. I open my eyes. "Mark said he jumped. He *was* very upset just before—"

"Carissima." Camille lays a beringed hand on mine and leans forward. "You hadn't just had a lover's spat?" I can feel a slight quiver in Camille's hand. This is the kind of romantic drama that Camille thrives on.

"Millie," I say, using the name her Polish immigrant mother christened her with. Roz always said that when you need to get Camille's attention, just remind her where she grew up: Greenpoint, not Montmartre. "He was my student, nothing more." I pause as Francesco delivers two steaming cups of coffee. Camille lifts her hand from mine and briefly pats the waiter's cheek, calling him by the same endearment she just called me, only in its masculine form. I take a deep breath and remind myself that if I sound too scandalized at her suggestion I'll offend her and she won't tell me anything more. And whatever I might think of Camille's . . . hobbies . . . , there's no doubt that she has her ear to the ground. "Besides," I say, "he had a girlfriend. A girl with pink hair named Zoe Demarchis. A boy who came here from Italy yesterday seemed to be jealous of Robin."

"Very handsome? With dark curly hair and a face like an Adonis?" Camille asks, her eyes sparkling.

"Yes, that sounds like Orlando. Where did you see him?"

"He came in here yesterday with a bald man in a white suit. They had their heads together, whispering like spies. You say he came all the way from Italy because of that pink-haired girl? I think I've seen the girl—" Camille purses her lips and narrows her eyes, assessing and dismissing Zoe Demarchis's charms. "I don t believe the young Adonis came all the way from Italy for *her.*"

"Perhaps not," I say, remembering, though, the way Orlando watched Zoe and Robin in the park yesterday. "He accused Robin of stealing something from him, but it had to do with the film and not Zoe. That man he was here with sounds like Leo Balthasar, a Hollywood producer. I think Orlando was trying to get credit for a script Robin had written."

"And where is the young Adonis now?"

"He ran out of the party after Robin . . . after Robin jumped." I don't mention seeing Orlando in the park afterward. "I don't know if the police were able to find him last night, but you might want to alert campus security if you see him in here again."

"Oh, yes, I'll make a code word to tell Francesco and then I'll keep him entertained until the police come." The lines around Camille's eyes crinkle with delight—she would have made a wonderful spy—but then her gaze shifts and she looks over my head to the bar, where Francesco is taking a long and complicated to-go order from a harried—and pretty—office worker.

"I've taken up enough of your time, Camille, and I need to read the newspaper story before going to the emergency faculty meeting this morning." I stand up with my coffee cup in my hand.

"*Va bene, bella,* I'll have Francesco get you a refill while I do this order for him. I'll send over something sweet." She kisses my cheek as she brushes past me on the way to the bar, where she plucks the office gofer's to-go list out of her hand and sweeps behind the bar in one fluid motion.

I take my coffee to a table in the back, in the corner between the fireplace and the window overlooking the cafe's little garden. The green metal tables and potted plants Camille put out in yesterday's sun are coated with a sheen of rainwater. I'm glad for the warmth of the fire. Yesterday's glimpse of spring seems like a winter's dream now. As I open the paper to Robin's picture for the second time this morning, I wish it really were a dream, that winter's long sleep had never been interrupted by the false promise of spring.

"Witnesses said that Mr. Weiss, who had won first prize in Hudson College's Invitational Film Show, was accused at the celebration following the show of plagiarizing parts of the film," I read in the paper. "According to Hudson College president Mark Abrams, an argument over credit for the film may have precipitated Mr. Weiss's suicide."

I'm surprised that Mark had ventured such a theory to the press without first interviewing Orlando Brunelli. Perhaps Orlando had gone to the police last night and given more information, but when I scan the rest of the article I find no mention of Orlando's name. I put down the paper and notice that Francesco is standing behind me, a plate of biscotti in his hands, reading over my shoulder.

"Camille told me to keep an eye out for that Italian boy who was here yesterday," Francesco says, putting down the plate. "The one who was talking to the film producer."

"You knew he was a film producer?"

"Well, I didn't mean to eavesdrop, but I kept hearing the words 'script' and 'film deal,' and since I've written a screenplay myself . . ."

"Yes, of course," I say encouragingly to Francesco, wondering whether there's a waiter in this city who doesn't have a screenplay or a head shot tucked under his apron, "your interest was piqued. What did you hear?"

"Well the bald man kept saying that he needed something concrete in order to get financial backing, and the Italian boy said he wasn't interested in making a deal, he just wanted what rightfully belonged to him, so the producer said, 'Well, we can kill two birds with one stone,' which the Italian boy didn't seem to get because he said, all serious, 'I do not think it will be necessary to kill anyone.' " Francesco lifts both eyebrows and approximates an Italian accent straight out of *The Sopranos*. "So the producer laughed—loudly—and said it was just a figure of speech."

"And what did Orlando say to that?"

"He said something like . . . let me think . . . that he took words very seriously and that Robin had broken a promise. But I couldn't quite make out what he meant. His English became worse the more emotional he got."

I'm about to ask another question when Camille calls Francesco's name. Several customers are waiting in front of the bar for their coffee orders. Francesco rolls his eyes and resumes his place behind the bar. I stare out the window at the rain-soaked courtyard, trying to make sense out of the conversation Francesco overheard and the bits of what Orlando said to me yesterday. What exactly had Robin promised Orlando? A credit in the script he sent to Leo Balthasar? Why wouldn't Robin just give it to him, then? What had Robin said about promises yesterday? *I think of it the way I think of most lovers' promises. That he speaks "an infinite deal of nothing."*

An infinite deal of nothing. I can't help but think that's what it all adds up to. All the speculations as to why a young man of Robin's promise would end his own life. Would he really have killed himself because of an accusation of plagiarism? But then I remember how upset Robin had gotten when I asked whether he wrote the poem at the end of the film himself. Was he trying to pass off a poem he wrote as a poem written by Shakespeare's Dark Lady? Or had someone else written the poem—Orlando, perhaps?—and Robin stole it for his film? I'd love to have another look at the poem. If only I had a copy of it.

Then I realize that I probably do. When I asked Robin for a copy, he'd said "Here" and pressed that envelope into my hands, which I assumed contained only my forgotten watch. But now I'd wager that he'd put the poem in there as well. And it's still unopened in my evening purse.

I get up from the table, leaving a generous tip for Francesco, and pull on my raincoat. It's already a quarter to ten, but if I hurry I can still make it back to my apartment, retrieve Robin's envelope, and not be too late for the meeting. What I'm hoping is that in addition to the poem there might be a note from Robin explaining where the poem came from—whether he wrote it himself or "borrowed" it from Orlando. That had to be what he wanted to talk to me about yesterday— it made sense after what happened freshman year. He'd made a promise to me then that he would never claim another writer's words as his own. I'd like to think that he held his promise to me a little dearer than the lovers' promises he'd dismissed in class.

Outside of Cafe Lucrezia, I pause to put up my umbrella before heading south to my apartment. Before I can turn, though, a hand grips my elbow hard and pulls me in the opposite direction.

"Good, I was hoping I'd run into you here. We can go into the meeting together. There's power in numbers."

I look down at the diminutive figure at my side, but all I see is the top of her head bent forward against the rain. I'd know her, though, from the iron grip on my arm and the sheer force of her will propelling us along MacDougal Street. Chihiro Arita, my colleague in comparative literature, may be a good head shorter than me, and I hate to think how many pounds lighter, but she possesses twice my strength. She's the one we call in the department to unstick file drawers and move the Xerox machine when something falls behind it. She's also the one I call on when I need help navigating the internecine politics of the comp lit department. I'm not sure whether it's her area of study—court poetry of the Heian era—or a childhood spent subverting her mother's determination to raise her as a traditional Japanese girl in the suburbs of Boston that has given her the diplomatic skills of a courtier. She knows who's had their last article rejected by the PMLA and who's gotten a prestigious grant. Two years ago when we collaborated on a paper for the MLA conference on courtesan poets ("The [Court]Ship of States: The Poetics of Prostitutes"), she predicted each question we would get and who would ask it down to the last syllable and inflection. I'm lucky to count

her as a friend; she's never steered me wrong. Still, I dig in my heels at
the corner of MacDougal and West Fourth Street to lodge a protest.

"I need to go back to my apartment first—" I begin, but Chihiro
only shakes her head, her dark hair whisking the collar of her bright yellow raincoat like a broom, and digs her fingers deeper into my flesh as
she propels me across the street.

"I wouldn't advise being late for this meeting, Rose. It will give people a chance to talk."

"Talk about what?" I ask.

"About you and Robin Weiss."

"What do you mean? There was nothing going on between us. You
know that, Chihiro."

"I know that," Chihiro says stopping in front of the Graham
brownstone and giving me a reproving look that lasts long enough for
me to take in her outfit: under the shiny yellow raincoat she's wearing an
orange T-shirt and a green vinyl miniskirt. ("You have your schoolgirl
look; I have mine," she is wont to say about our differences in style.)
"But you spent a lot of time with him during his freshman year. People
saw you together in Cafe Lucrezia—"

"I go there with lots of my students; lots of professors do—"

Chihiro pinches my arm so hard I yelp. "Those other professors
weren't seen in a clinch with a drunk student moments before he plum-
meted to his death."

"Who said we were in a clinch? Where are you getting this stuff
from, Chihiro? You weren't even there."

"I have my sources. The fact that Robin was whispering sweet noth-
ings in your ear moments before he jumped from the balcony is on half
a dozen student forums this morning. Also that Robin was accused of
plagiarism. The prevailing theory is that he'd signed a six-figure—some
say seven—deal with a Hollywood producer for a script that he'd written, and that you ruined it by telling the producer that Robin plagiarized the script. Some people think you wrote it—"

"That's ridiculous!"

"But there's also a speculation thread that the script was written by a handsome and mysterious Israeli who was at the party and who disappeared afterward."

"Orlando Brunelli. And he's Italian."

"Brunelli? Isn't that the name of your junior-year-abroad heart-throb?"

"Yes, Orlando's his son."

Chihiro rolls her eyes. "Thank God the shippers didn't get hold of that connection." I'm about to ask what a shipper is, but then I remember from a previous conversation with Chihiro that it's when bloggers posit romantic connections—relation*ships*—between characters in TV shows. I'd thought it was a funny word for a romantic. "Now, about this plagiarism charge," Chihiro continues. "Had Robin ever handed in a paper you suspected was plagiarized?"

"Well, yes, there was an incident freshman year—"

"That you reported to the dean?"

"Well, no—"

"Enh-enh." Chihiro cuts me off with the same guttural sound she uses to keep her huge Weimaraner, Suzie, from eating something off the street. "After the plagiarism scandal last year, a campuswide directive was issued by the dean that all plagiarism incidents were to be reported immediately—"

"Yes, but that was *after* the incident with Robin. There was nothing in the directive about retroactively reporting cases."

Chihiro frowns, considering my case. After a moment she delivers her verdict. "You may be technically correct, but I'm afraid it won't look good. Especially with the rumor going around that Robin had a bit of a crush on you—" She stops, seeing the expression on my face. "And please stop looking like you're going to cry. That's the last thing we need." She gives me a pat on the arm that I know is meant as reassuring but which I suspect will leave a bruise. Then she gives me a none-too-gentle push into the foyer of the Graham brownstone.

CHAPTER SIX

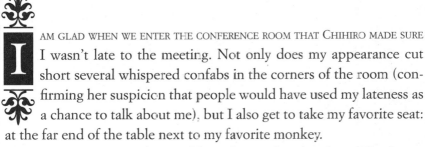

I AM GLAD WHEN WE ENTER THE CONFERENCE ROOM THAT CHIHIRO MADE SURE I wasn't late to the meeting. Not only does my appearance cut short several whispered confabs in the corners of the room (confirming her suspicion that people would have used my lateness as a chance to talk about me), but I also get to take my favorite seat: at the far end of the table next to my favorite monkey.

I've never quite understood how the monkeys got here. The fresco on the ceiling of this room—originally the formal dining room—is modeled on the one in the formal dining room at La Civetta. It depicts a lemon-covered pergola in a garden. An assortment of birds—doves, sparrows, and long-tailed peacocks—roost on the wooden struts. In the original fresco, fat cupids also frolic amidst the greenery, their chubby feet dangling precariously from their perches. In one corner a plaster foot even protrudes from the frescoed surface. In this New York version of the fresco, though, there are monkeys instead of cupids: monkeys peering out between leafy branches and monkeys dangling by their tails from the wooden slats of the pergola. If you look carefully (and I have had ample opportunity through long and tedious budget reviews to examine every inch of the palatial room), you can even find a few monkeys that have climbed down from the pergola and found their way into the formal dining room to perform rude and unspeakable acts. There's one painted in the china hutch defecating into a Meissen teacup and two copulating behind a Ming vase in the entryway. My favorite monkey, though, is the little one who peers out from behind the leafy fronds of an aspidistra, making an obscene gesture that I have seen only on the streets of Italy. I always sit right next to him. He gives me some relief for the sentiments I am unable to express in the course of departmental meetings.

Chihiro sits down next to me, bringing us both coffees and a napkinful of Mint Milanos from the spread set up on the sideboard. "The director of the counseling center has your name on his agenda," she says, spewing Milano crumbs in my direction. (When I once asked Chihiro not to talk while eating, she told me it kept people from being able to read her lips. "And it drove my mother crazy," she'd added.) "You come right after 'extended hours for counseling' but before 'dorm discussion groups.' "

"Were there any other teachers' names on the list?"

"Not that I saw, but I only saw the first page."

"His agenda is more than one page?"

Chihiro nods. She's just crammed two cookies into her mouth, a quantity that prevents even her from answering. "*Legal size* pages," she finally says. "I think we're in for a long meeting. I better get more cookies."

While Chihiro is laying in supplies, Mark comes into the room. He catches my eye but doesn't smile. Everything about him this morning bespeaks gravitas: the slightly rumpled gray suit, the dark circles under his eyes, and the faint suggestion of unshaven beard that shadows his face and brings out his cheekbones to advantage. He's never looked handsomer. I imagine him working through the night, preparing press releases and e-mails. *Poor guy,* I'm thinking when the young blond lawyer comes in wearing the same suit she was wearing last night, only very slightly rumpled, her hair scraped back into an unlawyerly pony-tail, the result, I'm sure, of not having access to her blow-dryer and flat-iron this morning. She takes the seat next to Mark's and opens a robin's egg blue leather portfolio filled with legal-size sheets in the same shade of blue, which also matches her eyes. Of course he'd need the lawyer to advise him on such a sensitive case, I tell myself. There's no need to be jealous. Still, I feel an uncomfortable sensation spreading in my chest and I find myself unable to take my eyes off this pretty blond woman.

"Thank you all for coming in on a Saturday," Mark begins, his eyes traveling around the table and seeming to greet each one of us sepa-rately. I'm not the only one who feels the spark of warmth when his eyes settle on mine, but I may be the only one who knows he's taking roll. He told me once that when he taught economics he never had to take attendance—he could tell in a lecture hall of a hundred students who was missing. His gaze does seem to stop a little longer when he reaches Gene Silverman, but that may be because Gene, slouched low in his seat and wearing opaque Ray-Bans, looks like he might be asleep. He straightens up when Mark's gaze stays on him, but doesn't remove the sunglasses.

"I realize you all had family obligations and better places to be this morning," Mark says, his voice a little hoarse, "but it was my hope that in the midst of our own blessings we could come together to make this tragedy more bearable to our larger family, as I have come to think of our college community. The death of a young person is a deep tear in the fabric of the community . . . and when that death is a suicide, the tear may spread even wider to those who may be wondering if they could have done anything to prevent that death." I feel Mark's gaze rest on me and know he's thinking of my relationship with Robin. "It's nat-ural, too, for there to be anger at someone who has committed suicide. I'd like us, though, to start with a moment of silence to honor the mem-ory of Robin Aaron Weiss and also to forgive him and to forgive our-selves for not being able to do more for him."

The low rumble of background noise, the shifting of papers and whispered conversations that accompany all such meetings, comes to an abrupt halt as we all bow our heads. The only sound in the room is the wet hiccups of the coffee urns. I lower my eyes to better think about Robin, but my gaze falls on the monkey in the aspidistra. *Not now,* I think, and close my eyes. I see the picture of Robin from the *Times,* standing at the end of the lemon walk, but he's turned away from the camera and is facing the Tuscan countryside, a patchwork of green and umber and gold laid out like a cobblestone road to the future. Had he, as I had, felt that a piece of himself would always remain there? Had he felt, as I once had, that he'd left the best part of himself behind and despaired?

I hope you'll leave more than your ghost here.

I flick open my eyes, sure for a second that someone has said the words aloud, and find Mark staring at me in the silent room. It's only then that I feel the tears on my face.

Chihiro reaches across me as if reaching for one of my cookies and knocks my cup of coffee onto the floor. "I'm sorry," she says. We both scramble to the floor to mop up the spilled coffee, and Chihiro passes me a tissue to dry my face. Is it really so shameful, I wonder, to cry for a young boy's death? But when I finish with the tissue I see that it's black with mascara and I'm grateful that I won't spend the rest of the meeting looking like a deranged raccoon.

By the time we surface, the director of the counseling center, Dr. Milton Spiers, is giving his report on the steps the counseling center is taking to handle the impact of Robin's death on the student body. Hours at the counseling center have been extended, and additional staff have been borrowed from neighboring hospitals.

"By the time your students show up to class on Monday morning, they'll have heard about what happened and they might want to talk about it. I would suggest making a brief statement about the event and posting the counseling hours on the blackboard. It's up to you if you want to open your classroom up to discussion—"

"Isn't that likely to get out of hand?" Lydia Belquist, the classics professor, asks, nodding her long patrician face up and down ("Lydia Equinus," Chihiro calls her).

Normally I find Lydia's comments in meetings irritating, but I've been mentally counting down Spiers's agenda and know I'm next, so I welcome Lydia's interruption.

"After all, we're not trained at *counseling*," she says, pronouncing the word as if it represented an arcane and slightly suspect skill, like dousing or feng shui. "Isn't it better to keep their minds on their studies? It's when they get distracted that these kinds of things happen. I plan to give my students extra passages of Tacitus to translate."

Someone tsks so loudly and explosively, it sounds like one of the urns has boiled over, but when I look in that direction I see it's Frieda Mainbocher, the women's studies professor and Lydia Belquist's bête noire. Frieda is a social historian whose work relies on statistics and other quantifiable data about the ancient world and the Renaissance. Her enmity with Lydia Belquist dates from an APA panel they both served on during which Frieda proclaimed that it was more important to know what the prostitutes in Rome were paid *per noctem* than what Caesar wrote in that silly book on Gaul. Lydia accused Frieda of having her mind in the gutter. Frieda accused Lydia of being a misogynist elitist. These are the two, I recall, that Mark has paired up to teach the Women in Italian History class. I can just imagine what fireworks that collaboration will produce.

"Sixty-five percent of suicides or suicidal attempts are made by students who have reported feelings of stress over academic performance," Frieda drones (I've heard students complain that her lecture style could put a meth addict to sleep). "Giving them more work is not the answer."

"I had Mr. Weiss in Latin 101, and he did not strike me as a scholar who subjected himself to pressure of any kind whatsoever. A shame, really, because he had a good mind." I could swear I hear a slight quiver in Lydia's voice, but then I remember that she has Parkinson's. "He was planning on majoring in classics before he went to Italy and got involved with all those film people." Lydia sends a purposeful look toward Gene Silverman, who is slumped in his chair sipping coffee from a Starbucks cup, but if the look penetrates behind his opaque Ray-Bans, he doesn't let on. Instead, Theodore Pierce, the English chair, responds to Lydia's comment.

"Really? He told me he was planning on majoring in English," Ted says at the same moment that three other professors attest that Robin was interested in majoring in their fields.

Mark holds up a hand to silence the commotion of wounded academic egos. It's not that unusual for a freshman to run through several majors before settling on one, but I've never seen so many professors so invested in that choice. Each sounds personally wounded by Robin's abandonment of his or her field.

"Clearly he was a confused young man," Mark says when the commotion has died down. "A compelling young man, charismatic even. He had a unique ability to draw people into his orbit." There's a reproving note in Mark's voice that I'm afraid is directed toward me, but when I look up I see that he's looking at Gene Silverman, who remains impervious to Mark's gaze behind his Ray-Bans.

"I'd like to ask if any of you encountered any irregularities with Mr. Weiss's written work—any cases of plagiarism." Now Mark's gaze does come to rest on me.

I raise my hand and describe the incident of the Oscar Wilde paper freshman year. "He seemed quite chastened, and he never gave me any reason to suspect his work again," I conclude.

"Did you continue to submit his papers to ithenicate.com?" Frieda Mainbocher asks.

"Periodically," I answer, not adding that I stopped after the rest of his papers that semester checked out okay.

"Did anyone else encounter any issues of plagiarism with this young man?" Mark asks.

Lydia Belquist, looking uncharacteristically abashed, clears her throat. "He handed in some Virgil translations that clearly had been cribbed from the Robert Fitzgerald translation, but that's not all that unusual . . ."

"He failed to attribute a few quotes in one of his papers," Ted Pierce volunteers, "but it seemed to be a confusion about MLA citation practices instead of a deliberate attempt to steal."

"He submitted a story to a workshop that sounded a lot like something by Bret Easton Ellis," our writer-in-residence says, "but to tell you the truth, so do half the things I get. Kids that age are so impressionable . . ."

A silence descends on the table. Another moment of silence for Robin, only this time I imagine we're all wondering whether we ever knew the boy we're mourning at all. I know I am.

Mark breaks the silence with a long-drawn-out sigh. "I think we can all see the necessity of reporting such incidents, however minor they may seem. Each on its own may appear innocent, but taken together they present a disturbing pattern. If this young man from Italy publicly accused Robin of plagiarizing this script that he'd just sold to Hollywood, all these other stories would have come out, and so he chose to take his own life instead."

"But are we absolutely sure it was a suicide?" Ted Pierce asks. "I was inside and couldn't see everything, but it looked to me like the Italian boy was running right at Robin and would have rammed into him hard enough to knock him off the railing."

"He would have if Mark hadn't gotten in the way," Gene Silverman says, pushing his sunglasses up onto the top of his head and turning his bloodshot eyes toward Mark. No wonder he'd worn the sunglasses; his eyes look ravaged. "Maybe if we hadn't been distracted by the other boy we could have kept Robin from falling. I know that I was paying more attention to him than to what Robin was doing. Even if he didn't push Robin, I think Orlando Brunelli has a lot to answer for." When he's finished speaking, Gene lowers his sunglasses, retreating behind them as if behind a stage curtain.

"Brunelli?" Lydia Belquist asks. "Isn't that the name of the family who is suing Cyril Graham for control of half the villa?"

At the mention of the lawsuit, a palpable ripple of excitement sweeps through the room. There have been rumors that Cyril Graham's ownership of La Civetta was being contested in the Italian courts, but this is the first I've heard the name of the other party in the suit. I can hear the words "illegitimate heir," "Sir Lionel Graham's mistress," and "slept with his wife's secretary" in the general melee. I turn to Chihiro and see immediately by her wide-eyed look (she always looks like an anime princess when she's trying to hide something) that she knew.

"Why didn't you tell me it was the Brunelli family that was suing Graham?" I whisper.

"Because," she says, "that name makes you crazy."

Of course she's right. Just the sound of the name, repeated in the fervid whisperings around the table, has the power to make my ears burn and my heart pound. The chattering swells and rises in the vaulted room until it seems as if the monkeys on the ceiling have come to life. Mark finally puts an end to it by pounding his fist on the table.

"This is exactly what we cannot have," he says, his voice tight with barely controlled anger. It's not like Mark to come so close to losing control—it must be the lack of sleep. "Yes, it's true that Orlando Brunelli is the grandson of Benedetta Brunelli, Lucy Graham's private secretary, who was rumored to have had an affair with Sir Lionel Graham. She was La Civetta's hospitality coordinator—and a fine one, I might add—for years and never seemed the least bit interested in suing for a piece of the estate, and neither did her son, Bruno Brunelli, who's taught at La Civetta for several years now. Brunelli's wife, Claudia, however, who took over the job of hospitality coordinator when the old woman died, filed a lawsuit in her son, Orlando's, name as soon as he came of age. They are contesting Cyril Graham's ownership of La Civetta and his intention to bequeath the entire estate to Hudson College, but our lawyers"—here Mark nods toward the pretty blond woman and she seems to glow under the attention—"are confident that the Brunellis will not be successful in their suit."

"Because the Italian government doesn't recognize illegitimate heirs?" Frieda Mainbocher asks.

"No," the lawyer answers, "because the villa and all the art collected by the Graham family were purchased by Lucy Wallace Graham, Sir Lionel's wife. This was her family home before she married Sir Lionel." The lawyer casts her eyes upward to take in the grand proportions of the room and seems startled to encounter the gaze of an impudent monkey. "She brought a great deal of money to the marriage, which Sir Lionel used to buy La Civetta and to finance his personal art and rare book collection."

"So if you can prove La Civetta really belonged to Lucy Graham you render the Brunelli suit impotent," Frieda Mainbocher sums up.

"But everyone knows it was Sir Lionel who was interested in art. Lucy Graham couldn't have told a Bellini from a Bernini," an art history professor points out.

"Ultimately that doesn't matter if the money was hers—but in fact we've discovered that Lucy Graham was more interested in her husband's collections than we might have thought. A number of important purchases—especially in the area of rare manuscripts—were made directly by Mrs. Graham. What would be helpful is more scholarly work on Lucy Graham's role as a collector—"

"What in the world does this all have to do with that poor boy's death!" The remark comes, surprisingly, from Lydia Belquist, whose head is nodding and quivering like a bobble-head doll's and whose rheumy old eyes are bright with tears.

Mark sighs and lifts his hands—pressed together as if in prayer—to the classics professor. "Thank you, Lydia. The answer is, nothing, absolutely nothing. It's just an unfortunate coincidence that Robin was involved with this young man. As for his involvement with Robin's death, yes, I agree with Gene that he was a precipitating factor in Robin's emotional state and I did ask the police to talk to the boy. Unfortunately, he was able to catch a plane out of New York early this morning and has returned to Italy. Given the negative publicity that would arise if a connection with Robin's death and the La Civetta lawsuit were made, I am asking everyone in this room to discourage this type of gossip. As far as I'm concerned, Orlando Brunelli was not responsible for Robin Weiss's death. Now, to get back to Dr. Spiers . . ."

Dr. Spiers, who seems wrapped up in an elaborate doodle on his notepad, startles at the sound of his name. "Oh, yes," he says, straightening up in his chair, "I think I've covered most of what I wanted to cover. Extended counseling hours, dorm meetings, refer troubled students to me . . ." As he ticks off each item on his list, I hope that he's doodled so heavily over my name that he can no longer read it. What in the world could he want with me anyway? I notice that a few people have gotten up to refill their coffee cups at the sideboard and some are packing their papers away in their briefcases and book bags, signaling that the meeting is drawing to a close. Mark is leaning across the table talking in hushed tones to the young lawyer. I notice that her skin pinkens at something he says and I feel another stab of jealousy. I suddenly remember that yesterday when he asked me to go to La Civetta with him he mentioned he would be working there with one of the lawyers to go over the terms of Cyril's bequest to the college. Was this the lawyer?

"Oh, yes, Dr. Asher," Dr. Spiers says, "I have a note to talk to you. You were very close to Robin, weren't you?"

"Well," I say, trying to sound neutral, "he was very interested in Renaissance sonnets." As soon as I say the words I find myself wondering whether they're true. Robin had apparently presented himself as a devotee of half a dozen disciplines. Perhaps his interest in sonnets was manufactured. Perhaps even his flirtation with me was part of an act.

"I was just his teacher," I say, trying not to sound as sad as I suddenly feel. "I wouldn't say that we were particularly close."

"Well, Robin must have felt differently," Dr. Spiers says. "I'm meeting with Robin's father as soon as this meeting's over, and he specifically asked that you be present. He said his son couldn't stop talking about you."

CHAPTER SEVEN

'LL BET YOU ANYTHING SPIERS DUMPS YOU WITH THE GUY," CHIHIRO TELLS me while we're standing at the foot of the staircase, waiting for Dr. Spiers to come back with Robin's father.

"He wouldn't."

"Oh, yeah? Then why is the meeting in *your* office?"

"Spiers said he thought it would be more intimate than the counseling center."

"And easier for him to bail. Just wait. Ten minutes into the session he'll get an emergency phone call, which he'll have to take because it's a distressed student. That way he gets to look caring while he's abandoning Robin's dad with you."

I'm about to protest, but Chihiro has an unerring ability to predict behavior so instead I enlist her aid.

"So, what should I do then?"

"Order in."

"What?"

"The poor guy probably hasn't had a bite to eat since he got the call last night. I'd recommend something light and nourishing, say, the borscht from Veselka . . . well, look at this." Chihiro points toward the glassed-in foyer, where Dr. Spiers is signing in at the security desk while talking on a cell phone. Next to him is a short man—no more than five feet six, I'd say—in a tan trench coat several sizes too big for him. Although he's wearing slacks and loafers, he gives the impression of being in his pajamas and of having just woken up. Maybe it's the way what little hair he has stands up on his head, or the dazed look in his eyes, or the way he keeps blinking like a newborn chick. "Spiers is already on the phone. I'd give you five minutes at best. Good luck, sweetie." Chihiro hands me a slip of paper and darts out the door before I can beg her to stay. I look down at it, hoping it contains some sage advice, but instead it's the phone number for Veselka on Second Avenue, which I slip into my book bag before coming forward to greet Robin's father.

"Mr. Weiss—" I begin.

"Dr. Asher? Please, it's Saul. I feel like I know you. Robbie talked about you so much."

I take Saul Weiss's soft, damp hand and hold it in both of mine. "I can't begin to tell you how sorry I am—"

He ducks his head, looking embarrassed to be the object of sympathy. I notice that under his tan raincoat he's wearing a washed-out plaid shirt in shades of tan and ecru and putty, colors that seem designed to blend in with some drab institutional setting. I rack my brain to remember anything Robin might have told me about what his father did for a living, but the fact is I can't remember Robin ever saying anything about his parents. Robin managed to give the impression of having sprung fully formed on his first day of college like Venus arising out of the sea.

"Is Mrs. Weiss—?" I begin, glancing toward Spiers for help, but he's still talking into his cell.

"Robbie's mother died when he was eight, so I've raised him on my own. Maybe I didn't do such a good job—"

"Don't say that. Robin was an extraordinary young man, so talented—"

"He was always good at school. Acting, writing, charming the girls," Saul says, managing a small proud smile, "but he had trouble settling down to one thing. He told me when he took your class on Shakespeare that he'd decided to write plays. I said that was fine, but how was he going to pay the rent until he became the next Mr. Neil Simon?" Saul shakes his head. "Of course I got it all wrong. That wasn't the kind of plays he wanted to write at all. I never could keep up with him."

I smile sympathetically, remembering all the times my mother would get it all wrong. When I first showed an interest in poetry, she thought maybe I could get a job writing greeting cards or jingles for advertising. When I told her I was studying Italian, she found me a summer job waitressing at an Italian restaurant in Astoria.

"I'm sure he appreciated the effort. Right, Dr. Spiers?" I say shooting Spiers a murderous look over Saul Weiss's head. He responds by clicking his phone closed and nodding vigorously.

"Yes, yes, absolutely—although the adolescent may overtly reject the parent's attempts to assimilate their cultural contexts, on a subconscious level they absorb the message."

"Shall we go to my office?" I suggest because Saul Weiss looks suddenly woozy. He's carrying a large shopping bag, and I offer to carry it up the stairs for him but he declines.

"Yes, you two go on up. I just have to check something back at the counseling center. I'm afraid my staff is being overwhelmed by the sudden demand. I'll check in with you later—or feel free to drop by my office on the way out."

Amazing, I think, as Dr. Spiers flees the building: he didn't even last the five minutes Chihiro predicted. I look down at Saul Weiss to see whether he looks insulted—or outraged, as he'd have every right to be—but the poor man looks apologetic.

"I suppose this is very upsetting for the other students." He takes a grayish handkerchief out of his coat pocket to blow his nose. "Dr. Spiers says they've had to hire extra counselors. That must cost a lot of money—"

"They've got it to spend," I assure Mr. Weiss.

"An accountant's habit," he says apologetically, "always adding things up. Robin used to hate it . . ." He falters and then gestures to the grand staircase.

"Whew!" he says, whistling. "Did someone really live here?"

"Cyril Graham," I say, starting up the steps. "He donated the townhouse to the college along with the funds to enlarge the film department—the windows are Tiffany." I pause on the second landing to point out the stained glass and to give Saul a chance to catch his breath.

"Cyril Graham's the fellow with the place in Italy, right? The school Robin went to last year. Is that place as fancy?"

"Fancier," I say. We've finally reached my office. Saul Weiss takes out his handkerchief to wipe his pink face. I unlock the door and gesture toward the Morris chair, leaning over it to open the window a crack. The sound of rain and traffic sluicing over the wet streets seeps into the room. "Let me know if that's too cold," I say, turning to sit behind my desk. When I see Saul sink into the green cushions, hugging his shopping bag to his chest, he looks so frail there that I don't have the heart to retreat behind the big imposing desk, and so I perch instead on its edge.

"No, it's fine," he says. "It must get stuffy up here." He looks up toward the ceiling. "And cost a bundle to heat in the winter. Now I know where all my tuition dollars have been going." He attempts a chuckle that curdles into a small strangled sob. "I'm so sorry," he says, rooting in his pocket for the much-used hankie.

"Please, Mr. Weiss—Saul," I say, handing him a box of Kleenex, "don't apologize. I can't even begin to imagine what you're going through. I only wish there were something I could do or say—" I break off, afraid that I'm going to start crying myself.

"You're a very nice lady," Saul says, his voice tight with the effort of controlling his tears. "Robin always said so. I'm sure you did all you could for my boy. It's a comfort to know he had someone like you to turn to. I always thought he missed having a mother—not that you'd have been like a mother—I mean, you're much too young—"

"Not really," I say, remembering that I could have had a son Orlando Brunelli's age if I'd stayed with Bruno twenty years ago. "I didn't realize that Robin's mother died when he was so young. She must have been quite young—was she ill?"

"Robin's mother took her own life," Saul says. "She turned on the gas oven while I was at work and Robin was at Hebrew school. Robin found her."

"I'm so sorry," I say, at a loss for anything else to say. "Poor Robin."

"I've always been afraid . . . You know, they say it runs in families." Saul sighs. "Pearlie was a sensitive girl who never really had a chance to do the things she wanted. Go to college, live in a big city, travel to Europe. I tried to make sure that Robin had all the opportunities to do the things she missed. I never wanted him to feel trapped the way she had—or like me, for that matter. I never thought about what I wanted to be. My father was an accountant, so I was an accountant. I never pushed Robin to follow in my path—even though he was very good with numbers. Now I don't know . . . maybe he needed a little direction. Maybe I should have kept better tabs on him these last couple of years, but he seemed happy—living here in the city and then getting to go to Italy—I figured he didn't need his old dad dragging him down."

I think of how desperate I had been to leave my mother's house on Long Island and escape to Manhattan. How I'd doubled up on classes in high school and studied through the nights to graduate a year early. Looking at this mousy little man—no trace of Robin's beauty in his face—I'm afraid he's probably right. Robin had reinvented himself and left his father behind. And now he'd left forever. What can I possibly say to this man to ease his grief?

"There is one favor I wanted to ask," Saul says as if reading my mind.

"Of course," I say, "anything."

"Robin wrote a lot. Poems, letters, journals . . . the kid never stopped writing. I don't know what to do with it all. I'd feel like I was invading his privacy if I read it, and I wouldn't be able to tell if there was anything . . . well, anything worth saving. You're an English teacher, right?"

I nod, sure that the distinction between comp lit and English would be meaningless to Saul.

"And a writer, too? Robin said you wrote poetry?"

I nod again, this time speechless that Robin had even known this. I never talk about my writing to my students.

"Would you look at this stuff?" he asks, patting the well-stuffed shopping bag. "I'd trust you to keep private anything that you should, and if you thought there was anything worth saving—" He holds the bag out to me.

Behind me on my desk I've got more than a hundred unread term papers. The last thing I need is extra reading. "Of course," I say, taking the bag from him, "I'd love to read what Robin was writing. Perhaps there's something we could publish in the literary magazine. I could talk to the editor about doing a memorial issue—" I falter, realizing that I'll have to go over anything Robin wrote to make sure he actually wrote it, but luckily Saul doesn't notice my hesitation. He smiles and for the first time I do see something of Robin in the shape of his mouth. "Yes, exactly, that would be nice. I knew you'd be the right one to talk to. Now, I probably shouldn't take up any more of your time . . ." He braces his hands on the arms of the chair to push himself up. He looks so weary that I hate to send him out into the rain. I'm thinking of what else I can say to him when there's a knock on the door.

"Maybe that's Dr. Spiers," I say, but when I open the door there's a delivery boy from Veselka, the aroma of beets and dill steaming up from the insulated bag he cradles in his arms.

"Stay here and have some soup," I say as I pay the delivery boy and read the message Chihiro has scrawled on the take-out menu ("You owe me, Asher!"). "I bet you haven't eaten since yesterday."

Saul Weiss leaves after finishing a quart of borscht and half a loaf of challah. The hot soup, the sound of the rain, and the emotions of the morning have left me craving a nap. After entering a few grades on my laptop and checking my e-mail (scrolling through a dozen messages with the subject line "Robin Weiss" that I can't face reading right now), I turn off the machine and start packing up to leave. I'm interrupted by a knock on my door. Hoping that Chihiro has thought to send coffee and dessert, I open it—but no such luck. It's the young blond lawyer, wrinkling her nose at the smell of beets that still permeates my office.

"Can I help you?" I ask, hoping my tone sounds cool enough to discourage her. She's holding a stack of folders and I suspect she's going to ask me, in the absence of Saturday office staff, to help her with the copying machine.

"President Abrams suggested I speak with you about a project I'm working on," she says, her eyes moving rapidly over the cluttered surfaces of my office. "Do you have a minute?"

I can hardly tell her I was planning on taking a nap, so I open the door and gesture toward the Morris chair. Since I don't have the same desire to make her feel comfortable as I had in Saul Weiss's case, I take the chair behind my desk, lean back, and treat her to the silent expectant gaze I reserve for students requesting a grade change. She shifts uneasily in the dent left by Saul Weiss in the upholstery and clears her throat. It occurs to me that she no more wants to be here than I want her to be.

"President Abrams thought this project might interest you because of your background in Italian Renaissance women," she begins. "You *are* interested in Italian Renaissance women, right?"

"Well, I'm interested in the poetry of certain Italian Renaissance women. Gaspara Stampa, Veronica Franco, Vittoria Colonna, to name a few . . ." I wait to see whether these names provoke any response from her, but I might as well be reciting a Greek declension. "Does this project concern poets?" I ask.

"Well, not poets per se," she says, "but it concerns documents pertaining to the lives of women in Italy during the Renaissance—letters, household accounts, nuns' chronicles—"

I hold up my hand. "I'm not a women's studies or history professor," I say. "Maybe you should be talking to Frieda Mainbocher."

"That's what I thought," she agrees "but President Abrams especially wanted you to handle this job."

I sigh, secretly flattered that Mark's still plotting to get me to Italy—and that this attractive lawyer is annoyed by Mark's preference for me. "Exactly what papers are we talking about?"

"Rare manuscripts collected by Lucy Wallace Graham," she says. "I'm sure there's some very valuable scholarly material—"

"I've seen Lucy Graham's collection," I tell her, "when I was at La Civetta during college. For the most part it's comprised of laundry lists from the Convent of Santa Catalina. I'm sure they're valuable from a historical point of view, but they're really not my kind of thing. No doubt there are plenty of scholars who have worked with them over the years at La Civetta who could help you inventory them—"

"The thing is," she says, squirming so hard in the leather chair that it creaks, "President Abrams wants someone completely trustworthy to ascertain the value—monetary and scholarly—of the collection. You see, it might be important for our case to establish Lucy as a scholar and discriminating collector."

"My understanding is that the only collecting Lucy Graham ever did was of the gin bottles she stashed in her armoire. The only reason she ended up with those papers from Santa Catalina was that when the convent's library was flooded in 1966 she offered to house the damaged manuscripts in the *limonaia* until they could be restored. She thought that since the original convent was once on the grounds of La Civetta, there was a special relationship between them. But then she never gave them back! If you ask me, the best thing to do is return all of it to Santa Catalina."

"If Lucy drank, it was because of how Sir Lionel treated her. He took all her money and then seduced her own secretary."

"You don't sound like a fan of the Graham family, Miss—?"

"Wallace," she says. "Daisy Wallace. Lucy Wallace Graham was my great-aunt on my father's side."

"Only one 'great'?"

"My father had me when he was already sixty," she explains. "He died last year."

"I'm sorry."

Daisy Wallace bows her head and to my shock and dismay begins to cry. I move around the desk and hand her the box of Kleenex that I'd given Saul Weiss and sit on the edge of the desk while she struggles to regain her control. "He wanted me to work on the Graham bequest," she finally is able to say. "He felt the key would be in establishing Lucy's role in Sir Lionel's collecting and that it would be an opportunity to rehabilitate Lucy's reputation. My father cared a great deal about family honor."

"Perhaps he felt that the Wallaces were owed a share in La Civetta as well."

"Oh, no," Daisy says, coloring deeply, "believe me, no one in my family wants anything to do with that villa. My father wasn't a superstitious man, but he said that the one time he was there as a young man he was sure it was haunted. He said that at night he could hear a woman weeping and that he saw blood spots appear on the tile floor of the rotunda—"

"Yes, I've heard those stories," I say, standing up. "The blood in the rotunda is an old legend about La Civetta, but if you look at the tiles you see it's just a mosaic pattern of rose petals in the marble that's faded over the years. When it gets wet it can look like blood—"

Daisy is staring at me as I recite this elaborate attempt at an explanation for the phenomenon. I stop myself before telling her of the time I saw the spots of blood glistening in the moonlight that poured through the oculus of the rotunda, but she must sense something of my horror at the memory.

"I completely understand you not wanting to go back there," she says, gathering her folders and getting up from the chair. "I told President Abrams that it really wasn't necessary. I'm sure I'll be able to catalog the books with a student intern to help with the Italian. I'll let President Abrams know what you said." She pauses in the doorway and smiles for the first time since she came into my office today. "I'm sure you have better things to do with your summer than spend it in Italy."

Sure, I think to myself as I listen to the sound of her footsteps echoing in the empty townhouse, *I can spend it in a mosquito-infested cabin in the Catskill woods deconstructing four-hundred-year-old lyrics.*

I gather my things and close the window, pausing to gaze out at the rain-drenched park. A fine mist hangs in the branches of the sycamores, muting the colors of pavement and brick to pale monotones. Gone are the bright dresses and T-shirts of yesterday; instead the few pedestrians crossing through the park are huddled under dull gray and tan rain-coats. The brick townhouses that briefly glowed ochre in yesterday's sun are now a faded rust color.

Yesterday's weather might have been a mirage, a tease of spring, but it's left everything a shade grayer. I believe that I was looking forward to spending the summer at my aunt's cabin in Woodstock; I believe I was hoping that once I made tenure in the fall Mark and I would get married; I believe I thought I'd done the right thing when I didn't report Robin's plagiarism to the dean.

I put on my raincoat, shoulder my book bag, and pick up the shopping bag that Saul Weiss left. I can hear its weight in the dull thud of my footsteps descending the stairs. I don't feel much like the heroine of a nineteenth-century novel today, but rather like one of the unnamed extras that people the margins of those sprawling epics: a scullery maid carrying down the slop buckets or a spinster aunt collecting castoffs for charity.

When I left La Civetta, I did see myself, however grief stricken, as the heroine of the story. I was Jane Eyre fleeing across the moors to keep from becoming Rochester's mistress. Soon after I came back to New York I heard that Bruno Brunelli had left La Civetta and gone to live in Rome. I suspected he couldn't bear to stay at the villa once I had left. Perhaps I maintained some small hope that someday I would hear his voice calling me, just as Jane does when Rochester calls out for her after he's been destroyed—and suitably chastened and de-wifed—by fire. But hearing that he's back at La Civetta, teaching that same class on the sonnet in which he so easily seduced me with a little Petrarch and Tasso, and that Claudia is there, too, feels like being forgotten.

And if he has forgotten me, I think, walking bareheaded in the rain because I can't handle an umbrella and Saul Weiss's enormous shopping bag at the same time, if it means nothing to him to be at La Civetta after all these years, why should I be banned from the one place on earth where I was ever truly happy? Why not go along with Mark's request to make nice to Cyril Graham? Why not take up Leo Balthasar's business offer and pick up a tidy sum for advising some Hollywood director on iambic pentameter? Mightn't there be in Lucy Graham's collection some worthwhile tidbit to flesh out my dry-as-dust book on Renaissance sonnets? After all, I've been asked three times—

I stop on the stoop to my building and drop the shopping bag to the pavement. No; no, I haven't, I realize. Daisy Wallace never really asked me to go. She got out of there before she had to because, I see now, she really doesn't want me to go. Mara was right: There is something going on between the lawyer and Mark, and she wants the field to herself.

I'm tempted to leave the shopping bag in the vestibule and come back for it later, but, then, what if someone takes it? So I drag it up five flights of stairs, wondering how on earth I'd ever been grateful for the lack of an elevator. That little bit of karmic spitefulness—begrudging my mother my home—would no doubt come back to haunt me someday, when, old and alone, I can no longer manage the stairs myself.

I am in so foul a mood when I finally drag myself into my apartment that the only respite I can imagine is Mara's white circles and ovals still wrapped in tissues in my evening purse. I take the bag and a bottle of Poland Spring into the bedroom and crawl into my unmade bed. For a while I just listen to the rain on the rooftop—an advantage of living on the top floor that today only seems to deepen my wintry gloom. I open my purse and sort out all the pills into two neat piles of ovals and circles on the bed. They lie on the floral-patterned sheet like late snow on spring buds. I close my eyes and remember the morning it snowed at La Civetta—a rare enough occasion to send Florentines out into the streets with cameras to document the effect of snow on centuries-old stone and stucco. At the villa the olive trees were glazed with silver, each tree casting a circular shadow of deep green where the snow didn't stick. The statues were dusted with a mantle of fine white powder, transforming Roman gods and goddesses into eighteenth-century bewigged courtiers. The students flocked into the gardens to take pictures, but Bruno took me into the *limonaia.* He made me close my eyes while he opened the huge green shutters. All around me I could smell the deep spicy scent of the lemon flowers and the sharper tang of the fruit. I could hear the rustle of the leaves as Bruno walked back through the potted trees to stand beside me.

"Open your eyes," he said.

When I did I was dazzled by the brightness. The light that poured through the falling snow was distilled, crystallized into liquid pearl that coated each leaf and petal and turned the hanging lemons into glowing orbs like a million candles burning in a dark church.

"I want you to remember this," Bruno said, "if you ever wonder if I loved you. Like the promise of spring buried beneath the winter's snow, I'll love you even when it most seems I don't."

Even when I've gone back to my wife, he might have said.

He didn't have to. I'd known then what he was going to do, and still I made love to him that day in the *limonaia,* beneath the lemon trees on the cold terra-cotta tiles, our bodies crushing the dried lemon flowers that had fallen to the ground so that afterward my skin smelled like lemons. Sometimes even now I imagine I can still smell their scent on my skin.

I open my eyes and realize that I do, in fact, smell lemon flowers. The scent is coming from my purse. Maybe it's some perfume that Mara uses that spilled on the Kleenexes from her purse. But no, Mara uses a cloying tea rose perfume without a hint of citrus in it. The scent is coming from the envelope that Robin gave me last night.

I sit up and hold the envelope to my face and breathe in the smell. When I tear the paper, a shower of cream-colored slivers drifts into my lap, a lemon-scented snow. A single sheet of paper is wrapped around my watch, a sheet of thick old parchment—the same cream color as the dried lemon petals. As I unroll it I see that it's bordered by an intricate pen-and-ink drawing of flowering lemon trees around a fourteen-line poem—I've read enough sonnets to instantly take in the quantity without having to count. The ink is so faded and the penmanship so antiquated that at first I can't read it, but then slowly, like a photographic image resolving in a tray of chemicals, the words emerge.

It's the poem that ended Robin's film. It looks like a genuine Renaissance manuscript, but I know such things can be forged. It's hard for me to believe that Robin would have the expertise, but perhaps he met someone at La Civetta who did. But what would be the purpose? To pretend the poem was written by Shakespeare's Dark Lady to sell his screenplay? Is that what this poem's supposed to be? The Dark Lady's invitation to Shakespeare to come to Italy?

When I hold the poem up, another sheet of paper, so thin it had clung to the back of the parchment, flutters to the bed. It's covered in script, but this handwriting I recognize as Robin's. It's a note addressed to me.

Dear Dr. Asher,

When I put this poem in my film I never dreamed how much trouble it would cause or how many people it would upset. I found it at the villa along with some other old poems and letters, but I left those where I found them because I didn't want to be accused of stealing. This was the only one I took, but I think now that I shouldn't have taken even this one. It must be very valuable—too valuable for me to hold on to. Would you keep it for me, please? I know that if you could read all the poems you would understand. If you could only come to Italy this summer, I could show them to you. There's another reason I think you should come, but I'll explain that later. Meanwhile, would you at least think about coming? Just read this poem. How can you resist going back there?

—Robin

I put down the note and read the poem again. It's a beautiful poem and quite possibly written by a Renaissance poet, perhaps by Ginevra de Laura, but there's no reason on earth to imagine it's addressed to William Shakespeare. But Robin said there were letters with the poems as well. Might they indicate whom the poems were written to? Would that explain why Robin thought the poems were so valuable—so valuable he was afraid to keep this one on his person? Valuable enough, perhaps, that someone would kill for one?

Was it possible that Orlando Brunelli had wanted this poem so badly that he pushed Robin from the balcony to get it? But Mark had said he hadn't pushed him . . . that Robin had deliberately jumped. Why would he say that if he wasn't sure . . . ?

Unless he was thinking about the lawsuit. What if Mark hadn't accused Orlando of pushing Robin because he was afraid that the Brunelli family would claim he was trying to discredit their lawsuit? Could he have been afraid that accusing Orlando would drag the lawsuit into the press? Hadn't he urged the faculty today not to talk about the connection between Robin's death and the Brunelli family? It's hard for me to believe that Mark would care more about good press than about the truth behind Robin's death, but then I know how much the fate of the college matters to Mark. He might even have been able to convince himself that he hadn't seen Orlando push Robin. And that look he thought he saw in Robin's eyes . . . maybe he had misread fear for despair.

I reread Robin's note. "I know that if you could read all the poems, you would understand." If the poems hidden in the villa could explain what happened to Robin, I owe it to Robin to go there and try to find them. And I owe it to Saul Weiss, who will go through the rest of his life thinking he somehow failed his son, that it was his fault Robin killed himself. Perhaps, too, I owe it to myself. I've avoided the villa, Florence, in truth all of Italy, since my junior year of college because of an unhappy love affair. Surely I've gotten over whatever lingering feelings I nurtured for Bruno Brunelli. Wouldn't it be better to go back and face the scene of our love affair—even face him—and know that I was over him and that I was ready to settle down with Mark?

I lie back in bed and read the poem over again. At the line "To be reborn amidst spring's gentle breeze" I feel something kindle inside of me. Whoever wrote this meant it not just as a promise and a gift, but also as an invitation. Robin is right; who could resist such a summons? I've received my third invitation to La Civetta.

CHAPTER EIGHT

VERY ONCE IN A WHILE NEW YORK GETS A SPRING THAT REMINDS US THAT our per annum rainfall is higher than Seattle's. The spring of Robin's death is one of those springs. It rained through Robin's funeral, turning the yellow soil that Saul Weiss shoveled over his son's grave into a viscous soup that stained the mourners' shoes a jaundiced hue. There was a high turnout among the faculty at the cemetery in Queens and I thought I detected in the following week that yellow mud tracked on the floors of the college: the ghostly yellow footprints a badge of mourning like the strips of torn cloth pinned over our hearts to show that something had been rent. Chihiro, who had never attended a Jewish funeral, was so fascinated by this practice that she decided to write a paper on the uses of textiles in mourning rituals.

It rained on graduation day, driving the ceremony indoors into an overcrowded and humid auditorium. When Mark came to the place where Robin's name would have been called (between Yung-ying Wei and Naomi Weissberg), we observed a moment of silence. Walking back home, I saw a circle of students standing in the fountain basin in Washington Square Park holding hands. When I came closer, Zoe Demarchis recognized me and broke the circle to let me in.

"We're singing songs that Robin liked," she explained to me. After a warbly rendition of "Hey Jude," there's a pause into which I find myself interjecting sonnet number 65, another of Shakespeare's assertions of writing's power to confer immortality. At the last lines, though—"O none, unless this miracle have might, / That in black ink my love may still shine bright"—I couldn't help but remember Robin's question that day in class, and when I closed my eyes I saw the yellow dirt falling on Robin's coffin and I knew how useless a trade it was—the living flesh for empty words. I would gladly have given up all the poems and all the plays in all the world for Robin to be standing there in that circle.

That night I have dinner with Mark at our favorite restaurant—Po, on Cornelia Street—and I tell him that I've decided to go to Italy after all. He's so happy that I feel churlish in having turned down his first offer and I'm glad to give him some good news. Since Robin's death he's been distracted and distant.

"I only wish you had told me earlier so you could have flown with me tomorrow," he says, reaching across the table to take my hand. "I could have found a way to get the college to pay for your airfare."

"Actually," I say, taking a sip of the Prosecco Mark has ordered, "that won't be necessary. I've accepted Leo Balthasar's offer to work as a consultant on Robin's screenplay. They're flying me to Florence next week. First class."

The smile on Mark's face doesn't change, but his hand tightens on mine. "Really?" he says. "That's . . . well, I'm impressed with Leo Balthasar's judgment. I hope he's paying you well." Mark's eyes flick away from me. I'm afraid that he's hurt that I've accepted the offer without consulting him, but then I see it's just that he's trying to attract the attention of the waiter. "Take this Prosecco away," he tells him when he comes to our table. "We'll have champagne instead—to celebrate," he says, turning back to me, "your good fortune."

"*Our* good fortune," I remind him. "Now we'll be able to spend the summer together. And I can have a look through Lucy Graham's archives like you wanted me to in the first place. Perhaps that's where Robin found the poems by Ginevra de Laura. Finding them would be a significant addition to my book on the Renaissance sonnet *and* a help to Graham's defense against the lawsuit. It would certainly establish Lucy as a collector of note if she had found the poems."

"Yes, it would be killing two birds with one stone," Mark says. I try not to cringe at the idiom he's chosen, remembering that it's what Leo Balthasar said to Orlando. What had Orlando answered? That it wouldn't be necessary to kill anyone?

"Or three, actually," Mark adds, beaming now. "Since the poems would substantiate Robin's screenplay. I gather you haven't found anything in the papers Robin's father gave you."

"No," I say. Technically I *am* telling the truth. The poem and letter from Robin weren't in the shopping bag Saul Weiss gave me. "Mostly there were just drafts of old term papers and some notebooks filled with poetry—all free verse—nothing in formal verse like the last sonnet of the movie."

"That's too bad," Mark says, "but perhaps you'll have better luck in Italy. I would like to ask one favor."

"Well, just one," I say, teasingly. "It is our last night together for a week. Are you sure you want to use it up now?"

Under the table Mark's leg presses against mine. "I'll have to count on my charms for later . . . but this is really important. If you find anything . . . any letters attached to the poems . . . say, by Lucy or Sir Lionel . . . would you show them to me before sharing them with Balthasar or anyone else?"

"You're worried about where the Grahams might have come by the poems?" I ask.

"Something like that. I just wouldn't want anything else to complicate the lawsuit right now. Those Brunellis are relentless. I'd just like to have first look." Mark looks tired again, bowed down by the myriad details he's had to take care of in these last few weeks, and I regret that this worry is tainting our last night together. I regret, too, that I haven't shared the poem Robin gave me, or his letter, or my worries that Orlando might have been trying to get the poem from Robin when he fell. But Mark's made it clear that he doesn't want to accuse Orlando Brunelli of pushing Robin off that balcony, and I don't want to ruin our last night together by voicing theories I can't prove yet.

"Of course," I say, rubbing my foot against his leg. "I'll show you anything I find first." It's an easy promise to make. After all, a cache of Renaissance sonnets might be a priceless discovery for me, but could it really decide the disposition of a billion-dollar villa? It doesn't seem likely. But then, as our appetizers are served, I remember that Robin had thought the poems were so important that just having one put him in danger. And he may have been right.

I decide, though, a week later on my last night in New York, to share Robin's letter and the poem with Chihiro over take-out Chinese food and a bottle of Australian Shiraz. First, though, we exchange going-away presents.

"So you don't freeze up north," I say, giving her a North Face rain slicker for her trip to the English Lake District, where she is spending the summer doing research on Dorothy Wordsworth.

"And here's something in an actual color to brighten up your usual nun-like wardrobe," she tells me, tucking a package wrapped in bright orange tissue paper into the zippered compartment of my suitcase.

"Speaking of nuns," I say, "have a look at this and tell me if it sounds like something written by a woman who spent the last years of her life locked away in a nunnery."

I hand her the poem and she puts on her lavender-rimmed cat's-eyes glasses to read it. "Well, she's obviously guilty about something she did to this guy. So guilty she's willing to hand over her villa—or at least the *limonaia*—to make it up to him. So, I'd say she's halfway to the nunnery already. Where'd you get this?"

I explain how I came by the poem and give her the letter as well. She reads the letter with as much attention and care as the poem. It's something I admire in Chihiro—she'll give as much textual analysis to a manga volume as to a poem by Wordsworth—but right now I'm anxious to get her verdict.

"He's playing with you," she says at last, "teasing you with little bits of information. Luring you to come to Italy. It's hard to say what he's really up to. After what I've heard about Robin Weiss, I could believe he made the whole thing up. Poems and all."

"So, you don't think I should be worried about someone trying to kill me for this poem," I say, laughing, making a joke of it.

"I didn't say that," Chihiro answers, looking serious despite her silly glasses. "If Robin's masquerade was successful and convinced someone the poems were real, you could be killed for a fake poem as easily as for a real one. It would just be . . . you know . . . a tiny bit more pathetic."

In the cab to JFK the next morning, hungover from the wine we shared, I'm not sure what to be more worried about: the driving rain and limited visibility, terrorism, or the fact that I'm carrying a poem—real or not—that someone might kill me for. I wish now that I'd saved at least one of Mara's Valiums, but I threw them all away a week ago when I realized I'd grown a bit too dependent on them. On the runway I decide that the thick blanket of cloud cover is definitely the more likely threat, but then, as our plane taxis into the line of aircraft waiting for takeoff, a thin band of gold appears at the horizon and the rain stops. The low-lying sun washes over the wet tarmac, flashes off the silver underbellies of the planes, and turns the gray clouds ink blue. By the time we lift into the stratosphere, I feel cocooned against turbulence, grief, and fear, insulated by the cool blue dusk that surrounds the plane with a cushion as soft as this plush first-class seat I accepted from Leo Balthasar's production company. Leo himself is sitting across the aisle from me, his seat fully reclined, a silk eye mask over his face, snoring loudly. I might as well take a cue from him and relax, I think, adjusting the footrest and accepting a glass of champagne from the flight attendant.

I can't help but compare this flight to the cut-rate Sabena flight I took to Italy twenty years ago, eight hours spent with my knees slammed into my chest because the seats in front of and behind me were occupied by basketball players on their way to a tournament in Brussels. They were so obviously more uncomfortable than I that I didn't dare recline or complain when the man in front leaned so far back in his flimsy seat that I could smell the Vitalis in his hair. And when the paltry meal was served, I joined in with the team as they donated their dinner rolls and processed cheese wedges to a fellow they all called "Buns."

I hadn't really minded, though. I had made my escape over my mother's objections (*Why do you have to go all the way to Italy to read poetry? They're shooting people in the kneecaps over there.*) and in spite of financial difficulties (I spent so many hours behind the bar at Cafe Lucrezia that there was a permanent ridge of espresso grounds beneath my fingernails) and a last-minute attack of conscience that my mother really wouldn't be able to cope without me.

"I'll take care of her," Aunt Roz assured me. "You go. You may never have this chance again—who knows how long any of us has?"

I've often wondered whether she had a premonition that she would be the one gone before I came back. Not my long-suffering hypochondriacal mother, but lively Roz killed in a taxi that ran a red light on Lexington Avenue, on her way back from buying a hat at Bloomingdale's. (*I don't know why she didn't take the subway,* my mother said at her funeral. *She always took the subway.*)

But I didn't know then that my aunt's death and my mother's diagnosis of lung cancer would call me back before the year was over. As far as I was concerned during that youthful journey to Europe, I might never come back. I was good at languages. Why not travel around and pick up a few while teaching English to pay my way? I felt as though I were escaping not just my mother's expectations for me but the self she would fashion me into: the cardigan-wearing, PBS-tote-bag-bearing high school teacher that had been the height of her unrealized ambitions for herself.

I wonder whether Robin had thought he was escaping the specter of becoming his father, poor stoop-shouldered Saul, who had been so frail at the funeral that he could barely lift the shovel high enough to clear the rim of Robin's grave. Leaving the cemetery, he had suddenly fallen to his knees and I thought he had fainted, but he was only pluck-ing a few blades of grass from the ground to throw over his shoulder— an ancient Jewish custom to ward off evil spirits, but also, I have always felt, a way of severing ourselves from the dead.

I take my leave of you I can imagine Robin thinking as he made his own journey to Italy. The sentiment was apparent in Robin's screenplay, which Leo Balthasar had sent me last week. In it the young William Shakespeare, burdened by a nagging wife and forced into unemploy-ment when the London theaters are shut down by the plague, receives an invitation from a mysterious woman. There are hints that she's a long-lost love, but the screenplay is vague on this point. She frames an invitation to her villa in Italy in the shape of a sonnet that proves just as irresistible to the Bard as it had been to me. In fact, it works so well as a catalyst for the action in the script that I find myself siding with Chi-hiro's theory that Robin had written the poem himself—or found some-one to write it—and pretended that it was a genuine Renaissance sonnet in order to pique Balthasar's interest in the screenplay. I wonder whether Leo had then demanded the original sonnet as proof of the his-torical basis of the script. I could try asking him, I think, glancing over at Leo to see whether he's showing any signs of awakening, but then I hear a familiar voice coming from behind the curtain that separates first class from coach.

"You don't seem to understand. I have a friend up there who will be most angry with me if I don't say hello," a woman is complaining in haughty tones to, I can only assume, a flight attendant. "If you don't let me by, I will complain to the management of the airline and see to it that you are fired."

The curtain bulges and parts, and Mara Silverman slips past a be-leaguered flight attendant into the empty seat next to me. When the at-tendant shows up at her side, Mara smiles sweetly, as if she didn't recognize her as the same person whose job she just threatened, and asks for a glass of orange juice.

"The fresh-squeezed kind you have up here," she says, "not that bottled stuff they gave me back there."

I exchange an exasperated glance with the flight attendant, who brings back a glass of orange juice for Mara, spilling only the tiniest bit on Mara's Juicy Couture jogging suit. If she'd planned the move as revenge, she miscalculated, because Mara then requests a bottle of club soda, towels, and some of the shower gel that she's sure must be in the toiletry cases the airline provides for its first-class passengers. Only when Mara has restored her velour hoodie to its pristine state and pocketed the toiletry case does she turn to me.

"Really, Rose, I'm surprised you're in first class. On your salary. Of course, you don't have children so I suppose you get to spend it all on yourself, but I'd think you'd want to be putting some away for your retirement. You're, what . . . forty now?"

I'm not sure what flaw to respond to first: my extravagance, my barrenness, or my age. I could, of course, tell her that Lemon House Films is paying for my seat, but then I realize that Mara's husband, Gene, is also working for them, and clearly they haven't provided him with first-class accommodations. Mara will be furious if she realizes that I'm being treated better than Gene.

"I had some extra frequent flier miles that were going to expire, so I upgraded," I say.

"Ah, we used all ours taking Ned around to colleges this year. Of course, the film company's paying for Gene's ticket, but not mine. Or Ned's."

"So, Ned's traveling with you?"

"No. The students had to go two weeks ago to start rehearsals. Ned insisted on going with this group who got budget tickets to Switzerland. They planned to hike in the Alps for a few days and then take the train to Florence. I've been going out of my mind worrying about him. They weren't even going to get sleeper compartments on the train! Can you imagine, wanting to sit up all night on a filthy Italian train eating salami sandwiches and drinking warm beer! That might be all right for some, but with Ned's asthma and psoriasis, he's bound to be a wreck."

I can, actually. It's how I first entered Italy, and after the cramped flight to Brussels I'd been happy for the legroom of a train compartment, even if it was occupied by three Mount Holyoke juniors who took up all the overhead luggage space with their matching pink duffel bags, which I later learned were stocked with six-packs of Tab and multiple cartons of Playtex tampons (*I'm not sticking anything foreign in there,* one of the girls confided to me later over a dinner of, yes, warm beer and salami). I'd woken up that morning surrounded by the pink light of dawn reflecting off the snow-topped Alpine peaks and the plains of Lombardy spread out below us. "Fruitful Lombardy," I'd remembered from *Romeo and Juliet,* "the pleasant garden of great Italy," and felt as if I were entering the illuminated pages of a medieval manuscript.

"You don't mind sitting up all night when you're young," I tell Mara, "or wearing the same clothes or sleeping in crowded hostels."

"Yes, well, easy to say from the comfort of first class," Mara says, reaching over and patting the fleece blanket I've got tucked around my legs and letting her hand linger on the pile of typescript in my lap. "Is that the script you've got there? The one that boy wrote? Is it really any good? Gene says he's sure it needs a lot of work. You really should let Gene have a look at it so he could do some work on it. You know he's been hired as a script consultant on the film by Mr. Balthasar."

She pronounces the producer's name loudly enough to wake up the man himself, and I see him stir a bit under his blanket, but if he's awake he chooses not to reveal that fact. I imagine he's waiting until Mara leaves. He'd told me last week on the phone that he'd given Gene the job of assistant script consultant. "It was either that or have him pop up in six months with a lawsuit claiming all Robin's ideas were stolen from him. I wouldn't put it past that shrew of a wife of his to goad him into a lawsuit to feed her designer-clothing habit. But I'm giving you first crack at the script; you decide when to give a copy to Gene Silverman."

"When we get to the villa I'll have some copies made," I tell Mara without mentioning that I've already scanned Robin's screenplay into my laptop. "I'm afraid this is my only copy right now."

"You really ought to have made copies in New York. What if the plane goes down? What if one of the stewardesses steals this copy while you're sleeping? If you like, I'll hold on to it when you go to sleep. I never can sleep a wink on planes, even after a couple of Xanaxes."

"That's all right," I tell Mara, looking past her to the flight attendant who's approaching with my dinner tray, "I'll be sure to put it securely away before I fall asleep. Right now I think you'd better get back to your seat or you'll miss the in-flight meal."

"Hm, maybe they can give me a tray here," she says, casting an appraising eye over my Chilean sea bass and braised endives served on real china with real silverware. I can hardly blame her for preferring this to the Saran-wrapped insta-meal that awaits her in coach, but if I let Mara stay now, I'll be stuck with her for the rest of the flight. And I wouldn't put it past her to wait until I fall asleep to take the screenplay for Gene. I catch the flight attendant's eye as Mara makes her request and shake my head. "I'm sorry, ma'am, we have only enough meals for our *ticketed* first-class passengers."

I almost feel sorry for Mara as she wilts at the emphasis the flight attendant puts on "ticketed," but not sorry enough to want her company for the rest of the flight.

"Well, then," Mara says, gathering up her toiletry case and free slippers and sleeping mask, "arrivederci until Italy, then. Maybe we can share a cab to the villa."

I nod noncommittally as Mara leaves, hoping that my proximity to the exit will get me through customs and immigration early enough to get my own cab. I've waited twenty years to see La Civetta again; Mara's the last person I want for company when I go through those gates. When I finish my dinner and the flight attendant has removed my tray and given me a scented hot towel and a handful of after-dinner mints, I pull out the screenplay again. As soon as I've got the pages in my lap, though, Leo Balthasar, as if awakened by the rustle of screenplay pages, slips his eye mask up onto his gleaming forehead and peers over at me.

"Oh, good, you're looking at Robin's script. Why don't we run through it together?"

Before I can protest that I'm still making notes, he's making himself comfortable in the empty seat by my side: adjusting the tubular pillow he wears like a pet boa around his neck, summoning the flight attendant for a pot of freshly brewed coffee, and angling the reading light on the pages in my lap so that I feel like an actor in the spotlight.

"So, what do we think?" he asks. "Does our boy have something here?" At least Robin's "our boy" now instead of my boy.

"Well, I'm very impressed with the language," I say, taking a sip of coffee, which is, to my surprise, nearly as good as Cafe Lucrezia's, "especially of the poem that he's included." I'd found when I read the script that only one poem was actually included: the *limonaia* poem that Ginevra sent to Shakespeare to invite him to the villa. There were numerous places in the script for other poems, but instead of the poems Robin had written in brackets. "Poem to come."

"And I like the characterization," I continue. "Robin has—*had*—a real feel for Shakespeare as a young poet and dramatist. I can't help but think he put a lot of himself in these scenes—"

"Yes, yes, but the plot line? What do you think of that?"

"Well, I have to admit that he's created a fairly plausible premise for what is essentially a fantasy. He has Shakespeare traveling to Italy in the summer of 1593 when the London theaters were closed because of an outbreak of plague. True, Shakespeare's company would have been touring then, but there's no way of knowing whether Shakespeare was actually with the company—"

"Aha! So, you admit it. Shakespeare could have gone to Italy."

"He could have gone to Timbuktu for all we know. It doesn't mean he did."

"Yes, but *Romeo and Juliet* isn't set in Timbuktu, is it? It's not *The Merchant of Timbuktu* or *Two Gentlemen of Timbuktu,* is it? All the writers I know are always writing off research trips. Why should Bill Shakespeare be any different? Wouldn't he want to scout out locations, gather material, check out Juliet's hometown to pick a good balcony for Romeo to scale?"

"Well, *Romeo and Juliet* was based on an Italian poem by Bandell, which was translated into English by Arthur Brooke, so Shakespeare could easily have written it without traveling to Italy. Besides, there's nothing in *Romeo and Juliet* that reveals a firsthand knowledge of Italy, nothing he couldn't have gotten out of Italian sources available to him. As for *The Merchant of Venice,* yes, some scholars have found the Venetian setting fairly convincing, although there's certainly no hard evidence in that. There's the scene at the ferry on the River Brenta in which Portia sees Balthasar off, but the fact remains that there's no evidence that Shakespeare ever went to Italy."

I'd thought Leo would like the reference to his Shakespearian namesake, but he only shakes his head angrily. "Tell me, is there a shred of evidence that he ever made the trip from Stratford to London? Can you show me the ticket stubs? But does anyone doubt that Shakespeare traveled back and forth between Stratford and London?"

I have to admit that there aren't any ticket stubs documenting Shakespeare's travels between Stratford and London that I know of.

"Right. So he could have gone to Italy—and what better reason to travel than to visit some beautiful Italian poetess living in a villa who's been writing him these sexy love poems. The Dark Lady is a great role. I've got top talent interested in playing her."

"Really?" I ask. "Have you actually ever read the Dark Lady sonnets?"

Leo Balthasar smiles at me as if I'd just asked him if he did his own laundry. "Honey, I've read the *treatment.*"

"Um . . . well, did you notice that they're not exactly flattering? In the nicest poem to her, he calls her hair black wires and her breasts dun. He accuses her of promiscuity and betrayal."

"Yes, yes," Leo says, excited. "It's just what we want. It was obviously a tempestuous relationship. She must have done something to enrage the Bard. What do you know about this Ginevra de Laura woman?"

"Not much," I admit. "She lived in the late sixteenth, early seventeenth century, was rumored to be the mistress of Lorenzo Barbagianni, who brought her to live at La Civetta, and some diarists of the period said she wrote sonnets, but none have survived—"

"But they could have been hidden at the villa, right? I was there last summer and the place is a rat's nest of paper—stuff crammed in every nook and cranny. An enterprising boy like Robin could have found them somewhere—"

"Did Robin ever show you these poems?" I ask.

"Well, not the originals," Leo admits. "He said he found the poems at the villa and hand-copied the one he used in the film because he couldn't remove it and if he took it down to the office to Xerox he'd attract attention. But he said he still had access to the poems and that if I needed the originals he could get them for me."

"You didn't encourage him to *steal* from the villa?" I ask, summoning all the outraged zeal of the scholar. A scholar who has in her carry-on luggage a possibly rare Renaissance manuscript page.

"Of course not!" Balthasar says, shaking his head reprovingly as if I had suggested that the Academy Awards could be bought. "But," he adds, lowering his voice conspiratorially, "I think *someone* thought he had taken something from the villa."

"Orlando Brunelli?" I ask and then, remembering something, add, "You met with Orlando the day of the film show, didn't you?"

Balthasar looks taken aback briefly but then smiles and taps his finger to his shiny skull. "Ah, I knew there was a reason I hired you. I'm never wrong about people. You don't miss a beat! Yes, I did meet with the boy at a cafe . . . uh, were you there? I don't remember seeing you until that night, and I never forget a beautiful woman."

"I wasn't there," I say, trying not to feel too pleased at Balthasar's flattery. "But I know the owner, and one of the waiters told me the next day—"

"Oh, yes, yes." Balthasar bobs his head up and down. "Orlando asked me to meet with him about Robin's script. He wanted a writing credit because he said he had helped Robin with the research. I told him that made him a research consultant, not a writer."

"Did he say anything about the poems?"

"What he said was . . . now let me make sure I've got this right"—Leo screws up his face in concentration—"he said that Robin had taken all the papers; yes, that's it. *Tutti i papiri.* My Italian's not so great, but I got that. I thought he meant that Robin had taken the only copy of the script. When he crashed the party, yelling at Robin for stealing something, I thought that's what he meant, but he couldn't have thought Robin had the whole script on his person; he must have thought Robin had the poems on him."

I nod, thinking that Orlando had been right. He just didn't know that Robin had already handed the one poem he had over to me.

"So, he could have been trying to get the poem from Robin on the balcony. He might have pushed him while trying to get the poem."

Balthasar widens his eyes at me. "Really? Do you think so?"

"Well, you would know better than I would," I say, exasperated. "I wasn't on the balcony."

Balthasar shakes his head. "I was busy with that girl—the one with the pink hair. She was between us and she was hysterical. I was afraid *she* was going to jump! And Mark had his hands full with Orlando Brunelli, who was demanding that Robin give him back something he'd stolen from him. If Robin did have one of those poems on him when he jumped, it would have been bloodstained pulp by the time they scraped him off the sidewalk."

I wince at the image and Balthasar shrugs apologetically. "Sorry. I know you were close to the boy."

I find myself unable to speak for a moment, my throat suddenly parched in the canned air of the airplane cabin. I look away from Leo Balthasar, out toward the vacant blue of twilight that is fast fading as we cross the Atlantic. I feel a wave of warmth steal over me and realize that it comes from Leo Balthasar's hand, which he has laid over mine on the armrest. I'm surprised more by the jolt of the physical contact than by the unexpected intimacy of the gesture. "I liked him, too," Balthasar says, squeezing my hand. "That's why I'm so damned set on doing this film. He'd have wanted his words immortalized on screen. You do whatever you need to, to make that script viable—I don't care if we've got to put Shakespeare in a time machine to get him to Italy—and keep an eye out for those sonnets. And I'll keep an eye on Orlando Brunelli. I'll tell you one thing. If it turns out he really pushed Robin off that balcony, I'll make damn sure he doesn't get a writing credit!"

Balthasar releases my hand after giving it another bone-bruising squeeze and goes back to his own seat. I feel suddenly overcome by fatigue, the effect of the stress of these last few weeks. I put the screenplay away in my book bag, cinching shut the brass toggles and tucking the bag under my other carry-on. I tilt my seat back and slip a pillow between my cheek and the cabin wall. When I close my eyes, though, the scene Leo Balthasar described rises up in my mind: Robin perched on the edge of the balcony and Orlando rushing toward him . . . accusing him of stealing from him . . . Mark trying to hold Orlando back . . . Robin's body falling, his body hurtling through space . . . The sensation jerks me awake. I must have fallen asleep, because outside my window the sun is cresting the curved horizon, limning a jagged line of mountains. I keep my eyes on the mountains as the cabin fills with the sounds of passengers yawning and the aroma of coffee and fresh-baked croissants. The mountains seem to spring out of the sea, massive and cragged and still peaked with snow in the heights. It's hard to imagine how anyone could ever have traveled over them on foot or by horse. Fynes Moryson, an English traveler, described travelers creeping over the Alps on their hands and feet with nails in their gloves and shoes, while their guides warned them not to look down into the deep abyss.

A good idea, I think, looking away from the beautiful, but bleak, scenery and toward the awakening cabin. Still, I can't quite dispel the notion that while my journey doesn't require crawling hand and foot over the mountains, it's likely to have its own perils and that the more I try to find the truth behind Robin's fall, the closer I bring myself to the edge of a precipice.

CHAPTER
NINE

I AM FOILED IN MY IGNOBLE PLAN TO DITCH MARA AT THE AIRPORT BY GENE Silverman's determination to catch up to Leo Balthasar. First he cuts the line at immigration, infuriating a French couple behind us who reel off a list of anti-American epithets at Gene's uncomprehending back. Mara smiles at the woman and tries to ask her where she purchased her Longchamps bag, but when the woman stares at her icily, Mara sidles closer to me and whispers, "The French, they're such snobs."

Although Mara, by all rights, should present her passport with her husband, she sticks to my side so that we end up approaching immigration together—forming an unlikely family unit in the eyes of the Italian government. Then, since Gene is too deep in movie talk with Balthasar to bother with Mara's luggage, I end up helping her collect five pieces of matching Louis Vuitton bags—including one that we are forced to return to the infuriated Frenchwoman.

By the time we reach the taxi queue, Gene has hopped into a cab with Balthasar and a German hedge fund manager who they've learned is also bound for La Civetta.

"Have you thought of investing in film?" I hear Balthasar say in perfect German. I wonder how many languages he knows how to say that phrase in.

"You girls probably want to plot out your shopping anyway," Gene tosses over his shoulder to us as he gets into the minivan. And then, turning to Leo Balthasar, "I should probably ask you guys for my re-tainer fee in cameos and small leather goods." He laughs at his own joke as the car drives off, leaving Mara and me to a tiny Fiat that visibly sinks to the pavement under the weight of Mara's luggage.

"Will we pass any good shops on the way to the villa?" Mara asks.

"No. La Civetta is in the hills north of the city. We're just skirting the northern edge of town right now. All the stores are south—along the Arno and the Via della Vigna Nuova, and, of course, the Ponte Vec-chio has dozens of jewelry shops." I peer out the window in the direc-tion of the river, but all I can see, past the brown and gold suitcases crammed into the backseat with us, are flashes of ochre walls and the metal shutters that cover the doors and windows of closed *tabaccherie* and cafes. It's early Sunday morning. The Florentines are still in bed or in church. Whatever life's occurring is going on behind thick stone walls and shuttered windows. A wave of sadness passes over me—a feeling of being shut out that I try to dismiss as jet lag or the melancholy that Boswell described upon viewing "the celebrated Forum . . . now all in ruins." My sadness, though, is not for ancient history, but for my own past, the life I might have had here.

Only when the car starts climbing do I realize we're on the street that leads to the villa. The road is narrow and curving, flanked by high stone walls that give no hint of the palatial villas that lie behind them. A fringe of olive branches, a spill of bougainvillea down an iron gate, or an enameled plaque inscribed with some whimsical name are the only clues that princes and dukes kept their summer homes here and, later, British peers and rich Americans, and now, colleges and universities. We pass the University of Paris's villa and I recognize the French couple from the airport standing before the gate shouting their names into an intercom box. La Civetta is just around the next curve of the road—which means that we'll be bumping into our new French friends at the bus stop for the rest of the summer.

Our driver swerves into a shallow half-circle depression, screeching to a halt inches from a pair of closed wrought-iron gates. I can see over the hood of our taxi the black face of an owl with hollow eyes staring at us as if we were intruders—part of the decorative pattern in the old metalwork.

"Is this it?" Mara asks. "You'd think Mr. Balthasar would have left the gates open for us." She doesn't mention that her husband was in the same car with him and might have been expected to think of his own wife's convenience first.

"Cyril Graham is fanatical about security," I tell her. "The gates are fixed to close automatically after each entrance. I'll have to get out and ring the bell."

I climb over a toiletry case and what looks like a hat box (who in the world still travels with a hat box?) and step out of the car. The intercom is the same antiquated metal box I remember from twenty years ago—a metal grate with a brass lever you turn to the right. I shout my name into it as though I were shouting down a well instead of speaking into a piece of late-twentieth-century electronic equipment.

The school took us all once to the Cave of the Sibyl at Cumae, and Bruno told me that there was a tradition that if you shouted your name into the cave and then listened very carefully, you would hear your destiny. I realized later that many of Bruno's "traditions" were his own fancies, but I didn't know that then. I threw my name into the dank sulfurous gloom as confidently as any tourist tossing lire into the Trevi fountain and then listened to the echoes dying in the still, flat air, waiting for an answering vibration from beneath the earth—from the gates of hell, as the ancient Cimbrians who once populated that part of Italy believed. Instead I felt Bruno's touch along the back of my neck and the coolness of his breath in my ear as he suggested how we might spend the rest of the afternoon. It seemed at the time all of the future I needed to know.

Now I don't bother to listen at the metal grate for any answering call. It's a one-way intercom (cheaper, Cyril Graham once told me); its only response is the slow opening of the iron gates. Mara beckons from the cab for me to get back in, but I lean in and hand her a twenty-euro note for my half of the fare.

"I'll walk," I tell her, closing the door before she can object. For a moment I feel the same childish glee I had back at Cumae when Bruno and I managed to slip away from the scheduled field trip and spend the rest of the afternoon at the Hotel Sibylla, and all because now I can approach the villa at my own pace with only my memories for company.

I step between two marble pillars that are surmounted by marble owls whose taloned claws grip three balls—icons that link the original owners of the villa (the Barbagianni family, whose name means "barn owl") with the symbol of the Medici family. These owls always frightened me. Their talons are long and sharp, their wings flexed for flight. As I pass underneath them it's hard not to imagine that they will follow me on silent wings, ready to sink their claws into the back of my neck. Even the sound the gates make as they close resembles the high-pitched screech of an owl.

To my right is the path that leads to the plain gray-stone building that once housed the Convent of Santa Catalina but now serves as a dorm for the students. Everyone just calls it the little villa. The main villa is lemon colored and lies at the end of a long avenue, or *viale,* of tall cypresses. It's a popular view featured in all the college's advertising brochures and on the Web site for the study abroad program. Maybe that's why I find myself curiously numb as I start down the *viale,* as if I am approaching a picture instead of the real thing, a painted façade that seems to slip in and out between its frame of gray-green cypresses like a woman hiding coquettishly behind a curtain.

"Like a high-priced whore," Cyril Graham once described the villa to our class, delighting, as always, in shocking *you naïve young Ameri-*

cans. "She's bled me dry keeping her up over the years. That's what La Civetta means. A whore."

"Isn't it Italian for 'screech owl'?" one of the students asked. "That's what the brochure says. That it was named that because the Barbagianni name meant 'owl' and that's why there are all the statues of owls and that goddess who's always got an owl on her head."

"I believe you mean Minerva," Cyril drawled, looking down at the boy as if he were himself an owl and the boy a tasty field mouse, "and yes, *civetta* means 'screech owl,' but it also means, in the vernacular, a coquette—a tease. Yes, I know, that's not what it says in the *brochure.* Not everything worth knowing is to be found in books, children; you must also listen to gossip—what the Romans called *fama*—a winged beast with a thousand eyes. And *fama* tells us that Lorenzo Barbagianni named La Civetta for his mistress, Ginevra de Laura, whom he had the gall to install here when his wife died. Of course, when Barbagianni died, his son and his guardians were able to throw her out. Some say she cursed the villa when she left. You'll see. La Civetta will imprint herself on your heart and mind, and years from now you'll be haunted by the time you spent here. You'll remember it as the most beautiful season of your life—"

Cyril paused, gesturing with his long, mobile fingers toward the garden. We were on the loggia; on fine days he always taught his Aesthetics of Place class on the loggia. We all looked out over the clipped yew hedges and rosebushes toward the view of Florence, the Duomo framed between two marble urns. We all thought we knew what he was going to say next. Wasn't everybody always telling us that these were the best years of our lives? Even the brochure for La Civetta claimed that the place would stamp an indelible impression on the minds of the students who studied here. But Cyril Graham had ended on a more melancholy note. "And you'll forever regret its passing."

In the twenty years since I'd left La Civetta, I have counted myself as reasonably happy. I've had success in my chosen career and even found time between writing for academic journals to pen a sonnet or two. I've dated men I liked, and just when I thought I might not marry before it was too late to have children, I met Mark. If we marry next year after I get tenure, there might be time yet to have a child. And even if there isn't, my students have, to a large degree, made up for that lack. I haven't, up until now, had any reason to think that Cyril Graham was right. And he was wrong about so much—for instance, I found out from Bruno later that *la civetta* may mean "a gossip" or "tease," but never "a whore," and even those meanings only attached to the word in the nineteenth century, too late to have had anything to do with the naming of this fifteenth-century villa—which at any rate already possessed the name before Ginevra de Laura came to live here in 1582.

So why, then, does my current life suddenly pale in the light of this strong Mediterranean sun? Is it because the colors here are so much more vibrant than anything back in New York? Too vibrant. I have a sudden urge to turn around, walk back down the *viale* to the Via Bolognese, and take a cab back to the airport. I'm afraid that if I go any farther I'll have to admit that Cyril was right. The best season of my life has passed.

But then the door to the villa opens and a woman is framed in the arched doorway. I recognize her immediately as Claudia Brunelli. If I turn now, she'll know I wasn't able to face her—or face La Civetta. I pass through the second set of gates—these flanked by statues of Minerva and Venus—and finally the façade of the villa comes completely into view. The placid ochre building regards me with equanimity behind the cracks in the stucco and the peeling paint on the wooden shutters. I could cry, I'm so happy to see its familiar worn face.

Claudia Brunelli comes forward and I see that she has weathered the twenty years that have passed much better than the villa has. She's only slightly curvier than I remember, and her skin—that lovely olive complexion that ages so well—looks more like that of a girl of nineteen than that of a woman in her late forties. She's wearing a cream-colored linen skirt and a sleeveless yellow silk blouse, with a blue and gold silk scarf tied around her waist—an outfit that looks so effortlessly chic, I'm instantly conscious of my wrinkled slacks and T-shirt that went saggy somewhere over the North Atlantic.

"*Cara* Rosa," she croons, brushing her cheek against mine, "*Che pi- acere.* How good to see you again after all these years. Orlando told me he met you in New York. Bruno and I were hoping you would come. We both wanted to talk to you about that poor unhappy boy who died."

"Orlando would know more about what happened than I would," I say coolly, thinking that *poor unhappy* Robin might still be alive if not for Orlando. "He was on the balcony; I was inside when it happened."

"Yes, yes, it was such a horrible shock for poor Orlando. Who knew the boy was so unstable? Although I have to say I thought he was a bit . . . *come se dice? . . . mutevole?*"

"Flighty," I say, instantly regretting the translation I've chosen. "Changeable. Yes, Robin seemed to change his colors with his sur- roundings. To become what people wanted him to be—"

"Exactly. Yes, I knew *you* would understand. Poor Orlando, he was charmed by the boy. He thought he and Robin were going to become writers for the movies, and then the boy went back to America and for- got all about his promises to Orlando. But I mustn't burden you with a mother's worries when you must be so tired from your flight. Look at me, keeping you standing in the doorway. And me, the hospitality coor- dinator! Can you believe it? You must have been very surprised when you heard."

I remember Robin saying that in Claudia's case the title was a mis- nomer. "Well, yes . . ." I begin, searching my jet-lag-addled brain for a polite response. "I remembered that you weren't exactly happy here at La Civetta, so I was surprised that you and Bruno had moved back from Rome."

Claudia doesn't say anything for a moment. Instead, she fingers the gold saint's medal (Saint Catherine, the same one I remember her wear- ing twenty years ago) at her throat and studies me as if waiting to see if the effort of pronouncing Bruno's name will have any effect on me, some tremor or aftershock that she'll be able to detect. I hold myself perfectly still and finally she shrugs, a movement that dimples her bare shoulders in a way she must know is attractive, and says, "I couldn't stand to see Bruno moping around the apartment in Rome any longer. He loves this place. So when his mother died I figured I might as well take it in hand and make it livable. You'll see I've made many changes since you were here, not that I haven't had to fight tooth and nail with the old man for every last euro spent on repairs." She holds up the thumb and forefinger of her left hand and rubs them together, giving me a nice view of her thick gold wedding band. "You'd think the plumbing was sculpted by Donatello to hear him talk. But really he just wants to spend as little as he can get away with until your university takes over and . . . oh, how do you say it? Foots the bill. He's in there with that American filmmaker and your college president—such a handsome man, your President Abrams!—trying to see who he can get to pay for repairs to the roof of the *limonaia.*"

I follow the tilt of Claudia's chin through the doorway, where the polished marble floor and Venetian glass mirrors gleam dimly in the cool light of the vestibule.

"They're in the *sala grande,*" she says, reading the look of reluctance on my face perhaps too well. "But the doors are shut. If you like I can whisk you up the stairs to your room. I've already had your luggage sent up."

"Yes," I say, "I think I'd like to wash up a bit before seeing Cyril. He was always so finicky about dress."

"He ought to be as finicky about the company he keeps," Claudia comments as she leads me over the stone lintel and through the thick arch of the doorway. The walls of La Civetta are two feet thick and made of stone under the orange stucco, an effect that always made me think of a seashell and which keeps the house insulated from the heat. As soon as the cool air hits my skin I realize how warm I'd been outside and how sweaty I am. I steal a look at myself in one of the giant Venetian glass mirrors that line the vestibule and wish I hadn't. The little bit of makeup I'd reapplied before landing has melted in the heat and my hair looks like I've just gotten out of bed. More Medusa hair than Botticelli hair, I think, glad that I'll have a chance to brush it before seeing Mark.

"*Vieni.* Let's get you upstairs," Claudia whispers, giving me a little push toward the rotunda.

Although I'm grateful to avoid meeting Cyril Graham right now, the way Claudia hustles me past the closed *sala* doors—beyond which I can hear the murmur of male voices—to the foot of the curving stairwell, makes me feel as though I were a concubine being smuggled upstairs to the master's bedroom. She even slips out of her high-heeled pumps as she steps onto the stairs and motions for me to take off my own shoes. Although I'm wearing crepe-soled loafers, I comply. The marble feels deliciously cool on my bare feet. If the walls of La Civetta are a seashell, then the rotunda with its curving staircase is the inner chamber of a nautilus. I look down to see whether the inlaid pattern I remember is still there. It is. Set into the white Carrara are mosaic petals fashioned of Eretria red and Rosetta pink marble. As I follow the cascade of petals up the winding stairs I remember Daisy Wallace telling me that her father believed he had seen blood spots appear on the tiled floor of the rotunda, and I look down and see the pattern of rose petals swirling around the antique Roman impluvium at its center. Before the rotunda was enclosed, the large basin collected rainwater from the open oculus, but now the skylight has been glassed over and the impluvium is dry, and whatever pattern the petals once formed has been lost under the eighteenth-century walls around the circumference of the rotunda. I can imagine, though, that when the rainwater splashed over the basin and wet the floor, the pattern of red and pink might have looked like splashes of blood.

At the top of the stairs Claudia turns left and takes me down a long hallway toward the northeast corner of the villa. "We house the students in the little villa near Via Bolognese," she tells me as she takes out a heavy ring of keys from her skirt pocket, "and most of the professors as well. I sent that other American woman over there, although she kept insisting that you'd want to be near her. If you really do—?"

"Oh, no," I say a little too quickly. "That's all right."

"*Bene*. President Abrams is on this floor—in the west wing—but I took the liberty of putting you in your old room." She opens the last door in the hallway. "For memory's sake," she adds, because clearly no one would have chosen this room for its size or decoration.

I remember thinking that I had been installed in a convent the first time I saw it: the cold terra-cotta tile floor, the bare white walls adorned only by a lunette-shaped painting of the Virgin Mary above the narrow bed, and for a desk, an old oak table below the only window. And yet, I think as Claudia crosses to the window and unlatches the heavy wooden shutters, I had come to love this room. Claudia steps aside and I rest my arms on the wide stone windowsill and lean forward. The view is exactly as I remember it—not the more celebrated view on the southwest side of the house looking over the gardens toward Florence, this view encompasses a corner of the *limonaia,* its yellow stucco walls and red-tiled roof surmounted by the bust of a woman who is looking away from the house and toward the Arno River valley. How many days had I looked up from my studies to see her profile, to follow her gaze out into the valley toward the blue hills of the Valdarno, until I came to feel that we were both waiting for something—or someone—to appear on the crest of the hill to come and deliver us from the penitential silence of this convent room?

"Of course, it *is* rather small—" Claudia says in the dolorous tones Italians use when offering to make some concession to the crassness of American tastes.

"No, no, it's perfect," I say too quickly, afraid she'll take the view away from me. "This is exactly where I want to work."

She smiles. "Yes, I thought as much. Perfect for a scholar. Bruno always likes to work someplace simple, too. But a woman has other needs, so . . ." She crosses the room—it takes only a few steps—and begins to unlock a door at the foot of the bed. When I stayed in this room the door was locked and covered by a wooden wardrobe, where I kept my clothes. It had often given me a creepy feeling seeing the edge of the locked door at the foot of my bed. I'd wake up sometimes in the middle of the night, sure that I could hear someone on the other side of it, testing the lock. What made it worse was knowing that the room on the other side was sealed and unused and had been since Lucy Graham had died there in the sixties.

Claudia opens the door and stands back, waving me in. I cross over the threshold and step onto a thick plush carpet (I'm still barefoot, so I can feel exactly how thick and lush it is). I find myself in a large, elegant bedroom decorated in shades of rose and green. The color scheme, I see, echoes the faded paintings on the walls, which depict scenes in a dark forest alternating with scenes in a medieval rose garden. Garden and grove: a common theme for a bridal suite—a *camera nuziale*—which this room was clearly meant to be long before it was Lucy Graham's room. Its furnishings and wall paintings are all designed to indoctrinate the bride into the culture of her new family. The garden theme is picked up in a painted trunk—a Renaissance *cassone,* which would have held the bride's trousseau—at the foot of the bed, and in a medieval tapestry that hangs on the left side of the bed depicting a knight handing his lady a rose. Lorenzo Barbagianni no doubt brought his short-lived bride here and, if the legends are true, outraged sixteenth-century Florentine propriety by installing his mistress, Ginevra de Laura, here only months after his wife had died.

"This is too much," I say to Claudia, who's smoothing the embroidered coverlet on the four-poster bed.

Claudia sits down on the edge of the bed. "President Abrams told me, specifically, to make sure you had a good room and one in the main villa," she says, tilting her head and smiling slyly at me. "I got the impression that he wanted you close to him—he's just down the hall. Such a handsome man, your president, *bellissimo* . . . You are perhaps . . ." She allows her voice to trail off suggestively and I feel the force of her charm urging me to confirm her suspicions. Leave it to Claudia to pick up on whatever stray bit of gossip is in the air. She'd been equally quick to learn of my involvement with Bruno twenty years ago.

"Colleagues," I say, returning her smile. "I imagine he wanted me to be near Lucy Graham's archives. I'm sure he had no idea you'd give me such an elaborate room. Surely there are more important guests staying here this summer who are more worthy of it. Some of Cyril's prospective film investors, for instance."

"Yes, but I wanted you to have it." She looks up at me and for the first time today I can see the last twenty years in her face. The colors in this room are meant to flatter a young woman—a blushing bride. Claudia's skin looks a little sallow and her eyes look tired. I can think of nothing to say but what I'm really thinking. "But why?" I ask. "Why are you being so kind to me?"

"I've always felt you were the one who suffered the most in the . . . situation. That you were the victim caught between Bruno's and my estrangement that year. And given how difficult your situation was, I thought you acted quite well. If you hadn't gone back to America, I don't think Bruno would have come back to me."

"But you were married," I say. "What else could I have done?"

Claudia smiles and rises from the bed. She reaches out her hand and touches my cheek. Her hand is warm, but still her touch makes me shiver. "*Cara* Rosa, you could have done anything you pleased with him. But you didn't. And for that I am thankful. So"—she hands me two silver keys, one large, one small, tied together with a blue ribbon—"enjoy your suite. There's a private bath through that door, and Lucy's archives are housed right across the hall. There's a computer there—although I see you've brought your own—and a scanner. And, of course, you've got your funny little convent room for when you want to be serious."

"That's how I always thought of it," I admit as I walk Claudia to the door, glad for a change of subject. "It's funny it was attached to Lucy Graham's bedroom. What could she have used it for?" I ask. "Praying?"

Claudia laughs. "Really, Rose, you Americans are so adorable. It was her maid's room, of course."

CHAPTER TEN

THE BEST THING ABOUT THE SUITE TURNS OUT TO BE THE BATH. THE YEAR I stayed here I used a hall bathroom that featured a hip bath and a rubber hose that dispensed a thin trickle of rust-colored water, while all that time this enormous antique marble tub lay empty behind locked doors! I fill the tub with hot water and pour in a capful of *aqua di rosa,* a potion made by the Farmaceutica Santa Maria Novella. The scent of roses rises with the steam as I sink into the hot water, and I say a little prayer of thanks to the Dominican friars who have been making this magical elixir since the thirteenth century. This same fragrance might have scented the baths of the Renaissance women who first lived in the villa. Ginevra de Laura, Barbagianni's mistress, might have soaked in this very tub, inhaling this same "perfumed tincture of roses." Watching the steam rise to the high-domed ceiling, I feel suddenly dizzy, as if the perfumed cloud held the ghosts of all the roses that ever bloomed in the gardens below, a heady potpourri gathered over the centuries.

It's only the jet lag, I tell myself, closing my eyes and sinking deeper into the perfumed water, jet lag and the disorientation of my former lover's wife thanking me for handing her back her husband. *You could have done anything you pleased with him.* She'd made it sound as if I had been the one in control back then, and yet, I'd never felt more out of control in my entire life. From the first day of class, when the handsome dark-eyed professor (I hadn't yet realized he was still in graduate school) had looked up from his roster after calling my name and recited, "The rose looks fair, but fairer we it deem / for that sweet odour which doth in it live."

Later, when I knew Shakespeare's sonnet number 54 better, it would strike me as ironic that Bruno wooed me with a poem that praised the beloved for his truthfulness when our love affair was founded on a lie.

I'd like, even now, to pretend that the lie was Bruno's, that I didn't know he was married. But he'd mentioned "his wife"—dropping the words like a boy drops stones off a bridge just to watch the ripples they make—the first time he kissed me.

The sonnet class was taught at the little villa near the Via Bolognese. Most of the students would rush out the minute class ended, in a hurry to get to the main villa, where lunch was served. I was a lingerer, though, the student who stayed behind with questions. In truth, I lingered because the sound of Bruno's voice entranced me each class and I found it hard to tear myself away. I spent my evenings, when I should have been studying, thinking up questions to ask after class so that I could walk back to the main villa with Professor Brunelli, discussing Petrarch and Shakespeare as we walked through the olive grove that lay between the main villa and the road. Instead of eating lunch at the villa, Bruno (as he soon told me to call him) liked to bring bread and cheese and a little flask of red wine and picnic under the shade of the olive trees. He invited me to join him, and I started collecting the small, sweet plums that grew in the walled fruit garden—the *pomerino*—so I'd have something to share in exchange for the bread and cheese and wine he gave me. I brought, too, the little journal I wrote my poems in and, after a few weeks, admitted to him that I wanted to be a poet. He didn't laugh or ask, as my mother always did when I confessed my ambitions, how I planned to make a living doing *that*. (*What are you going to do? Open a poetry store?*) Instead he looked at me for a long time, his dark brown eyes reflecting the silvery green of the olive trees, and asked, "Why?"

"To make something that lasts," I answered.

"Let me show you something," he said, getting up and brushing the dust from his pants, "about the lasting powers of poetry."

He led me into the gardens, onto the lower terrace with its famous view of Florence, down the lemon walk and through a gate that the students were told not to enter, and down a flight of crumbling steps into a sunken rose garden so overgrown, it appeared to be an underwater pool of pink and red and coral sea anemones.

"Most people think the rose garden is a later addition," he told me, "an English affectation. But in fact it dates from the late sixteenth century. Ginevra de Laura, Barbagianni's mistress, designed it herself based on an Elizabethan knot garden. There's a story that she had visited England and had a lover there and that as she walked through this garden she composed love poems in his memory. The paths are supposedly shaped in her lover's initials."

I had an idea then of why he'd brought me here. He wanted me to understand the immortal power of poetry. "Do you come here to write?" I asked.

He smiled and tapped his finger under his eye. "Ah, you've found me out. How did you know I wrote poetry?"

"Well, when you teach Petrarch and Shakespeare you speak with such passion—"

"And that *passion*," he said, his voice lingering over the word, "you think that's where poetry comes from?"

I blushed as pink as one of the damask roses arching over the path and nodded. "Yes . . . yes, I do." I tore the rose off the vine and buried my face in it to hide my embarrassment. I wasn't used to discussing passion with my professors—or with anyone, for that matter.

We had come to a ruined fountain at the center of the knot. Bruno sat down on the edge of the fountain. "Then in order to write poetry one has to experience that passion—even if it causes pain and sorrow?" he asked.

When I looked up from the rose I saw that he was staring at me with a hunger in his eyes that unnerved me. I realized that these weren't academic questions—these were life-and-death questions for him, and he seemed to think that I had the answers. The scent of so many roses baking in the hot sun was so strong that I suddenly felt dizzy. I must have swayed slightly, because he put his hand on my arm to steady me and then, when I continued to sway, he pulled me down beside him and kissed me. The rose I held in my hand, already past its bloom, was crushed between us, and its scent seemed to swell around us, a cloud that would shield us from the rest of the world but that also made it hard to breathe. When he pulled away from me, the very air felt heavy with perfume—I could see it—a thick gold haze that trembled all around us.

"You're not going to faint, *cara,*" he said, laughing. "You do know I have a wife, don't you?"

"Yes," I lied, instantly and without thinking, afraid he wouldn't kiss me again if he thought the first kiss was a mistake.

"We're separated, of course," he went on, picking up a rose petal and rubbing it between his thumb and forefinger as if it were a piece of cloth he was considering having a suit made from. Watching his fingers stroke the soft pink flesh made my stomach ache. "We met at the University at Rome and she goes back as often as she can. She finds Florence—and especially La Civetta—too provincial. I'm afraid she's not cut out to be a professor's wife."

"Do you have children?" I managed to ask. When he told me no, I asked, trying to make my voice sound casual, whether he was planning on getting a divorce. He shrugged and pursed his lips in that way Italian men have of dismissing a question as silly. Instead of feeling dismissed, though, I was looking at his lips and remembering how they felt pressed against mine.

"It's not so easy for Catholics," he told me. "If it bothers you, perhaps we'd better stop right now."

I shrugged, too, trying to imitate his gesture down to the little purse of the lips, although I was finding it hard not to smile. *We'd better stop right now.* His words implied we'd already started something, that our first kiss was not an anomaly, but the first in a *series.*

"No," I said, telling my second lie, "if it doesn't bother you and she knows—"

"Our understanding is that we are both free to lead our own lives," he said, lifting his hand and caressing my cheek.

And so I began my affair with Bruno with my eyes open. He hadn't lied to me. I was the one who lied—who told him I was content with being the mistress of a married man when I knew already that day in the rose garden that I was falling in love with him. I thought it would be okay if the only person I was hurting was myself. I hadn't counted on him falling in love with me.

The bathwater has gone cold by the time I get out, dripping to the floor in oily splotches. I look down and see a splash of red and think for a moment that I must have gotten my period—that the air travel and the hot bath have brought it on early—but when I kneel to wipe up the stain I see it's embedded in the marble floor: a red rose petal made out of dark red marble, the same as the ones on the stairs. *Is this where the pattern starts?* I wonder.

I follow the inlaid rose petals out of the bathroom and into the bedroom, where they end at the edge of the thick Aubusson carpet. I lift a corner of the rug and see that the pattern continues underneath. I can't help but wonder whether the pattern extends over the whole floor and whether it consists of only random petals or takes some other shape. I also can't help wondering why anybody would cover up such a beautiful mosaic of *pietre dure,* even with an expensive French rug. Expensive *and* heavy. It takes all my strength to peel it back and then, kneeling on the cold marble floor, to roll it to the edge of the room, beneath the windows. When I'm done, I sit back on the rolled-up carpet, wearing nothing but a towel and a sheen of sweat from my exertions, and survey the floor.

The cascade of petals is thickest around the bed, a deep red circle that surrounds the massive wooden posts like a crimson moat. From there the petals trail off in two directions—the bathroom and then the front door, and to the wide windows overlooking the gardens. I get up and walk around the bed, feeling with my bare feet where the marble has buckled and, in some places, cracked with age. Perhaps this is why the floor's been covered with a rug—to protect the mosaic from further deterioration. It looks old, centuries old.

The visual arts are not my specialty. When I was here at La Civetta, the professors and students divided themselves into two camps: the word people and the stone people. I was in the word camp, but I secretly loved the art and archeology classes we all had to take and I especially loved *pietre dure*—mosaics crafted out of carved semiprecious stones that became popular under the patronage of the Medici in the late sixteenth century. I try to think of a mosaic that looks like this floor, but the pieces that I've seen at the Opifizio delle Pietre Dure or at the Uffizi of this quality are usually small tabletops. The only time I've seen an entire floor made out of such intricately carved stone is in the Capella dei Medici in San Lorenzo—and that took hundreds of years to complete. Also, there's something about this design that feels profoundly *personal,* obsessive almost, beyond mere ornament. The pattern seems to be telling a story—but of what event?

I circle the bed once more and notice that the rose petals are thickest on the side of the bed farthest from the window. There's only a light scattering on the floor between the windows and the bed, as if they had blown there from the open windows. I notice, then, that the rolled-up carpet is covering some kind of border. I push it away and find two mosaic faces on either side of the windows, their cheeks swelling and their lips pursed as if they were blowing out air. Thin, nearly transparent lines (carved from delicate chalcedony) stream out from their lips, rose petals fluttering in their wake. These faces do look familiar to me. They look very much like the figures of the winds in Botticelli's *Birth of Venus.* So, I figure, the rose petals are supposed to be blown in from the garden, through the window, and then onto the bed. That makes at least some sense. I open the window and step out onto the little wrought-iron balcony. Below me, beyond the lemon walk and to the right of the *teatrino,* at the foot of a long flight of marble steps that are even more derelict and overgrown than they were twenty years ago, I can just make out the old rose garden where Bruno and I first kissed. If I lean over the railing, I might even see the fountain—

I refrain from leaning over when I remember that I'm still clad only in a bath towel. I quickly retreat back inside, pick up my suitcase, and haul it up onto the bed. Although I'd fully planned to spend the day napping and recovering from jet lag, I'm now determined to go out and explore the grounds first—specifically the old rose garden. Not, I tell myself as I rifle through my clothes, because of my *personal* history with the rose garden, but because of the story Bruno told me there that first day. He had told me before we kissed (for years I divided my life into two parts: the time before that kiss and the years after) that Ginevra de Laura had fashioned the knot garden out of her English lover's initials, but it wasn't until we were leaving the garden (having agreed that I would come later that night to his apartment above the *limonaia*) that I thought to ask what the initials were.

"No one has ever been able to make them out," he told me. "She made the design so complicated that no one even in her time could read them. And, of course, over the centuries the roses have so overgrown their original beds that there's no way to make out the initials now."

"What a shame," I said, "that all traces of their love affair are gone."

Bruno formed his lips into that little dismissive pout—a gesture I would come to know all too well over that year—and drew me to him. We were almost within sight of the house, and it both thrilled me that he was willing to take the chance we would be seen (his wife couldn't mean that much to him in that case) and scared me.

"All any lovers have is *this,*" he said, pressing his lips to mine. "It's only poets who try to pretend otherwise, who think they can trap warm flesh in words."

"But what about the poems Ginevra de Laura wrote to her lover? Isn't that a kind of immortality that we know about their love through her poems?"

"Alas, none of her poems have survived. The story is that she burned them when Barbagianni died and his son's guardians forced her into the Convent of Santa Catalina." Bruno pointed toward the house, to a small iron balcony covered with climbing roses. "That was her room," he told me. "Some say she built a pyre out of broken furniture and firewood right on top of her bed and burned all her poems and all the roses her lover had sent her over the years so that everyone for miles around could smell the scent of burning roses."

"Wow," I said, imagining it—the dead rose petals catching fire, their scent rising on the air. "What happened to her after that?"

"Oh, she went along to the convent. Another legend says that she went dressed in nothing but a linen shift, into which she sewed her poems."

"Couldn't she have gone somewhere else?"

Bruno shrugs. "Where? What choice did she have other than to become another man's mistress? And although it was said she wrote some beautiful poems, it was no easier to make a living as a poet then than it is now. She spent the rest of her life kneeling on cold marble floors with only the remembrance of her past passion to keep her warm."

"Repenting, do you think?"

"Oh, I hope not," he had said, laughing and kissing me again.

I pause in my search for clothes and look up, alerted by some shift in the air. Through the windows, which I'd left open, a breeze carries the sound of voices from the garden, a man's laugh that sounds almost like Bruno's. *It could be Bruno.* For the first time, that fact finally gets through to me. For years after I came back from Italy I would imagine I saw him or heard his voice on the street. I had to school myself to ignore those mirages, but now it's possible—well, more than possible . . . *inevitable*—that I will see him again. I'd shut out the thought over the last few weeks by telling myself that he probably left Florence in the summer and, like most Italians, fled to the seaside or the northern lakes. But Claudia hadn't said he was gone. In fact, she'd said that they *both* wanted to talk to me about Robin.

And so, if I ever choose an outfit and leave this room, I'm likely to run into him.

I look down at the pile of clothes I have been sifting through like a homeless woman picking through Salvation Army castoffs and suddenly feel defeated. My God, do I own anything that's not black or white? Is this my *summer* wardrobe? Black linen dresses and black cotton capris, white button-down shirts (three-quarter sleeve instead of winter's long sleeve), and white T-shirts. Is this what I've worn through nineteen New York summers except when I go to Woodstock, where I live in cut-off denims and my aunt's old peasant blouses? All of this seems too dreary and heavy to wear in the lambent Italian air, which, coming through the open windows now, seems to bathe my skin. Even this towel is feeling too heavy.

I've gotten to the bottom of the suitcase when I remember Chihiro's going-away present. *Something with an actual color,* she'd said, to brighten my usual schoolgirl uniforms, which is exactly what my drab clothes look like to me.

I unfold the thick tissue paper—itself a beautiful shade of vibrant orange that I recognize as the packaging of the Tibetan store Do Kham in Nolita—and lift up a delicate dress of pink gauze embroidered with gold thread; it flutters in the breeze like a rare butterfly. I slip it over my head before it can fly away—and before I can heed the little voice inside telling me I should probably wear a bra. I do put on panties and the gold Tibetan sandals I find nestled in the tissue paper along with a prayer from the Dalai Lama.

Now all I have to do is find a way to slip into the garden without running into Cyril Graham and company.

I grab a comb and run it through my wet hair on my way to the door, scattering water drops in my wake. When I stop at the full-length Venetian mirror by the door, I look back and notice that the water drops have turned the mosaic rose petals a brighter red. I turn to the mirror and look at myself. Chihiro chose well. The pink suits me. It's brought out the pink in my skin (or maybe that's just the effects of the hot bath), and the gold threads in the fabric catch the gold in my hair, which is quickly drying and beginning to curl in the hot, moist air. I begin to tie it up into a knot but then decide to let it hang loose. I am not, I remind myself, going to the rose garden to meet Bruno. I am going there to look for the poems Robin found.

On the day I first kissed Bruno, he had taken me into the garden to show me an inscription on the marble rim of the fountain at its center. He had wanted me to read the lines there as a warning against thinking that writing poetry was a way of making something that lasted. Ginevra de Laura, he told me, had spent her whole life writing poetry, but out of all those poems only two lines, carved into crumbling marble and hidden beneath tangled vines, had survived. What if before she left for the convent Ginevra decided not to burn the poems but to hide them? What better repository for those love poems than that same fountain, hidden at the center of a garden designed in the shape of her lover's initials?

CHAPTER
ELEVEN

I MANAGE TO MAKE IT TO THE STAIRS AND DOWN TO THE FIRST FLOOR OF THE rotunda without running into anyone, but as I'm passing the *sala grande* I hear voices approaching and the door opening. Fortunately, I learned years ago that when I wanted to avoid running into anyone in the rotunda, there is a convenient hiding place just at the foot of the stairs: a niche covered with a medieval tapestry. This one depicts a peasant snaring a bird for a lady on horseback. I step into this recess now and look out through a narrow gap between the tapestry and the wall. The doors to the *sala grande* open, and out step Cyril Graham and Leo Balthasar.

Although I feel suddenly like Polonius hiding in Queen Gertrude's bedroom, I'm glad I have this chance to see Cyril Graham for the first time while remaining unobserved myself. I know exactly what he would expect—*demand*—as tribute from a guest who had been long absent.

You haven't changed a bit. He was famously vain about his "figure," as he called it, and lectured us on the advantages of a Mediterranean diet long before it became fashionable.

And he is thin. I can say that for him. His mandarin-collar jacket (no doubt made by the special tailor in Hong Kong he had always bragged about) hangs off his thin, sloping shoulders, and his linen slacks swish around his bony ankles as he escorts Balthasar to the *ingresso*. He passes so close to me that I can see the liver spots on his bald head and smell his cologne.

"Good, it's settled, then," Cyril says, clapping his hand onto Balthasar's shoulder in a gesture that's supposed to be hearty but ends up, as Cyril's hand drifts trembling down Balthasar's arm, looking as if he's trying to hold on to the younger man for support. "You can start filming in the *limonaia* once you pay the roofers. After all, you don't want all that expensive film equipment water damaged."

"I'll pay the roofer's bill, Graham, and any other little home improvement project you can cook up, as long as you keep to your end of the bargain."

"A gentleman always honors his word." Cyril draws himself up, trying to square his thin shoulders, but succeeds only in swaying from side to side.

"But you thought the boy had the papers," Balthasar says, putting out a hand to steady Cyril. I can see an expression of pity mixed with irritation on Leo Balthasar's face.

"I'm sure he found something."

"Well, if he did, their whereabouts have died with him, I'm afraid. Are you sure you've looked everywhere?"

"You can't imagine the amount of papers stuffed away in this old place." Cyril lifts his hands, palms up, and looks toward the ceiling of the rotunda as if he expected a rain of paper to flutter down from the glassed-over oculus. "Are you sure he didn't tell the Brunelli boy before he died? That would be a disaster."

"I don't think he told Orlando anything. They weren't exactly on speaking terms at the end. But I think he might have told Dr. Asher something. She certainly changed her mind about my offer quickly after Robin died."

Cyril says something I can't make out, and I hear the front door open and close. I wait to see whether Cyril is coming back, but after a moment I conclude that he must have gone outside with Balthasar. I slip out from the niche and into the *sala grande,* which has, I remember, doors leading out into the garden.

The *sala grande* looks so exactly as it did twenty years ago that I feel as if I really have stepped back in time. It's not just the Louis Seize furniture—artfully arranged in conversational groupings—or the early medieval paintings on the walls that are the same. I could swear that even the knicknacks—or *tshatshkes,* as my mother would call the porcelain shepherdesses, ivory netsukes, and majolica lemons—and silver-framed photographs are arranged on the ormolu tabletops and chinoiserie cabinets exactly as they had been on my last day at La Civetta. I pick up a framed photograph of a minor British royal with a not-so-minor British writer and notice that the wood of the table is a darker color in the spot where the picture was positioned. I move a faience bulldog and a millefiori paperweight and see that they, too, have been sitting on darkened shadows of themselves while the wood around them has bleached in the Tuscan sun.

The sound of someone coming down the stairs in the rotunda startles me out of my communion with the inanimate objects. Whoever it is, I don't want to be kept from my errand in the garden. The fountain there might be the one place Cyril Graham and Leo Balthasar would not have thought of looking for Ginevra's poems. I unlatch the glass doors and slip outside, feeling, as the sultry air wraps around me, more insubstantial than those sepia-toned images in the *sala.*

A short flight of mossy steps takes me down to the lemon walk, which is lined with lemon trees, each in its own terra-cotta pot from the Tuscan village of Impruneta, where the high iron content of the clay makes their pottery resistant to frost. The flowers have fallen from the trees, and small green lemons are ripening in the sun. On the terrace above the walk is a walled fruit garden—the *pomerino*—and across from the *pomerino* is the *limonaia,* where the lemon trees spend the winter, and above the *limonaia,* on the second floor, is the apartment where Bruno lived the year I was here. It was a large and elegant apartment with terra-cotta floors and views of the garden and the Valdarno, but I somehow doubt that it would be enough for Claudia.

I see that the old wooden gate that used to be at the top of the staircase leading down into the rose garden has crumbled away. Instead there's a sign strung on a chain between two marble pillars warning *Pericoloso!* I'm surprised that this part of the gardens has not been renovated, but then, from the conversation I just overheard between Cyril and Leo Balthasar, I gather Cyril hasn't had enough money to even keep up the buildings. Something will have to be done about this staircase, though, when Hudson takes over. You can't expect students to heed a little wooden hand-painted sign. I certainly don't. With a quick backward glance at the villa, I step over the chain and start down the stairs.

They *are* dangerous, I quickly realize. There are whole steps missing and some that rock when you step on them. Small green lizards, which have colonized the ruined steps, dart under my feet, nearly causing me to trip several times. At the first landing, where the steps turn sharply right to descend into the rose garden, a statue of some ill-fated goddess or nymph has toppled over into a heap of broken limbs. Her face is half covered with vines, one eye staring up toward the top of the stairs as if waiting for someone to come down and save her.

"No one's coming, honey," I say stepping over her. At the bottom of the steps is the tomb of the veiled woman. I realize that this is also the back entrance of the *teatrino* and would have been an easier way to get into the rose garden. *Next time,* I think, reading the Shakespearian inscription carved into the stone, the one added by Cyril's father, Sir Lionel. "My father was quite the romantic," Cyril would tell us. "He liked to imagine the Bard himself wandering through these shaded walks or his lovers meeting under cover of night in the *teatrino.*"

The notion had struck my imagination then and it still has power now. This could be the forest of Arden from *As You Like It* or the enchanted woods in *A Midsummer Night's Dream.* The gardens of La

Civetta seem to exist outside time and place, just as Shakespeare's characters transcend their age and circumstances. As if to confirm my
thoughts, I hear, from the *teatrino,* a voice reciting lines I recognize
from *Romeo and Juliet.*

> *If I profane with my unworthiest hand*
> *This holy shrine, the gentle sin is this,*
> *My lips, two blushing pilgrims, ready stand*
> *To smooth that rough touch with a tender kiss.*

I can just make out from where I stand the boy's white shirt fluttering as
he gestures on the grassy stage and the swirl of the girl's spangled Indian
skirt as she answers:

> *Good pilgrim, you do wrong your hand too much,*
> *Which mannerly devotion shows in this:*
> *For saints have hands that pilgrims' hands do touch*
> *And palm to palm is holy palmers' kiss.*

I don't wait for the kiss that ends the scene. I move past the *teatrino,*
feeling insubstantial again, like a ghost spying on the living, and enter
the knot garden. As I follow the narrow, curving paths I realize that the
latter part of Robin's film was made here—the part in which Zoe runs
through the ruined garden after she has been betrayed by Orlando.
From the film I recognize the broken statuary strewn across the paths.
Arms and legs are scattered in the overgrown rosebushes as if there had
been some massacre and these were the bodies of the dead. No heads, I
notice. No doubt the garden was plundered for salvageable busts. I
imagine Cyril selling them for pocket cash to his antiques dealer in Florence, and that now those marble faces—women's faces, I gather, from
the delicacy and curve of the broken limbs—lie atop coffee tables and
bookcases in apartments in Rome, New York, and Paris, like exiled
princesses.

　　When I get to the fountain at the center of the garden, I remember that this is where Zoe sees Orlando and the other woman reading the Moroccan-bound notebook. When I saw the film in New York, I'd read the scene as a generalized depiction of betrayal. The book stood for the lover's innermost thoughts about the beloved. The lines of Shakespeare's poems that the audience hears might be the poems in the book—or they might be meant to suggest the *sort* of love poetry to be found in the lover's notebook. It didn't seem necessary to know for sure in order to feel the sting of betrayal when another woman sits with the beloved and laughs at the contents of the book.

Now, though, as I tug at the thick underbrush that covers the rim of the fountain, I wonder whether Robin was re-creating his discovery of the lost poems in the film. Perhaps Robin had shown the poems to Orlando and Orlando wanted to use them for his own purposes—to sell them or write his own story about Ginevra de Laura and William Shakespeare . . . I pause with a vine in my hands, realizing that it's far more likely that Bruno would write a book like that. In fact, it would be the perfect book for him to write. If Orlando told him about Robin's discovery, Bruno might have asked him to get the poems for him. Perhaps it was Bruno who sent Orlando to New York.

The idea upsets me so much that I tug too fiercely on the tangled vegetation that is still keeping me from the center of the fountain, releasing a thick, thorny vine that snaps back at me, snagging my hair and wrapping itself around my head. I cry out and step back, but that only entangles me further.

"Stay still," a man's voice says from behind me, "and I'll get you out."

I try to turn toward the voice, but the thorns scratch my face. I feel hands moving through my hair, slowly unraveling the vine from each strand. I'm reminded, oddly, of the medieval tapestry in the rotunda that depicts a man releasing a bird from a net into a gilded cage. As I turn around I feel as one of those birds must, freed from one trap only to find itself caught in a larger one. In my case, it's Bruno's eyes that have snared me, the fine lines that have grown around them only making them a wider net. I feel myself falling into them, but then I remember that he could have been the one to send Orlando to hound Robin for the poems. Which would mean that he could be the one responsible for Robin's death.

"Rose," he says, making of my one-syllable name a long, drawn-out sigh.

"Bruno," I say, trying to make my voice cool, but it's hard to sound imperious with tangled hair and scratched hands.

"You've torn your dress," he says.

I look down and see a small tear-shaped rip in the gathers of the bodice.

"It's along the seam," I say—inanely! Am I really, after all these years, talking to Bruno about clothing repairs? "I can sew it back together easily."

"*Brava.* It's a lovely dress. The color of your name. And all these years I've been afraid you'd become one of those New York women who dress only in black."

"As though I'd gone into mourning?" I ask, arriving now at the tone I'd meant to assume in the first place.

Bruno smiles—a small, reserved smile. "Well, you did return upon the death of your aunt, I remember, and your mother died sometime after, no?"

"Yes," I say, disarmed by the sympathy in his voice. "And I heard your mother died. I'm sorry. It's hard to imagine anyone replacing her here . . ."

I falter, remembering who *has* replaced her. It hasn't taken us long to get to the heart of the matter. Bruno winces as though he's been trapped, and I remember another detail from the tapestry in the rotunda. The man who kneels to unsnare the bird from the net is watched by a lady carrying a falcon on her arm. In the language of love practiced in medieval art, the tethered falcon is a reminder that even the hunter can be trapped. It's some relief to see that he's not totally in control of the situation, that he's been unnerved by my presence as much as I have been by his. My heart is racing. But then, I tell myself, maybe that's because it's just occurred to me that he might be involved in Robin's death.

"No one imagines that Claudia is a replacement for my mother," Bruno says, "least of all Claudia. But it suited her purposes to come back here when my mother died."

"You mean because of the lawsuit?"

"Ah." Bruno tugs at the skin under his right eye, skin that has become darker since the last time I saw him affect this fundamentally European gesture (its meaning, I learned over time, ranging from "You can't fool me" to "You've caught me"). "I see you've been keeping up with La Civetta's abundant store of gossip."

"Actually, I only heard about it a few weeks ago. I was surprised that you and Claudia would be here and that Cyril would allow it when you're suing him."

"Cyril and Claudia are both believers in the maxim 'Keep your friends close and your enemies closer.' Technically, I'm not suing anybody. The Brunelli family trust is suing the estate of La Civetta. It's all civil enough, and in the meantime, where else would I go?" He holds up his hands and, although I know he means to include all of La Civetta in the gesture, I imagine he means the rose garden, the fountain, this very moment. Perhaps it is what he means, because as he lowers his arms, he says, "I see it's drawn you back as well."

"I was offered a job on the film," I say primly, "as a research consultant."

"Ah, I see. And you've come to the rose garden to do research?"

I look down at the fountain, at the torn-up shrubbery; the center is still covered by thick vines. I'll have to come back to look in the basin for the poems, but for now I have to invent another reason for being here.

"Yes, I remembered the lines of poetry that are inscribed on the fountain. You were the one who showed them to me." I say it as if it's his fault I'm here—not just in the rose garden, but in Italy. I suddenly feel immensely tired and a little dizzy—the jet lag catching up with me. Surely that is what keeps making me feel *flimsy*—as if I'd left part of myself somewhere over the Atlantic and it hasn't had time to catch up with me yet. "The boy who wrote the screenplay used them in one of his poems. Perhaps you showed them to him?"

"Ah, Robin. *Povero raggazo.* Orlando told me what happened. It's upset him tremendously."

"You know, the police wanted to speak with him after Robin died, but he disappeared," I say. "And we've all wondered what he was doing in New York."

Bruno shrugs his shoulders. "Teenagers—who can make any sense of what they do and why? I tried to tell him it was foolish to go to New York, and look at what happened. And then he was afraid of the American police. He watches too much of your American television shows, *CSI, Law and Order* . . . He was afraid they'd find some speck of Robin's hair on his lapel and send him to prison. I've taken Orlando to the American ambassador and he answered his questions. He wants now to act in this movie the Americans are doing. You know, he was working with Robin on the script."

"Yes, Leo Balthasar told me there was some disagreement over the writing credit for the screenplay. Perhaps he wrote the poem that's in the script," I say. "If so, he's inherited your poetic talent. It's very good."

At the mention of the poem, a change comes over Bruno's face, a stillness that freezes his usually mobile features as if he were posing for a picture, and I wonder whether it's because he thinks I know where the poems are.

"You mean you don't believe the poem is by William Shakespeare's Dark Lady, Ginevra de Laura?" he asks.

"Well, I've only read one of the poems . . . but perhaps you've read others."

Bruno hesitates. "I've heard one of the poems described, but no, I'm afraid I'm at an even greater disadvantage. I haven't read any of these poems."

"But you've heard the stories about Ginevra de Laura. You were the one who told me about her—" I blush, remembering the circumstances under which he imparted that particular lesson. "Finding those poems and proving that they were by Shakespeare's Dark Lady would be a real scholarly coup for you, wouldn't it?"

"And for you as well," Bruno says. "Is that why you're really here, Rose? To make your academic reputation?"

It's exactly what I've just accused him of, so I shouldn't be surprised—or as hurt as I feel by the sudden coolness in his voice. This *is* what I wanted, I remind myself, to establish right away that there was nothing between us. He's also provided me with a chance to explain my presence here—and my search for the poems—that doesn't involve Orlando and my suspicions about Robin's death.

"Yes," I reply, "I'd like to find those poems—if they exist. Not because I think they're by the Dark Lady, but because I'm writing a book on Renaissance women poets. The discovery of a previously unknown poet would be a valuable addition to the book. I remember that you told me that Ginevra was Lorenzo Barbagianni's mistress. Isn't it more likely that if she wrote a series of poems they were addressed to him rather than to William Shakespeare?"

"Not if you knew anything about Lorenzo. He was a bit of a brute. No, according to references in contemporary diaries, she wrote to an unnamed lover. Someone she met as a young girl—an Englishman, it was thought, since the poems were written in English—before she became Barbagianni's mistress and came to live here at La Civetta. After Barbagianni's death she went to live in the Convent of Santa Catalina. It was believed that she destroyed the poems, but I came across a letter recently from the mother superior of the convent in the early seventeenth century referring to the 'creative outpouring' of one of her nuns, and it occurred to me that she might have been speaking about Ginevra de Laura and that Ginevra could have taken the poems with her to the convent. And if that were so, it's possible they were brought here after the 1966 flood when Lucy Graham 'saved' the water-damaged books by bringing them to La Civetta and appropriating the ones she thought might be valuable."

"If they've been in Lucy Graham's archives since then, why haven't I heard of it? Why hasn't anyone—you for instance—published it?"

"Because they're not in the archives. I've looked, of course. It's possible, though, that Lucy hid the poems when she realized how valuable they were. I've been looking for them for years. It's one of the reasons I came back."

I look away, up toward the villa, not wanting to ask what his other reasons might have been. All I can see of the building from here is a glimpse of golden ochre shimmering through the holm oaks and yew hedges. "It would make a great story, wouldn't it? An undiscovered sixteenth-century Renaissance woman poet who wrote sonnets in English. And you've never found a single poem? You said you heard one described . . ."

"Just an old family story," Bruno says. "My mother said Sir Lionel gave her a poem once, but she wasn't really sure who it was by, and when I tried to ask her about it she refused to say more. No, the only lines of Ginevra's I've read are these two lines . . . Do you remember them?"

While I've been looking up at the villa, Bruno has been excavating the fountain, pulling out handfuls of twisted rose vines, not gently as he removed the vine from my hair before, but roughly, so that all the roses on the vine have shed their crimson petals over the marble fountain and his hands are scratched from the thorns. There's a hunger in his eyes that I recognize from the first time we met here and he asked me whether I thought one had to experience passion in order to write poetry. It occurs to me now that I'd never answered the question.

He holds back a last tangle with one hand and with the other circles my waist to draw me closer. Through the thin fabric of my dress I can feel the warmth of his arm penetrate my skin, setting off a vibration that radiates across my back like a net woven of electricity. In pulling the vines from the rim of the fountain, Bruno has also cleared the basin, which is empty. I barely have time to register my disappointment that the poems are not here before Bruno reads the two lines out loud.

"Our bed awaits thee, strewn with wisps of rose," Bruno recites, "my longing more than any the wind knows." I feel an answering throb in the wind as it picks up the scattered rose petals and blows them toward the villa. One petal catches in Bruno's hair and my hand moves toward it as if it, too, had been lifted by the wind, but before I reach it, the wind blows back from the house, carrying with it the sound of voices coming toward us.

CHAPTER
TWELVE

RUNO'S ARM TENSES BEHIND ME, BUT HE DOESN'T PULL IT AWAY IMMEDIATELY. He takes a moment to lift his hand to my hair and smooth back a lock that the wind has blown across my face. Then he turns toward the approaching voices and leans against the rim of the fountain with his arms folded across his chest, his head tilted down as if he were studying the tips of his soft leather loafers. I turn, too, and try to adopt as casual a pose as he has assumed so effortlessly. Is it just his innate elegance, I wonder, or practice at dissembling, that gives him such an air of nonchalance, whereas I feel as if I've been caught pillaging the garden?

I make out a girl's voice as it comes closer to us on the path. "But isn't your father, like, working on the movie? Can't he get us something better than extra work?"

"My father won't do a thing," a boy's voice, young and petulant, answers, "because my mother doesn't want me to be an actor."

I recognize the voices as the same two I'd overheard playing Romeo and Juliet in the *teatrino*—only now instead of advancing through a web of metaphor toward their first kiss, they are, apparently, bickering over the politics of family and influence. As they come in to the clearing, I recognize the boy as Ned Silverman, Mara and Gene's son. He's got his father's height but his mother's pale skin, dark hair, and delicate bone structure. The girl I recognize by her raspberry-colored hair as Zoe Demarchis. She startles when she sees Bruno and me and drops something on the path that she screws into the ground with the sole of her rubber flip-flop. The smell of pot and burning rubber joins the hundred varieties of roses, and I wonder what the Dominican friars of Santa Maria Novella would make of that addition to their line of perfumes.

"Professor Asher." Ned turns as bright pink as the rose petals that litter the ground. "Wow. I didn't know you'd arrived. Are my mom and dad here, too?" Ned's eyes dart back and forth as if he expected Gene and Mara Silverman to jump out from behind the fountain and yell, "Surprise!"

"I'm sure they're up at the villa resting. Which is what I should be doing, only I was so excited to be back at La Civetta after twenty years that I had to come out and look at the garden and I ran into Professor Brunelli."

Zoe widens her already dilated eyes—I think, for a moment, at my explanation of how Bruno and I happen to be here together in the most secluded part of the garden, but that isn't what she finds incredible. "Twenty years! Man, that must be so weird coming back after all that time."

She's made it sound like centuries, but I'm forced to agree with her. "Yes, it is strange, but what's strangest is how it feels like it could have been yesterday—" I realize I'm stroking the rim of the marble fountain. Bruno is looking at me, remembering, I feel sure, that this was where we first kissed.

"Do you all know each other?" I ask, my voice a little high and brittle sounding to my ears. "Professor Brunelli, Ned Silverman and—" Before I can say her name, Zoe steps forward and does it for me.

"Zoe Demarchis," she says, extending her hand to Bruno. "You teach that poetry class, right? I was going to take it because I write poetry all the time, but then I got the part of Juliet and realized that I wouldn't have time"—she gives Bruno a flirtatious smile—"but maybe you could give me a private tutorial?" Zoe catches my eye and her smile fades as if I'd scowled at her, although I hadn't been aware of doing so. She quickly adds, "I really liked that sonnet you recited, Dr. Asher . . . you know, at the thing for Robin in Washington Square? I remember that it had something in the last lines about black ink and love lasting."

" 'O, none, unless this miracle have might,' " Bruno recites, " 'That in black ink my love may still shine bright.' "

"Yeah, that's it. I thought it was cool because Robin was always talking about being remembered for what he wrote. You must have really liked him, huh? Was he, like, your favorite student?" She slides her eyes toward Ned and then, looking back at me, widens them in an attempt to look sincere. It's always amazed me how young people—especially stoned young people—think adults don't notice when they're being laughed at. Ned, though, looks pained at the insinuation in her voice. Poor Ned. Mara was unfortunately right about the effect of roughing it on his physique and complexion. He looks too thin and his skin is mottled and rashy—what I'd taken for a blush at first being a permanent strawberry blotch on his cheeks.

"I'd be saddened by the death of any of my students," I say in my best prim schoolmistress voice.

Zoe and Ned nod seriously and I think I've gotten away with my evasion, but then Bruno says, "Yes, but you haven't answered Ms. Demarchis's question. Was Robin your . . . *prediletto?*"

He chooses the Italian word that means "dearest" or "pet," giving it an inflection that makes it sound vaguely dirty, maybe because of that *letto* at the end, which means bed. Zoe giggles and Ned turns so pale that the rash on his cheek stands out like the angry mark from a slap. I turn to Bruno and meet his gaze. Does he really think I was having an affair with one of my students? And if I were, who is he to call me to task? He'd had an affair with me when I wasn't any older than Robin. At least I'm not married.

"I suppose he was," I say coolly. "Who could help but take an interest in a young person of such talent? I think he would have become a great writer. If he kept to it."

I've meant only to make Bruno a little jealous—to let him see that I haven't spent the twenty years since I left him in mourning (despite that suitcase full of black clothing back in my room at the villa)—but the look of hurt in his eyes goes beyond jealousy. It's the jab about Robin's potential as a writer that's gotten to him. But only for a moment. He shrugs and lifts his hands, palms up, to the sky. "But now we'll never know. What a shame, eh?"

"Maybe it's better," Ned says. "Now everyone will remember him as this beautiful guy with all this promise and he'll never get old or fat and give up his dreams and take some awful job he hates and live in the suburbs. He'll never have to be a failure." Ned finishes in a gasp that makes him look like an angry fish.

"Yes," Bruno says, pushing himself away from the fountain, "there is a beauty in that. Some flowers are more beautiful as buds than full blown. And memories are often best left as memories. I hope you don't regret coming back to La Civetta, Professor Asher. Reality so rarely measures up to our memories."

"No," I say, looking down at the ground strewn with scattered rose petals, "I guess not." I look up too quickly, and the heat-struck garden seems to blur around me, dark, petal-shaped blotches superimposed over the thicket of green. I feel myself swaying, and Bruno touches my elbow to steady me.

"You're not going to faint . . . ?" Bruno asks. I think we both hear the echo of the word *"cara"* at the end of his sentence and remember it's what he asked me after the first time we kissed.

"No," I say, pulling away from his touch. "It's just jet lag. I'd better go back to my room and rest."

"Yeah, you don't want to miss the big party tonight," Zoe Demarchis says. "It's to celebrate the summer solstice and officially open the summer term. Mr. Graham's had a crew of chefs cooking for a week and we've been rehearsing day and night to get the entertainment ready. The theme is the Capulets' masked ball from *Romeo and Juliet* with a little bit of *A Midsummer Night's Dream* thrown in—those are the two plays we're doing here this summer. I'm playing Juliet and Ned's Romeo. We've been rehearsing day and night for two weeks and we've only got three more days before opening night, so we'd better get back to it, right Ned?"

"Oh, right." Ned shakes himself as if waking from a dream. He is still, I think, imagining poor Robin, frozen for all time in the moment of youth and promise like a figure on Keats's vase. There's a strange light in his eyes that makes me uneasy, but then maybe it's just the pot he's smoked. "I'm her Romeo . . ." He starts to laugh and Zoe pulls him away, heading down the path toward the villa, first shushing him and then giggling herself. Bruno and I follow a few steps behind. At first I think Bruno's slow pace is to give them time to get ahead, but even when they're out of sight he keeps his eyes on the ground and loiters a half step behind me. I can think of nothing to say to break the silence until we reach the gate that leads out of the rose garden.

"What you said just now about me regretting coming back to La Civetta . . ." I begin. "Is there any reason why I should?"

He turns to me but instead of looking at me he tilts his head back, his hands in his trouser pockets, and looks up at the sky. I remember that this is what he'd do in class if you asked him a difficult question. Perhaps I learned my evasion tactics from him. After a long moment he looks at me and smiles.

"I suppose it depends on why you came. If your plans are strictly academic—"

"Of course they are," I say perhaps a little too quickly. Let him think my interest in the poems is scholarly and not that I've begun to suspect he might have been the one who sent his son to New York to get the poems.

Bruno gives me a long look—the same look he'd give a student in class if they'd sounded unsure of their answer. I almost expect he'll ask, as he would then, "Is that your final answer?" but instead he says, his mouth curving into the same secret, mysterious smile I saw once on an Etruscan funerary statue ("My ancestors," Bruno had said when I pointed out the resemblance), *"Bene,* if that's why you're here, I can't see that you're in any danger at all."

Back in my room I close the heavy wooden shutters on my windows to block out the afternoon sun so that I can take a nap. Otherwise, I reason with myself, I'll never get through tonight's reception and dinner. Clearly I need to keep my wits about me. For a moment there in the garden when Bruno recited the lines of poetry on the fountain and the air had filled with the scent of roses, I'd been close to falling into his arms. What had I been thinking? How could I possibly trust a man who deceived me twenty years ago and whose son might have killed someone dear to me, let alone fall in love with him again? I had forgotten his power to charm and dissimulate. When I asked him whether he'd ever seen any of the poems, he had hesitated and then offered that lame explanation of hearing his mother talk about a poem Sir Lionel had given her. Wasn't it far more likely that Orlando had shown him the poems that Robin found? No, I couldn't trust Bruno, and I'd better get some rest before jet lag and exhaustion compromised my judgment once again.

Before I climb into the old four-poster bed, I roll the rug back over the *pietre dure* pattern of scattered rose petals. I can see now why Lucy Graham chose to keep the floor covered. In the dim half light the pattern really does look like splotches of blood rather than wind-scattered rose petals.

When I close my eyes, though, I see the rose petals in the garden drifting over Bruno's hand and see myself turning to him. I open my eyes and stare at the faded frescoes that line the walls, counting the repeated pattern of arch and tree, bird and flower, that marches across the cracked and faded plaster. Only the stiff medieval figures change in each scene, and they seem to move in jerks and stops in the wavering bands of light that creep in through the slatted shutters. A young man and woman part from one another in a garden, the youth wanders through a grove, a knight appears on horseback, a young woman runs naked through the woods, there's a flurry of activity with dogs in the foreground in the painting between the two windows that's partially blocked by the heavy curtains, and then they're all back in the garden again, seated at a banquet table. The scenes seem vaguely familiar, but I can't follow the story or remember its source. Each time I close my eyes I'm back in the rose garden with Bruno and our movements have acquired the same jerky quality. We turn to each other as if to kiss and then turn away, over and over again, like windup dolls.

I'm not sure whether I sleep or not. I notice after a while that the strips of light from the shuttered windows have moved across the room, stretched, thinned, and, finally, faded into the painted walls. I check my travel clock, but since I haven't changed the time yet I can't make any sense of what it says. I can hear, though, from the creaks and groans of La Civetta's ancient pipes, that preprandial preparations are going on around the villa. So I get up, splash water on my face, and start to get dressed, cursing at myself for not hanging up my clothes before my so-called nap so the wrinkles would have had time to fall out.

Luckily, one of the dresses I packed is made from a wrinkle-proof jersey. It falls straight from shoulder to knee, and I thought, when I bought it in New York, that it was the height of elegant simplicity. As I slip it over my head, though, I can't help but think of what Bruno said about New York women dressed in black, and I feel suddenly as though I were dressing for a funeral instead of for a party. Worse, when I turn to look at myself in the mirror, the dress's straight cut reminds me of a nun's shift. I notice, then, that draped over the back of one of the chairs is a black silk shawl embroidered with red rosebuds and green vines. I pluck it off the chair, the fine old silk moving like water through my hands, and tie it low around my waist. Instantly my plain black shift is transformed into a flamenco dancer's costume. When I move I can feel the silk hugging my hips and the shawl's fringe brushing against my bare legs like a caress. Before I can change my mind, I twist my hair up into a knot, baring the dress's one daring element—a low-plunging back—and step out onto my balcony.

The sky has softened to a lambent lilac and the air smells like lemons and roses. Torches have been lit along the lemon walk and Chinese paper lanterns strung along the garden paths: a river of light moving on the soft evening air between the dark, flamelike shapes of the cypress trees. I pluck a red rose from the vine growing on the balcony and slip it into my hair. As I turn to go back inside, I feel the breeze touch my bare back like a hand urging to me to hurry on downstairs and join the party.

As I come down the curving stairs of the rotunda, I see Cyril Graham look up—away from Gene and Mara Silverman—and startle. For a second I think there must be someone else behind me or that he's mistaken me for someone else, but he bows his head toward me and, when I've reached the foot of the stairs, lifts my hand ceremoniously to his lips.

"Rose," he says when his dry lips have grazed my skin, "you have bloomed. You were a very pretty girl, but you've become a beautiful woman."

I smile back at him and say, "Cyril Graham. You haven't changed a bit," and even though it's a line I've been practicing, I find I actually mean it. His flattery (with a sly nod to my increased age) and the combination of admiration and malice in his eyes more than make up for his infirmity. In fact, Cyril seems more himself than ever, as if age had boiled him down to his essential self—a crafty spirit who loves gossip and pretty things above all else.

"Ah, you can flatter all you like," he says wagging a finger at me, "but I'm still very angry with you for staying away from La Civetta for so long. When you left you promised you would help me put the villa's archives in order, but you never came back."

It's not exactly true. Yes, I had, a few months before my aunt died, agreed to work as Cyril's research assistant and had even started the laborious work of sorting through both the old record books that belonged to the villa and the archives that Lucy Graham had "saved" from the Convent of Santa Catalina, but I was hardly essential to the project and I found a replacement before I left. There's no point arguing with Cyril, though.

"I'm sorry I took so long returning," I tell him, accepting a glass of Prosecco from a waiter in a white tunic, "but I was unavoidably delayed."

Cyril laughs, recognizing the formulaic excuse he gave our class nearly every afternoon when he would arrive as much as half an hour after the appointed time. He would always stroll out onto the loggia, a demitasse of espresso and saucer in one hand, a Dunhill cigarette in the other, the picture of unhurried elegance, and recite the line as if he were a character in a Noel Coward play.

"You are forgiven," he says, bowing to me, "but only if you promise to take up exactly where you left off."

"Take up what?" I hear someone ask.

I turn and find Mark, in an elegant dark gray suit I haven't seen before, standing behind me. He's directly in front of the tapestry I hid behind earlier today, and it reminds me of how I felt when I turned around in the garden and found Bruno behind me. Mark looks nothing like the pale medieval youth in the tapestry, though. Since I saw him just a week ago in New York, he has lost his city pallor and his skin seems to glow, the result, no doubt, of a diet rich in olive oil and the Mediterranean sun.

"My research in the villa's archives," I answer. "Cyril was just reminding me that I abandoned my work with them twenty years ago."

"Your loss was our gain," Mark says, moving close enough to me so I can feel the warmth he gives off.

"Well, I'm glad you've agreed to loan her to us for the summer. I'm looking forward to seeing what Rose turns up in the archives. I feel they've been neglected and that they will be especially valuable for Mr. Balthasar's film project—not just the ones from Santa Catalina, but the villa's archives as well. There are inventories going back to the quattrocento listing every painting, every vase, every statue, that ever passed through this house. Each room can be made to look exactly as it did in the 1590s when Shakespeare himself stayed here. There might even be proof somewhere in all the record books and letters and diaries of his visit. Imagine what luster it would add to your university, President Abrams, to own not just any Italian villa but the one in which Shakespeare visited his Dark Lady."

Mark's eyes catch mine with that same look of skepticism I've seen in faculty meetings when professors propose ambitious and expensive programs. "Hudson College will be happy to acquire La Civetta, in due time, with a minimum of controversy and fanfare. I think we can all agree that it's a jewel just as it is." Mark gestures toward the *sala grande,* where the wide doors are open, taking in with the sweep of his arm the torch-lit garden, the violet sky, and the domes and red-tile rooftops of Florence laid out below us like a fairy-tale city. He has that same proprietorial look he had surveying Washington Square Park from my office window, only here instead of NYU's purple and gold flags, the intruder he spies is Bruno Brunelli, standing in a circle of students just outside the doors, the lilac evening light reflected in the fine white cotton of his dress shirt and the pale linen jacket draped over one shoulder.

"I would think he'd feel awkward working here while the lawsuit's pending," Mark whispers to Cyril. "I wonder that you've allowed him to live here all these years."

"Ah, but the lawsuit is entirely his wife's doing. I don't blame Bruno at all. If not for the difficulty of divorce in the Catholic Church, he wouldn't even be married to her. They live quite separately, you know, since the boy is grown up. I can't say I blame Bruno for seeking refuge at La Civetta. Like me, his best memories are here." Cyril finishes with a sly smile in my direction. Luckily Mark is looking at Bruno and doesn't notice. "Besides," Cyril continues, "my mother made me promise that Bruno would always have a place here."

"Really?" I ask. "I'd never heard that. It's unusual, considering—"

"Rose," Mark says, cutting me off, "you haven't seen the gardens yet, have you? You'll be impressed with the renovations the college has financed since you last saw them in your undergraduate days. I think we have just enough time before dinner . . ."

He pulls me toward the open French doors before I can finish ask-

ing Cyril what he'd meant. Why would Lucy Graham have wanted the
son of her rival—and possibly the illegitimate son of her husband—
assured a place here forever? I'm distracted from the question, though,
when I see the direction Mark has chosen. He's heading straight toward
Bruno. I try to think of something to deflect him from his course—a demand for a drink? Tripping over one of the ornamental urns? But
Bruno has already noted our approach, and his gaze wraps around me
like a gossamer-thin net reeling me in.

"Ah, Professor Asher," he says, ignoring Mark completely. "I was
just telling my students that we're fortunate to have in our midst such
an adept practitioner of the art of sonnet writing." And then, turning to
Mark, he says, "Perhaps President Abrams will prevail on her to give a
reading of her poetry this summer?"

"I didn't realize Dr. Asher's reputation as a poet was . . . interna-
tional," Mark says, "or that you were so familiar with her poetry." The
air between the two men is lit with a tension I can feel in my bones. I assume Mark's hostility comes from the lawsuit, but I wonder at the
source of Bruno's animosity. Has he, as Claudia clearly had, heard some
rumor about my involvement with Mark? But then why would he care
whom I was involved with after all these years—unless he really did believe I'd gone into mourning after our affair and remained a black-
garbed nun in New York.

"I took Professor Brunelli's course on the Renaissance sonnet when
I was at La Civetta," I say, gratefully accepting another glass of Prosecco
from a passing waiter. "It set me on my course of study."

"Ah," Mark says, holding a glass up to Bruno in a toast, "then we
have you to thank for one of our most prized teachers. Do we also have
you to thank for inspiring her to write love poetry?"

"I can hardly take credit for Dr. Asher's writing talent," Bruno says.
"That's something you're born with."

"Really?" Mark asks, furrowing his brow skeptically. "You think
writing talent is innate? That it can't be taught? That's bad news for our
writing program." Mark grins amiably and the few students who are
still standing in our orbit laugh, but then Mark cuts off his smile—so

quickly it's as if a mask has descended over his face. The students, sensing a change of mood, drift away from us to groups of their own. "But then, according to your theory, you *can* take credit for your son's writing talent."

"Orlando?" Bruno asks.

"Yes, Orlando. Do you have another son?"

"No, Orlando's my only child," Bruno says, squaring his shoulders as if he's getting ready to block a tackle. "He's talented at many things, but acting is his heart's desire—an art I have no talent for whatsoever—"

"But I thought he was also a writer. When he came to New York recently he was claiming that he had worked with Robin Weiss on his screenplay. In fact, he was so vehement in his assertions that the poor boy killed himself."

"I've heard a slightly different version of the story," Bruno says slowly, enunciating each word carefully. "Orlando never said that he wrote part of the screenplay; he said he helped Robin do the research for it."

"Ah, so he's inherited your scholarly aptitude. Tell me, did you help with the research for Robin's screenplay? Because if you did, Leo Balthasar might want to know before he has another lawsuit on his hands—"

"I have no intention of suing—"

At the sound of the words "lawsuit" and "suing," Cyril Graham appears on the loggia and slips in between Mark and Bruno. "Oh, let's not have any such talk," he says, placing a bony hand on each of the men's shoulders. "Not on a night as lovely as this one. Look," he says, taking his hand off Mark's shoulder and waving it toward the darkening garden, "isn't it magical? Like the woods in *A Midsummer Night's Dream*."

Indeed his gesture seems to transform the party for an instant into the revels of otherworldly spirits. Laughter rises out of the shadowy groves, and sparks of light—from the torches and lanterns, perhaps, but also from the cigarettes or joints students are sneaking behind the hedges—flare up out of the dark like winged fairies. Cyril removes a torch from its holder to lead the procession in to dinner. With his wizened old face lit up by the torch he carries, Cyril looks for a moment like an aged version of "that shrewd and knavish sprite" of *A Midsummer Night's Dream:* the hobgoblin Puck.

Mark waves Bruno on ahead of us, but then, instead of staying by my side, he excuses himself, saying he has to oversee the seating arrangements. As I join the crowd following Cyril, I try to sort through the threads of Mark and Bruno's argument. Tension over the lawsuit certainly explains some of the hostility between the two men, but something else is going on. What I'm afraid of is that Mark shares the same suspicion that I do: that Bruno sent Orlando to New York to get those poems back from Robin.

CHAPTER
THIRTEEN

DINNER IS SERVED IN THE *LIMONAIA,* EMPTY NOW OF ITS LEMON TREES, ITS floor-to-ceiling windows open to the night. The building was designed to let in as much sun as possible during the winter months and so works as well to let in the evening breezes. Lit by the flicker of candlelight, the wall of tall arched windows overlooking the lemon walk and the *teatrino* appears insubstantial, a painted scrim hanging above the stage of the *teatrino.* Even the way the tables are set up—in a U shape with the open end facing the windows—suggests that we are seated for a performance. Students dressed in Renaissance garb and silk masks are dancing to the strains of dulcimer and lute. Only the faces of some of my colleagues from Hudson dispel the illusion that I've wandered into the Capulets' masked ball at which Romeo and Juliet first meet.

When I find my seat—marked by a name card bound to a silver

napkin holder with lavender ribbons and silver wire—I feel a bit as if I'm taking my place onstage for a drawing room comedy. I see by the place cards that I've been seated between Mark and Bruno and across from the lawyer Daisy Wallace, Leo Balthasar, and Mara Silverman. I'm tempted to switch my place card with one at another table—even Frieda Mainbocher and Lydia Belquist lecturing to a group of Japanese businessmen at the next table look like restful company in comparison to this table.

I look around and see that several people are grabbing their name cards and switching them to other tables, so why shouldn't I? I notice that Mark, in fact, is leaning over Gene Silverman, who's seated at a table of pretty young students. Mark is whispering something in Gene's ear. Mara, who's hovering over my chair, is watching them.

"Isn't that thoughtful of Mark?" Mara says when she sees Gene get up and walk with Mark back to our table. "He's invited Gene to sit at our table. I'm sure Gene would rather sit with me and Mr. Balthasar."

I'm wondering whether this is what Mark meant by overseeing the seating arrangements—making sure that Gene Silverman wasn't hitting on any of the students—but still I agree with Mara. "Yes, it's very thoughtful. In fact, he can have my chair," I say, raising my voice so Mark and Gene can hear me as they get closer. "I don't mind sitting somewhere else."

"I've already asked the waiter to bring an extra chair," Mark says, holding my chair out for me, and then, in a lower voice, "I'd prefer that you stay here."

I slide into my seat just as Mara lets out an earsplitting shriek. "Hermès scarf rings!" she cries, holding up a silver-plated ring that I had taken for an ordinary napkin ring. "They go for over a hundred apiece in New York. Now *that's* class."

"Cyril likes everything done with style," Bruno says, sitting down next to me.

"A ridiculous extravagance," Daisy Wallace says, sliding her napkin out of its silver ring and briskly snapping out its folds before smoothing it over her lap. She herself is wearing a white cotton shift so austere in its simplicity, it might be a nightgown. With her long light hair, she reminds me, tonight, of the sickly Mary in Dante Gabriel Rosetti's *Annunciation*. "No wonder this place is falling apart." I notice, though, that she's carefully slipped her scarf ring into her evening purse. Since I don't have a purse, I place my ring to the right of my plate.

"Careful you don't lose yours, Rose," Mara says. "Gene, can you put mine in your jacket pocket?"

"Do you want me to hold yours for you?" Mark asks as he sits down.

I see Bruno and Daisy watching us and realize that the offer to carry this silly overpriced bauble in his pocket, where it would surely spoil the line of his suit jacket, has a husbandly aura that these two have picked up on.

"That's okay," I say, holding the ring up. "My name is firmly attached to it."

"You'll find that your initials are inscribed on it as well." Bruno smiles his Etruscan smile. He seems pleased that I've rebuffed Mark's offer.

"Signora Brunelli's work, no doubt," Mark says. "And look, she's even gotten the middle initials right. What careful attention to detail. How lucky to have a wife who pays attention to every little thing."

Bruno's smile disappears and I reach for the glass of Prosecco that's just been poured for me. I'm already exhausted. My God, if we can't even put our napkins on our laps without sparring, how are we ever going to get through the antipasto, let alone the six courses of a traditional Italian dinner? And I know that Cyril would never present anything less than a banquet. The antipasto itself is a feast, including a half dozen cured meats in the *salumi misti*, three types of *crostini*, sundry pickled vegetables, figs, peppers, and olives.

Fortunately, Cyril is as generous with wine as he is with food. Leo Balthasar, holding up a glass of the local Chianti that comes with the *primo piatto*—taglierini pasta with black truffles—makes a backhanded toast of sorts to our host. "Cyril Graham certainly has a free hand with the booze. I hear his mother was quite the lush."

Daisy Wallace, who is still nursing her glass of Prosecco, tilts her head and looks at Balthasar with the same disdain with which she regarded the fat-marbled salami and wrinkled peppers of the antipasto. "And yet it was Lucy who had the presence of mind in the 1966 flood to rescue the archives of Santa Catalina while Sir Lionel was posing in front of the Biblioteca Nazionale and flirting with the mud angels."

"Mud angels?" Mara asks, wrinkling her nose. "Is that some Catholic thing?"

"Not exactly," I answer because Daisy is staring at Mara blankly. "That's what they called the volunteers—many of them women librarians from the States—who came to help save the books that had been damaged in the flood. It was amazing, really. People from all over the world came. The city had no electricity, there was a food shortage, fear of epidemics, tons of mud, oil and sewage choking the streets. The volunteers had to sleep in railway cars, but they stayed anyway, forming human chains to pull books out of the Biblioteca Nazionale, the State Archives, dozens of private collections, museums, galleries, and ecclesiastical archives. It's estimated that at the Biblioteca Nazionale alone over a million books or manuscripts were damaged."

I finish breathlessly and take a gulp of the Chianti, embarrassed to notice that the whole table is staring at me. At least I haven't confessed my lifelong regret that I was born too late to be a mud angel.

"Unfortunately many of the flooded churches in the Arno valley were neglected," Daisy continues. "Lucy Graham personally supervised the evacuation of manuscripts from Santa Catalina, a small convent in the Valdarno, about an hour southeast of the city. She felt it was her duty because the convent was once located here on the grounds of La Civetta, but not everyone would have acted so conscientiously. She let the nuns stay in the old convent here on the grounds until the convent in the Valdarno was habitable again. She organized training sessions at the *biblioteca* in cleaning and restoring books for the nuns and her own household staff. They used this building to dry the folio leaves on laundry lines strung over the lemon trees." Daisy lifts her eyes to the ceiling with the fervor of a saint ascending to heaven and we all follow her glance up to the rafters, where dark shapes flutter in the shadows, and I can almost imagine that the ghosts of those old manuscript pages still linger in the cavernous space. "Even now," Daisy says, "the books in Lucy's archives smell like lemons."

"It would have been even nobler if Lucy had returned the archives after she'd restored the books," Bruno says.

"Oh, but the convent library was so damaged in the flood. For a long time it was closed for restoration."

"Ah, *chiuso per restauro,*" Leo Balthasar says. "Practically my only Italian phrase. I learned it trying to film a miniseries on location here a couple of years ago."

Gene tries to ask Balthasar what miniseries—clearly he is dying to change the subject from convents to movies—but Daisy goes on as if it's a brief she's prepared to deliver in court.

"Well," Daisy says, "the convent is open now, but the nuns there are devoted to wool production and tapestry weaving. They're far too busy to care for such an important collection. I'm sure it's better off here at La Civetta, especially now that it will belong to the college."

"But I don't understand," Mara says. "What could possibly be that interesting about some nuns' writing from the dark ages?"

It's practically the same sentiment I expressed to Daisy Wallace back in New York, but when I hear it voiced by Mara, I'm ashamed at my previous dismissal of the library of Santa Catalina. "Actually," I say, "it's surprising how varied the works are. The nuns wrote plays, diaries, histories . . . A seventeenth-century nun by the name of Arcangela Tarabotti wrote a moving and eloquent condemnation of fathers who immured their unwilling daughters in convents just to avoid paying their dowries so they could add to their own wealth."

"Oh, how awful," Mara says, a hand to her chest, her voice raspy as if something was constricting her breathing. "I didn't realize those girls were put in the convents against their will."

"Not all," Daisy says. "Some had a calling." And then, turning to me, "I see you've revised your valuation of the archives. Have you found something of interest?"

"I only just arrived today; I haven't had a chance to look in the archives. I confess, though, that the fact that Ginevra de Laura spent the last years of her life at Santa Catalina has piqued my interest in those records."

"Ah, our Dark Lady," Leo Balthasar says. "I'd forgotten that she ended up in a convent."

"Really, though," I say, "Professor Brunelli's the expert on Ginevra de Laura."

"Bah, hardly an expert, so little is known about her. Barbagianni's heirs destroyed all the letters and poems they could get their hands on when he died and they kicked Ginevra out of the villa. Legend has it that she went to the Convent of Santa Catalina wearing a shift lent to her by a serving woman and that she sewed some of the pages of her poems into the cloth."

"A woman who was having an affair with a married man went to live in a nunnery?" Mara asks. "Wasn't that unusual?"

"Mara would have had her burned at the stake," Gene comments to Leo Balthasar in an all-too-audible aside.

"The Renaissance convent was the last refuge for women who didn't wish to remarry or who were no longer considered desirable on the marriage market," Bruno replies, ignoring Gene and addressing his comment directly to Mara, perhaps, I think, to distract her from her husband's boorish behavior. The second-course wine is poured while Bruno talks—a Brunello di Montalcino—known sometimes as the king of Tuscan wines. When I raise the glass to my lips I can smell the oak from the cask it's been aged in. "It's possible that Ginevra de Laura brought her collected poetry with her to the convent—or even wrote in her remaining years—and that it survived in the convent's archives. Unfortunately, the library's catalog was lost in the flood and no inventory has been made since then, when the collection was brought here. Cyril began cataloging the material two decades ago, but then complained that one of the student researchers he hired stole a rare manuscript. He's been very cautious about who he lets have access to the archives since then. Naturally that has slowed up the cataloging process."

"But of course you've had access to them all along," Gene says. "You've had plenty of opportunity to find the Dark Lady poems. I bet it would be pretty tempting if you found them to sell them to a private dealer. After all, we all know how low paying this job is." Gene chuckles and pours himself another glass of the Brunello. The rest of the table is silent. Only Mara seems oblivious to how insulting Gene's last comment was. Perhaps she's just learned how to tune him out.

"No scholar worthy of the name would trade in the black market," Bruno says in a tightly controlled voice.

"Really? Not even if it got his son a part in a Hollywood movie? Hey, I know what it's like to have a kid with the acting bug. Who wants to see him waiting tables for ten years—"

"What exactly are you implying—?" Bruno begins to ask, but Mara interrupts, suddenly announcing to the whole table, "Our son, Ned, is going to Cornell in the fall. He's going into the premed program."

Another silence descends on the table, but this time, thankfully, it's filled by the rising notes of a lute and a lowering of the lights throughout the *limonaia*. The waiters, who are now bringing out plates of cheese, are also extinguishing the candles at each table. "Oooh, what's happening now?" Mara asks the waiter when he comes to our table.

"Una sorpresa," he replies. A surprise.

"A student performance," Gene informs the table. "The miracle will be if they don't all fall over each other. I'd better have a last check backstage."

"That's a good idea." Mark pushes his chair away from the table and stands. "Cyril said something about 'pyrotechnics,' so I'd better go make sure the students aren't going to burn down the villa."

I look up at Mark, trying to catch his eye before he goes to see whether he's as shocked by Gene's behavior as I am—and whether his real reason for going is to privately reprimand him—but a sudden flash of light from the open windows throws him into shadow. I turn toward the garden in time to see a waterfall of sparks drift down from each of the arched windows, its fall accompanied by a rising murmur from the crowd. When I look back, Gene and Mark are gone.

I had thought the Capulet ball was the main entertainment for the evening, but I see now that the dancers have formed two groups on either side of the *teatrino,* as though they were spectators watching a performance prepared for their entertainment. It's a clever play-within-a-play frame—one worthy of Shakespeare himself. A chorus of oohs and aahs draws my attention back to the windows. Another waterfall of light descends, but this time the tiny sparks seem to settle on the privet hedges and marble statues on the green stage of the *teatrino,* where they swell into glowing globes. Each globe tumbles for a moment, vibrating to a chord of a distant melody, and then, as if at a signal, they begin to dance. Some of the guests behind our table stand up and move toward the windows for a better view, thereby blocking ours. I hear Daisy Wallace hiss a command to sit down, but no one pays her any mind.

"Let's move closer," Bruno whispers in my ear. "Orlando's in this."

I hesitate, but then curiosity gets the better of me and I get up to follow him through the crowded, darkened room. The only lights are the dancing globes, which, I see, have multiplied and become iridescent with color—indigos and violets, the same colors the sky had been just before dusk, as if the hues of twilight have effervesced into airy bubbles. When we get close enough I can see that the bubbles are, in fact, paper lanterns and that each one is held aloft by a figure in a black body stocking and blackface. Although seeing the dancers peels away a layer of illusion, it doesn't ruin the effect. It feels, rather, as if the shadows in the garden have come to life, grown muscle and sinew, for this one purpose: to make light dance. When the light from the lanterns passes over their costumes I see they're not entirely black but of the same iridescent violet and indigo as the globes. Translucent wings flutter and billow at the dancers' backs. They're fireflies, I think, or dark fairies.

"It's the second act of *A Midsummer Night's Dream,* isn't it?" I whisper to Bruno.

"Yes, this is Oberon's train," he says, the purple light from the lanterns catching the curve of his smile, "and here comes Titania's retinue."

The dark-winged dancers have paused, listening to the faraway call of trumpets. Then they hold their globes above the ground, illuminating what appear to be crouching statues. When the light touches them, the figures, dressed in lighter suits of pearly pink and lavender, stretch and rise, unfurling elaborate sparkling wings. I take advantage of the lull in the dance to say to Bruno, "I don't know what came over Gene. I mean, he's an ass, but even for him that display was pretty bad."

"It doesn't matter. As you say, the man is an ass—and I think he is annoyed that Orlando got this part instead of his son, Ned—there he is now." Bruno points toward the center of the *teatrino,* where a statue poised on a marble plinth is suddenly lit up by a floodlight. It might be a statue of Eros or the young Dionysus, but then it comes to life, vaulting off the plinth into the middle of the dance, scattering the fairies like dewdrops.

"Orlando is playing Puck?" I ask.

"Yes."

"He's good," I say as the boy dances in a circle made up of the dark and light fairies, the lanterns now placed at their feet a ring of ghostly footlights. "You must be very proud of him."

Bruno doesn't reply at first and I'm afraid that my praise has come out sounding stinting. I don't mean it to. Orlando's dance is beautiful, heartbreakingly so. He would, in this part of the play, be telling of the quarrel between Oberon and Titania, a petty fight over the prize of a changeling boy, but his dance seems to evoke some deeper rift, as if some fundamental element of nature had been ripped asunder by the warring king and queen of fairies.

"He's been working himself to the bone," Bruno finally says, "trying to get this part right. You see, it was Robin's part last year and Orlando feels as if it's some sort of memorial to him. *Dio,* I almost forgot"—Bruno slaps his hand against his forehead—"I was supposed to take pictures. My camera's back at the table. I'll be right back."

Of course, I think turning back to watch the performance as Bruno goes, the grief in this dance is not for Titania and Oberon, but for the original Puck—Robin Weiss. I should have known it was originally Robin's part. Robin would have made the perfect Puck; even his name

echoes one of Puck's aliases: Robin Goodfellow. When Orlando has finished his dance, he sinks to the ground, wrapping his arms around his
knees in exactly the same pose he'd assumed that night in the park after
Robin's death. I'm relieved when the actors playing Titania and Oberon
appear and enact their quarrel. "The parts will be spoken in the final
performance," Bruno, who's returned to my side, whispers in my ear,
"but the director wanted this wordless prologue to precede the play."

"It's beautiful," I say as Titania and her retinue leave the stage, their
lights slowly dying as they fade into the *teatrino*'s green stage wings.
Oberon's dark fairies remain, but curl into tight balls around their
lanterns, extinguishing the lights one by one. Only Oberon and Puck
remain at the center of the stage, lit by a single lantern. Oberon per-
forms a slow stately dance around Puck, telling him, I remember from
the play, of how he saw Cupid shoot an arrow at the young virgin queen
and miss, the bolt falling on a "western flower," turning it from milk
white to "purple with love's wound." Oberon points toward the *limonaia* to send Puck on his quest for this love potion—the touch of which
will make any man or woman love the next creature that he or she
sees—and Orlando springs to life, runs uphill, and then grabs a rope
held by another fairy, and suddenly he is airborne, swinging over our
heads into the *limonaia.* The crowd gasps at the stunning leap, but I am
painfully reminded of the moment when Orlando rushed from the balcony after Robin's death. I don't have time to ruminate on the memory,
though. I hear a rustling sound above my head. Again I think of the
manuscript pages that had once been strung to dry in the *limonaia,* and
when I look up I see they're raining down on us. Only it's not paper, but
a shower of purple and white petals, Shakespeare's love-in-idleness, settling over hair and eyelashes and shoulders. Everybody is clapping and
laughing in the downpour, the fairies taking their bows in a final explo-
sion of purple fireworks and then scampering offstage while the Capulet actors resume their dancing and the waiters light the table candles
and serve Vin Santo and almond cookies. Bruno plucks a petal from my
hair and touches it first to his eyelid and then to mine, and I can feel the
echo of that velvet touch in every atom of my flesh.

I open my mouth to speak, but the voice I hear isn't my own.

"Rose, I told you to be careful," a voice admonishes me. "And now look!"

I turn around and see Mara standing at our table, her arms open wide. "It's gone! Your Hermès scarf ring is gone."

I sigh and leave Bruno to make my way back to my seat, scanning the petal-strewn table, and then, pulling out my chair, I spy the glint of silver. "It's just been moved to my chair, Mara . . ." I begin, and then stop, because I've noticed that what I thought was my napkin rolled into the ring is actually a piece of paper—the same type of yellowed parchment I found in Robin's package back home.

CHAPTER
FOURTEEN

ARA PEERS OVER THE TABLE TO SEE FOR HERSELF THAT MY HERMÈS SCARF
ring is safe, but before she can see it I slip the rolled parchment out of the ring and into the fold between my shawl and
dress. Then I hold up the silver ring for her to see. "It's definitely mine," I say. "Here are my initials."

"Well, you're lucky," she says, frowning at the espresso cups being
laid out on the table. "You really should put it away someplace safe."

"You're right," I tell her. "In fact, I'm going to take it up to my
room right now." I turn to say good night to Bruno, but he's vanished
into the crowd. Mark hasn't returned and Daisy Wallace has also left. I
suppress a niggling suspicion that she's gone off to find Mark. Really, it
must be the atmosphere at La Civetta that breeds jealous thoughts—or
these magic petals strewn across the tabletops and floor.

I leave Mara looking for Gene, and Leo Balthasar trying to negotiate decaf American-style coffee from the waiters. As I walk through the *pomerino* toward the villa I see that all the interior lights have been turned off, no doubt so that they wouldn't interfere with the light show in the garden. The library—also known as the Sala dei Ucelli because of the frescoes of birds that adorn the ceiling—is lit only by the moonlight coming in from the windows. I can just make out the profusion of painted songbirds fluttering through the branches of a painted grove and, at the top of the domed ceiling, a great horned owl, its wings spread and talons extended, about to descend on its unsuspecting prey. I consider switching on a lamp and reading my mysterious missive here, but the room has always made me uneasy. As I cross the tiled floor I can hear the parchment crinkling under my shawl, and the sound, like mice running through dry brush, makes me feel like the owl's prey. Better to wait for the privacy of my own room.

When I enter the rotunda, though, I see that it's empty, and although it's also unlit, the moonlight pouring through the oculus is so bright, I can see clearly. I find I can't bear to wait any longer. At the foot of the steps I take the parchment out and unroll it. The sonnet is written in the same antiquated hand that penned the poem I read in New York. The drawing that forms the border is in the same faded ink, only now instead of lemon trees the poem is framed by roses shedding their petals. I read as I walk up the steps, the sound of my footsteps keeping time with the meter of the poem.

> I long for thee more than the wind can know,
> More desperately than roses for the sun;
> I crave the grace thy kisses can bestow
> Upon my fallen self's scarred flesh and bone.
> My violation was no fault of mine;
> My lowborn fate turned woeful in this bed
> In contradiction of divine design;
> My blood announced my anguish as I fled.
> But on these very stairs once streaked with shame,
> Thy trail of petals starts, leading up to

Our destiny to merge; pink wisps proclaim
Perfection greater than what Adam knew.
For blood is fleeting but love's perfect rose
Blooms from eternity, as sunlight knows.

I pause at the top of the stairs and read the poem over again. The opening line echoes the closing couplet that's on the rim of the fountain, as
do the rose wisps in the eleventh line, suggesting that the poem is either
by Ginevra or by someone imitating her. Here, though, the bed strewn
with roses has become the site of violation the rose petals have been
transformed into the blood of defiled virginity, and then that blood is
turned into a marble trail to lead her lover to her bed.

I look down at my feet. At the top of the stairs the pattern of rose
petals ends at the border of narrow carpet that lines the hallway. I hook
my foot under the edge of the carpet and kick back a corner. Yes, the
pattern continues under the rug. I look down the hall toward my
bedroom—the nuptial suite with its frescoes of garden and grove and
its *cassone* painted with traditional wedding scenes to celebrate a marriage. If the poem in my hand really was written by Ginevra de Laura in
the sixteenth century, then perhaps the pattern of roses embedded in
the bedroom floor, in the hall, and down the steps of the grand staircase
was commissioned by her to commemorate her own deflowering in this
house and to turn the shame of that blood into a path her lover can follow up to the bedroom to find her.

It's far more likely, though, that such a fanciful idea came from
Robin Weiss's fevered imagination and that he has concocted these
poems out of the myth and gossip that surround La Civetta. The floor,
the wall paintings, and the *cassone* were probably all there before
Ginevra de Laura was even born. Certainly the *cassone* must predate
her, since *cassoni* went out of fashion by the early sixteenth century and
the wall paintings look like they're from the same period. As for the
floor . . . well, I suppose it's possible that the floor is later, because *pietre
dure* became popular in the late sixteenth century. But I shouldn't have
to depend on stylistic clues alone. The villa's archives include the ac-

count books and inventories of the Barbagianni family going back to the fifteenth century, when the villa was built. I should be able to find out when the bridal suite was painted, which bride brought the painted *cassone* into the house as her dowry, and when the tiled floors were laid. Even if they were created during Ginevra's time, it seems unlikely that she, a mistress, not a wife, would have had anything to do with their commission.

Whoever has written these poems has finally made a mistake by including a detail that can be verified or disproved through a little historical research. I decide to go back to my room and turn in for the night so that my head will be clear in the morning. As I turn down the hallway, though, I'm startled to see Daisy Wallace coming out of my room. I imagine she must be startled to see me as well, but if she is, she recovers quickly. She squares her shoulders and approaches me, head up, very much as if I were the intruder and she were the lady of the manor. Her attitude makes me wonder whether she had been totally honest when she claimed her family had no interest in La Civetta. It also makes me feel sufficiently wary of her that I tuck the sonnet back into my shawl before she can see it.

"Was there something in my room that interested you?" I ask when she's reached me.

"Your room? Oh, I didn't realize it had been assigned to you. My apologies. I wanted to see it because it was Lucy's room. Perhaps you've forgotten that she was my great-aunt?"

"No, I haven't forgotten. I also remember you saying that no one in your family wanted anything to do with this villa. I'm surprised you're so interested in Lucy's old room."

Daisy looks pale, but then I realize that the moonlight has bleached her face, her blond hair, and her white dress so that she looks like an apparition. "I've been reading Lucy's letters," she says, "and she mentions several times that she believed the room was haunted. She said that at night she could see the figures on the walls moving and that she heard sounds coming from the *cassone* at the foot of the bed. She believed that a young bride who was brought to this house was murdered on her wedding night because her husband discovered she wasn't a virgin and that he stuffed her body into the *cassone* and returned it to the family."

"Then what's the *cassone* still doing here?" I ask.

Daisy opens her mouth but says nothing.

"And as for the moving figures on the wall," I continue, "I think you have to remember Lucy's drinking problem."

"It's not that I think the room is actually haunted," Daisy says, recovering her composure. "Obviously, Lucy was imposing her own feeling of imprisonment at being forced to marry against her wishes and made to move to a foreign country."

"I didn't realize she was forced to marry Sir Lionel."

"Yes, the marriage was arranged by her mother, who liked the idea of having a titled son-in-law. And Sir Lionel liked the idea of her money."

"It sounds," I say, "like the plot of a Henry James novel."

"But these were real people. That's what you academics never get. Lucy had dreams of her own. She attended the Pennsylvania Academy of the Fine Arts in Philadelphia and came to Europe to study art. Instead she ended up embalmed in this museum." Daisy sweeps her arm in an arc to indicate the rotunda. I had thought, earlier in the evening, that her pale, loose dress made her look like Rossetti's Mary, but now she looks like one of Burne-Jones's hungry sylphs reaching up though the water to drag an unsuspecting sailor down into the watery depths.

"So, what did you make of the room?" I ask. "It seems like an awfully pleasant prison to me."

"Have you looked closely at the paintings on the walls and on the *cassone*?" she asks.

"No," I answer, "I haven't had the time."

Daisy smiles. "When you do, I think you'll see what I'm talking about. They're downright creepy. I can't imagine what kind of sick mind would put a young bride in there. It almost makes me believe my father's story about the steps . . ." Daisy looks down toward the marble steps I've just come up and I see her eyes widen. As I turn I almost expect to see someone coming up them—some apparition conjured out of

Lucy Graham's alcoholic delirium—but instead I see that the steps are stained with crimson drops. I'm trying to reconcile these pools of red with the faded pattern I saw before, but then a current of air—stirred by the opening of a door in one of the rooms leading into the rotunda— spirals up the steps and the pools of red quiver like raindrops falling into a pool. Only when one strays over my foot and I feel its velvety caress—so like the petal Bruno stroked over my eyelid earlier tonight— do I realize what they are. I kneel and pick one up and hold it out for Daisy to see.

"Look, they're just rose petals," I say.

"But where did they come from?" she asks, her eyes still wide. "They weren't on the steps when I came upstairs a few minutes ago."

I touch the back of my head and feel a bare thorn embedded in my hair. "It's from the rose I was wearing in my hair," I tell Daisy. "Its petals fell while I was climbing the stairs."

Daisy nods, accepting my explanation, but as she says a hurried good night and heads down the hall in the opposite direction from my room, I have the feeling that the fact that the ghostly phenomenon has come from me is no relief to her. Looking down at the petal-strewn steps, I have to admit, it doesn't make me feel any easier either. Nor, as I make my way down the darkened hall, do I find that I'm able to dismiss from my mind Daisy's hysterical description of the paintings in my room. I could, of course, choose not to examine them now, but her account has piqued my interest, and when I open my door I have, for just a second, the unsettling impression that the figures on the walls are waiting for me. I turn around in a slow circle, scanning the scenes, looking for where the narrative begins. I find it, I think, in the large painting on the right side of the bed, where a courtly young man, expensively dressed in gilded tunic, embroidered tights, and a hat adorned with peacock feathers, takes his leave of a beautiful young damsel in a walled rose garden. The youth passes through an arched doorway and then reappears in another painting on the east wall wandering through a dark and mysterious forest. The sequence appears to proceed clockwise from the perspective of the bed.

I look around for a chair to stand on so I can examine the pictures more closely, but all the furniture in this room is too fragile and expensive looking, so I go into my old room—the convent room—and drag back its serviceable desk chair and place it under the painting of the forest. Even when the painting is at eye level it's still hard to make out the details, so I climb down from the chair and get my flashlight (*Always pack a flashlight,* my mother's voice had reminded me while I was packing back in New York; *you never know when your hotel might catch fire*) out of my suitcase and, back on the chair, shine the heavy metal Maglite into the branches of the painted grove.

Immediately a hundred amber eyes stare back at me from behind the tangled branches. The trees are full of sharp-taloned owls hunting for prey. Beneath them the youth looks vulnerable and lost. When I shine my flashlight on him the light catches the glint of fear in his eyes and the gleam of tears on his dewy cheek. An innocent—and yet there's something in his stance and his richly adorned clothes, his cloak tossed jauntily over his milk white shoulder, the sparkle of jewels on his fingers, those gaudy peacock feathers in his hat, that makes him appear arrogant and callous. Looking back at the previous scene I can't tell whether he's been rejected by his lover or he's rejected her, but it's clear that having been exiled from the garden of love, he's chosen to reject all bonds of civilization for the lawless wilderness. How lawless becomes apparent in the next scene, in which the youth watches from behind a tree as an armored knight appears on horseback chasing a naked woman.

Of course, I realize, it's the story of Nastagio degli Onesti from Boccaccio's *Decameron,* a common enough theme for Renaissance wedding *cassoni* and nuptial suites despite—or maybe because of—its grisly content. Dragging my chair to the fourth painting, which is between the garden windows and directly across from the bed, I should be prepared for the gruesome scene. No wonder Lucy Graham partially concealed it behind the curtains.

The story, as I remember it, tells of a young nobleman, Nastagio degli Onesti, who, rejected by his beloved, runs off to lead a wild and irresponsible life in the woods outside Ravenna. While wandering there alone, he sees a knight on horseback pursuing a naked woman. Then, to his horror, he watches what happens when the knight catches her.

I push back the curtains and shine my flashlight on the scene. The knight, having leapt from his steed onto the back of the screaming naked girl, lifts his sword and slits her in two from the nape of her neck to the small of her back. The hunting dogs snap and growl over her scattered entrails. Horrified, Nastagio watches from behind a tree, while the yellow-eyed owls descend from their perches to snatch their share of the offal.

Oh, yeah, this must have been a pretty sight for the blushing bride to contemplate from her nuptial bed while waiting for her new husband to ascend from his drunken revelries downstairs to the bridal suite.

I've read that the story is not directed solely at a female audience or meant to cow young women into obedience. It's the future bridegroom, Nastagio, who learns how the knight, rejected by his lover, killed himself, causing, in turn, his beloved to kill herself and condemning the both of them to reenact this grisly cycle of butchery and resurrection each day just at nightfall. Learning this, Nastagio invites his family and the family of his beloved to a banquet at which the horrified dinner guests witness the gory scene—reenacted here on the west wall of the chamber. When Nastagio explains the knight's story, his beloved agrees to bed with him immediately, but Nastagio, a changed man, says he wants an honorable marriage.

I get down from my chair and approach the final scene, on the left side of the bed, which is covered by a tapestry. The tapestry itself depicts a familiar trope of courtly love: a young man in richly embroidered doublet and hose offering a rose to a blushing maiden. She reaches for the rose shyly, her gracefully long fingers resting on the air like a dove perched on a branch. I expect that the painting under it will be the traditional last scene in the series—the marriage of Nastagio degli Onesti. It should be another garden scene, ordered and calm. Instead, when I hold back the tapestry and shine my flashlight on the wall, I surprise two naked figures in a lewd and compromising posture. Nastagio degli

Onesti, his pose cruelly echoing the pose of the knight disemboweling his beloved, mounts his fiancée from behind as the horrified banquet guests look on. In this version of the story, Nastagio takes his fiancée at her word and avails himself of her offer of a night of unmarried lust. He has learned not obedience from the knight's tale but bloodlust. Moving closer to the picture I see that the guests have the same yellow eyes as the owls in the forest scene and that only some of them are horrified. Others are laughing and pointing at the ground beneath the copulating couple, where the hunting dogs have come to lap at the blood that pools beneath the violated virgin. Bile rises to my throat. It's by far one of the nastiest pieces of pornography I've ever seen. I drop the tapestry over it, struck by the contrast between the sweet scene on the tapestry and the ugliness it hides. Instead of masking the scene beneath, though, I feel now as if the corruption from the painting is seeping up, polluting the innocence of the two young lovers. The proffered rose now seems obscenely red, its stem fleshy and thick, its thorns threatening to the maiden's white hand that reaches for it. I'm forced to agree with Daisy Wallace's verdict that whoever installed a new bride in this room—in the fifteenth century or the twentieth—was a sadist.

I no longer feel so comfortable in the room. I double-check the locks on the door leading to the hall and the one into the convent room. I leave the windows open for air but close and lock the slatted wooden shutters. Even then I feel on edge as I sit down at the dressing table. I take the rolled-up parchment out of my shawl first and flatten it so I can put it in a file folder in my book bag, but as I'm smoothing it out I realize that there's a thin sheet of tissue paper clinging to the back of it. When I peel it away from the parchment, I realize it's the same kind of airmail stationery as the note Robin included with the last poem. And it's in Robin's handwriting. A note from the dead, then.

"This house is stained with the blood of innocence," it reads, "that will never bloom again."

I read the single line over several times. Whatever Robin meant by the comment, someone else has chosen to send it to me, but is it a threat or a warning? It's an infuriatingly oblique line of prose and I suddenly wish I had Chihiro here to analyze it. I'm too tired now, though, to puz-zle through its meaning. It will have to wait until the morning.

I crawl into bed, placing the heavy Maglite on my night table, and try to put the images from the paintings from my mind, but they follow me into my sleep. In my dream I wander through a dark wood. Al-though I can't see anyone, I know I'm not alone. I hear the rustle of mice through the dry underbrush and glimpse yellow eyes in the branches. Then the yellow lights swell and become the dancers from the *Midsummer Night's Dream* pageant—only instead of fairies they've be-come sinuous demons twining themselves through the tree branches—and the rustle becomes the thunder of horse hooves bearing down on me. I start to run in the sickening slow motion of nightmares, but I can already feel the hot breath of the horse on my neck and I know that it's only a matter of seconds before I feel the steel of the knight's blade cleave my back in two.

As I feel myself falling under the horse's hooves, I startle awake, flinching away from the weight of a hand at the back of my neck. Before I can untangle the skeins of the dream from reality, I've reared up against the headboard and grabbed the heavy metal Maglite from my night table to strike at the intruder.

"Rose, it's me, Mark," I hear before I can bring my arm down. "I didn't mean to scare you."

"Mark? Jesus, how did you get in?"

"I finagled an extra copy of the key from Claudia Brunelli. I thought . . . well, I thought you might be expecting me." Even though he's whispering, his voice has regained the formality he uses in faculty meetings. He's clearly hurt that I hadn't been expecting this surprise midnight visit.

"I thought you might . . . Claudia said you were on this floor . . ." I stammer, feeling like I've been caught out in an indiscretion. "I must have been in a very deep sleep," I explain, "and then I was confused when I woke up. Being in a strange place and all."

My eyes have adjusted to the darkness enough to see his shoulders relax. He moves toward me and takes the flashlight out of my hand and lays it down on the night table. "Jesus, that thing's heavy. I'm lucky you didn't hit me with it. Look how tense your shoulders are." He starts to massage my shoulders and I try not to flinch at the feel of his hands on the back of my neck. I still can't quite banish the images from my dream. Even when we make love I can feel the yellow eyes of the owls watching us, and when Mark tries to turn me over—into the position I know he favors—I let him know that's not something I want to do tonight. I can't quite make myself turn my back to him.

CHAPTER
FIFTEEN

ARK IS GONE BY THE TIME I WAKE UP THE NEXT MORNING. FOR A FEW
moments, lying in the strips of pale gray light from the slatted
shutters, I wonder whether his visit wasn't a dream—an ex-
tension of my night journey through the woods—but then I
notice a Post-it note anchored beneath the flashlight on the
night table.

"I'll tell the kitchen to leave a breakfast tray outside your door so
you don't have to come down to breakfast. I know how anxious you are
to get to work on the archives."

He's signed the note "Mark." No "love," in case anyone should see
it. Although we've agreed that such discretion is as much for my benefit as his, I can't help feeling disappointed at his caution. Maybe it's the
love poem I read last night that's made me want to hear my lover de-
clare boldly, as my supposed sixteenth-century poet did, "I long for
thee more than the wind can know, / More desperately than roses for

the sun." I repeat the lines to myself as I open the shutters and step out onto the balcony, closing my eyes and turning my face up to feel the morning sun on my skin and breathing in the scent of lemons and roses on the air. Opening my eyes, I watch the sun crest the ancient hill town of Fiesole, setting the red-slate roofs on fire, and then wash down into the shallow bowl that holds Florence, the light turning the city into a sparkling mirage of tower and dome, the arched bridges that span the Arno springing into life as gracefully as deer leaping a stream. "The air trembling with clarity," as the poet Guido Calvacanti put it.

Most people looking at this city think of the masterpieces of art contained within its churches and museums. Michelangelo's *David,* Botticelli's *Birth of Venus,* Brunelleschi's great dome. But even though I'm not immune to those attractions, I look at Florence and think of the poets of the late thirteenth century: Guido Calvacanti, Lapo Gianni, Gianni Alfani, and the young Dante. It was they who made the sonnet into a visionary and moment-centered love poem. It was here that Dante first set eyes on his Beatrice. It's the city more than any other where love poetry was born. No wonder I awoke this morning hungrier for love poems than for Post-it notes.

I go back into my room and open the door to find a tray waiting outside in the hall. It might not be a love poem, but the thermoses of steamed milk and coffee, the basket of fresh-baked *cornetti,* and the blue and yellow majolica bowl of fresh figs come pretty close. Besides, I remind myself as I drink my coffee and get dressed, the love poem I read last night spoke of blood and violation and it came with a warning—or a threat, depending on how you read Robin's cryptic note. The poem might be a fake as well. My plan for this morning is to look at the inventories to see when all the curious and morbid decorations— the paintings, the *cassone,* and the *pietre dure* floor—were installed. I suspect that the paintings and *cassone* will turn out to have been purchased years before Ginevra's lifetime, and if the floors were installed after her residence at the villa, then it will prove that the reference to rose petals on the floor is a modern one derived from the legends that have grown up around the curious decorations.

I'm curious, too, to see whether I can trace the references in the poem back to the inventories themselves. Whoever faked the poems might have done his research there, and he might have left some trace of himself in the archives. The most likely author of the poems is Robin—since the note attached to the poem is in Robin's handwriting even if the poem is not—but it's possible that Orlando wrote them, or even Bruno. He is the one with the most talent and the most access to the archives, which is what Gene was drunkenly implying last night—that Bruno could have stolen the poems to sell them on the black market or used them to get his son an in with a Hollywood producer. What if Robin, though, somehow found out and managed to get the poems away from Bruno? Would Bruno send Orlando to New York to get them back? The Bruno I knew would have too much integrity to do something like that, but then, I knew Bruno before he was a father. He looked so proud last night watching Orlando perform. What did I know of that kind of love or what it might drive one to?

I shake my head, trying to unwind the scenario I've woven. It's the secretive atmosphere of this place—a wasp's nest of gossip and suspicion. Certainly the last person whose suspicions I should be listening to is Gene Silverman.

I finish my coffee and try to put away my doubts. As I dress, though, I have an unwelcome thought. Gene was close enough to Robin and Orlando on the balcony to hear what they were saying. What if Gene's suspicions of Bruno came from something Robin said to Orlando? Or what if Orlando accused Robin of stealing his father's poems? I promise myself to keep my mind open while searching through the archives and then see what I can find out from Gene—or from Mara, who was also there on the balcony and is far more likely to tell me what she heard.

I finish getting dressed and then pack the thermos and some of the pastry and figs wrapped in a napkin into my book bag along with my laptop. It's only a few steps across the hall to the upstairs library. When I open the door I'm greeted by an aroma even stronger than the Italian coffee. Maple syrup, I think, sniffing the air, with a touch of nutmeg and . . . yes, Daisy was right . . . there's a hint of lemon from when the pages were dried in the *limonaia.* Even with the scent of lemon, though, the dim, dusty room I step into feels miles away from the sunlit gardens.

The three-storied library at La Civetta takes up the entire northeast corner of the building. In this, the third floor, the room is austerely plain, the walls whitewashed, as though in respect for the religious nature of the collection. The windows overlook the dusty olive trees in front of the villa and the funereal cypress trees that line the *viale.* It's here that Lucy Graham stored the books she saved (or looted, depending on your point of view) from the flooded Convent of Santa Catalina, stacked on metal shelves, in no particular order. Little has changed since I first saw them twenty years ago except that someone has dusted them recently. As I remove one of the volumes from a shelf, I have the dreadful feeling that they've been waiting here for me, an impossible task set for me, like the mountains of grain Psyche was supposed to sort into piles of wheat, barley, and millet.

I look at a long row of nuns' chronicles—mostly dry histories of the founding of the convent—and account books that record the number of sheep bought and born and sold and slaughtered each year, the amount of wool produced, and the money earned through the weaving of tapestries. I take down one chronicle, by a Suor Benedetta Fortino in the beginning of the seventeenth century. It describes the founding of the order of Santa Catalina in the hills above Florence in the fifteenth century and then the removal of the order in 1581 to the Valdarno, giving as a reason for the move the desire of the sisters to expand the wool production and tapestry works of the convent. I flip through the whole of the handwritten chronicle, skimming for mention of Ginevra de Laura or of any nun who wrote poetry, but it seems as if the nuns of Santa Catalina were too busy raising sheep, spinning wool, and weaving tapestries to do much writing.

I move on to a shelf of prayer books, taking down each one and flipping through to see whether all they contain are prayers. I know that sometimes more than one work may be bound into the same book, but if this were the case with Ginevra de Laura's poems, then why were the one that Robin gave me and the one I found last night on loose manuscript sheets? They hadn't been torn from a bound book. Still, I know I should go through each one of these missals carefully and I have just made up my mind to carry a stack of them to the library table set beneath the windows when I hear a knock on the door.

"Come in," I call.

The door opens and Zoe Demarchis appears, her pink hair jarringly bright in the plain whitewashed room. "Um, Professor Asher? President Abrams sent me up to see if you needed any help with the books. Like, if you needed me to move anything or . . . I don't know . . . help you sort through them."

"Don't you have a class?" I ask, torn between my relief at being offered help and compunction at subjecting poor little Zoe to such a tedious task.

"Just Early Christian Art," she answers, making a face, "and I took that last fall. I mean, like, how many crucifixions and bleeding saints can a girl take? Besides, I helped out last year dusting and reshelving the books, so President Abrams thought I'd be the right person to do it." She moves to a shelf and runs a finger along the spines of a row of account books. "They could use another good dusting. To tell you the truth, I'm allergic to dust . . ."

"You're right," I say, looking at the actually fairly dust-free books in my hand. "I'll tell you what. Why don't you go down to the kitchen and get a dust cloth and come back up here and give them all a good going over. I've got some things I want to check out in the lower floor of the library in the meantime."

"Yeah, okay," she says, "anything to get out of another lecture on Christian symbolism. I'll have them nice and clean for you. Do you want me to organize them in any particular order?"

"Well, you could pull out any folios with loose pages and leave them stacked on the table over there."

"Sure," she says, "that'll be easy. Robin and I put all that stuff on the bottom shelves last fall."

"Robin? Do you mean Robin Weiss? He worked with you reshelving these books last fall?"

"Uh-huh, but I know what you're thinking. He didn't find any of those old poems in here. I was with him the whole time and all we found were lists of sheep and stuff . . . It was pretty boring. Robin was always saying that the really interesting papers in the villa would be hidden and that we should explore the other rooms."

"And did you go exploring other rooms?" I ask.

"Uh-uh," she says, shaking her head adamantly. "Not me. I'm here on scholarship and I didn't want to get in trouble. But Robin . . . I think he did later . . . which is how he found those poems he was going to put in his screenplay. But he never told me where he found them . . . Well, I'd better go get those dust cloths . . ." Zoe shifts uneasily from foot to foot and appears to be blushing—although it may just be the reflection of her pink hair in this white room. She certainly seems anxious to be away from me, so I let her go, wondering what she and Robin got up to in here while sorting through these dusty dry tomes. Concocting Renaissance love poems, perhaps, or acting them out? I bend down and glance at the stacks of folios and boxes on the lowest shelves. I'll have a look at them later, I think, straightening up and kneading a crick in my lower back. I'll let Zoe pull them out and dust them off before going through them. First I'll have a look at the record books from La Civetta to find out when those awful paintings in my room were created and see whether there's any mention of when the rose-petal floors were made.

I cross the room to the spiral staircase that leads down to the two lower levels of the library. When I step onto the first cast-iron tread, the whole staircase trembles. The staircase was installed by Lucy Graham during the Second World War as an emergency route into a secret cellar in case the family needed to flee from the Nazis. Bruno once told me that Lucy had seen nothing ironic about ordering the staircase from Hamburg. When it arrived, the Italian laborers who had been hired to install it couldn't read the German instructions—or didn't bother, at any rate—instead assembling it according to some aesthetic principle only they understood. Perhaps they wanted it to vibrate like a plucked violin string.

I navigate the first flight as gingerly as I can, hoping not to draw the attention of anyone on the library's main floor. I can't hear voices as I descend, and when I peek out between the shelves that screen the staircase from the rest of the library, the room appears to be empty save for the painted birds that made me so uneasy last night. In the early morning they look harmless enough; even the painted owl on the ceiling looks half asleep, drowsing on his perch instead of keeping an eye out for prey.

I descend to the next, and lowest, level of the library—into darkness. Fortunately I thought to bring my Maglite—an item that is turning out to have more uses than even my overcautious mother would ever have imagined. I use it to find the chain to the bare bulb that hangs from the ceiling. I'm surprised that it actually works. Someone must have been down here recently, although, looking around at the cobwebs and dust-coated bookshelves, it's hard to imagine why.

The bottom floor of La Civetta's library is actually part of the villa's ancient cellar. The walls are bare stone, the floor dirt, the only window an unglazed porthole covered by a metal grate high on the wall. A dungeon, really, like something out of the Museo della Tortura in San Gimignano. Instead of the pleasant smell of old books in the upper stories, this room's predominant odor is mold and mouse droppings. I should talk to Mark about having these books moved to a drier location. Although they're only record books, they no doubt contain information that would be valuable to social historians. The French scholar Christiane Klapisch-Zuber, for instance, has used tax documents and family records to illuminate nuptial practices in fourteenth-century Florence, and Frieda Mainbocher has assembled data from hundreds of last wills and testaments in Siena to document the increase in female bequests to the church after the Black Death. And though it seems odd to come looking for marriage rites in this underground tomb, the Florentines were a practical people who orchestrated family unions with complex rituals of contracts and dowries, trousseaus and bride gifts. The people who invented double-entry bookkeeping kept as careful records of their familial alliances as of their banks and businesses.

Shining my flashlight on the metal shelves, I see that the books are covered in dust and mold, but one appears to be slightly less encrusted—the inventory for 1581, the year Lorenzo Barbagianni's father died and left him the villa and all its contents. If the paintings and the floor in my room were done before Lorenzo brought Ginevra de Laura to the villa, then they would be described in this inventory. I also take down a thick leather-bound ledger that lists the accounts—the *libri dei conti*—for the villa for the years 1581 to Lorenzo's death in 1593, and transfer the books to the table beneath the lightbulb. It, too, appears a bit less dusty than the other books, but I can't tell for sure whether that's because it's been consulted more recently.

It would be pleasanter to take them upstairs to the main floor, but I'm reluctant to meet anyone and have to explain what I'm looking for. I pour myself a cup of coffee from my thermos to ward off the chill and open the inventory.

After five minutes my respect for social historians such as Klapisch-Zuber and Frieda Mainbocher has trebled. Presented in seminars and conferences, neatly arrayed in charts and tables, their findings have always appeared to me so neat and rational compared to the more amorphous impressions of literary analysis. I've often envied the historical ethnologists their color-coded pie charts and PowerPoint presentations, but I no longer envy their working conditions. Whatever notary Lorenzo Barbagianni hired to take an inventory of the possessions he inherited from his father in 1581 was not hired for his handwriting. It's tiny and cramped and employs abbreviations I can't, at first, begin to guess at. I take a quick glance at the account book and nearly despair when I see that it's written in the same hand. It strikes me as unusual that the same notary who did the inventory kept the accounts (usually a *computista* would be hired for the latter chore), but then Renaissance bookkeeping is not my specialty.

I turn back to the inventory and find after a few minutes that at least it's organized by types of objects. There are lists of statues in the house and in the garden, rugs, mosaics, embroidered cloths, jewelry, paintings, furniture, and tapestries—including two described as hanging in the rotunda, "depicting scenes of courtly love," woven by the nuns of

Santa Catalina. One of these must be the one that still hangs in the rotunda that I hid behind yesterday. The other, I suspect, is the one that now hangs in my bedroom, the *camera nuziale.* I scan ahead to the list of frescoes and find a description of the birds painted on the walls of the library. In fact, the notary took pains to list each bird in the room by species and color, an account so thorough, it's as if he were afraid one of them would take flight and escape into the garden. There's a description of the garden fresco in the *sala grande* that itemizes each flower and tree in botanical detail and half a page devoted to a still life in the dining room that reads like a shopping list for last night's banquet and makes me hungry enough to dig into my bag for some figs. I wonder whether the notary was naturally this meticulous or Barbagianni demanded this thorough an accounting of his new possessions. Whichever, I can probably assume that nothing has been left out.

Which is why, when I get to the description of the frescoes in the *camera nuziale,* the first thing I notice is that only four paintings are listed. It is possible, though, that the two paintings on the north wall, which are separated by the bed, are counted as one. So I carefully read the description of each painting.

> *Four frescoes in the wedding suite to celebrate the marriage of Asdrubale di Tommaso degli Barbagianni to Caterina di Albertozzo degli Galletti in the month of May in the year of 1511, depicting the story of Nastagio degli Onesti. The first fresco depicts the rejection of Nastagio degli Onesti by his beloved in the garden of her father. Various flowers and fruit trees . . .*

I skip the botanical details and read ahead to the description of the second painting, of Nastagio wandering through the forest (no mention, I notice, is made of the birds in the trees—a surprising lapse for this thorough notary), and the third, of Nastagio watching a "noble knight" pursuing an unclothed maiden through the woods.

It is clear from the description of the third painting, the one in which the knight disembowels his former lover, that the notary must have described the painting while standing right in front of it. In fact, he seems to have taken a morbid interest in each gory detail as though the grisly subject matter had taken possession of him just as it had of Nastagio degli Onesti. He even adds an odd little editorial note to the inventory: "And so the young man learns of the perfidy of women and that he is not the first to be so thoughtlessly scorned by one of them."

A rather unorthodox reading of the tale, I think, and not what I imagine Lorenzo was paying his notary for. Perhaps the notary was admonished for embellishing his account, because the next painting, of the banquet scene on the west wall, is described in a perfunctory manner. Or maybe the notary just had little interest in the happy finale of the story. "And so," he writes laconically, "Nastagio declines the lady's offer of a night of unhallowed lust and agrees to marry the lover who first rejected him." Obviously he wasn't aware of the existence of a fifth painting that suggested a different ending for the story.

Was it possible that then, as now, the painting was concealed by a tapestry or other wall hanging? But I can't imagine this particular notary not lifting a piece of cloth to look beneath. And there's no mention in the inventory of tapestries of one that hung in the *camera nuziale*. Clearly the tapestry in the rotunda was later moved to cover the fifth fresco.

I can only conclude that the fifth painting must have been added later, although it strikes me as odd. Wedding *spalliere,* like *cassoni,* had gone out of fashion by the late sixteenth century. Why would Lorenzo Barbagianni add another to the *camera nuziale?* And why such a horrible one? I'll have to go through the account books to determine whether it was ever listed there. First, though, I turn back to the listing of furniture to see whether the *cassone* is listed and find a *forziere*— which, I remember, is the term that was used for wedding chests at the time—commissioned in 1511 to celebrate the marriage of Asdrubale and Caterina. The chest is described as *"depinto e adorni d'oro,"* painted and adorned with gold, but nothing else is said about the content of the paintings. There is, however, an odd little note added beneath the entry. "Although such objects have gone out of fashion today they should be preserved, if not for their artistic value, then for their power to teach valuable lessons and to contain the baser instincts of any new bride who may come to this house." I shiver reading the words. Was the painting of Nastagio degli Onesti raping his fiancée also supposed to teach a valuable lesson?

At least I know now that the wall paintings and *cassone* predate Ginevra's residence at La Civetta by a good seventy years. Now for the inlaid floors. The only category that comes close is mosaics, but when I look there I find only a description of a few mosaics in the garden. Nothing in the house at all. Still, it doesn't prove that the floors weren't commissioned during the years Ginevra lived at La Civetta. I'll have to go through the whole account book.

I open the account book and read on the first page, *"Rincontro di Cevole dal 1581 al 1593."* The next page is so covered in black ink that the words swim together into a dark blot and the column of numbers on the far right of the page sways like a cobra to a snake charmer's pipe. I lower my head and cover my eyes with my hands, pressing the palms into my lids. Sparks fly into the blackness, a sure sign of an impending migraine. I'll have to take a break soon, go upstairs for a couple of Advil, and lie down, or I won't be able to work for the rest of the day. With my eyes closed, I become aware of voices in the library above me. They could have been there for the last hour, but I'd been too intent on the inventory to notice. Or maybe it's that the low rumble of masculine voices is suddenly punctuated by a louder, high-pitched female voice.

"I thought we had a deal."

"You and I certainly did not have anything of the kind. *Your husband and I* had reached a tentative agreement."

"Is that right, Gene? Did we come all the way to Italy in the middle of the broiling heat of summer, spending money we can ill afford on your salary, on the basis of a *tentative agreement?*"

The reply is too low and garbled for me to make out, but now at least I've identified two of the library's occupants—Gene and Mara Silverman. And when the third party speaks again, I recognize his voice as Leo Balthasar's.

"Yes, I said I thought I could get you a fee for working on the script once Dr. Asher had a go at it, but I never said anything about getting you a producer credit. Frankly, I don't see that you've got the qualifications."

This time Gene raises his voice enough for me to hear it. "My screenplays have won numerous awards at film festivals nationally and internationally. I worked with Robin on the first draft of the script whether he chose to acknowledge it or not. I should be working on it now, not Rose Asher. She has absolutely no experience in screenwriting."

"But the period is her specialty and we need to have someone with historical clout to give the project credibility. And besides, Cyril insisted on her, and without Cyril there's no film."

"I don't understand that," Mara says. "I thought Cyril was in debt up to his eyebrows, so how does he come by the money to make a film—and where does he get the money to throw around Hermès scarf rings as party favors?"

"It's not Cyril's money per se, but the LLC, Lemon House Films, he put together with investors he drew in. The old boy is friends with half the nobility in Europe. Bored, rich playboys and dowager duchesses who love the idea of being part of a movie. They love to feel like they're part of the 'artistic process.' But the only reason they trust us with their money is Cyril's say-so."

"Is that because your last production company went bankrupt?"

"Mara!"

"I'm just saying. And when are the actors going to get here, anyway?" Mara asks.

I hear Balthasar sigh before answering Mara's question. "We've nearly finished attaching the talent, but we certainly don't want to have actors and crew sitting around on their salaries before we've got the script ironed out—and I want to have those poems you told me about when the investors show up. They've been told this isn't just another imitation of *Shakespeare in Love*. They've been promised Shakespeare's Dark Lady, and I want the proof in my hands when they get here. So if those poems you told me about don't really exist . . ."

"What else do you think Orlando Brunelli was going on about? He had them, I tell you, or his father had them and then Robin stole them and took them to New York."

"I was on the balcony as well as you," Leo begins, but then he lowers his voice to an angry hiss that I can't decipher. Both men converse in a low rumble for several minutes and then Mara's higher-pitched voice breaks in.

"But I don't understand why you're protecting him."

"We are protecting him, Mrs. Silverman, because we have a thirty-million-dollar film project hanging in the balance and if we come forward with what really happened on that balcony he will come forward and publicly reveal that the poems were stolen."

"But he killed that poor boy—"

"As I recall," Gene says, "you weren't overly fond of that *poor boy* five minutes before he died."

"What happened on that balcony was a terrible tragedy," Leo Balthasar says, "but I don't believe it was premeditated, and nothing we do will bring Robin Weiss back to life. But bringing his words to an audience—a worldwide audience—is the closest we can get to giving him life. I honestly think it's the best thing—the right thing—to do."

The library is silent and I imagine that Mara and Gene aren't quite sure how to respond to such lofty sentiments. Then Gene says, "So the three of us agree to stay silent, but there's another witness—"

"He won't be a problem. He has his own reasons for staying quiet."

There's another brief silence, and then Gene says, "I think my wife and I need a little better incentive for keeping quiet."

"Very well," Leo replies, "how about a producer's credit and one percent of revenues?"

Yet another silence ensues during which I imagine Mara and Gene are tallying up their take and whether they could get more. I find myself staring down at the columns in front of me, aghast at how the three people upstairs have arrived at a dollar valuation of Robin Weiss's life. Who else could they be protecting but Orlando Brunelli, who must have known that Robin stole Ginevra de Laura's poems from the villa and killed him in his attempt to get them back? Balthasar said that it wasn't premeditated and I imagine that's true—that he pushed Robin in a moment of passion—but that didn't mean he should go unpunished. The world shouldn't go on thinking Robin took his own life. Saul Weiss shouldn't go on thinking his son had killed himself. What seems even more cold-blooded than the crime itself is the calculated cover-up being perpetrated by the three people upstairs, who, I gather from what I now hear, have just made a deal.

"All right," Gene says, "but I want to be an executive producer."

"Shouldn't we get this in writing?" Mara says.

"If it would make you more comfortable—" Balthasar begins.

"No, no, a handshake's good enough for me," Gene says, his voice suddenly jovial. "After all, we're all friends here, right? After what we've been through, we're all in this together."

Gene's voice is so thick with innuendo that I don't have to be upstairs to picture the wink that no doubt accompanies the handshake. Then I hear footsteps and a door closing. At least now I can go upstairs unobserved. Barbagianni's account books can wait. I feel sick to my stomach. Although I don't completely understand the conversation I've just overheard, I gather than Gene must have seen Orlando push Robin from the balcony—that must be what Mara was referring to when she asked why they were protecting a murderer. Why Gene stayed quiet about what he saw at first, I'm not sure. Perhaps Mark asked him to . . . or he just followed Mark's lead in calling the death a suicide. Balthasar, too, must have realized that Orlando pushed Robin, but he agreed to stay quiet . . . why? Because he thought his film project would be jeopardized if a scandal was attached to it? Whatever their original motives for remaining quiet, though, clearly Leo and Gene and Mara have agreed that it's in the best interest of the film project not to tell the truth about what happened on the balcony and that Mark—who must be the other witness Gene referred to—could be counted on to remain quiet because of "his own reasons." What exactly those are, I'm not sure; all I know now is that I've had enough of accounting for the day.

Before I close the book, though, my eye strays to a phrase midway down the page. "Forty florin paid for me to the *commettitore* Pietro for a table inlaid with precious stones."

Although it's not a floor, it sounds as if this was a work made in *pietre dure.* I remember that in the 1570s Francesco I de' Medici was importing *pietre dure* craftsmen to Florence and housing them in his new residence, the Casino di Marco. When he succeeded his uncle in 1587, Ferdinand I would move the workshop to the Galleria dei Lavori in the Uffizi and continue his uncle's vision of decorating the Medici chapel in San Lorenzo in precious stones. *Pietre dure* workshops sprang up in major cities across the Continent, often overseen by Florentine craftsmen who trained in the Medici workshop. The workshop still existed today as the Opificio delle Pietre Dure, a museum and conservation center located just down the street from the Accademia and only a few blocks away from Francesco's *pietre dure* workshop in the Casino di San Marco. That a wealthy nobleman like Lorenzo Barbagianni, who had just inherited a villa as impressive as La Civetta, should want to decorate it in the new fashion is not surprising.

What surprises me here is the use of the personal pronoun. *"Per me."* The account book—and therefore the inventory—wasn't written by a notary or a *computista;* it was written by Lorenzo Barbagianni himself. So it was Barbagianni who performed the obsessively thorough inventory and Barbagianni who described the grisly episode in the Nastagio degli Onesti story as if the disemboweled woman had gotten only what she deserved, and it was Barbagianni who thought the *cassone* would be a proper vessel for containing the baser instincts of *his* future bride. Apparently I'm not the first person to make this discovery. When I look closer at the inventory, I notice faint indentations in the paper. I hold the book up to the light and I see that the looping scratches form words in English. Someone wrote something, leaning against the inventory book, not realizing that his—or her—pen pressed hard enough to leave an impression on the page beneath. The phrase—and the handwriting—is the same as in the note I found last night: "This house is stained with the blood of innocence."

CHAPTER
SIXTEEN

I TAKE THE MAIN STAIRS UP TO THE SECOND FLOOR BECAUSE I'M AFRAID THAT the humming of the spiral staircase might make me more nauseous than I am already, but I'd forgotten about the rose-petal pattern on the steps. I feel as if I'm following a trail of blood back to my room. Even when I get to the top of the stairs and the carpet covers the pattern in the hall, I imagine that I can feel the drops of blood beneath my feet. Robin must have felt it, too, as he began to uncover the story of Ginevra de Laura, a sense of what this house had witnessed. Somehow by following her story he must have figured out where her poems were hidden in the house. If I can only follow in his steps I might be able to find the poems. I need to remember, though, that his steps might have ultimately led to his death.

I open my door and my eyes fall right on the big *cassone* at the foot of the bed. This is where the blood trail ends, I think, walking over to the big chest. Or perhaps it's where it begins.

They've always given me the creeps. I know, of course, that the elaborate chests were designed to hold the bride's linens and clothes, that they were carried through the streets in a procession from the bride's house to the groom's, that as sumptuary laws sought to curb the display of public wealth the *cassoni* were conveniently employed to hide the richness of the bride's clothing while at the same time hinting, through their ornate and gilded exteriors, at the riches within. I've studied the iconography of the stories that appear in painting and carving on their sides and lids: stories from classical mythology and Italian folklore exhorting obedience to the bride and celebrating the social bonds of marriage. I fully appreciate their value as works of art and cultural icons, but they have always looked like nothing so much as giant coffins to me.

This one is no exception. From its huge gilded claws—great fleshy paws with obscenely long talons—to its heavy domed lid, it looks better suited to hold the bride's corpse than her wardrobe.

Nor have I ever been able to fathom the subject matter usually chosen for these monstrosities. The rape of the Sabine women, for instance, was a popular choice because it celebrated the reconciliatory power of marriage between enemies. Kneeling down to examine the painted panel on the front of this *cassone,* I find another popular Renaissance choice: Boccaccio's story of Griselda. Although it's not as gruesome as the story of Nastagio degli Onesti, I've always thought it was a particularly depressing story to use in celebrating a marriage.

A wealthy marquis named Gualtieri shuns marriage in favor of hawking and hunting. It strikes me how often the stories of this period start with a reluctant bridegroom. Even Shakespeare's sonnets start with poems beseeching a wealthy young man to do his duty and procreate. In Gualtieri's case, it's his vassals who urge their master to marry lest he die without an heir.

Like a petulant teenager forced to attend a family gathering and so making sure that everyone suffers in his company, Gualtieri makes a deliberately perverse choice of bride. He picks a poor peasant girl, beautiful but penniless, named Griselda. He invites all his friends and relatives, and all the nobility from the surrounding countryside, and brings them to the rustic hut where Griselda lives with her father. Then, in front of all the assembled company, he orders her stripped naked so that he may clothe her in new expensive clothing.

It's this moment that painters loved to depict: the naked Griselda in the midst of the richly attired company. Here it takes up the entire left-hand side of the *cassone*. Klapisch-Zuber has called the dressing of the bride a rite of passage, a rite of integration. The husband's gifts of jewels and dresses mark her as a part of his family. Therefore, it makes perfect sense to celebrate this moment on the very trunk that carried the bride's robes. Gazing at Griselda's lovely bare form against a backdrop of lush velvet and fur robes, I can't help but feel, though, that the painter meant us to feel a little frisson of prurient excitement at her nakedness. She stands like an Oriental slave at market, so much flesh for sale. How, I wonder, did the bride whose trousseau this chest carried look upon her? Did the image remind her that she would soon stand naked before a man who was probably little more than a stranger to her? The depiction of Griselda strikes me as half brutal and half tantalizing, but unlike the wall paintings of Nastagio's story, the scenes on the *cassone* seem to follow the conventional course of the story. On the front of the *cassone* Griselda undergoes the tests of obedience that Gualtieri designs for her. When she gives birth to a girl, he tells her his vassals are unhappy with such lowborn offspring and in order to satisfy them he must have the child put to death. Griselda submits to his judgment, just as she accepts, in the next two scenes, the same treatment of her son and her husband's decision to have their marriage annulled. When I move around to the right side of the *cassone,* I find Griselda naked again, this time going home to her father's hut, her head bowed in obedience to her husband's will.

I stand up to look at the lid and find the finale. On the far left Griselda is shown sweeping Gualtieri's sumptuous villa—which, I realize, looks an awful lot like La Civetta—while wearing rags. She's been ordered to act as servant in her own former home while her husband brings a new bride to take her place. The next scene shows the bridal procession—a young, childlike bride riding a white horse followed by servants, gaily attired in brightly colored tunics and tights, carrying her *cassone.* Bending down to look closely at the *cassone,* I find a sly hall of mirrors trick. It is painted with the story of Griselda—miniature versions of the same paintings on the real *cassone.* If Griselda herself, as she bows humbly before her "replacement," would only raise her downcast eyes, she could read her own happy future on it. But she doesn't. In this ultimate sign of obedience and trust she seems to deliberately look away from her own future—as if her fate were as much a part of her husband's possessions as the clothes that he provides and takes away as it pleases him.

Griselda is, of course, rewarded in the end for her long ordeal. The child bride turns out to be Griselda's own daughter restored to her (the little son, as well, follows in the procession). She is reinstated in her former place. In the last scene she is shown dressed in finery, seated at a banquet table at her husband's side. All she's lost is her children's childhood, but then, I remind myself, it was common for Florentines to send their infants out to wet nurses for extended periods of time. Missing your child's infancy might not seem such an unusual deprivation to the audience for which this *cassone* was intended. In fact, Griselda's acceptance of being parted from her babies might be another part of the lesson taught here.

I glance over the *cassone* again and notice that there are family crests on either side of the heavy brass lock—the Barbagianni crest with its owl perched on three balls and the Galletti rooster. Clearly this is the *cassone* made for the same marriage celebrated in the *spalliere* on the wall. The *cassone,* though, does not appear to have suffered any subsequent alterations. At least not on the outside. I remember, though, that the insides of the lids are usually painted—often with a nude reclining woman as a charm to guarantee the conception of beautiful children. Perhaps that is where Lorenzo Barbagianni has chosen to add another "valuable lesson to contain the baser instincts of a new bride." When I grasp the heavy rounded edge of the lid and try to lift it up, though, it doesn't budge. The chest is locked.

What, I wonder, could be in it that required the chest to be locked? Remembering that this was Lucy Graham's room, I realize that it might have been a convenient hiding place for liquor—in which case she would have kept a key somewhere. I'm just opening the top drawer of the dressing table when I hear a knock on the door. I'm tempted not to answer it, but then I hear Mara Silverman calling my name, and although Mara is the last person I feel like spending time with, I also realize, after hearing Gene and Mara's conversation with Leo Balthasar, that I shouldn't pass up an opportunity to try to find out what she knows about what happened on the balcony in New York. As I go to the door, though, I'm preparing to excuse myself from any errand Mara might have for me by pleading a headache. I realize, though, that my headache is gone. Sometime during my investigation of the *cassone* it vanished.

"I've got a cab waiting downstairs," Mara says when I open the door. "Do you want to get out of here and go shopping?"

I'd have wagered two weeks ago that my first trip into Florence proper would be to visit the Uffizi or the Accademia, not the Hermès store in the Piazza degli Antinori.

"I didn't pack any of my Hermès scarves, and I have to have one to wear with my new scarf ring," Mara tells me as she hops out of the taxi (leaving me to pay the fare because she hasn't converted any of her money into euros yet), "and it would be rude not to show Cyril how much I appreciate his gift."

As I follow her into the Hermès store I wonder whether Mara's sudden need to buy expensive French silk scarves really comes from a desire to flatter our host or has more to do with the deal she and Gene made with Balthasar in the library just an hour ago. Perhaps she's shopping in anticipation of that one percent of revenue Balthasar promised Gene and Mara in exchange for keeping the truth about Robin's death a secret. Whatever her true motive, there's no doubt that shopping seems to agree with Mara. As soon as she walks through the heavy glass doors, her shoulders relax and she approaches the saleswoman behind the glass cases of scarves with an ease in her step I haven't seen . . . well, since the last time I went shopping with her, at Bergdorf's in New York. It's as if the atmosphere of the luxury store—the thick carpeting, the polished wood cabinets, the slither of silk as the saleswomen unfold the richly colored scarves—acts as a narcotic on her. I'll have to wait until lunch to try to get any information out of Mara; she's totally absorbed in the shopping process.

"I need something to go with my yellow St. John's dress and my apricot Chanel suit," she tells the wide-eyed saleswoman in English. "And I want you to show me different ways to use the scarf ring," she adds, taking out the silver ring from her purse and laying it down on the counter. "Rose, did you bring yours? This will be fun. They'll show us tricks for how to wear the scarves."

I shake my head and greet the saleswoman, a young pretty girl who clearly hasn't understood half of what Mara has just said, translating into Italian as much as I think will be useful.

"Oh, but you speak English, don't you?" Mara demands, her shoulders already tensing. Before the saleswoman can answer, an older woman appears from the back of the store and, murmuring something into the younger girl's ear, quickly takes her place. "*Sì, signora,* I speak English. My name is Simona. Let me show you our newest design. I think it will suit your complexion perfectly."

Mara relaxes again as Simona flips through folded scarves and extracts one in shades of gold, russet, and umber. With a deft flick of her wrist, the silk billows into the air and settles over the glass counter like a swan landing on a still pond. The pattern is of swirling leaves against a rich yellow ground.

"That's pretty," I tell Mara, "and the colors suit you."

Simona folds the scarf diagonally and drapes it over Mara's shoulders, nimbly tying a loose knot and then twitching it sideways so that it lies perfectly over Mara's thin collarbones. "*Bellisima,*" she croons. "*Guardi!*" She points Mara to a full-length mirror on the paneled wall. Mara half turns, her fingers fluttering up to the silk at her throat and then, before she could possibly have really seen how the scarf looks, turns back to the saleswoman. "Good. I'll take it. What else do you have?"

Since there are perhaps a hundred heavy silk twill scarves beneath the glass counter, Simona might be expected to appear confused, but she removes another scarf—this one in deep burgundy with a pattern of racehorses and jockeys—without batting an eye. Before long the glass counter is littered with a dozen scarves in lush puddles of color. Simona has demonstrated how to wear a scarf as a headband, belt, necktie, choker, halter, or, for someone as slim as Mara, a sarong. Each time Mara selects one, the younger saleswoman folds the silk into a square and lays it in a nest of tissue paper in its own shallow orange and brown box.

When she's picked out six scarves, she turns to me as if suddenly recalling my presence. "Rose! Aren't you going to get one? You've got the scarf ring, and after all, you're making all this money working on the movie."

Simona and her assistant pause in their folding and draping, immaculately plucked eyebrows lifted with sudden interest in my direction. I see myself transformed in their eyes from drab academic to movie person! Yes, I suppose I could afford maybe one of these scarves. I finger the rolled, hand-sewn edge of one of Mara's discards and say, "Well, . . ."

Instantly the air is alive again with the flutter of silk, only now the colors are cooler—blues and greens, which, Simona insists, will bring out my eyes. One scarf is printed in a mosaic pattern of flowers and vines against jewel-like lozenges of emerald, sapphire, and peridot.

"This reminds me of the mosaics at Santa Constanza in Rome," I say.

There's an appreciative murmur from the saleswomen at my classical learning while the scarf is coiled around my neck and tied in a manner that I already know I will never be able to duplicate on my own. But what does it matter? How many articles of clothing flatter both my eyes and my brain?

Fifteen minutes later I leave the store with my own slim orange envelope secured with a brown ribbon, still trying to convert the euro charges that have just been entered on my MasterCard into dollars. Passing a *cambio,* I pause to read the day's exchange rate posted in glaring red LED lights. It's worse than I thought. I try to catch up to Mara to warn her, but she's already veering into another store on the Via Tornabuoni. "Oh, look," she says, when I catch up to her at the doorway, "I read about this store in *Lucky* magazine. They've got all the newest Italian designers and they serve espresso!"

I follow Mara into the spacious modern store, where the clothes seem to hover in midair like exhibitions in an aerospace museum. A slim man in impossibly narrow black jeans and black T-shirt appears with a tiny demitasse of espresso for each of us, both cups garnished with a lemon peel the size of a nail clipping.

"I think I'll sit this one out," I begin, edging toward the espresso bar at the back of the store.

"Oh, look, Rose," Mara croons, "this blouse is exactly the color of the scarf you just bought." Mara has managed to untie the ribbon of my Hermès bag before I can object and extract a corner of my new $350 scarf.

"Che meraviglia!" the man in black exclaims as if an angel had just descended from the track lighting. What a miracle!

"And look," Mara says, pulling out a softly gathered skirt with a pattern of gondolas floating on a green lagoon, "it would be perfect with this skirt. Isn't this the new Prada line? It was sold out before we left New York."

The salesman—Cesare—explains in a hushed whisper that this particular line is done by one of Prada's designers but for "much, much less." I steal a glance at the price tags as he plucks out a handful of skirts and blouses and slacks for me and notice that "much, much less" is about a week's worth of my salary. But then I *am* making the script consultant's fee, and, as Mara explains as we follow Cesare back to the dressing rooms, pieces like this are really an *investment.* And when I try on the well-tailored slacks in teal sateen and the sleeveless silk blouse in jade trimmed with the slightest whisper of pale green chiffon at the throat, I have to admit that they make my clothes back at the villa seem drab and shapeless. Everything seems to fit a little better, drape a bit nicer, and make my skin glow. The emerald green cocktail dress Cesare brings back to me falls over my hips like water, and the slingback sandals in butter-soft kid hug my instep like a masseuse's hand. Within an hour I've said yes to an entire new wardrobe. By the time Mara and I stumble back onto the Via Tornabuoni—exchanging kisses with Cesare like old friends—my head is spinning. Thankfully, all the shops are closing.

"What's going on?" Mara asks at the sight of drawn shutters and *Chiuso* signs.

"They're closing for the *riposo,*" I say. "For the afternoon rest. You know, the siesta."

She turns to me, an empty look in her eyes, her shoulders slumping under the weight of half a dozen shopping bags. She looks like a woman waking up the morning after a drinking binge and discovering there're no Bloody Marys waiting for her in the fridge. I'm afraid I probably have the same hungry look in my eyes.

"It's okay," I say soothingly, "I know a lovely trattoria near here—if it's still here. We'll have lunch."

Mara nods meekly and, managing a small smile, follows me down a narrow side street. Lunch is a close second to shopping. The restaurant I'm thinking of is a small, family-owned trattoria on a quiet side street with a secluded fifteenth-century courtyard garden in the back. Bruno introduced me to it, of course; it wasn't the kind of place you'd find in a guide book. He said that during the war it had been a meeting place for Delasem, the Italian Jewish refugee assistance organization that had hidden Jewish refugees in convents, churches, and homes throughout Italy. The restaurant had been owned by the same family since the middle of the last century, he'd told me. Surely having survived that long—and withstood fascist raids—it will still be here. It should be the perfect place in which to prod Mara in her limp post-shopping daze to talk about the night of the film show.

If only I can figure out where it is. I've turned us into the maze of side streets that run parallel to the river. I know it's not far from the Arno and that it's somewhere between the Ponte Vecchio and the Ponte Santa Trinità, but whenever I came here with Bruno I'd followed him, listening to the stories he told about every statue and fountain and cornerstone we passed.

"Are you sure you know where you're going?" Mara asks. "My feet are killing me. Maybe you should ask directions."

I nod, but the trouble is, I don't remember the name of the restaurant. I remember an old wooden sign painted with a knight on horseback hanging above an arched doorway and a wrought-iron gate dripping with brightly colored bougainvillea, beyond which was a low-ceilinged cavelike room with paintings on the whitewashed walls. But I can't remember the name on the sign.

"The name started with a *G*," I say. "Il Grotto, maybe?"

"Haven't we passed this building already?" Mara says, pulling on my arm. "We're going around in circles."

I look up and see we're standing in front of a five-storied palazzo faced in rough gray stone. "This is the Palazzo Davanzati," I say, as happy as if we'd just run into an old friend. "It has some beautiful wall paintings—"

"Does it have a restaurant? Can we get something to eat there?" Mara whines.

Unfortunately it looks like the Palazzo Davanzati is closed for restoration, which is too bad because I've remembered that the paintings in one of the bedrooms are similar to the ones in my room at the villa (minus that last horrific scene beneath the tapestry). The good news, though, is that I remember now that the restaurant I'm looking for is just around the corner. I turn down a narrow street—an alley, really—and there it is. The arched doorway, iron gate, the bougainvillea, all just as I remembered it, and three steps down is the cool white cavern with the strange writhing figures painted on the walls. I remember now that the name had something to do with Dante's *Inferno,* but there's no name on the sign. A maître d' in a gleaming white shirt greets us at the bottom of the stairs.

"Potremo mangiare al fresco, per favore?" I ask, the words Bruno always used when we dined here coming back to me as if they were the magic incantation that ensured entry.

"Ma certo, signora," the maître d' replies, bowing deeply and sweeping his arm toward the back of the restaurant. We follow him down a long, low corridor, past the wraiths of Dante's dead undulating on the walls beneath incongruously cheerful banners.

"This is kind of creepy," Mara says, clutching her shopping bags closer to her. "Who are these people supposed to be?"

"The sad spirits who lived without praise or blame," I tell her. "In Dante's *Inferno* they occupy a kind of vestibule before hell. And those"—I point to the ceiling, where dark-winged angels wheel above us—"are the coward angels who neither opposed God nor stood by him. The paintings were done during the war," I say, lowering my voice, "and were probably meant to condemn those who let the fascists take control without opposing them or trying to save the Jewish refugees."

"A little grim for a restaurant," Mara says. "Are we going to hell now?"

"Well, yes, but only the pleasanter part. The bar through there is limbo," I say indicating a room paneled in dark wood and lined with deep red banquets, "and cut here in the garden is the second circle for the lesser sins of lust and gluttony."

The maître d' opens an old wooden door at the end of the corridor and waves us into a tiny courtyard, enclosed on each side by espaliered pear trees and climbing roses. In the center is a fountain of two lovers entwined together in an eternal kiss.

"Paolo and Francesca," I tell Mara as the maître d' seats us at a small table underneath a grape arbor. Each one of the tables is in its own small bower to ensure privacy.

"Well, this is pretty," Mara admits, sinking into her chair and letting her shopping bags settle to the ground around her, the layers of tissue paper inside rustling like roosting pigeons

I order us a bottle of sparkling mineral water and a carafe of the house red. "There's no menu," I tell Mara "but I remember they made a wonderful pasta with cream and grated orange peel. Oh, but I forgot—

you don't eat dairy." Or drink, I remember as the waiter returns and pours us each a glass.

"Oh, well, when in Rome," Mara says, taking a sip of the wine. "Order whatever's best. I'm exhausted. Shopping always makes me tired."

I can see why. The energy that had propelled Mara through her purchases had a frantic quality to it—a compulsive quality—and now that it's abandoned her, she seems somehow deflated.

"But what good bargains we got," she says. "I know those scarves cost over three hundred dollars at home, and here they were only two-eighty."

The waiter has appeared so I don't answer right away. I order us both salads and the *pasta del giorno*. When he goes I take a sip of mineral water and say, "Well, actually, Mara, that was in euros. With the current exchange rate, that makes it well over three hundred dollars."

"Oh," she says, waving her hand again. "Oh, well. I suppose I'll have to listen to Gene rant and rave when he gets the Amex bill, but at least he can't make me return anything without sending me back to Florence." She smiles conspiratorially and clinks her glass of red wine against mine as if I were her comrade in deceiving her husband. I'm alarmed to see that she's finished the glass and I wonder whether it's a sign of guilt over concealing the truth about Robin's death. "And he really shouldn't complain. My parents bought us the house we live in, so it's not like we've got a big mortgage, and it's not my fault academics make so little. When we met he told me he was going to make movies. I thought it sounded so glamorous, but I should have listened to my mother and married a doctor or at least an orthodontist. Do you have any idea what Ned's braces cost us?"

Thankfully, our salads arrive and Mara takes a break to exclaim over the nearly translucent shavings of parmesan, the crisp white fennel, and the sweet figs. "What did you say this restaurant was called again? I want to tell my friends about it."

"I honestly can't remember. The name had something to do with Paolo and Francesca, though."

"Who?"

"Two lovers Dante met in the underworld. Francesca tells Dante how they fell in love while reading the tale of Lancelot and Guinevere, how when they got to the moment where Lancelot kisses Guinevere, Paolo kissed her. *'La bocca mi basciò tutto tremante.'* All trembling, he kissed my mouth. It's very sensual in the Italian . . ."

I pause because the waiter has brought our pasta—cream-drenched tagliatelle flecked with tiny orange specks and garnished with purple nasturtiums. A dish, I suddenly remember, called Pasta alla Francesca.

"I'm not sure I should eat all this dairy . . ." Mara says, but she's already twirling the gleaming noodles and bringing a forkful to her mouth. She closes her eyes at the first bite and moans. "Oh, my God, that is the most delicious thing I've ever eaten. So, tell me, why are Paula and Francesca in hell?"

"Well, Francesca was married to Paolo's brother, Gianciotto."

"Ah, so they were adulterers," Mara says, wiping a dab of cream from her chin.

"Yes, but in their defense, there's a story that Gianciotto sent Paolo to Ravenna to bring Francesca back to Rimini to marry him, and Francesca fell in love with Paolo thinking *he* was her husband-to-be."

"Still," Mara says, "once she knew . . ."

"Yes, well, they are in hell," I say, annoyed with the way Mara always turns everything into *her* story—the story of the aggrieved wife of a philanderer—but then I realize that I can perhaps use the story to serve my own purposes. "But the husband, Gianciotto, is in a lower circle for killing Paolo and Francesca. Dante organizes the circles of hell so that the worst sinners receive the worst punishment. The figures we saw coming in, for instance, were of people who saw evil but did nothing to stop it. Like the citizens who did nothing to stop the fascists from killing the Jews here in Italy."

"Oh, it's just too awful to think about," Mara says, wiping the cream from her lips. "You know, I read Anne Frank's diary four times in the year I was preparing for my bat mitzvah. It had such a big impact on me that I brought it up in my dvar Torah speech. I'd gotten the worst

Haftorah portion—that part of Leviticus with all the gross sacrifices? But then my Hebrew tutor pointed out that it was all about responsibility and I was able to relate it to Anne Frank and the rabbi said it was one of the best dvar Torahs he had ever heard. There wasn't a dry eye in Temple Beth-El."

"Yes, I can imagine that was a very powerful subject," I say, delighted that Mara has grasped the concept of bystander guilt so quickly. I think, from my own dim memories of Hebrew school, that the passage of Leviticus she's talking about (the one with all the "gross sacrifices") actually says something about a witness's obligation to report what he has seen. Now I just have to connect that lesson to her responsibility to report what she knows happened on the balcony in New York before she starts in with her bat mitzvah theme and color scheme.

"Accountability is something I've thought a lot about since Robin's death," I say. "You see, I was inside, so I didn't see what happened. But you were out on the balcony. Maybe you saw something then that didn't really register—"

"I didn't see anything," Mara says abruptly. "Gene pulled me away."

"But Gene saw what happened . . . Is he sure Robin jumped?"

Mara has been twirling the same forkful of pasta for the last thirty seconds, staring at the strands as if they had turned to snakes. "What difference does it make?" she asks, putting down her fork. "I mean, the boy's dead. What difference does it make if he killed himself or someone pushed him?"

"Well, for one thing, Saul Weiss, Robin's father, wouldn't have to go through the rest of his life thinking that his son killed himself. Imagine if it were Ned—"

"Ned would never hurt himself. I've made sure he's had all the best therapists, and when they wanted him to go on Prozac last year I said no because of the cases of teenagers on antidepressants killing themselves. We put him on Wellbutrin instead. It has a much lower incidence of suicidal thoughts and it helps you lose weight at the same time."

I realize I've touched a nerve more sensitive than I'd counted on and I feel a twinge of guilt using Mara's maternal protectiveness to make her come forward with what Gene told her. I also realize how much pain I'll be causing Bruno if Mara does accuse Orlando of pushing Robin off the balcony. For a moment I wonder whether it's worth it—trading one parent's grief for another's, but then I think that Bruno might well have sent Orlando to New York to get those poems. Why should I spare him? And as for Mara, she hasn't just concealed the truth surrounding Robin's death; she stands to profit from it. She's just gone shopping on it.

"So, think how you would feel," I say, "if after everything you did, you thought Ned had taken his own life. If it weren't true—if it had been Ned who was pushed off that balcony—wouldn't you want to know the truth?"

Mara nods her head meekly. She looks suddenly very young. I can picture her at thirteen delivering her dvar Torah to the congregation of Temple Beth-El. "I really didn't see anything," she says, sounding for all the world like a schoolgirl caught cheating, "but Gene . . ." She stops, reluctant, I imagine, to give too much away to me. A full confession is more than I need, though, as long as she convinces Gene to come forward with what he saw on the balcony. I put my hand on hers. "If Gene saw something that's different from what Mark told the police, he should say so."

Mara nods. "Well, I'll talk to him about it," she says weakly. "I suppose we ought to be getting back. Garçon!" She summons the waiter and wiggles her hand in the air to indicate that she wants the check. We lapse into silence waiting for it. Mara, I hope, is busy thinking of how she will tell Gene that they need to tell the police about Orlando, and I'm reluctant to push her any further.

"Oh, sweetie, could you put this on your card?" she says when the bill arrives. "I don't want Gene having a hemorrhage over our balance. You're so lucky that you don't have anyone looking over your bills."

Or paying them, I think, laying my MasterCard on the silver tray. Since I may have just sabotaged the Silvermans' lucrative film deal with Leo Balthasar, I figure the least I can do is pay for lunch. In order to stoop to such a deal, the Silvermans must be fairly desperate for the cash. Which isn't hard to fathom if Mara regularly shops like this on an academic's salary.

I sign the credit card slip and leave a generous tip in cash. When I'm folding my receipt I notice the name of the restaurant printed on the top: Il Galeotto. Of course. It's the Italian name for the Arthurian knight who encouraged the love affair between Lancelot and Guinevere. In *The Inferno* Francesca calls the very book she and Paolo read from a "Galeotto"—the go-between that prompted their unlawful love. Bruno told me that the restaurant took its name because it was a place where Jewish refugees could go to make contact with antifascists, and then, after the war, it became a place where lovers met. The owners didn't have to advertise the name, relying on tradition, word of mouth, and, most of all, discretion, to provide their clientele.

As we walk back down the hall of those souls who lived without praise or blame, I try to feel that having just maneuvered Mara into making her husband confess what he saw on the balcony, I've avoided at least one sort of purgatory.

CHAPTER
SEVENTEEN

HEN WE COME OUT OF IL GALEOTTO I LOSE MY SENSE OF DIRECTION ONCE again, and instead of heading toward one of the major streets where we stand a better chance of getting a cab, we find ourselves wandering through the streets just south of the Duomo. I realize how close we are to the Duomo when we turn onto the Via dello Studio, so named because it housed the workshop for the artisans who worked on the great church.

"I'm sorry. Mara, I don't see any cabs, but we can get a bus on the other side of the Duomo. It will take us right up to the villa gates."

To my surprise, Mara agrees. "At least I can tell Gene I took the bus," she says. "He's always complaining I take too many taxis in New York." Poor Mara. I feel like I'm sending her into the lion's den. If Mara really does confront Gene, he's unlikely to take the news that Mara wants to break off their deal with Balthasar better because she saved on cab fare.

"We just have to buy a ticket in a *tabaccheria,*" I tell her. "I think I saw one on the last block."

Mara nods but I see that her attention has drifted to a paper goods store—one of the few shops that haven't closed for the *riposo.* "I just want to get a few of those darling little paper boxes to bring home for gifts for the maid and Ned's tutors and all. Why don't you meet me back here?"

"Okay," I tell her, amazed that she still has the will to shop. Maybe, though, it's her way of calming herself in preparation for her showdown with Gene. I only hope she hasn't changed her mind about talking to Gene. I go back to the *tabaccheria* on the Borgo degli Albizi and buy a book of tickets. After what I've spent on clothes today, I should take the bus for the rest of the summer.

When I come out of the *tabaccheria* I notice the art store directly across the way. It's the same store where the art students at La Civetta bought their supplies back when I was a student. Figuring that Mara's probably not done with her shopping yet, I wander in, drawn by the shelves of powdered tints that line the back wall. It's as if all the colors in the Uffizi—the golden hair of Botticelli's Venus, the limpid blue mantles of Fra Lippo Lippi's translucent madonnas, the rich red velvet cloaks of Raphael's noblemen—had filtered through the air and settled into the glass jars. I remember being sorry when I came in here that I wasn't a painter.

But Bruno said I was lucky. The art students often went home overwhelmed by the centuries of genius crammed into this small city on the Arno. The stacks of drawing pads they bought here (embossed with the name of the art shop and a drawing of the Via dello Studio) would remain blank. Not that their time in Florence would be wasted, Bruno said when I protested that he was being too cynical; they would become teachers or curators or maybe just well-educated tourists bringing their own children to visit their favorite paintings at the Uffizi. Only a handful would absorb the lessons of the masters, take what they needed, discard the rest, and continue painting. Of course, it could happen to writers, too, Bruno told me. The literary critics even had a name for it: anxiety of influence.

I leave the art store, but instead of going back to the paper store, I turn back down the street to the little church of Santa Margherita and go inside. It's a plain medieval church, a single rectangular room with little of architectural interest, its only real claim to fame being that Beatrice Portinari, Dante's beloved, is buried here and that it was here that Dante first glimpsed her.

I sit down in the last pew in back in a dark corner, grateful for the cool gray stone, the dimness, and the silence. I remember coming here one day after Bruno had told me about the anxiety of influence and thinking, yes, I could feel it here where Dante first met Beatrice. I could *hear* it: the whispering of the poets from Ovid to Petrarch to Shakespeare uncoiling down the narrow streets along the rough-scored paving stones like a mist rising to envelope me. I imagined I could see the high-water marks, like the plaques commemorating Florence's floods, but instead of feeling overwhelmed I had thought that if Shakespeare could take what he wanted (the influence of the sonnet tradition, Ovid's stories, and Renaissance Italian sources), why couldn't I?

I wonder whether that's what Robin thought when he found Ginevra de Laura's poems—that he could appropriate the legacy of the past and so link his voice to the chorus that I heard in these streets when I was his age. Little did he know that taking the poems would lead to his death.

Although I'm not particularly religious, I bow my head and try to pray for Robin. I tell him that I'm sorry I didn't listen to him the night of the film show and that I'm sorry I wasn't able to rescue him as he asked me to. I promise that I'll do everything I can to find out the truth of what happened to him and make it known—publicly, but most of all, to his father. And then I whisper out loud, because it feels like these heavy walls are the best audience for the admission, "I'm sorry, Robin."

I'm startled to hear his name echo in the church. I look up and see that two people, a man and a woman, have entered the church and are wandering along the wall farthest from where I'm sitting, looking at a display of paintings that depict the meeting of Dante and Beatrice. It takes me only another second to realize that the woman is Claudia Brunelli and the man is Mark Abrams.

I immediately duck my head again, leaning my forehead against the back of the next pew, and shield my face behind clasped hands so that I can listen to their conversation unobserved.

"I don't know why we couldn't have met at the villa," Mark says. "Do you think Cyril's got it bugged?"

"Of course not," Claudia answers, "but La Civetta was built for spying. There are hidden niches covered by tapestries and stairs behind shelves and false cabinets leading to secret rooms. Cyril knows them all."

"And you wouldn't want Cyril to hear that you're willing to settle out of court?" Mark asks.

"I think it best we don't involve Cyril in this at all."

"That's probably wise. I imagine you wouldn't want your husband knowing either. He doesn't know anything about this, does he?"

"Don't worry about Bruno—he's been punishing himself for that fling he had with Rose Asher for twenty years now. He's really become quite boring. I could never have gotten him to see the wisdom of my plan. No, I sent Orlando to New York, so of course I feel partially responsible—that's why I thought we should talk. After all, the boy's dead. We can't bring him back. I see no reason why anyone else should be made to suffer, *capisce*?"

"I understand completely. I'm sure we can come to an agreement, but why not over a glass of wine? I find these gloomy old churches depressing."

I hear their footsteps pass down the aisle into the noise of the street. Still I keep my head pressed against the back of the wooden pew in front of me. There's a slight depression in the wood, worn smooth by generations of supplicants, that feels oddly comforting—like a hand pressed to my forehead. I'm reluctant to leave it, but then I remember Mara in the paper shop. She must think I've abandoned her.

I leave the church and head back toward the Duomo. When I get to the paper store I see with relief that Mara's just paying for her purchases. As I come into the shop, the salesgirl is handing two heavy shopping bags across the counter. "There you are," Mara says when she sees me. "I was just wondering how I was going to carry all this."

Since I already have two bags from our earlier shopping expedition, I'm not sure how we're going to manage, either. When we emerge onto the Via dello Studio I feel as if we're taking up half the narrow street with our large rustling bags fanning out around us like hoopskirts. I look nervously up and down the street for Mark and Claudia, afraid they'll see us. Why I should be afraid to be spotted by them, when they're the ones who seem to be bartering truth for money, I'm not sure, but I'm relieved when we get around the Duomo and see the bus waiting that we're getting out of the city without running into them. Mark is unlikely to take the bus since he got his pocket picked the last time he was in Italy. And besides, he and Claudia are in some cafe. I imagine that they're working out how much Claudia is willing to reduce her lawsuit in exchange for Mark's silence about what he saw on the balcony. With any luck he should be able to get her to drop the suit entirely to ensure her son's safety. This must be what Gene referred to as Mark's "own reasons" for not accusing Orlando of killing Robin.

The only La Civetta residents I see when we get on the bus are a couple of students sitting up front. I steer Mara toward the back to the last remaining seats just as the bus lurches into motion. While Mara lists for me her purchases—this oval box covered in blue and gold Florentine swirls for Esmerelda, the housekeeper, and this ledger bound in hand-marbled paper for Ned's math tutor—I replay again the dialogue I overheard in the church, searching for some other explanation than the one I have arrived at. Was Mark really cold-blooded enough to sell his collusion for getting La Civetta free and clear of a lawsuit? I knew that the lawsuit was a thorn in his side—and how much he wanted Hudson to acquire the villa—but I never would have dreamed that he'd stoop to making such a callous exchange.

A group of students gets on at the Piazza San Marco, clutching bags from the Accademia's gift shop. They crowd close to us, falling and giggling as the bus fills up. Instead of looking annoyed, Mara asks them what they bought in the shops, and soon they're pulling out T-shirts emblazoned with naked Davids and boxer shorts silkscreened with selective parts of David's anatomy. Mara shrieks at the boxer shorts and makes me promise I'll take her to the Accademia so she can buy a pair for Gene. It occurs to me that for all Mara's complaining about Gene, she manages to work him into the conversation as often as possible, like a teenager writing the name of her most recent crush over and over again on her notebook covers. It makes me wonder whether she'll really ask Gene to reveal what they saw on the balcony. Why should they? Gene and Mara will get rich on Robin's film; Mark will get his villa without legal entanglements. Everybody is cleaning up on Robin's death. Including me. I've been paid a very nice fee to work on his script and look for those lost poems.

I suddenly feel as if I might be sick.

"I just remembered something I have to do," I tell Mara, getting up. "Some research at a museum near here. I'm sure these nice girls will help you with your bags."

The nice girls eagerly agree to help Mara with her bags and even offer to take mine back to the villa as well. The bus has started up, but I pull the stop cord and it comes to a screeching halt. Before Mara can object, I've squeezed my way out into the Piazza San Marco, where I lean against one of the columns in the square until the nausea passes. All around me tourists stream past, heading toward the Accademia to see Michelangelo's David. I think longingly of the quiet of Santa Margherita, but it seems far away now. I remember, though, that just down the street from the Accademia is the Opificio delle Pietre Dure, a less popular tourist destination, and, I think, peeling myself away from the support of the column, I can do some actual research there. I can find out whether there are any *pietre dure* floors like the one at La Civetta. Perhaps there's even a record of who laid the floors and when, since the museum is also a center for restoration.

I know even as I locate the museum and buy an admission ticket that I'm trying to take my mind off what I've just learned, but still I'm absurdly grateful for the coolness of the museum, the effect, I think, of all the marble and precious stones that line the walls and cases. I'm grateful, too—almost to the point of tears—for how beautiful it all is.

I've seen examples of *pietre dure* in the Uffizi, but I've never been surrounded by so many beautiful pieces: tables and vases crafted of multicolored precious stones—marble, agate, jasper, heliotrope, lapis lazuli, and chalcedony carved into flowers and birds and butterflies. In the courtyard stand great chunks of stones—the raw materials collected and hoarded by the Medicis. There's something audacious about the whole enterprise of *pietre dure*—mining the earth for precious stones to fill the artists' palette instead of paint.

A guard walks through the courtyard announcing that the museum is closing in ten minutes. I make a more scientific search then, instead of letting myself be dazzled by the colors. So far nothing resembles the rose-petal floors at La Civeta at all. The patterns here are all symmetrical and ordered, nothing like the free-flowing cascade of rose petals. I'm just about to give up when I find, in a corner behind a block of Carrara marble, a fragment of white marble floor with what looks like a scattering of rose petals across its surface. It's hard to tell, though, because the stone is cracked and covered by a fine layer of pine needles from a nearby tree. I kneel to brush away the needles.

"*Scusi, signora, non si può toccare.*"

I turn around and find a woman in a navy skirt and pinstriped blouse standing over me. I apologize and introduce myself as a resident scholar at La Civetta.

"Ah, La Civetta," she says, her stern expression softening. I've noticed how often just the name of the villa evokes for Florentines an ideal of beauty. "No wonder you're interested in the rose-petal floor. You recognize it from the villa, *sì*?"

I turn back to the fragment and look at the surface I've cleared. The petals are unmistakably the same as the ones at the villa. "Yes, do you know who made this floor?" I ask while taking out my digital camera to photograph the floor, "and the ones at the villa?"

"*Sì*, he was a very famous *commettitore*—one of Franceso de' Medici's favorites in his workshop at the Casino di San Marco, and then too of the Grand Duke Ferdinand when the *pietre dure* workshop was moved into the Galleria dei Lavori in 1588—"

"So he was definitely active in the 1530s?"

"Yes, but he died soon after the move to the Galleria, by 1590 at least."

"I see—can you look up his name?"

"Oh, no, *non è necessario*—I remember his first name was Pietro because I've always wondered if he was named that because his family were stonemasons."

I remember that Pietro was the name of the *commettitore* mentioned in the account books. Of course it would make sense that it was the same one. "Do you know his last name?" I ask.

"Oh, yes, that I remember because it's such a pretty name, like Petrarch's girlfriend. His name was Pietro de Laura."

On the bus ride back up the hill, my mind shifts between two sets of images as the bus sways back and forth on the twisting road. One is a picture of the wealthy Lorenzo Barbagianni standing in the Casino di San Marco watching the *commettitore's* pretty young daughter as she helps her father with his work. Did Lorenzo begin by flirting with her? By bringing her little presents? Did she understand that a man of his class would never marry a girl of hers?

The other picture I see, again and again, is Mark telling me that Robin killed himself. How he'd looked straight at me and lied. When I'd started to believe that Orlando might have pushed Robin, I hadn't wanted to face what that said about Mark. I'd allowed myself to believe that he might have been mistaken . . . or that he'd been afraid of accusing a young man of murder when he wasn't sure, but now I have to wonder whether he had realized he could use what he'd seen as a way to get Claudia Brunelli to drop the lawsuit from the beginning. Had he already been planning, with Robin's body still on the sidewalk below, to use his silence as a bargaining chip? How could I love someone capable of such callous deceit?

The bus rounds the last curve before La Civetta, and at the sight of the gates my eyes fill with tears just as they did twenty years ago when I looked back at them for what I thought was the last time. I'm forced to wonder whether I ever really did love Mark. To wonder whether the last time I really loved someone was twenty years ago when I walked out of the gates of La Civetta and took this same bus down the hill and got on a train to take me across the Alps and home.

What an idiot I've been, I think, getting off at the gates to La Civetta. I speak my name into the intercom, thinking how little good it had done to call my name into the sibyl's cave all those years ago. I might as well have dropped my heart into its dank pit while I was at it. The gates creak slowly open and I walk up the long, mournful cypress *viale* and then up the long curving staircase. I remember how it was on that last night—after I'd gotten the call that my Aunt Roz was dead— that I'd crept down these stairs in the dark. When I was halfway down, the moon had appeared in the oculus and lit up the marble, turning the rose petals beneath my feet into splotches of blood. *This place is cursed,* I'd thought, rushing from the house and wiping my feet on the mat outside the door as though I might leave a trail of bloody footprints.

In my room I find my shopping bags and mechanically begin unpacking them. In spite of myself, I'm comforted by the touch of the expensive fabrics. I spread out the Hermès scarf on the bed, admiring its mosaic pattern, and lay the slacks and dress and blouses I've bought next to it, fingering the rich textures of the silk and polished cotton. The colors are as vibrant as the powdered tints in the shop on the Via dello Studio and the colored stones in the Opificio.

I sit down on the bed next to my purchases, and admit to myself that for all my horror at what I've witnessed today, there is one piece of welcome news: Bruno had nothing to do with sending Orlando to New York, and he probably had no idea that Orlando pushed Robin. It's not much comfort, but it's something. At least, unlike Mark, he hadn't been revealed today to be a total cad.

I'd had plenty of reason to think Bruno was a cad twenty years ago when Claudia came to my room and told me that she was pregnant. I'd thought at first that she was telling me that she and Bruno would finally be divorcing. When Bruno had told me that he and Claudia had an understanding, I thought that meant they both saw other people and lived apart. I thought it meant they didn't sleep together. And surely even the antiquated conventions of the Catholic Church wouldn't demand that they stay together if she were pregnant with another man's child. I said as much to Claudia. Then Claudia took my hand and told me that the baby was Bruno's.

So Bruno wasn't exactly a saint—but at least he wasn't hiding a murder. Right now, I think ruefully as I slide my newly purchased clothing into a dresser drawer, that makes him the more honorable of my ex-lovers.

I give the drawer a hard push to close it and hear something chime against the wood. Opening the drawer again, I run my hands under the tissue paper and feel something flat and metallic at the back. When I pull it out, I see it's a small brass key. I look down at the dresser to see whether it matches a lock on any of its drawers, but there are no keyholes on the drawers. Nor is there a keyhole on the single drawer on the dressing table. I turn around in the room, scanning the rest of the furniture, but nothing else is locked. Nothing except for the *cassone* at the foot of the bed.

It hardly seems possible, but then, it seems to be a day for surprises. I kneel in front of the *cassone* and fit the key into the lock. As I turn it I wonder what kind of surprise might lie inside—would it be the kind of thing that I'll be sorry later that I uncovered? Griselda's humble downcast eyes as she greets her husband's new bride seem to rebuke me, and I open the lid. I recall Barbagianni's dictum that *cassoni* ought to be preserved, "if not for their artistic value, then for their power to teach valuable lessons and to contain the baser instincts of any new bride who may come to this house" and wonder what object lesson may have been added to this *cassone* to teach Barbagianni's new bride subservience. I'm expecting some profane variant on the Griselda tale—perhaps the children slaughtered after all, or Gualtieri really marrying his daughter—but instead I find, stretched out on the reverse of the lid, a reclining nude of surpassing beauty and delicate modesty. Her arms are crossed in front of her breasts, one hand tucked beneath a satin pillow against which her smoothly curved cheek . . . not so much rests, as gently hovers above. Her deep-lidded eyes are closed, her lips curved into the faintest of smiles, as if she were dreaming. I sit back hard on my heels, as if the beauty of the figure had been a hand that laid itself on my chest and pushed, knocking the breath out of me. I've stood in front of paintings at the Louvre, the Uffizi, the Met, and *admired,* but none of those paintings have ever had the power of this simple reclining figure, painted by an anonymous *cassone* painter, not for a million eyes but for only two eyes, those of the bride who in contemplating such physical beauty would bring forth beautiful children.

I lean forward to look at her more closely and notice that the *cassone* isn't, as I first thought, completely empty. A single sheet of paper lies at the bottom. When I pick it up I notice that the wood at the bottom of the cassone is covered with dark stains, as though it had at some time suffered water damage. Odd, I think, if it's been in this room all along. Then I turn to the poem, which is in the same handwriting as the two other poems I have read so far.

> *Thy words are what I crave, not velvet, silk,*
> *Bestowed to gloss me as prime property,*
> *In fevered art of lust; a minute's talk*
> *With thee means more than bartered luxury.*
> *These garments, even mine, will wither, fade,*
> *Spun-silk worm-feast someday in my dark grave;*
> *While sonnets, by which time's cruel hand is stayed,*
> *Thy lustrous jewels free-given to me, save*
> *Our love from all decay; thy wordrich gifts*
> *Exceed the whole of wealth on this bleak earth.*
> *Ah love, this rosy sunset breeze which lifts*
> *My spirits, is a poem to thy great worth.*
> *As you approach, may words grow wings and fly*
> *To thee across the north Italian sky.*

I look up from the poem to the figure on the *cassone* and notice for the first time that running along the curve of her hip is a delicate scroll of words. I lean in closer and see that it's two lines of the poem inscribed in the wooden panel. "These garments, even mine, will wither, fade, / Spun-silk worm-feast someday in my dark grave." Running my fingers along it I can feel the grooves where the words were carved, the paint cracked where the fine blade pressed into the wood. Clearly it was done after the *cassone* was painted. I look back at the sheet of paper in my hand and see that it's the same handwriting. I run my hands along the words again, feeling a thrill as if I were really touching flesh, and notice that there are other marks in the surface of the wood, little crescents in the faded blue background, which I think at first might have been meant to represent tiny moons, until I notice that they're all over the surface, in the flesh of the nude and her hair and on her pillow, and then I realize what they are. They're nail marks. Made by someone inside trying to claw her way out.

CHAPTER
EIGHTEEN

I DECIDE TO WEAR THE GREEN DRESS TO DINNER. IT'S A LITTLE TOO FORMAL FOR even Cyril's idea of dressing for dinner, which I've always suspected he got more from watching the BBC than from his own threadbare childhood, but I have a feeling that this is going to be an evening for drama—and I feel a sudden need to *gird* myself to face it, to clothe myself against the dangers of this house. And this dress is dramatic. It's cut for a Grecian goddess, pleated over my breasts, skimming my waist, and then fluttering across my hips. The skirt is lined with a thin layer of chiffon that just grazes the tops of my knees as I make my way down the steps of the rotunda. I can hear it whispering against the heavy satin, silk talking to silk in iambic pentameter of transience and mortality. "These garments, even mine, will wither, fade, / Spun-silk worm-feast someday in my dark grave."

When I get to the bottom of the stairs I can hear voices from the dining room, but before I turn in that direction someone calls my name from the library. I turn and see Mark standing by the French doors leading out to the *pomerino,* a champagne flute in his hand.

"Join me for an aperitif," he calls to me, and then, as I come into the room, he says in a low whisper, "Close the door behind you."

I hesitate. After what I learned about Mark earlier today, I'm not in the mood for an intimate moment, but then this is as good an opportunity as any to confront him with what I know. As I close the door behind me I'm not sure what I'm hoping for—that he'll somehow be able to explain everything or that the confrontation will mark the end of our relationship.

"You look lovely," Mark says, pouring me a glass of Prosecco. "Is that a new dress?"

"Yes," I tell him, "I went shopping with Mara Silverman today."

"Really? I can't imagine that you and Gene's wife would have much in common, but if shopping with her yields such beautiful results . . ." He strokes the silk pleat above my collarbone and a chill passes through my body. The words "spun-silk worm-feast" rise unbidden in my mind. I look at Mark, at his handsome, chiseled features and glossy hair, the muscular physique so carefully controlled in his well-cut suit, and feel no spark of attraction to him. His physical charms leave me cold. I wonder again whether I ever really loved him.

Mark takes his hand away when I fail to move closer. "You're right," he says, glancing over his shoulder out the glass doors, "this place is alive with gossips."

"Yes," I say, "La Civetta was built for spying."

I see a vertical line appear between his eyebrows. Does he recall Claudia saying the same thing this afternoon? If so, he dismisses the coincidence and smiles. "You're in an odd mood this evening. Perhaps you should have rested instead of going into town with Mara."

"Perhaps, but I was also able to do some research in town and I learned something interesting. Something upsetting, actually." I wish now that I had spent more time planning what I would say to Mark, but then I hadn't realized I'd be alone with him so soon. I sigh, suddenly tired of having to measure each word so carefully.

"Have you found something so soon? I didn't realize that you'd had a chance to look through the archives."

"No, it wasn't anything I learned in the archives. I went into the church of Santa Margherita after lunch and I saw you there with Claudia." If I'd expected Mark to look abashed, I'd be disappointed. His smile wavers only slightly, but otherwise he doesn't look alarmed.

"Really? I didn't see you. You should have said something—"

"The two of you didn't look like you wanted to be disturbed."

"Oh, Rose," Mark says, his face creased with concern now, "you don't think there's anything going on between me and Claudia Brunelli, do you?"

"No, that's not what I meant . . ." I begin, but falter, suddenly confused. *Is* that what I meant? Is that what this is all about? Was I merely jealous of Claudia—again?

Mark puts down his glass on a side table and moves close to me, drawing me to him and away from the glass doors in one fluid gesture. I struggle to extricate myself, but his arm tightens around my waist.

"I overheard you talking about what happened on the balcony . . . and earlier I heard Mara and Gene making a deal with Leo Balthasar. Mark, I know what happened on the balcony in New York."

With one arm still gripped around my waist, Mark uses his other hand to tilt my chin up to look at him, and I meet his steady gaze. "What do you know, Rose?" he asks.

If a minute ago I thought I'd gotten over feeling anything for Mark, now I'm not so sure, but the heat that moves through me feels closer to fear than attraction. "I know that you saw Orlando push Robin from the balcony and that now you're using that knowledge to get Claudia to drop the lawsuit. It's blackmail, Mark, and I can't stand by and let the world think Robin killed himself when it isn't true."

I feel the tension in Mark's arm relax, and something slackens in his face. He closes his eyes briefly and exhales. I realize I've been holding my breath, and I, too, breathe out now—a long sigh that warbles into an unexpected sob.

"Rose," Mark says, opening his eyes and pulling me closer to him.

"I'm so sorry. I shouldn't have lied to you. It's just that I knew how much the boy meant to you—"

"That isn't the point." I lay my hand on his chest to push him away. He grabs my hand and squeezes it, then drops it and sinks onto a couch.

"You're right, but it clouded my judgment. And then I knew Orlando was Bruno's son and I thought . . . well, I thought you still had feelings for Bruno and that you'd be devastated that his son had killed Robin. I just wanted to think about what to do . . . and then it was too late because I hadn't spoken up right away."

"Why would you think I still had feelings for Bruno?" I ask looking down on his bowed head. "It's been twenty years."

Mark looks up at me. "Because I've always felt you held a piece of yourself apart from me. I confess at first I thought you were in love with Robin, but then I realized that you had far too much integrity to allow yourself to feel something for a young student. It made me think, though, that you'd loved someone at that age and never gotten over it. Then I noticed how you reacted whenever Bruno Brunelli's name came up. Was I wrong? Are you over Bruno?"

I look out the glass doors, across the *pomerino* toward the *limonaia.* There's a light on in Bruno's apartment, and I remember the last time I went there to ask him whether it was true, whether the baby Claudia was carrying was his.

"No, you weren't wrong," I tell Mark. "I didn't realize until I came here, but I think now that I left a part of myself here. I'm sorry, I suppose it's the part I've always held back from you."

Mark nods. I've never seen such a look of defeat on his face. "We should have talked about it before this, and now . . . Is it too late, Rose? I know what I did was wrong, but if I made things right . . . What do you want me to do? Go to the police right now and make a statement that Orlando pushed Robin? I'm willing to, but I'm afraid that with the lawsuit . . . it will look like I'm trying to discredit the family. I'm certain that Professor Brunelli will see it that way."

"But Mara and Gene will back you up—and Leo Balthasar—"

"Ah, but you just said that they've made a deal. Did Mara tell you . . . ?"

I shake my head and tell him what I overheard in the library. He nods. "Yes, that sounds like a deal Balthasar would make. All he really cares about is his film, and he wants to film it here at La Civetta. If the Brunellis win their lawsuit, how likely do you think it is that they'll allow that? And there's still the question of the stolen poems."

"Yes, it's complicated," I admit. "I can see that."

"And Orlando . . . well. I'm afraid of what he might do if confronted. He might flee—or worse. He's very volatile. You didn't see his face when he pushed Robin. He was like a madman."

I remember Orlando's face when he fled the balcony—his eyes wide like a frightened horse's—and then how he'd looked in the park, curled in on himself in grief. Then I recall Bruno's expression watching his son perform last night. This would destroy him.

"You're right," I say. "We'll need to call the police before we confront him and we'll have to talk to Gene and Mara and Leo Balthasar." And Bruno, I add to myself. I know Mark will argue that it will only give him an opportunity to warn Orlando, who might then flee, but I have to give Bruno some warning of what's to come. I owe him that much.

"All right," Mark says, getting to his feet. "I'll talk to Gene and Leo. Mara will go along with whatever Gene says. I'll tell them that I won't give my permission to use the villa for the film unless they go along with us and that we'll bring up Robin's history of plagiarism. It won't be easy, but I promise that I'll do everything in my power to make this right. I only hope it's not too late to make things right between us."

He reaches out his hand and touches my arm lightly, tentatively. I try to return the faint smile on his lips. "We'll have to see, Mark . . ."

"Of course," he says, lowering his arm. "One thing at a time." Then he holds out a crooked arm for me to take. "Now I think we'd better get to dinner. Or people will be gossiping about us."

I do a better job of returning his smile this time, but I shake my head. "Then we'd better not go in together. And I need a moment . . ."

"Yes, you're right." He turns to leave and then, as if he'd just remembered something, turns back. "Oh, and Rose, it would help if you found those poems Robin supposedly stole. Have you had any luck?"

"No," I lie. "I haven't found any poems yet."

———

Although I told the truth about needing a moment to collect myself, I had an ulterior motive for wanting Mark to go on ahead without me. I want to go back down to the cellar to check the account book one more time. Mark is right—it would be better if I could find Ginevra's poems to prove at least that Robin didn't steal them from the villa, that he left them where he found them, including the one in the *cassone*. If he was led to the one in the *cassone* by what he read in the account books, then maybe there are hints in the account books of where the other poems were hidden.

I gingerly make my way down to the cellar in high heels that weren't made for navigating spiral stairs. Without a flashlight I have to grope in the air for the string to the lightbulb, batting my way through spiderwebs. When I finally get the light on, I see that I've acquired a netting of grime along my arms, but at least nothing has touched my dress. I find the account book where I left it and open it on the table, standing over it because I don't want to risk soiling my dress on the chair.

Scanning through the first few months of daily accounts, I quickly see that Lorenzo Barbagianni was planning to marry. It was, after all, the perfect time for him to take a bride. He'd inherited his father's villa, which included not only this house but the surrounding farmland of olive groves and vineyards, and the convent of Santa Catalina and its wool and tapestry works. He was lord of the manor, responsible for the lives of dozens of servants and farmworkers, who, like Gualtieri's vassals in the Griselda story, would have wanted him to produce an heir, but unlike Gualtieri he had obliged them by becoming engaged to a woman of nobility, Cecelia Cecchi. Betrothal presents were exchanged between the two families in the spring of 1581, one of which, I notice, is a small jewelry box inlaid with the finest gemstones, produced in the *pietre dure* workshop of the Casino di San Marco.

So, I think, while Lorenzo was preparing for his marriage to Cecelia Cecchi, he was, no doubt, flirting with the *committitore's* pretty daughter. Flipping another page of the account book, I see that as part of getting his villa ready to welcome his new bride, he commissioned, on April 21, 1581, a *pietre dure* floor for the dining room. And so, I think, closing the book for now, when Pietro came here to lay the floor, perhaps he brought his daughter with him to help. It would have given Barbagianni ample opportunity to seduce her.

The antipasto has already been taken away when I finally arrive in the dining room, and the diners appear to be halfway through their pasta when they all look up to watch me make my late entrance. Frieda Mainbocher looks so pointedly at her watch, I'm afraid she's going to haul out a grade book from the folds of her wooly tartan wrap and mark me tardy.

"Ah, Rose," Cyril says, holding up his glass to me, "I would chide you for being late, but to see you so beautifully attired was worth the wait."

I can't help but notice that all the other men at the table—Gene, Leo, Bruno, and Mark—watch me as I take my seat. Even Daisy Wallace murmurs something about my dress being a fantastic color. The only occupant of the table who pointedly does not look at me is Mara. She is staring at her untouched pasta sullenly. Her eyes look red and her normally creamy complexion is splotchy. Clearly she's been crying.

"It's certainly lucky you got that consulting job with Leo," Gene says. His look, I realize now, is more resentful than admiring. "I can't imagine you could afford that dress on a professor's salary."

I open my mouth to reply to Gene's taunt, but Bruno beats me to it. "You seem quite preoccupied with academic salaries, Professor Silverman. Perhaps you'd be happier in another line of work."

"As a matter of fact, I've written a number of award-winning screenplays," Gene says indignantly, "and unlike poetry, screenwriting pays. I think you'll be impressed with the results once I've gotten a go at that script," he says to Balthasar. "And you won't see me squandering my time here shopping."

I'm more worried than insulted by Gene's spiteful attack on me. It seems likely that Mara has tried to persuade Gene to break his deal with Balthasar and failed.

"Actually, I believe Dr. Asher spent some time today doing research," Mark says, directing his comments pointedly to Balthasar, "and has already made some important discoveries." Some tacit message seems to pass between Mark and Balthasar that I imagine has to do with what happened on the balcony in New York. But Leo's question to me stays on the topic of the film.

"Have you?" Leo asks me. "Have you found the love poems of William Shakespeare's Dark Lady?"

"I honestly don't know if I can promise you the Dark Lady," I say, sidestepping the issue of found poems, "but I am beginning to believe that Ginevra de Laura was a significant poet and lived a life that would be worth telling whether she ever met Shakespeare or not."

"The Dark Lady without Will Shakespeare?" Leo Balthasar shrugs, rippling the folds of his soft white dress shirt. "It might make an interesting independent film." He says "independent film" with as much condescension as he can fit into the two words. "But we're talking a thirty-million-dollar project minimum, top talent attached. For that we need the Bard."

I laugh. "I can't produce William Shakespeare out of a hat," I say. "And I think you might be underestimating Ginevra de Laura's story. She was the daughter of a craftsman—one of the artisans who created this very floor." I wave my hand toward the repeating pattern of the Barbagianni crest inlaid in colored stone. "She may have even helped her father in his studio, where she could have met Barbagianni when he came to commission a wedding present for his fiancée, and she might have come here when her father worked on this floor." I pause. I'm running way ahead of anything I know, but I'm intoxicated with the picture that's emerging with my words. I only half know where they're coming from. I see the girl kneeling over a workman's table, her bare arms and plain cloth shift stained with dust from the stone she's cutting: blue lapis lazuli, yellow jasper, orange carnelian, white Carrara, and black chalcedony. I imagine the colors suggesting to Barbagianni the colors of the silks he would dress her in when she became his mistress.

"When she came here with her father, Barbagianni seduced her—raped her, probably. What could her father have done—"

"Well," Frieda Mainbocker says, "he could have brought Barbagianni to court and sued for the lost marriage value of a virginal daughter. He would have asked for money to increase her dowry to make up for her decreased value on the marriage market or for Barbagianni to marry her."

"Ugh," Daisy Wallace says, "you mean she would have had to marry her rapist?"

"That would have been considered a positive outcome," Frieda says, "but it's unlikely that a man of Barbagianni's station would have agreed to marry an artisan's daughter."

"And," I add, "he was already engaged to a woman from a wealthy family. A Cecchi."

"An old family indeed. Yes, these old families stick together," Claudia says, glancing at Cyril. "They have little use for commoners. They make promises they don't keep—"

"Exactly," I say, startling Claudia by agreeing with her so vehemently. "It's another possibility. Perhaps Barbagianni pretended that he intended to marry Ginevra." I take another sip of the bubbling Prosecco and the idea begins to percolate in my mind. I look around at the dining room table and it calls to mind another banquet, the one painted on the wall of my bedroom upstairs and the next painting in the grisly cycle of Nastagio raping his fiancée before the wedding night. "He lured her to the bridal suite with presents and false promises and then raped her."

I pause, noticing that my audience is as morbidly entranced with the scene I've conjured as Nastagio's guests are with the bloody scene they're forced to witness. "When she knew that he had tricked her, she ran from the bridal suite. She ran down the hall and down the steps of the rotunda, her own blood marking the path of her flight. 'My blood announced my anguish as I fled.'" I pause, realizing that I'm quoting Ginevra's poem. I look around the table to see whether anyone gives any sign of recognition at the line, but I meet only the wide-open eyes of interested listeners. If the person who gave me the poem is at this table, he or she isn't letting on. "Although she never became Barbagianni's bride, she did become his mistress, and after Cecelia Cecchi died he installed Ginevra here in this house. I think it was she who commissioned the pattern of rose petals in the nuptial suite, along the upstairs hallway, and down the steps of the rotunda."

"I think you've got it all wrong," Mara says, suddenly breaking her silence. "You say that Ginevra was sleeping with Barbagianni before he married Cecelia Cecchi—well, what if she plotted to kill her so she could take her place?"

"Well," I say, trying not to sound condescending, "for one thing Cecelia Cecchi died in childbirth—"

"So? The Laura woman could have bribed the midwife to poison her . . . or let her bleed to death . . . I bet that's what the bloody petals on the floor are supposed to represent—that whore's triumph over poor Mrs. Barbagianni!"

During Mara's increasingly hysterical speech, the server has come in to deliver the *piatto secondo*—a beefsteak Florentina. When Mara looks down at her plate, she shrieks at the sight of the bloody meat and pushes her chair away from the table. Gene reaches out a hand to restrain her, but she bats it away, screaming, "No, it's unclean, and if you touch a carcass or you're a witness you're supposed to confess." Then she runs through the open doors of the dining room out onto the loggia.

Gene looks around the table, his face baffled, and meets Mark's gaze. Mark tells Gene that he'd better go after her.

"Yes, yes," he says, getting up and laying his linen napkin over his plate. I wonder whether he covers the meat because of Mara's calling it unclean. "It's just the jet lag, you see, and this new medication she's on, and"—his gaze falls on his plate, where the red blood of the steak is seeping up through the white cloth—"and she doesn't eat red meat."

When he leaves, the rest of the table is silent for several minutes. None of us has much of an appetite, I imagine. Only Cyril seems undeterred by Mara's unflattering description of the entree and is happily tucking into the rare steak. Mark finally excuses himself, saying, "I think I'll go see how they are. Maybe I can help."

"It's funny," Frieda Mainoocher says after Mark's gone, "but what Mara said about the meat sounded very familiar. I believe it's from the Old Testament. Leviticus, I think."

I nod. Yes, Mara had been quoting from her Haftorah portion, the section that stipulates what sacrifices are expected for what sins, including what's necessary of a person who has witnessed a crime. I can only conclude from Mara's outburst that Gene hadn't been amenable to sacrificing his producer's credit and one percent of the film's revenue to come clean.

CHAPTER NINETEEN

FTER COFFEE IS SERVED, THE GUESTS DISPERSE QUICKLY AS IF EAGER TO DISPEL the mood of the dinner. Some wander out onto the loggia to enjoy the night air—or in Leo Balthasar's case, to enjoy a good cigar—but I excuse myself, pleading jet lag, and head into the rotunda. Bruno catches up with me, though, at the foot of the stairs and, laying his hand over mine on the banister, says, "Rose, I need to speak to you."

I turn to him and am startled by the worry in his face. I almost say no, knowing that what I have to tell him will only cause him more pain, but then how much worse will it be to learn about Orlando's role in Robin's death with no preparation at all? "Yes, I have to speak to you, too," I say, stepping down toward him.

"Not here," he says, glancing around the rotunda. At the very center of the house—open to all the main public rooms on the first floor and the hallways of the second—the rotunda is indeed the worst place in which to have a private conversation.

"Where?" I ask, half afraid he'll suggest my room—or his apartment.

"In the garden in half an hour, at the fountain. Can you find it?"

"I think so," I say, "but why can't we just go now?"

"I have to find Orlando first," he says, "but I promise I'll be there in half an hour. You should put on something warmer. As lovely as you look in that dress . . ." His eyes linger over my dress and I blush.

"Okay," I say, "half an hour, then."

"Oh, and Rose, that poem you quoted at dinner tonight about the blood in the rotunda"—we both look down at the rose-petal pattern on the floor swirling around the impluvium—"is that one of the poems in Robin's screenplay or have you found something?"

Looking into his eyes, I find myself unable to lie. "It's a poem I found—or rather that someone gave me last night. I don't know who."

He nods. "Did it come with a note?" he asks. When I nod he asks me to bring it with me.

"Okay," I say. It seems little enough to give him in return for destroying his life. "I'll bring it."

I turn around then and go up the stairs. It's not until I get to the top that I hear his footsteps echoing in the rotunda and I know that he watched my ascent

When I get back to my room, I quickly retrieve the poem I was given last night and the other original poems I have so far—the one Robin gave me in New York and the one I found in the *cassone*—from my book bag. Then I pick up the embroidered shawl I wore around my waist last night and turn it over. I'd noticed that the black silk lining has come unstitched along one side, creating a sort of pocket that's just the right size for the poems. I slip them into the lining and then arrange the shawl so that the poems are close to my body and the black lining faces out. Then I change my high-heeled shoes for the flat Tibetan sandals

Chihiro gave me, wondering whether she imagined me using them for clandestine night journeys. I wish, for a moment, that she was here instead of in England so I could go over with her everything that's happened in the short time I've been here, but then I realize that if she were here she'd probably be telling me that sneaking off to the garden in the middle of the night to meet the father of the man who killed Robin is not the smartest move I could make.

Although I'm ready, it's still too early to go. I sit down on the bed, facing the painting of Nastagio degli Onesti wandering through the woods. I've left only the night light on, so the room is too dark to make out much of the painting, but the shadows only seem to bring out the lurid yellow eyes of the owls in the trees tracking Nastagio's progress through the woods. I can't help wondering whether Barbagianni had these eyes added to the wall painting for the benefit of his new bride so that she would know that wherever she went, he, Barbagianni the owl, would be watching her. It's a creepy thought and makes sitting here all the more unbearable until I remember that I have another place to wait. I get up, open the door, and cross into the plain little cell I lived in twenty years ago. My little convent room. I'd almost forgotten about it.

In the moonlight its whitewashed walls have a nacreous glow—like the inside of a pearl. I sit down at the desk by the open window without turning on a light. There's no need. A full moon has risen over the hills of Valdarno, silvering a path through the river valley to the rooftop of the *limonaia,* which, I notice, is still dark inside. The bust on the corner eave seems to be looking directly toward the path of moonlight. I always felt that she was waiting for someone to appear at the crest of the hill, and now that I've read Ginevra's poems I imagine that she felt that way, too, that she sat in this very room—her only escape from Barbagianni's paintings—penning the poems that would bring her lover across the Alps to her. Who could resist such invitations? I certainly hadn't.

But did he come? The three poems that I've found so far are all by a woman asking her beloved to visit her. The fact that these poems are here at all is not a good sign. They might be copies of the poems she sent, or maybe she never sent them at all. And if she did send them, did he ever respond? Did he heed her summons and come to La Civetta? And if he did, what happened? When Ginevra left this house it wasn't on the arm of her lover. It was alone, in a threadbare shift, and she didn't flee to England; she followed the river thirty miles to the east—a path that would have closely followed the path of moonlight I can see now—to the Convent of Santa Catalina, where she lived out the rest of her life in a cell that was probably even smaller and colder than this one. What went wrong? Did her English lover never come? Or did he come only to find that it was impossible to revive their lost love? To forget their history of betrayal?

My thoughts are interrupted by the sound of voices rising from the *pomerino.*

"I'm not crazy. I know what's right."

It's Mara's voice. I lean closer to the window to look out and I see Gene and Ned standing by Mara in the center of the walled garden. Leo Balthasar is a little ways off on a marble bench, smoking his cigar and looking impassively on as the two men try to calm Mara.

"Mom," Ned says, extending his hand to Mara, "we can go inside and talk about it. You know how you always say that talking about things makes them better."

Even from here I can see Mara's face soften. "Neddy." she says, taking his hand, "that's absolutely right. Let's go inside and talk. Let me tell you what your father wants me to do—"

I see Gene and Leo exchange a look, and a second later Gene has Mara by the shoulders and is pulling her away from Ned and into the library. "I think your mother is too upset to talk right now, Ned. I'd better get her into bed, and you . . . I'm sure you'd rather be with your friends . . ."

A burst of laughter comes from the opposite side of the *pomerino,* from inside the *limonaia,* and a boy and girl come tumbling out in a little cloud of marijuana smoke, which I can smell from here.

"There—isn't that the girl you like, Chloe?" It's a mark of how desperate Gene is to keep his son away from Mara—and from what she might tell him—that he'd rather send him off to smoke pot.

"Zoe," Ned corrects his father. His face looks suddenly wistful and

I see why. Zoe is with the handsome Orlando. I guess they've made up the argument they were having in New York—or now that Robin is gone, Zoe's seeking solace in her former suitor. "And Orlando."

The two teenagers stop short when they see the group of adults in the *pomerino.* Zoe erupts in a fit of giggles, but Orlando looks serious. He straightens up and walks across the walled garden, his posture and stance reminding me forcibly of his father. He's walking straight toward Ned.

"We were looking for you—" he begins, but Mara hurls herself between the two boys, snarling at Orlando. "Stay away from him. Haven't you caused enough trouble?"

It takes Leo and Gene both to hold Mara back from scratching Orlando's face. She struggles for a moment and then collapses between the two men, sinking to the graveled pathway.

Orlando holds out his arms and looks toward Ned. "I don't understand," he says.

"I think you'd better leave, son," Leo says. "In fact, why don't you come with me." He lays a hand on Orlando's shoulder, but Orlando shrugs it off and with a last parting glance in Ned's direction leaves the *pomerino* by the side gate leading onto the lemon walk.

"I'd better follow him," Leo says. "Can you handle her?"

"Sure," Gene says, bending down to help Mara up. Mara, though, suddenly springs to life.

"I don't want to be *handled,*" she spits at Gene, and then, before either man can stop her, she runs out of the *pomerino,* taking the same side gate that Orlando walked through a minute ago. Ned tries to follow, but Leo grabs his arm. "I think it's better that I talk to your mother right now. She seems to be angry about your . . . relationships. Let me talk to her. I've had some experience with these things."

"I don't know what you're talking about—" Ned says to Leo's retreating back, but the producer's already through the side gate.

"Son, we should go inside," Gene says, looking up at the villa as if suddenly aware that there are windows facing onto the *pomerino.* I move back a few inches into my darkened room, hoping Gene hasn't seen me. "It's nobody's business—"

"A minute ago you said I should go off with my friends," Ned says defiantly. He moves over to Zoe, who's been watching the whole scene goggled-eyed as if it were a reality TV show, and drapes his arm around her shoulders. He glares at his father as if daring him to intervene, and Gene throws up his arms in an exaggerated display of parental pique. "Fine—do whatever you like," he says. He turns and goes into the library. Ned whispers something in Zoe's ear that makes her giggle, and they head toward the *limonaia,* but before they reach it Zoe whispers something into Ned's ear and they veer off to the side gate. I keep staring at the deserted *pomerino* as if waiting for the next act, but when no one else appears I realize I'm going to be late for my assignation with Bruno. I can only hope that all the people who have just headed off into the garden aren't going in the direction of the fountain.

Hugging the dark folds of the shawl close to me, I cross the hall and enter the top floor of the library. With a qualm I notice that Zoe has neatly arranged manuscript boxes and folios on the table by the window and remind myself that I'd better start sorting through them tomorrow. Not now, though. I descend the spiral staircase to the main floor of the library, glad to see that the room below me is dark. I should have brought the flashlight with me, but once I'm outside the moon will light my way. As soon as I reach the bottom of the stairs I can see the reflection of moonlight on the marble floors—a path leading to the doors to the garden. I'm almost there when a voice stops me.

"Ah, Rose, I knew you wouldn't be able to resist the garden on such a night. I've been waiting for you."

I turn slowly, careful to keep the shawl with its cargo of poems close against my body, and face Cyril, who's sitting so far back in a velvet club chair that I can make out only the tips of his loafers and the long waxy fingers of his left hand lying on the arm of the chair.

"You know me too well, Cyril. Who could resist the gardens of La Civetta under a full moon? I'm surprised you came in from the loggia."

"Even these warm summer nights are too chilly for my old bones," he says. "I needed a little *restorative* to warm me up." His right hand appears from the shadows cradling a silver goblet etched with spirals and set with opalescent stones. "Would you join me in a little nightcap?" he asks. I'm about to tell him that I've had more than enough to drink when he adds, "Unless, of course, you have some more pressing engagement?"

Even without being able to make out his face, I can guess he's smiling. I'm caught.

"No, no engagement except with the gardens under the moonlight, and the moon's just risen." I sink into the chair opposite him, angled into the moonlight so that he can see me, while I still can't see any more of him than his disembodied hands, which now lift a decanter, made of the same design as the cup, from a hammered silver tray on a pedestal table set beside his chair, and pour the liqueur into a silver goblet that's set on the tray as if he'd been expecting me. He pours a little water from a ceramic pitcher and hands me the cup; his fingertips when they graze mine feel as cool as the metal. It's impossible to tell the color of the liqueur, but when I sip it I taste licorice. Sambuco, perhaps, or any of the half dozen Italian liqueurs that are flavored with aniseed. The slight metallic aftertaste comes, I imagine, from the silver.

"I don't think I've ever drunk from a silver cup before," I say. "I think I read somewhere of a wife poisoning her husband with ground-up silver."

He makes a dry sound that could be a laugh or a cough. "You'd need quite a bit more silver, my dear; it's not like the lead cups that made the Romans mad, although"—he chuckles—"I have been having my after-dinner drink from these since a Turkish pasha presented them to me in 1956 as a thank-you for giving him some rose cuttings for his garden. Perhaps the silver has addled my brain."

"Your brain doesn't seem the slightest bit addled," I say. Cyril must have sat through the scene in the *pomerino,* quietly watching the drama from his dark corner. I wonder what he made of it. Does he know that Mark is blackmailing Claudia into dropping the lawsuit? I take another sip of the curiously warming liqueur. It feels like liquid silver slipping down my throat, like moonlight stealing under my skin. "You've come to a comfortable arrangement with Hudson College and now you've put together this movie deal. You seem quite on top of everything . . . except, I suppose, for the lawsuit."

Cyril steeples his long fingers in front of his shaded face. "I wouldn't worry about the lawsuit, my dear. I've always got something up my sleeve." For a second the moonlight hits his fingertips in a way that makes them look like claws, but then I blink and they're just the yellowed, cracked fingernails of an old man again. An old man who's willing to hide the truth of a boy's death to protect his property, I'd wager.

"Is it worth it, do you think?" I ask, taking another long sip of the liqueur for courage. Cyril's not an opponent to take on lightly. "When you think about a young boy's life—"

"What's one young life compared to all this?" Cyril asks, holding up his hands to indicate the villa. "My only aim has been to leave a legacy. To preserve La Civetta for posterity. If Claudia has her way, it would become a glorified Hilton, full of tourists sporting their dreadful soccer shirts and buying underwear emblazoned with David's penis. My God, the last time I ventured into town during the tourist season I saw a vendor selling a calendar of penises. *Famosi piselli.* And the streets are full of Eastern Europeans dressed up as statues and gladiators—like at Disneyland! Claudia's own son was romping about town last year with that American boy in see-through tights. Can you blame me if I want to preserve La Civetta for scholars instead of letting it fall to the Philistines?"

I take a long draught of my drink to give me time to think of an answer. Of course, I want to see La Civetta preserved as a place for scholars to study instead of as a playground for rich tourists, but I'm remembering the students today with their David boxers and picturing the fairies dressed in tights and troubadours dressed in doublet and hose for last night's performance. I'm not sure, really, how far Cyril and Mark's vision of La Civetta is from Claudia's. Not enough of a difference, really, to justify hiding the truth of a boy's death.

"Maybe there's another way to settle it. Maybe all Claudia wants is an acknowledgment that Orlando belongs to your family," I say, thinking that such an acknowledgment will be little enough once Orlando's part in Robin's death is revealed.

Cyril leans forward, his face, rising out of the gloom, alarmingly yellow, his eyes bloodshot. He looks like a drowned man surfacing out of the dark water. "What that bitch wants is to make us all suffer. You tell your friend President Abrams that there's not enough money under the sun to buy her off. She'll take my last chance at happiness and yours, Rose, just like she did twenty years ago. We can't sit around waiting for her to give us what we want; we have to take it—" Cyril's invective is interrupted by a coughing fit. I get up to pour him a glass of water from the ceramic pitcher and nearly lose my balance. The room seems to slide a bit, the moonlit surfaces as slippery as glass.

"Here," I say, handing Cyril the glass and steadying myself on the arm of his chair. "Calm down. I'm sure you'll come to some sort of arrangement with Claudia . . . and as for what happened between Bruno and me . . . well, I can hardly blame her for that. She got pregnant—"

"Do you think that was an accident? She knew she was going to lose Bruno to you and that the only reason he'd stay was if she were carrying his child. Or at least if she made him believe it was his child."

"That may be," I say, "but she couldn't very well have made him believe it was his if he hadn't slept with her, and no one forced him to do that." I pour myself some more of the liqueur, which, I notice, looks cloudy in the silver cup, and take another long drink. This isn't what I want to be reminded of on my way to meet Bruno.

"It's a lapse I'm sure he's had occasion to regret. Personally I've always suspected that she drugged him."

"That's ridiculous." I try to laugh, but the sound I make comes out tinny and my mouth is suddenly full of the bitter taste of metal. I finish the rest of my drink and put the silver goblet down on the tray, metal ringing against metal like a bell tolling. "She's not Lucrezia Borgia. And even if he had been drugged, that's no excuse."

I gather up my shawl, and the poems in the lining crackle angrily. I see Cyril's ears actually twitch at the sound. His hand shoots out and grabs my arm, the long, yellowed nails pressing into my skin. I imagine he's going to rip the poems from their hiding place, but instead he stretches his mouth into a wide, lupine smile. "You're a strong woman, Rose—not everybody has your strength of character—but we all have our weaknesses." He lets my arm go and grasps the edge of the shawl, rubbing the material between his fingertips. "I hope this will keep you warm enough. Don't stay out too late. The gardens grow damp after midnight."

I nod. "I'm only going to take a short stroll," I say, pulling the shawl around me as if its blackness could make me invisible from him. "Thanks for the drink."

"You're most welcome," he says, holding up his cup and inhaling the aroma of the liqueur. Although it's probably just a trick of the moonlight, I imagine for a moment that the cloudy liquid casts a green-ish light on his face. "It's difficult to find the real stuff nowadays, but there's an order of Benedictine monks in the Val-de-Travers where it was invented by a French doctor who had fled the Terror . . ." He must notice the look of confusion on my face. "Oh, I thought you knew. *Artemisia absinthium*. Or as some call it, the Green Muse. It's *my* per-sonal weakness."

CHAPTER TWENTY

HEN I STEP OUT INTO THE *POMERINO* I THINK, FOR AN INSTANT, THAT I have stepped back in time to the winter of my junior year, to the night it snowed. The statue at the center of the walled garden—a half-nude goddess with a leaping deer at her side and bow strapped across her bared breast—is blindingly white, as if dusted by snow. But when I come close enough to lay my hand on the cool marble, I see it is only an effect of the moonlight—and perhaps of the two glasses of absinthe I've just drunk. Leave it to Cyril to imbibe not just any after-dinner drink, but one redolent of history and mystique. "The Green Muse," it was called by the artists and writers who favored it in nineteenth-century Paris. Granter of visions and corruptor of virtues. All myth, I've heard. Most of the reported effects came from the adulterants used in cheaper brands, which the lower classes—all those laundresses and prostitutes in Toulouse-Latrec's paintings—drank all the more to match the alcohol content of the more expensive brands. And, I've read, the chemical similarity between *Artemisia absinthium* and cannabis has been greatly exaggerated.

Still, the last time I found myself so fascinated with the texture of stone was the last time I smoked pot. I realize that I've been standing here in front of this statue for . . . well, I'm not really sure how long. I feel as if she's cast a spell on me, willing me into the same stony rigidity as her. Of course, I suddenly realize, she's Artemis, the namesake of the herb I've just drunk. I nearly laugh at the coincidence (the way I recall laughing at such epiphanies when stoned) but remember that Cyril is probably still watching me from the library. Just as he must have watched the whole scene with Mara and Orlando and realized that she was trying to interfere with the plan to blackmail Claudia into dropping the suit. Claudia was right—La Civetta really is built for spying. The walled *pomerino* feels suddenly like one of those glass snow domes and the child shaking it is Cyril.

I turn to the right, hearing a creak that could be my bones coming rustily to life, but is actually the sound of paper rustling in my shawl. I walk through the same gate that Orlando, Mara, Leo, Ned, and Zoe all passed through before, out onto the lemon walk. Under the moonlight the glossy leaves of the lemon trees shine like polished jade and the lemons like globes of yellow quartz. It is as if I've wandered into a world carved out of precious stone—a *pietre dure* landscape. For a second I think the two figures pasted up against the wall farther down the walk are part of the stone inlay. Cupid and Psyche embracing, perhaps, only this Psyche has Zoe Demarchis's raspberry-colored hair and her Cupid is the gangly Ned Silverman. They are so engrossed in each other that they don't notice me, even though the moonlight lights up the path between us. As soon as I move, though, they're bound to hear the crunch of the gravel, and I find myself loath to disturb them, so I step off the path into the soft grass.

To my left is the yew path that leads down to the *teatrino*. I'd planned to go into the rose garden that way, but I hear voices coming from there and glimpse shadowy shapes on the grassy stage. Some of the shapes, I know, are the statues of Shakespearian heroines, while others must be students performing impromptu theatrics, but I find it hard to tell them apart. The absinthe has affected my perception in a way that makes solid objects appear to shimmer with an otherworldly life and live things freeze into stone. When I turn right, stepping over the chain, to take the staircase down into the sunken rose garden, the marble steps seem to undulate like an escalator. I reach out to hold the railing, but the piece of decorative carving I touch turns scaly and skitters away under my hand. *The lizards,* I remember with a shudder. I concentrate on placing each foot carefully on each step, feeling for the wide cracks and loose paving stones and praying that I don't step on a lizard.

On the landing I find the broken statue. She's mostly in shadow, but as I step over her, a splash of moonlight falls on her vacant eye, making it glitter reproachfully. Another streak of moonlight seems to bring a broken hand to life. I feel something graze my ankle, and in leaping away I nearly fall headlong down the next flight of stairs. I manage to catch myself just in time. I creep down the rest of the stairs, clinging to the railing no matter what brushes against my hand, until I reach the tomb of the veiled woman.

In the silver moonlight I can just make out the lines: "So long as men can breathe or eyes can see / So long lives this, and this gives life to thee." I remember that Robin thought Shakespeare's promise to his beloved to immortalize him through art was "an infinite deal of nothing." I'd put Robin's bitterness down to some trifling love spat, as though I didn't know how thoroughly one could have one's heart broken at nineteen.

I look up at the statue of the woman reclining on the tomb. She's wrapped head to toe in diaphanous drapery—a winding sheet or shroud, perhaps. Even her face is covered in the material, her features faintly visible beneath the tightly stretched veil. I walk around the tomb in a slow circle, noticing how the figure seems to be straining against her wraps like a mummy struggling to free herself of her winding sheet. I realize that even though the night is warm, I've wound the black shawl around me just as tightly in an unconscious imitation of the tautness of the statue's drapery. Although I know that the lines of the poem were added later to the tomb, it feels as if they were written for her. "So long lives this, and this gives life to thee." She seems, though dead, to be struggling against the bonds of death as if her lover's promise will indeed bring her back to life. Resurrection by the pen! I'd laugh at the thought if it didn't suddenly chill me to the bone. I've turned Shakespeare's eighteenth sonnet into a Hollywood B zombie movie. I stop in my tracks, dizzy from walking in circles, and hear the question Robin asked me that day in class.

If you lost someone you loved, would reading something about him— or by him—lessen the loss one iota? Wouldn't you trade all the poems and all the plays in all the world for just five minutes with him again?

Wouldn't I?

I grasp my shawl closer to me and hear the crackle of paper. Isn't that what I'm doing right now? Carrying Ginevra de Laura's poems to Bruno as an offering for . . . what? As compensation for what I'm about to tell him about Orlando? As if some old poems could make up for the loss of his son?

I shake my head, trying to shake free of the morbid turn my thoughts have taken. It's Cyril's fault. Cyril the poisoner. He's poured his evil thoughts into my ear while pouring bitter wormwood into my cup. The motion does nothing but make my ears ring—a tinny, jangling sound that's maddening and growing louder by the minute. Just when I think the absinthe has produced auditory delusions along with the visual ones I've been suffering, two figures appear on the other side of the statue accompanied by the sound of bells and laughter.

I really am hallucinating, I think, staring at the diaphanous bell-trimmed wings fluttering around them and their crowns of tangled branches—or else the gardens of La Civetta really do possess fairies and sprites. One of the fairies pirouettes in front of the statue and recites:

"You spotted snakes with double tongue,
Thorny hedgehogs, be not seen,
Newts and blind-worms . . .
Shit, how did the rest go?"

Her companion answers, "Newt and blind-worms do no wrong, / Come not near our fairy queen."

"Yeah," she spins again, wobbling a little, and curtseys in front of the statue.

"Come on, let's find our Puck," the boy says. "Zoe said he went into the garden."

The two drama students evaporate into the shadows without seeing me, taking the path back to the *teatrino*. Hopefully that means Orlando's in that direction and not in the rose garden, which I head into now.

I hadn't noticed when I was here yesterday how close together the rosebushes had grown, so close that they brush against my arms, thorny branches catching at my shawl. I pull it tighter to me, the paper crackling in the lining, and think immediately of the yellow eyes in the painted woods, of the talons waiting to strike. When I peer into the thick bushes, which are speckled with white flecks of moonlight, I can see long hooked thorns gleaming in the silvery light. It's as if the rosebushes had mated with owls and sprouted talons. A breeze moves through the garden, stirring the foliage. The whole garden seems to be breathing, coming to life, a green monster with eyes the color of absinthe and claws wrought of silver. The Green Muse, indeed—not the muse as a winsome girl in floating drapery, but an angry winged harpy riding its prey to ground and then devouring it.

I come to a place where two paths cross and realize I have no idea which way to go. The paths in the rose garden are laid out like a labyrinth. Even in the daylight they're difficult to navigate. I could be wandering in here for hours. Why in the world had I told Bruno that I'd be able to find the fountain? And why had he picked such a difficult spot to meet? If it was to ensure privacy, he picked the wrong night. Several times I hear laughter and whispering—more students, I imagine, frolicking through the garden as if it were their private enchanted wood.

I can't say I blame them. I remember my days and nights here at La Civetta like a gilded dream, a stage set designed especially for my romance with Bruno. I think that up until the end I'd believed that we were characters in a story. I didn't necessarily expect a happy ending, but I thought that whatever the conclusion to our drama, it would be a beautiful work of art—something I'd treasure like the watercolors I brought home and put on my walls or the brightly covered pieces of pottery that now sit on my shelves. Souvenirs. I didn't realize I'd spend the rest of my life missing what I'd lost here.

Which is what I've done, I realize now as I walk in aimless circles on these paths carved out of another woman's longing for her lost beloved. I've never allowed myself to love anyone else. What I'd valued most of all in Mark was the distance he let me keep from him. It's Bruno I've loved all along. I only hope that I can find him in this maze and that he hasn't given up waiting for me.

I walk faster—practically running now—my heart hammering against my hands where I'm clutching the poems to my body. My dowry. Not all the poems and all the plays in all the world, but just these three poems. My breath grows ragged, choking on the heavy air, which is perfumed with roses and marijuana and something else—a richer and more complex aroma. Cuban tobacco.

I pull up short on the path because I can hear voices around the next bend. There's no place to go but into the thorny rosebushes, and I'm not about to ruin my new dress to hide. Why should I? I've done nothing wrong. I hold my ground, but the voices, which I recognize now as Leo Balthasar's and Orlando's, don't come closer.

"You made a deal," Balthasar is saying. "You can't back out of it now."

"But Mrs. Silverman knows what happened and is going to tell—"

"Don't worry about Mrs. Silverman. I've got that situation under control."

Orlando says something I can't make out, and Leo replies, "Just stick to your end of the bargain and find those poems—"

"You'll get the poems," Orlando says. "Robin showed them to me. They're somewhere in the villa. If Robin could find them, I can. I just need a little more time."

"Alas, I'm afraid that the amount of time you have depends on Mrs. Silverman . . ."

I miss the rest of what Balthasar says because they've started walking away from me. I consider following them to hear more, but I'm so disgusted by their machinations that I turn around and head in the opposite direction. I don't want to hear what bribe they'll come up with to buy Mara's silence. I can't imagine it will have to be much. Then I'll be alone claiming that Orlando pushed Robin. I won't be able, though, to say I saw it myself.

I walk more slowly now, no longer in a rush to reach Bruno. It *is* too late, I realize, whether he's waiting for me at the fountain or not. When I tell him what I know about his son and what I intend to do with the information, I'll effectively put an end to any possibility of a future together. The only good thing I could hope for from the encounter is that I might finally admit that it's over and get on with my life.

I've all but given up on ever even finding the fountain when the dark path suddenly opens into a wide bowl filled with light, an open glade into which the moonlight has poured itself as though into a cup, the dry fountain at its center brimming over with silver light. I'll never know whether Bruno would forgive me for betraying his son, though, because the glade is empty. I stand still for a few moments, willing myself to breathe in the silence and accept that whatever future I might have imagined for me and Bruno is as empty as this silver fountain. I've just begun to accept that truth when a voice breaks the silence.

"I thought you'd decided not to come."

The words so mirror my own thoughts that for a moment I think they're another illusion brought on by absinthe and garden magic. Even when I turn and see Bruno standing in the shadows at the edge of the glade, I still think he's a vision I've conjured. Then he steps forward out of the shadows into the moonlight and his face—creased with time and worry—is all too real. I can read in every line of it what he's been through in the last twenty years. What had Claudia said in the church? That he'd spent the last twenty years punishing himself for our affair.

"I got lost," I say, and it seems the most truthful thing I've said in a while.

"I'm sorry, I shouldn't have asked you to meet me here. It was sentimental of me."

"I thought it was so we'd have privacy, but I think half the residents of La Civetta are wandering through the garden tonight."

"Yes," he says, coming closer, "that's why I stepped out of the moonlight while I was waiting for you. I saw Mara Silverman wandering through here a few minutes ago."

"Mara? She's still loose?" I laugh because I've made her sound like a stray cat. "I saw her run out of the *pomerino* earlier, but I didn't think she'd last outside too long. She's afraid of the dark."

"Perhaps I should have spoken to her, but I was afraid of scaring her. She's not too fond of my son."

"You saw that scene in the *pomerino* earlier?"

"Yes, from my apartment window. I can't imagine what she has against Orlando. He's usually very charming."

"It must run in the family," I say and then instantly regret it when Bruno smiles and steps toward me. What am I doing flirting with him when he's just given me the perfect opportunity to explain exactly what Mara has against Orlando?

"I think I know why Mara was so upset with Orlando," I say, drawing my shawl closer around me.

"Are you cold, Rose?" Bruno asks, stepping even closer and putting his arm around my shoulders. "You're shivering."

Although I hadn't thought I was cold, I feel suddenly drawn to his warmth, as though I'd been frozen. His arm tightens around me as he pulls me against his chest, where I rest my cheek. Just for a moment, I think, and then I'll tell him. When I lift my head, though, his lips are there to meet mine, those full, curving lips I've never forgotten that feel like they fit the shape of my mouth. I feel his hand on the nape of my neck as I press my mouth against his, and as I lift my hand up to touch his face, my shawl flutters to the ground, releasing its cargo of old parchment.

"You're molting," he says. I can feel his lips smiling under mine, but he doesn't let me go. It's only after another long kiss that I break away and say, "I'd better get those."

He's faster than me. He kneels down on the ground to retrieve the three pages, holding each one up in the moonlight to read. I sit on the rim of the fountain and look up at the sky.

"Where—"

"Robin gave me the one about the *limonaia,* then someone put the one about the rose petals in my napkin ring last night, and I found the clothing one in the *cassone* in my room. You've never seen any of them?"

He shakes his head. "This one about the *limonaia* is very like the one my mother described to me. She said that Sir Lionel sent it to her."

"If he gave it to her, how could Robin have found it?"

"She didn't keep it. When she told me about it, of course I wanted to see it, but she said she no longer had it . . . was there anything with this poem?"

"A letter—" I begin.

He stands up abruptly. "Do you still have it?" he asks.

"Back in my room," I answer, startled by his urgency. He hadn't shown as much excitement about the poems. "But it's just a note, really, from Robin, saying he left the rest of the poems where he found them and that I should come to La Civetta to see them—"

"Then I am thankful to Robin Weiss," Bruno says, caressing my face, "for bringing you here."

"In the note Robin said he was afraid that having the poems had put him in danger and then . . . then he died—"

"I think he was right," Bruno says. "I don't think you should keep these. Let me keep them for you." He's already rolling them up and slipping them underneath his shirt.

"Bruno," I say laying my hand on his chest, as much to steady myself as to comfort him for what I'm about to tell him, but before I can say anything else we're both startled by a sudden scream coming from the direction of the villa.

"It could be one of the students," Bruno says, "playing one of their games." But then we hear another scream and another. There's nothing playful about them.

"Come on," Bruno says, grabbing my arm, "I know the fastest way back."

Bruno navigates the maze without a moment's hesitation, steering me over broken statuary and holding back thorny branches. When the paths narrow he walks ahead of me, but I keep a hand on his elbow so I won't lose him. We seem to be getting closer to the screams, which have not let up, only hoarsened. When we reach the bottom of the staircase, Bruno stops abruptly and holds his arm up to keep me from coming any farther. I can see around him to the steps, though, and I can't understand what he's keeping me from. They're empty except for scattered rose petals, which gleam darkly in the moonlight.

"I think you should stay here, Rose," he says. "Let me go up first."

I look up the steps and see the broken statue on the landing, only she seems to have changed position. Instead of looking up the steps, she's craned her head over the edge of the landing and is looking down. Ned is crouched by her side, wailing into the night. It's then that I recognize Mara, her neck twisted like a broken branch, and realize that the rose petals on the steps are her blood.

CHAPTER
TWENTY-ONE

 HEN I WAKE UP THE NEXT MORNING, THERE'S A SICKLY GREEN GLOW TO MY room, an absinthe stain that seems to have permeated my eye sockets and seeped into the crevices of my brain. After a few minutes I realize that I'd hung my green dress over one of the half-opened shutters when I came in last night and it's the light filtering through it that's given the room a greenish cast. I stare at the dress, at its tattered hem and dark stains, and feel nausea rise as I remember what happened to ruin it. How I'd pushed back Bruno's protective arm and rushed up the steps to kneel beside Ned, my knees scraping on broken marble, and leaned across Mara to feel for a pulse even though it was clear from the angle of her neck that it was broken. When I brought back my hand, it was covered with blood. Not only had the fall broken her neck, but she had also cracked her skull on the edge of the landing.

I had wiped the blood off on my dress so that Ned wouldn't see it and put my arm around him. When Bruno reached us he knelt down, put his hand on Ned's shoulder, and suggested we all go back up to the villa to call the police, but Ned had recoiled from him.

"It's all your son's fault," Ned had said before dissolving into those awful shrieks again, reminding me horribly of the sounds that Mara had made the night Robin died. I told Bruno to go up to the villa and that I would stay with Ned. A moment after he left it occurred to me to tell him to get Gene down here. I turned away from Ned and Mara to call after Bruno, but when I did I saw that Bruno had paused at the top of the stairs, looking at something on the ground. As I watched he stooped down, picked something up, and put it in his pocket; then he turned and walked quickly toward the villa. I didn't call after him.

When he was gone I told Ned I'd be right back and I went up the stairs, scanning the steps for . . . for I didn't know what. At the top of the steps I noticed that the chain holding the *Pericolosa!* sign had been broken. Had Mara tripped over it and fallen down the stairs? I stared down into the grass where Bruno had picked something up, but there was nothing more there. Then Ned's sobs drew me back down the steps to sit with him until the police came.

The rest of the night was a blur. Gene came and added his lamentations to his son's. Then Cyril and Leo Balthasar appeared, and finally a swarm of Italian policemen who asked questions in a language I suddenly seemed to have forgotten. It was Leo Balthasar who helped Ned to his feet and led him away. I heard Ned again saying something about it being Orlando's fault, but Leo only patted his arm and told him that it was no one's fault, just a horrible accident. I started following them, but when I got to my feet I found that my legs had gone numb from kneeling so long. Frieda Mainbocher caught me.

"Now, we can't have another casualty tonight, can we?" Frieda said briskly. She practically carried me up the stairs and into the villa, up the steps of the rotunda and into my room. She would have undressed me and tucked me into bed if I hadn't told her I was able to do it myself. I don't remember though, taking my dress off and getting into bed. Maybe Frieda did do it for me.

Now I drag myself out of bed and over to the window. I ball the green silk dress up and toss it in the garbage. This disposal of clothing feels so good that I open a drawer, scoop up an armful of clothes, and dump it onto my bed. I'm hauling my suitcase up on the bed when I hear something slither under the door. I turn, half expecting to find dried rose petals drifting across the lintel, but it's a piece of paper.

Basta, I think, kneeling to pick up the paper, enough! I've had enough anonymous notes. But this one, I see right away, is signed. It's from Bruno.

"I have to talk to you today away from the villa. Will you meet me at the State Archives? I need you, Rose."

I sit down on my bed and look at my scattered clothing. I should go on packing and put as much distance as I can between myself and this place. I came thinking I would solve Robin's death, but instead I've caused another one. I don't believe that Mara's death was an accident. I think Orlando pushed her so that she wouldn't tell anyone that he had pushed Robin. If I had gone to the authorities right away with what I knew about Orlando, he'd be in jail now and Mara would be alive. And why hadn't I?

Although I'd allowed myself to be swayed by Mark's reasoning, the real reason was that I wanted to spare Bruno. I wanted to be with him again. And wasn't that really why I came back here, not to avenge Robin's death or find any poems—what did I care for some old poems? I'd given them over quickly enough to Bruno last night.

I look down at Bruno's note. There's no reason on earth why I should go. Last night Bruno had seen something at the top of the steps, which he picked up and put in his pocket. Why would he remove something from the scene of an accident unless it indicated that it wasn't an accident—and who would he be protecting but his son? Wouldn't he do anything to protect his son? There's no point in me telling him about what happened in New York; it's the police I should be telling. And yet, when I try to muster all the evidence I might take to the police— overheard conversations, which everyone will deny, cryptic notes, and old poems—it seems so scant and incoherent that my head spins. The only way anyone will ever believe that Robin didn't kill himself and that

Mara didn't trip down the stairs in the garden because she was over-medicated and hysterical is if Orlando himself confesses, and the only person who might convince him to do that is his father. I can at least try.

I look down at my pretty new Italian clothing and remember how happy Mara had been with each piece I'd picked out. She'd been as excited about my purchases as about her own. I don't realize I'm crying until I see a tear darken a jade green blouse and then I start crying harder because it seems so awful that my only memory of Mara happy is of Mara shopping. I cry the whole time I'm getting dressed, picking out an outfit—the green blouse, the gondola-print skirt—that I think Mara would agree is much too pretty for a trip to the State Archives.

The Archivio di Stato is on the east side of town in a modern building on the Viale Giovine Italia, which follows the line of the old city walls. It's not in an area much frequented by tourists and so I'm fairly sure that once I switch buses in the Piazza della Libertà I'll be able to make my trip without running into anyone from the villa. I'd managed to get out of there this morning without seeing anyone, and it's doubtful that anyone else is going sightseeing today. I'd forgotten, though, that the bus goes by the English Cemetery, a popular site for anglophiles and fans of Elizabeth Barrett Browning, who is buried there, and, as it turns out, the place where Zoe Demarchis heads when things "get really screwy," as she tells me when I find her slumped in a seat by the window reading EBB's long novel in verse, *Aurora Leigh*.

"Ned's just so messed up over this," she tells me when I sit down next to her, "but he won't talk to me because he's guilty we were making out while his mother was falling down those stairs. Like I'm to blame. Anyway, I thought I'd visit Elizabeth's grave. She always helps me put things in perspective."

I would have thought Zoe Demarchis more likely to have turned to the ballad of some punk rock band—something by AFI, for instance, whose T-shirt she's wearing—for solace than to the poetry of a neurasthenic English invalid, but I remind myself that I shouldn't be so quick to make assumptions about people. Beyond the raspberry-colored hair that looks like it's been hacked by a razor blade, the nose ring, the faded AFI T-shirt with its glaring white skull, and the tattered crocheted scarf that is ineffectually hiding several large hickeys on her neck, might well lurk the soul of a poet.

"What happened to Ned's mother is not your fault," I tell her.

"Oh, I know. Everyone's saying it was Orlando's fault."

"They are?"

"Yeah, because Mara caught him with Ned and she freaked out that her son's gay and fell running away. But of course I know that's not true because I was with Ned last night and he's definitely *not* gay." She adjusts her scarf, less to hide the hickeys on her neck than to call attention to them.

"That's what people are saying? Gossip can be mean and move fast," I say. *"Fama volat."*

"Huh?"

"It's from Virgil. Rumor flies. He describes Rumor as a monster covered with eyes and tongues. Why ever would anyone think that Orlando and Ned were gay?"

"Well, because Orlando is. He had this big tempestuous affair that blew over because . . . well, because of me. Robin was bi and we hooked up. Orlando was in a total snit over it. I mean, he came all the way to New York and made a big scene in the park."

I remember the scene I'd watched in Washington Square Park. I'd been sure that Orlando was jealous that Robin had taken Zoe from him, not that Zoe had taken Robin from him. How had I completely misunderstood? It's like I'd watched a foreign movie with the wrong subtitles.

"Anyway," Zoe goes on, "Orlando and I are friends again now. We just made up last night." I recall Zoe and Orlando coming out of the *limonaia* in a fog of pot smoke last night and the scene that followed. Could Zoe be right about Mara lashing out at Orlando because she was afraid that he was corrupting Ned? Had I misread that scene as well?

"Zoe, are you sure about Orlando and Robin?"

"Oh, yeah, Robin told me everything—more than I really wanted to know, to tell you the truth. I couldn't really blame him for liking

Orlando—I mean, he *is* gorgeous—and Robin was so into the whole Dark Lady mystery, which Orlando told him about . . . oh, hey, this is my stop."

She's gotten up and is standing in front of me, holding on to the bar above our heads and swaying with the motion of the bus. "Have a—" I stop myself before telling her to have a good time in the cemetery, but she's already completed the thought for me.

"Oh, I will. I came here like every week last year to visit EBB's grave. She's a big inspiration to me because I had all these horrible allergies and asthma growing up and my parents would hardly even let me leave the house—just like Elizabeth Barrett Browning! But even though she was sickly and her father tried to make her stay at home and wouldn't even let her get married, she ran away with the great love of her life and got to live here in Italy with him until she died, just like I finally convinced my parents that I could go away to college and come to Italy and then I hooked up with Robin and even though that ended so sadly, now I've got Ned. I know this is going to sound stupid, but I've always thought of Elizabeth as the protector of hopeless love affairs or something. Like if you made an offering to her she'd help you out."

The bus comes to an abrupt stop and Zoe half falls into me. I catch a whiff of the fruity shampoo she uses and then she rights herself and gives me an unexpected hug. Before I can react, she's gone. As the bus pulls away, I watch her cross the street and go in through the tall iron gates of the English Cemetery, which rises in a jumble of marble tombs and tall cypresses on its crowded island in the middle of the busy avenue. What an unlikely pilgrim to Elizabeth Barrett Browning's grave site, I think, and yet, I'm sure she's not the first lovelorn teenager to find her way there.

Poor Zoe! If Ned really does connect her to his mother's death, he may not want to have anything else to do with her. Besides, it's likely that Gene will bring him home after this—whisk him into therapy and dose him up on antidepressants until it's time to go to Cornell. Ned will probably think he's obliged to fulfill his dead mother's dream for him of becoming a doctor.

I'm so wrapped up in the Silverman family drama that I nearly miss the stop for the State Archives and I have to scramble to get off the bus in time. As I walk into the clean, well-lit building, I guess why Bruno wanted to meet me here. It's a relief to be away from spying eyes. A relief, too, to be in a place devoid of personal history, since the State Archives were still housed in the Uffizi when I was a student here. I'm enjoying the feeling of anonymity until I take out my Hudson College ID to show the clerk at the reception desk.

"*Bongiorno,* Professoressa Asher," she says, making of my title something royal and pretty. As close to a *principessa* as I'm likely ever to get. She switches easily into English but still gives Bruno's title lovingly in Italian. "Professore Brunelli called to say he would be late, but he asked me to get some materials ready for you. I've brought them to the desk the *professore* always uses."

I wonder what could have held him up as she escorts me through the large *sala di studio* with its row after row of polished wood desks, each desk equipped with a wooden book stand to hold delicate archival materials. Has Orlando come under some suspicion for Mara's death after all? I find myself thinking that if he has, then at least I won't be the one who has to break it to Bruno that his son is involved in a murder. Not a particularly noble thought, I realize.

Bruno's desk is in a small separate room—a mark of preference he must have earned with his considerable charm—under a window facing southwest and overlooking the neighborhood of Santa Croce. I can just make out, over the red-tile rooftops, the white and green Gothic façade of the church of Santa Croce itself. *I always have to have a window wherever I work,* I remember Bruno once saying, *to give my mind space to dream.*

I thank the clerk and sit down at the desk, facing the window, and stare at the dozen or so books and document boxes Bruno has ordered for me. I see that he's requested notarial records for the the last quarter of the sixteenth century. At first the thought of conducting research after what happened to Mara last night seems inconceivable, but after a few minutes I find myself scanning the materials. I quickly notice that Bruno has selected records from notaries who worked in the neighbor-

hood around the Uffizi, a quarter once known as a working-class neighborhood of wool dyers and artisans. When I raise my head and look out
the window, I can see the long twin rooftops of the Uffizi galleries,
which today hold one of the most impressive collections of Renaissance
and Baroque art in the world, but in the late sixteenth century housed
the offices of Florentine government and the workshop of the Medici.
It's possible that Ginevra de Laura and her father lived in this very
neighborhood.

I find myself lifting my head often to look out the window, to give
myself a break from the painstaking work of searching the notarial
records for mention of any de Laura, to rest my eyes on the red rooftops
and the distant hills, to picture what life would have been like for the
daughter of a stonecutter—not just any stonecutter, but a *commettitore*
of fine inlaid marble—and to check the street below for any sign of
Bruno. I can see from here the arrivals and departures of the bus he'd
have to take, and I've soon memorized its schedule, but an hour goes by
without any sign of him. If something really did come up with Orlando,
he might not be able to get away at all. I decide to check one more
record book before giving up on him.

And that's where I find the reference to Pietro de Laura, *commettitore* of *pietre dure,* employed in the workshops of Francesco I de'
Medici. It's a record of a lawsuit, filed on the second of May, 1581,
against the nobleman Lorenzo Barbagianni for the *defloratio* of Pietro's
fourteen-year-old daughter, Ginevra, and a claim for restitution for the
crime committed—either for Barbagianni to marry the girl or for him to
provide a substantial enough dowry to compensate for her nonvirginal
state on the marriage market. I recall Frieda saying last night at dinner
that these were the options for the family of a rape victim, but still it's
shocking to see them in print.

The witnesses to be called in the case were the girl herself, a nun
of the order of Santa Catalina, and one of Barbagianni's servants
who claimed to have cleaned up the blood shed by the distraught girl
as she fled from Barbagianni's bedroom. 'Such an abundance of
blood," I read, "that she left a trail all along the hall and down the steps,

on the floor of the rotunda, and through the *ingresso* where she fled through the front door and then down the dirt road of the cypress *viale* toward the Convent of Santa Catalina where," according to the nun who gave testimony, "she stained the floor of the vestibule with her blood."

Such a lot of blood that it's hard to imagine how the girl was still standing, let alone how she made it all the way down the viale to the Convent of Santa Catalina. It's hard not to wonder whether the accounts of the blood are exaggerated. I'm familiar enough with Renaissance accounts of rape to know that evidence of blood was key to proving that the violated girl was a virgin—as if the rape was somehow a lesser crime if the victim had had sex before. Of course, in Renaissance terms the proof of her virginity was so important because that was the marketable commodity that had been stolen by the rape. Ginevra's father was seeking restitution for that commodity—through either marriage with the perpetrator himself or a sizable dowry so the damaged goods could still be sold to someone else.

I page through the rest of the witness accounts to find Ginevra's testimony. I've just found it when something makes me look up and see Bruno's reflection in the window. I turn around, wondering how long he's been standing behind me.

"You've found something," he says. "I can tell by the look in your eyes." He draws a chair next to mine and leans close to see the record book on the table in front of me. His arm presses against mine and I can feel the heat of his body through the thin cloth of his shirt—as if he ran all the way here from La Civetta. He looks exhausted enough to have run here from a greater distance than that. His face is lined with worry and the shadows under his eyes are deeper than they were yesterday.

"Has something happened?" I ask.

"Orlando has disappeared," he says, "since last night. I went to look for him after we found Mrs. Silverman and I couldn't find him. I've been looking for him all night—so have the police."

"Why do the police want him?"

"You saw that argument he had with Mrs. Silverman earlier in the evening. Well, so did half the guests at the villa. So of course they wanted to speak with him. I'm afraid . . ."

He pauses to mop the sweat from his brow. I put my hand over his. "What are you afraid of?"

"I'm afraid that when Orlando heard about Mara's death, he ran away—because he thought the police would suspect him—just as he did in New York." Bruno shakes his head. "He's never been able to stand anyone being angry with him. Once, when he was five, he broke his grandmother's favorite mixing bowl. He hid for the rest of the day. It was midnight before I found him, hiding in one of the big lemon tree pots in the gardener's shed. He told me he couldn't bear to see Nonna angry at him." A heartbreaking look of fondness passes over Bruno's face, replacing for a fleeting instant his anxiety.

"It makes it look very bad that he's run away," I say.

"Yes, yes, I know, but it's ridiculous. Orlando wouldn't have hurt that woman—even if she was so horrible to him. And you know why she attacked him like that?" he asks me, but before I can answer—before I can say it's because of what happened in New York—he answers his own question. "Because she thought he was corrupting her precious son."

"She thought Orlando was gay . . . um . . . I heard . . ." Bruno sees me struggling and puts me out of my misery.

"Yes, I know my son's gay," he tells me, patting my hand, as if I were the one who needed comfort. "I've known, I think, since he figured it out himself, about three years ago. At first . . . Well, like most parents I suppose I thought it might be a stage that would pass, but then when he was with that boy Robin last year, I saw . . . I saw what my son looked like when he was really in love. How could I wish him not to follow his heart?" He looks at me and then he looks away. "I know too well what comes of denying one's heart."

"And so that's what Mara was angry with Orlando about?" I recall standing with Mara at the film party in New York. Her telling me that she didn't want Ned to go to the Hudson acting program because there were *too many gays*. Then the jealous fit she threw on the balcony—

I had assumed the target of her jealousy was Zoe, but I realize now that Gene had his arm around both young people: Zoe and Robin. What if she were actually jealous of Robin? Had I misread the scene on the balcony just as I had misread the one in the park?

"But it seemed to me that Mrs. Silverman was angry with Leo Balthasar and her husband as well as with Orlando," Bruno says. "I'm sure her husband had far more cause to want her dead than my son, especially if she were interfering with his movie deal. I heard Balthasar say to Mara that she had to be quiet until they had the papers. He must have meant Ginevra de Laura's poems—"

"Bruno, do you really think Gene Silverman would kill his own wife? Or that Leo Balthasar would kill Mara because of some poems?"

"I know—whoever cared that much for poetry, eh?" He attempts a smile, but his face is so ravaged by fatigue that it's only a weak flicker that fades from his face in an instant. "But I think there may be something with the poems—a letter—that might be very valuable. It's something my mother told me about when she described the *limonaia* poem. That's why I wanted to know if there was a letter with the poem when Robin gave it to you."

"There was only the note from Robin," I say. I can see that he's working hard to construct some alternative scenario for Mara's death. All I have to do to topple his shaky edifice is to tell him that Orlando pushed Robin from the balcony—that Mara knew it and was trying to make Gene go to the police, and that's why Orlando killed her—but I find I can't do it right now while he's so obviously frightened for his son. What good would it do while Orlando is missing? It might even encourage Bruno to help Orlando stay hidden. When Orlando shows up there will be time enough for Bruno to learn the extent of his son's crimes. If he wants to spend these last hours in ignorance, trolling through archives and looking for Ginevra de Laura's poems, so be it. I know I'm staying silent for my own reasons as well—to give myself a few more hours with him—but don't I deserve at least that after all these years? "But I have found a record of the rape," I tell him, "and of Pietro's lawsuit against Barbagianni."

"Ah," Bruno says, looking glad for something to distract him, "did he want Barbagianni to marry her?"

"Yes, can you imagine being forced to plead in court to get your attacker to marry you?"

Bruno shrugs. "It was not uncommon. I'd imagine that a wealthy man like Barbagianni would have settled for paying the girl's dowry instead. Is this her testimony?" he asks, nodding at the book.

"Here," I say, sliding the book over so that it's between us. "You read it. My Italian may not be up to the nuances of her testimony."

He gives me a skeptical look. My spoken Italian might be a little rusty, but we both know I don't have any trouble with the written language. If he suspects that I'm afraid of what my voice will reveal of my feelings about Ginevra's case, he doesn't say so.

" 'On the first of May in the year 1581—' " Bruno begins, translating as he reads.

"Less than two weeks after Barbagianni commissioned Pietro de Laura to lay the floor in the dining room of La Civetta," I interject.

"Yes, he didn't wait long. On this day he saw his opportunity. She says, 'I came with my father to the Villa La Civetta to help him in laying a floor in the dining room. On this day he had forgotten one of the knives he needed for cutting the smaller pieces in the design and I volunteered to retrieve the knife from his workshop. Ser Barbagianni insisted that it was not safe or proper for a girl to walk the streets alone and so sent instead a servant to escort my father to his workshop while suggesting to me that I amuse myself by looking at many of the fine paintings in the villa. When he had shown me the paintings in the *sala* downstairs he told me that upstairs in the *camera nuziale* were many fine *spalliere* that told wonderful stories. He knew I was especially fond of stories.' "

"Betrayed by her love of literature," I say.

"Yes," Bruno says, summoning a small smile. "Another Francesca. 'And so I accompanied Ser Barbagianni upstairs to the *camera nuziale,* never suspecting what he had planned for me there. At first he seemed only interested in showing me the paintings. They told the story of a young man who, rejected by his first love, refused all marriage and was forced to witness a scene of savage butchery to learn the price we pay for shunning honorable love. Ser Barbagianni spoke so movingly of the lessons conveyed in the paintings that I never would have suspected that he was planning his own savagery. When he showed me the scene of the banquet where Nastagio degli Onesti's fiancée offers him her unwed body, he asked me what I thought his answer would be. "What any honorable man would answer," I told him. "He will refuse her offer and wait until they are married to consummate their union." "Ah, you have read your Boccaccio," he said, praising me. "But see here, this story has a different ending." Then he lifted a cloth from the wall—a tapestry showing decorous lovers engaged in polite and proper courtship—' "

"That sounds like the tapestry that's in the room now," I interrupt. "But in the inventory it's described as hanging in the rotunda. Barbagianni must have had the new painting done and moved the tapestry to cover it sometime in the first few months after he inherited the villa."

"He probably thought it was a good joke to cover such an obscene picture with a depiction of courtly lovers—and it sounds as if he relished the surprise of revealing it to Ginevra. Certainly she found it shocking: 'Imagine my horror when I saw that beneath this tranquil scene lay a picture of such unspeakable shame that I cannot here describe it, only to say that looking at it seemed to inflame Ser Barbagianni's desire and that he looked to the picture as a justification of what he wanted to do. "That woman should not have offered what she was not willing to give freely," he said, and then he took hold of me from behind and forced me down onto the bed—which I only noticed then had been strewn with fresh rose petals as people are wont to do for a marriage bed. Such a cruel touch, indeed! As if what he planned to do to me was a marriage! Then he pressed himself so heavily against me that my face was pushed into the bedclothes so I could barely breathe, let alone scream. Although I struggled, he lifted my skirts and pushed himself inside of me, causing me great pain and making me bleed. When he was done, I wept so hard and made such a commotion that he threatened to lock me up if I didn't leave off with my lamenting, and when I still didn't stop he picked me up and carried me to a painted chest at the foot of the bed and dropped me into it, closing and sealing the lid so that I was trapped, alone in the dark empty chest.' "

"The stains at the bottom of the *cassone*," I say. "I thought it was water damage—"

"But actually they are from Ginevra's blood," Bruno says, shaking his head. "What a brute! 'I was there so long screaming and trying to claw my way out, that I thought it would be my coffin, but finally one of the servants came and let me out. The servant offered me water with which to wash myself, but instead I ran from the room. I could feel the blood running down my legs and see the trail of blood I left behind me, but I only wanted to get as far away as I could from Ser Barbagianni and the scene of my disgrace. In my confusion I thought of the drops of blood I shed as the rose petals he had strewn upon the bed and I thought that this would be the only marriage bed I ever lay upon now that I was no longer a maid.' "

Bruno stops reading, but he doesn't lift his head from the book. Neither do I. I know he's thinking of that first time we made love in his apartment above the *limonaia*. Of course, it was nothing like what happened between Barbagianni and Ginevra—I had been more than willing—but when I'd gotten up from his bed, a splash of blood had hit the tiled floor and Bruno had been unable to conceal his surprise. He hadn't known it was my first time. *"Poverina,"* he had said, "now you'll have to remember me forever," and I had wept because I'd realized that if I'd have to remember him it meant we weren't always going to be together.

Now I feel something wet fall against my hand. I look up, half expecting to see the red splash of Ginevra's blood, summoned by her words, staining my hand, but it's only Bruno's tears. I put my arm around his back, which trembles with the effort of holding back a sob, and lay my head against his shoulder.

"It's all right," I say, not sure whose loss of love and faith I'm consoling him for—mine, or Ginevra's, or his—and although I'm afraid it's untrue, I tell him that there's still time to make everything all right.

CHAPTER
TWENTY-TWO

IT WASN'T UNTIL YOU WERE GONE THAT I UNDERSTOOD HOW MUCH I HAD LOST through my stupidity," Bruno says when he has wiped his face with his handkerchief.

"You don't have to do this," I tell him, " especially not today. You don't have to explain. We were both . . . foolish. You never promised me more than the present."

He shakes his head. "Only an idiot thinks he can put such limits on love"—he makes chopping motions with his hand on the table as if he were dicing carrots—"this is how much love there will be and this is how long it will last and then—*poof*! It will vanish, leaving only sweet memories and no scars."

"It's not your fault I fell in love with you," I say.

He turns to me, his face washed by his tears into an openness that makes him look both younger and older than when he arrived here thirty minutes ago. "It wasn't you I was speaking about," he says, and then shrugs, trying to retreat back into his worldly persona, only the gesture turns into more of a shiver. "You seem not to have suffered any grievous injury from my folly. I don't presume that you've thought of me all these years—"

"I've done little but," I say, grabbing his hand and pressing it hard. I want to hold on to the naked look I'd seen in his eyes a moment ago; I know I may never have an opportunity to say these things to him again. "I thought the worst part would be at the beginning, that as time passed I would get over you, and for a while I thought I had. I threw myself into graduate school and writing my dissertation and then teaching and more writing. I dated, of course, but you know how graduate school is—there's not a lot of time for that sort of thing and everyone knows they'll be heading in different directions afterward and I knew I'd do better if I was entirely focused on my work—"

"I've read your articles on the sonnet, by the way. They're excellent."

I smile, pleased at the compliment, but I go on, determined to tell him everything today—before it's too late. "I felt at times when I was working—reading, researching, writing—that I had no body, as if I was floating outside of my body and had become only mind. And then six or seven years ago, when I began teaching at Hudson, I started having dreams about you. Not just once in a while, but every night, and they felt . . . well, not like dreams, but like you were actually *visiting* me. When I woke up it felt as if you'd really just been there—" I stop, unable to convey the immediacy of those dreams.

"I know what you mean," he says. "I've dreamt of you as well."

"And then for days after I'd dreamt of you I wouldn't be able to stop thinking about you. I realized then that all those years I had thought I was getting over you, all I had done was *delay* grieving for what I had lost. My subconscious was catching up with the reality of what had happened years before, and the dreams were my way of working you out of my system."

"Like a splinter?" he suggests, a faint smile curving his lips.

"Well, not entirely unlike a splinter. I thought . . . well, that I was simply a slow learner."

"Anything but," he says. "And after dreaming those dreams these last seven years, did it finally work? Did you *work me out of your system,* as you say?"

"I thought so," I say, resolved to be honest. "The dreams became less frequent. I . . . I started seeing someone a few years ago . . ." I hesitate. Despite my resolve to be honest, I don't know whether I should tell him about Mark. It turns out I don't have to.

"President Abrams?" he asks, lifting one eyebrow.

I nod. "How did you know?"

"I didn't think he could despise me so much for the lawsuit alone."

"You're wrong there. I think he cares more about the lawsuit than—" I'd been about to say "than me," but I stop myself. Again, Bruno knows what I'd been about to say.

"Well, then he's an even bigger idiot than I was twenty years ago." He takes my hand in both of his and leans closer to me. "I'd like to think I've gotten a little smarter in the interim."

His lips have just touched mine when a noise from the door alerts us to the fact that we're not alone. The young receptionist who greeted me earlier is standing in the doorway, looking flustered.

"*Scusi,* Professore, but there are some men—police—here to see you downstairs. I asked them to wait—"

I see Bruno turn very pale. "They might have good news about Orlando," I say. "Perhaps they've found him."

Bruno nods and tries to smile, but when he gets up I notice that his hand is trembling. "I'll go with you," I say, starting to get up.

"No." He puts out a hand to keep me in my seat and then, turning to the receptionist, says, "Could you go down and tell the policemen that I will be right down, please?" When she's left, he sits back down and takes both my hands in his. "If they've found Orlando and taken him in for questioning I may be stuck all day at the police headquarters. You should stay here to see if you can find any clue to where Ginevra would have hidden the poems and then go back to the villa. I'll meet

you back there tonight . . . if you would come to my apartment . . . ?"
He leaves the question open and I answer by pressing my mouth onto
his. As I watch him leave I can only hope that by tonight he still wants me.

After another two hours of scouring the record books of Ser Cosimo
Guasconi, I can find no conclusive ending to the de Laura/Barbagianni
lawsuit. In the first court appearance, Barbagianni's lawyer went about
systematically destroying Ginevra's reputation. Witnesses were called
forth who claimed that she was a woman of low character and that she
had bedded several of her father's clients for money. Barbagianni
claimed that she had been the one to suggest going to the second-floor
bedroom and had lured him into bed. Obviously, her intent was to trick
Barbagianni into an ignoble marriage. As for the evidence of the blood,
the servant recanted her testimony, and the nun who had found
Ginevra bleeding at the door of Santa Catalina took an oath of silence
and, when the convent was relocated to an obscure town in the Valdarno, became a hermit. And then Ginevra and her father disappeared.
Ser Guasconi noted on June 1 of 1581 that the de Lauras failed to appear at a hearing and that attempts to locate them at their residence
proved unsuccessful. At the same time, Barbagianni informed the
podestà that he was engaged to be married—to a young woman of the
noble Cecchi family—and argued that the case ought to be dropped.
But the *podestà* decreed that the case should merely be suspended until
such time as Ginevra and her father reappeared before the court "in the
event that Pietro de Laura had been compelled to leave the city to follow his craft abroad."

I wondered where the *podestà* got the idea that Pietro and Ginevra
had gone abroad and whether there was any basis to his supposition. I
find myself wondering whether they could have gone to England. Perhaps Pietro received a commission to create a floor there and he
thought it was a good idea to get out of town for a while. He might have
thought it was a good opportunity to get his daughter out of town while
Barbagianni was spreading rumors about her.

I'm interrupted in these conjectures by the receptionist, Sylvia, coming to tell me that the library is closing in half an hour, early for the *festa,* and that if I want to copy anything she'll be pleased to help me. I ask whether the library has a scanner I could use to transfer material directly into my laptop, and she tells me she has one in her office that I'm welcome to use. As we go down to her office I try to think of a way to ask whether she overheard what the police said to Bruno without implying that she was an eavesdropper, but then she solves my problem for me. "Imagine, I was so silly before. I thought perhaps the *professore* was in trouble with the police!" She laughs at herself as she opens the door to her office. "But it was nothing like that—just a little . . . how do you say? *Una scappata* of his son's."

The word can mean escape, or flight, but I realize from her demeanor this isn't what she intends. "An escapade?"

"*Sì,* a little joke."

"What kind of escapade?" I ask.

"He was using his father's credit card to buy train tickets," she says, shaking her head. "I did the same thing when I was younger because I wanted to go with my boyfriend to ski in the Alps. Stupid, yes, but harmless. I hope his father won't be too angry with him when they find him."

I nod in agreement, but I'm thinking that Orlando wasn't trying to go skiing. He was probably trying to leave the country.

By the time I've finished scanning the records I want into my laptop, it's four o'clock. The bus to the Piazza della Libertà is just pulling out as I come out of the archives and I know, from watching the comings and goings of the bus from the window, that there won't be another for half an hour. I can probably walk to the stop at the English Cemetery and catch up to the bus there.

After consulting my map, I walk west and then north, a route that takes me past the synagogue. Its nineteenth-century Moorish design was generally overlooked in the art and architecture classes I took here, but I had visited it often—if only so I could write home and tell my mother I was still going to temple. Florence's Jewish neighborhood is small compared to Rome's, but I'm happy to see that there's still a kosher restaurant on the Via Farini. I'm less happy to see the elaborate security booth and armed guards installed in front of the synagogue.

I continue walking north alongside a neighborhood park full of speckle-trunked sycamores and children waiting their turns for a ride on the carousel. This area feels more like a regular middle-class neighborhood that you might find in Brooklyn or Queens than an art capital of Europe. One block north of the park I run into a wide avenue and find myself directly across from the English Cemetery. I check the times on the bus stop and see that I've got fifteen minutes until the bus arrives, just enough time for a quick visit to Elizabeth Barrett Browning. Zoe's not the only one whose love affair is in need of a little kindly intervention.

Even on a summer afternoon, the English Cemetery feels gloomy, an effect, I think, of the many cypresses standing like gaunt, black-coated mourners above the graves of displaced foreigners. The graves of these Swiss exiles (despite being known as the *English* Cemetery, it was founded and is still owned today by the Swiss Evangelical Reformed Church), Russian princes, and Anglo-Florentines exude a melancholy mixed of mortality and homesickness, the sadness of being buried in foreign soil.

Elizabeth Barrett Browning's sarcophagus, held aloft by six columns, seems to float above these sorrows, perhaps because the fifteen years she lived here with Robert Browning were a reprieve from the half-life she endured until she fled her father's house. Her presence here in a foreign grave seems more victory than defeat. "I love Florence," she said in her last days. "I cannot leave Florence." And she hadn't.

I notice that someone has left a small bouquet of wildflowers tied with a pink ribbon and wonder whether it's Zoe's gift to the poet. I wish

I had something to leave as an offering, but when I close my eyes I realize that all I've got is the memory of Bruno's lips on mine and a simple wish. *Let it not be too late.* And then, as an afterthought, I silently tell EBB that, after all, I'm the same age now as she was when she met Robert Browning. If she could get off her invalid's couch and defy her draconian father at that late stage, why can't I start over again with *my* poet?

Ginevra, too, I think as I wander farther up the cypress-lined path, must have fled the court-induced marriage her father was trying to coerce out of Lorenzo Barbagianni. Why else would she have disappeared in the middle of her own trial? Perhaps her flight was the reverse of EBB's. Perhaps she *did* go to England and meet the English poet to whom she later addressed the poems I've read. And really, why couldn't it have been Shakespeare? The timing was perfect. Ginevra disappeared from Florence in 1581, a year that the young William Shakespeare was absent from Stratford and unaccounted for. Some scholars—most recently Stephen Greenblatt—believed he was a private tutor in the north of England during that time. If Ginevra's father had received a commission to lay a *pietre dure* floor somewhere nearby . . .

I am so deeply engrossed in this line of conjecture that I trip over a slab of marble embedded in the ground. When I look down at the offending tombstone, I am more than a little shocked to find the name of the poet whose biography I have been happily reinventing: William Shakespeare.

"Well, that can't be," I grumble out loud, "he's buried in Stratford."

I hear laughter come from behind one of the graves—an unnerving sound beneath the gloomy cypresses—but then a gray shape unfolds itself from the marble tombstones. It's an old woman dressed in the same shades of white and gray as the weathered marble: a long homespun gray robe, a soft white cloth tied over her head, and, despite the warmth of the day, a gray and white alpaca poncho woven in Incan patterns. A specter in gray and white that could be the spirit of the cemetery, except that when this woman smiles there's nothing remotely sepulchral about her round, dimpled face and clear blue eyes. They seem to defy both her old age and the gloomy atmosphere of the cemetery.

"My predecessors," she says, wiping her grass-stained hands on her robe as she comes over to stand by me above the gravestone, "and descendants of the poet.'

I look down and read the entire gravestone: "Beatrice Shakespeare and Claude Shakespeare Clench, last *descendentes* of William Shakespeare."

"Descendentes?" I ask.

The nun chuckles. "Italian stonecutters," she explains.

"Were they really the last descendants of William Shakespeare?"

"Well, only in a misogynist sense. There are more descendants; they just don't carry the name. Are you another Shakespeare scholar come to prove Will visited Italy?"

"Another?"

"Yes, there was a lovely American boy who frequently came to this grave site this past fall. I made him come into the library for tea so he wouldn't ride the bus back half frozen, and he told me his ideas about Shakespeare and an Italian poetess who lived in one of the old villas up in the hills. A bit fanciful, I thought, but he read me some lovely poems by the Italian poetess."

"That must have been Robin Weiss," I say, imagining Robin in the thin jackets he wore in winter crouched here at this grave site with the lonely cypresses as his only companions. "I'm sorry to tell you . . . well, he died this spring."

"Oh, no, the poor lamb! Was it drugs? I'm afraid he often smelled of cannabis when he came to visit."

"No, it wasn't drugs. He fell from a balcony at the college where I teach."

The nun's face, which had looked so smooth a moment ago, creases into a maze of lines. I've aged her a good ten years by thoughtlessly blurting out the news of Robin's death. "I'm sorry, I shouldn't have told you."

"No," she says almost sternly, "of course you should have. Now I can pray for his soul. I'm just a little shook . . . Was it . . . ? Did the poor boy take his own life?"

"That's what the police decided—" I stop when I see the nun's chin begin to wobble and dig a tissue out of my pocket. She blows her nose loudly and shakes her head as if trying to shake her tears away.

"I'm sorry," she says. "It's just that I thought the conversations we had were a help to the boy. I could see he was troubled, but if I had thought he was in that much trouble—"

"You mustn't blame yourself," I say, laying my hand on her arm. "I don't think Robin *did* kill himself. I think someone might have pushed him. If it's anyone's fault, it's mine. If I had listened . . ." I stop, startled at how close I am to tears.

The nun's soft hand steals into mine. "Would you like a cup of tea?" she offers. "I think we both could use one."

I'm about to say no—I can see by the angle of the sun slanting through the cypresses that it's growing late, and I'd promised Bruno I'd look for Ginevra's poems—but then I look down at the nun's softly crumpled face and realize I can't possibly run off after dropping such a bombshell.

"Tea would be nice," I say.

We introduce ourselves on the way down to the gatehouse. "Sister Clarissa," she says, "of the Anglican Church." And then, with a sly smile, she adds, "Clarissa Dalloway that was."

I laugh and then feel instantly ashamed to have regained my humor so soon after telling her about Robin. But Sister Clarissa seems pleased at my reaction.

"Yes, I know. My mother was a fan of Virginia Woolf. I've always suspected she married my father so that she could name me after her favorite literary character. If she'd had a suitor named Woolf, I'm certain my name would be Virginia."

We've reached the gatehouse, which contains on one side a little souvenir bookshop. She ushers me into the other side, into a room filled with books. "This is the library," she says, moving a stack of books off a small deal table by the window and plugging in an electric kettle. "I live upstairs, but I find it's cozier to have tea down here. And such interesting people come to visit. So you're a teacher at Hudson College. In English literature?" she asks, offering me a seat.

"Comparative literature," I answer. "My specialty is the Renaissance sonnet—English and Italian."

"Ah, the sonnet. 'What lips my lips have kissed,' " she quotes from Edna St. Vincent Millay, " 'and where, and why, I have forgotten.' "

I'm beginning to learn not to be surprised at Sister Clarissa's unorthodox literary interests, but her next statement does startle me.

"Did Robin's death have anything to do with that boy he loved?"

"You knew about that?" I ask, abashed that even a nun knew that Robin was bisexual while I didn't.

Sister Clarissa smiles. "He talked and talked about William Shakespeare's love for the young man and the Dark Lady of the sonnets, and I surmised after a while that Robin himself was in a similar triangle and that it was tearing him apart."

"He may have been," I allow. "There's this girl at the school now who says that Robin was involved with another boy at the villa last year . . ." I stop, not wanting to give away Orlando's name, but Sister Clarissa is clearly well informed.

"Orlando, wasn't it? *My* favorite Woolf character"—I try not to gape. A nun who's read and admires Woolf's gender-switching adventurer!—"and the girl . . . Zoe Demarchis, isn't it? They were here today."

"They?"

"Orlando and Zoe. They didn't come together. Zoe was here first—" The teakettle whistles and Sister Clarissa's attentions are occupied for several excruciating minutes of tea preparation before she's ready to continue her story. "Oh, yes, what was I saying?"

"Zoe Demarchis came first . . ."

"Yes, she came to put flowers on Elizabeth's grave. She was crying and I wondered if I should go talk to her, but I thought I'd give her a little time to herself. Then Orlando showed up—"

"Did it look like they had planned to meet?" I ask.

"Oh, no, I think not. She looked quite startled to see him, but, now that I think of it, he didn't look surprised to see her." Sister Clarissa's blue eyes narrow, thinking. "No, I'd wager he came to find her. That he knew she'd be here. Zoe always came here last year when she was upset. . . . Has something happened at the villa?" she asks, training her sharp blue eyes on me. While I'd like to spare her the news of another death, I realize I'm not likely to get anything past her.

"Yes, a woman died last night—an American woman." And then, feeling that I owe Mara this much, I add, "She was a friend. She fell down a flight of stairs in the garden, but I'm afraid the police might have reason to think that Orlando pushed her."

"Oh, no, I can't believe that! He's a little wild, perhaps, but I can't believe him capable of that. No, dear," she says, patting my hand, "you must have that part wrong. But, yes, Orlando *was* very upset. Maybe he saw someone else push this woman."

"Why do you say that?"

"Well, I wouldn't want you to think I was eavesdropping, but just like today when I overheard you, I happened to be doing a little bit of weeding near Elizabeth's grave—I like to keep it nice because it's where the tourists head first—"

"Yes, and what did you hear?"

"Orlando was saying that he had to find out where the poems were—the ones Robin had found last year—and that no one would be safe until he did."

"Did it sound as if he were threatening Zoe?"

"I think he was warning her. He kept saying that if she knew something, she should tell him."

"And did she?"

"No. She said—and this I heard quite distinctly—that he was the last person she would tell the whereabouts of the poems."

"And what did Orlando say to that?"

"Oh, dear, this *is* going to sound like a threat, although I didn't think of it as one at the time. I just thought the boy was angry, and of course I didn't know about poor Robin."

"Sister Clarissa," I say, grasping the nun's soft, plump hand. "Please tell me exactly what he said."

"He said that if she didn't tell him where the poems were, she would be in danger—that she was making the same mistake that Robin had made."

CHAPTER
TWENTY-THREE

I CATCH THE BUS OUTSIDE THE CEMETERY, BUT WHEN I GET TO THE PIAZZA DELLA Libertà I learn I've just missed the bus that goes up the hill and because of the *festa* there won't be another one for an hour. I remember, though, that when I was a student I sometimes hiked up the hill with a couple of girls from Cornell who claimed it was the best way to burn off all the pasta we were eating. They set a brisk pace that got us up to the villa in under thirty minutes. Surely I can make it in forty and still beat the bus and hopefully reach Zoe before anything happens to her.

The difference between nineteen and thirty-nine, though, proves to be more than ten minutes. Although I walk a lot in New York, it's all on flat terrain. I'm winded in the first ten minutes and after fifteen the backs of my thighs feel like someone's holding a match to them. Every time I look up, the brick wall that borders the road seems to curve into infinity as if I've entered some Dantesque punishment in which professors who don't listen carefully enough to their students are doomed to tread in an ever-looping circle, their backsides licked by the flames of hell.

When Zoe said to me on the bus this morning that she and Orlando had made up last night, I should have wondered what had prompted the sudden reconciliation. She had also said that Robin told her *everything.* From what Sister Clarissa told me, it's clear that Zoe must know something about where the poems are—or at least that Orlando thinks she does. Sister Clarissa also said that Zoe had left upset and crying and that Orlando had tried to follow her, but then he had stopped at the gate and stayed behind while she boarded the bus. I had asked whether, by any chance, there had been a policeman near the bus, and she hadn't remembered. It seems, though, the most likely explanation of why Orlando hadn't followed her. He could easily have waited, though, and taken the next bus.

By the time I make it to the gates of La Civetta, I've worked myself into a lather of sweat and anxiety. The hollow eyes of the owls carved into the iron gates stare at me accusingly. When I press the buzzer and shout my name into the metal grate, I half expect to be denied entrance, but the gates swing slowly open onto the *viale.*

I don't go down the *viale,* though, but turn instead into the narrow path that leads to the little villa where the students are housed, the original Convent of Santa Catalina before Lorenzo Barbagianni resettled the nuns in the Valdarno. In one chronicle I read, the nun claimed that the move was prompted by the sisters' desire to expand the wool production of the convent, but it occurs to me now that Barbagianni was punishing the order for the testimony of one of its nuns in Ginevra's lawsuit against him. As I approach the heavy wooden doors I think of Ginevra running here, scared and bleeding, seeking refuge. But when the door swings open, instead of a black-robed nun, a gaggle of teenage girls in navel-baring shorts and skimpy T-shirts spills out into the stone-paved courtyard.

"Excuse me," I say raising my voice to catch their attention. "Do any of you know which room is Zoe Demarchis's?"

"The best room, of course," one of the girls answers, rolling her eyes at her friends, "because she was here in the fall and has seniority."

"And she *had* to have a single because of her asthma and food allergies—like a roommate might slip peanuts into her mouth at night."

Poor Zoe, I think, she's obviously not popular with the other students—at least not with the girls. "I see," I say with a level, humorless stare meant to discourage any more criticism. "And what would be the room number?"

"Oh, it doesn't have a number, but you can't miss it. It's at the end of the hall on the second floor. The one with the picture of a woman with a face like a cocker spaniel." The rest of the girls double over in spasms of laughter that crease their bare, taut midriffs, and then they practically run from the courtyard, shrieking that they hear the bus coming.

Whatever would the nuns of Santa Catalina make of them? I wonder as I enter the cool stone foyer and pass the old refectory, which is now used as the student dining room. What would they have made of the strains of Coldplay that drift down the worn stone steps where once the nuns would have chanted hymns as they made their way to chapel? Or the torn-out magazine pictures of bare-chested boys on the doors of what were once convent cells? Teen idols vying with the ceramic saints that remain from the period in the 1960s when the nuns of Santa Catalina were housed here after their convent in the Valdarno was flooded.

No wonder Zoe had complained about being stuck on this stuffy hall. It's hot and airless and smells yeasty—a brew of overactive hormones, greasy snack foods, and Noxema. I easily identify Zoe's door by the postcard of Elizabeth Barrett Browning, who does, I have to admit as I raise my hand to knock on Zoe's door, bear a certain doggy resemblance to some kind of spaniel. When I knock, though, no one answers. I try again, knocking harder in case she's asleep—or worse—until the door next to hers opens and a girl in sweatpants and rumpled T-shirt appears rubbing her eyes.

"She's not here," the girl tells me in a groggy but pleasant voice.

"She got called down to the main villa while she was getting ready for tonight's dress rehearsal. She looked pretty upset."

"Do you know who asked to see her?"

"The message said President Abrams wanted to see her in the archive room. Zoe said she was afraid that something was missing and that she was going to get blamed for it. Which wouldn't be fair"—the girl stops to yawn—"because, Zoe said, all that stuff went missing last year."

"Okay, thanks, sorry I woke you up," I say, heading down the stairs and outside as fast as I can. The *viale* stretches in front of me impossibly long. I wonder whether the trip felt this long to Ginevra de Laura when she ran it in the opposite direction. I tell myself that there's no need to run, that Zoe's safe as long as she's with Mark, but I'm unable to dismiss the sense of urgency that's taken hold of me—a sense that I'm figuring everything out a step too late. I should have questioned Zoe more about the documents Robin sorted through last year and not taken her word when she said they didn't find anything in the archives and that Robin never told her where he found the poems. Clearly Orlando thinks she knows something, and now so does Mark.

When I reach the villa I go straight into the library and start up the spiral staircase, but a sound from below brings me back down into the library. It's a plaintive, half-strangled weeping, as if someone were trying very hard not to cry but couldn't stop himself. The sound is coming from the club chair in the shadowy corner where I found Cyril last night, but when I get close enough I see it's not Cyril; it's Gene. He's got Cyril's silver decanter of absinthe, though, and one of Leo Balthasar's Cuban cigars.

"Gene," I say, "I'm so sorry about Mara." He looks up so that the light from the *pomerino* falls on his face, and I'm shocked at the damage grief has done there. Although I never shared his infatuated students' regard for Gene's looks (he always seemed a little *too* pretty to me), I'd recognized in an abstract way that he was a handsome man—toothy and blond, tan even in winter—but now his face looks like a piece of paper that's been crumpled, his eyes bloodshot and puffy, and his nose as pink as a rabbit's. He holds up a silver tumbler full of cloudy liquid. I think he is going to make a toast to Mara, but instead he makes one to me. "Here's to kindhearted Rose. You were the only one of the faculty who gave Mara the time of day." He swallows the entire glass in one gulp. "Oh, *ex-scuthe* my bad manners," he slurs. "You don't have a drink. Here, let me pour you one. This stuff will knock the socks off you."

"No, thanks, Gene, I had some last night. I think it has an unusually high alcohol content. Perhaps you should go easy—"

"Yeah, trust Cyril to get the real thing. Everything's got to be authentic. Can't do a movie about Shakespeare without finding the real Dark Lady."

"Gene, have the police come to any conclusions about Mara's death?"

"Accident," Gene says, refilling his glass. "She fell down the steps. All the medication she was on upset her balance. Of course, if Cyril had maintained the garden the way he should . . . Hey, you know, I could probably sue. Why not? Everybody else does! Oh, but no," Gene slaps his head in an exaggerated display of forgetfulness, "I just remem-membered, I can't make Cyril unhappy because then we can't make our film here, and I can't make Leo Balthasar unhappy or I won't get my producer's credit, and I can't make President Abrams unhappy or I'll lose my fucking job—"

"Gene," I say, kneeling directly in front of him so he has to look at me. "Mara was going to make a number of people unhappy when she told what really happened on the balcony. Do you really believe it was an accident that she fell?"

Gene places a finger to his lips and makes a shushing sound. Then he points up with his index finger. "The walls have ears," he says. I look up and meet the yellow gaze of the painted owl on the ceiling, but I realize that Gene's talking about Mark, who's supposed to be upstairs in the archive room with Zoe.

"I'm going to talk to Mark," I tell Gene. "If someone pushed Mara—" But Gene's eyes have acquired the same cloudy film as the absinthe in his cup, and I can tell he's not listening.

"It was a regrettable accident," he says loudly, "most regrettable. Poor Mara never had any luck. She was always saying so herself. After all, she could have married the rich orthodontist her parents picked out for her, but instead"—Gene smiles up at me to show me he's in on the joke—"instead she got stuck with me."

I go up the spiral staircase, the metal steps twanging under my feet. I figure a loud approach will give Mark and Zoe a warning that I'm on my way, but when I come up into the archive room they don't look as if they were aware of my approach. Zoe, attired in her Juliet costume for tonight's dress rehearsal, is seated in the desk chair by the window, her head—her own ragged pink hair she hasn't donned her Juliet wig yet—buried in her hands, weeping. Mark is standing in front of her, his back to me, staring at the ceiling. They could be a tableau from *Romeo and Juliet,* the part where Juliet's father threatens to disown her if she won't marry the man he's chosen for her.

This is exactly the kind of scene I didn't want to come in on. I know that Mark's manner with students can often be intimidating. He says that I'm too easy on them and that they benefit from a firm authority figure, but I've always thought he could be a little rough. It's too late to back out now, though, so I clear my throat and step forward.

"President Abrams," I say, "can I be of any help? Zoe was working for me here in the archives, so if there's any problem—" I stop because I've just noticed that the room is in total disarray. All the portfolios that Zoe had so neatly stacked and dusted are lying in a disordered heap on the floor; some of the pages have even come loose and slipped out of their bindings. They look as if someone had taken each one by the binding and shook hard.

Mark turns to me, startled and, for just a moment, furious. I'm so stunned by his expression that I freeze on the spot, but then the anger is replaced by an emotion I can't quite read. I could almost swear that it's *amusement.*

"Ah, Dr. Asher, perhaps you can be of assistance. It turns out that

Miss Demarchis was an accomplice in stealing some valuable documents from the villa last year—"

"But I told you I didn't take them—"

"No," Mark booms the single syllable out so loudly that I hear the stairs behind me vibrate and Zoe gulps back whatever she was going to say next, "but Robin showed you the documents he was stealing and you didn't tell anyone. That makes you an accomplice."

"But it wasn't a poem. Everybody's been asking about poems—"

Mark whips his right hand up in the air between them and Zoe flinches as though he were going to slap her. Of course he's only motioning for her to be quiet, but for a moment I, too, had flinched.

"That's enough," he says. "We won't talk about this any longer until you can tell me where Robin found the papers."

Zoe seems about to say something else but thinks better of it when she looks up at Mark. I've never seen him look this enraged.

"In the meantime," Mark says, taking his voice down to a calmer register, "about the play you're in—"

"Please, President Abrams, I've worked so hard on this part and Ned's making such an effort to go on with the performance even after what's happened. He says he wants to do it as a tribute for his mother. How can I not be there for him?"

Mark sighs and holds up his hands to me in a gesture of defeat that's supposed to be a softening. I've seen him do this before, though, seen him become conciliatory and gentle at the end of a grueling interview, and it occurs to me now that he does it on purpose. That after wearing down the student he suddenly acts warmly so that the student will feel he's really a friend. It's at such moments, he's told me himself, that he's most likely to get a confession. It's a tactic not unlike the methods of medieval inquisitors.

"Of course you should go ahead with tonight's dress rehearsal. Especially since Ned is making such a valiant effort to go on. You're a fine Juliet to his Romeo. I've watched you both rehearse." Zoe practically beams at this crumb of praise. "That is, if you feel up to it."

"Oh, yes, President Abrams, I'll be fine. I'll just take a Benadryl for the hives," she says, wiping her face, which is, I notice now, pocked with red spots.

"Some cool water on your face should do the trick," Mark says. "Benadryl will just make you sleepy. And we wouldn't want Juliet falling asleep before the fourth act when she takes the friar's sleeping potion, would we?"

Zoe shakes her head and smiles, getting unsteadily to her feet. Mark escorts her to the door, his hand on her elbow. She turns toward me in the doorway and starts to say something, but Mark presses a finger to his lips and says, "You'd better rest your voice now." The gesture reminds me uncomfortably of the one Gene made a moment ago in the library.

When Zoe is gone, Mark turns to me in the open doorway, shaking his head. "This job can really get to you after a while. You want to do your best by these kids, but then they go and do such stupid things." He moves to a shelf and begins reordering the books there. "Here they have an opportunity to live in an authentic Renaissance villa in one of the most beautiful cities in the world, and they abuse the privilege by stealing private papers."

"How did you guess Zoe had seen the poems?" I ask.

"Oh, I guessed all along, but last night I happened to catch her and Orlando smoking pot in the *limonaia,* and so I sent for her today and told her that on top of the pot-smoking I'd noticed that some things were missing from the archives where she worked and that if I thought she'd committed two infractions I'd have to seriously consider expelling her."

"So basically you intimidated her into confessing that Robin showed her some of the poems last year."

Mark looks up from the jumble of portfolios he's stacking back on the lower shelves. I wonder whether he really thought he'd find something here among the nuns' chronicles of Santa Catalina or he just wanted Zoe to witness the effects of his search. I realize that I've come to distrust every word Mark says and every gesture he makes.

"That's an awfully harsh way of putting it, Rose. It's not easy being an administrator, you know. I don't have the luxury of befriending my students. And in the long run you're not really doing them any favors."

"So we're back to me and Robin again. Are you suggesting, Mark, that I could have prevented Robin from killing himself? But, oh, wait, Robin didn't kill himself, did he? You and I both know that Orlando pushed him. I thought you were going to tell the police. Did you mention it to them when they came to investigate Mara's death? It seems unlikely that they would be dismissing her death as an accident if you had."

"I'm surprised you're so anxious to get your lover's son convicted of murder, Rose. I can't imagine it will make for a happy reunion with him."

I open my mouth to deny that Bruno's my lover, but then I recognize the implicit threat behind Mark's words. If I persist in insisting he tell the police what really happened in New York, he'll tell Bruno that I was the one to seal his son's fate.

"So that's it? You've made another deal with Claudia? I imagine with this second potential charge you were able to get her to dismiss the lawsuit entirely. Mara's death was pretty convenient for you, wasn't it?"

"What a truly awful thing to say, Rose. If you want to manufacture a fight so you won't feel bad about leaving me for your Italian lover— your *still-married* Italian lover—fine. But accusing me of having something to do with that poor woman's death—"

"I didn't—" I start to object that I hadn't meant that Mark had caused her death, but then I remember what he just said about catching Orlando and Zoe smoking pot in the *limonaia* last night. Had Mark evicted them from the *limonaia* into the *pomerino* so that Orlando would run into Mara there? Mark must guess at the thoughts forming in my head; I can see him clenching his jaw, something he does when he's very angry.

"I'm sorry, Mark, I didn't mean to imply you had anything to do with Mara's death. And I'm sorry things had to end like this."

"So it *is* over between us? Do you really think Brunelli is going to divorce Claudia *now*? Because you're wrong about her agreeing to settle for free. She's just come into quite a bit of money, and unlike the money that would have come from the lawsuit, this is solely in her name. Bruno won't get a cent of it if they divorce."

"What happens between me and Bruno now isn't important," I say. "I think things were over between us long before this."

Mark nods, lowering his head to the stacks of portfolios on the table so that I can't see the expression on his face. When he lifts it up I see that he's assumed a mask of concern. "I do wish you the best, Rose, no matter what happens between you and Brunelli. The man's not all bad. He certainly looked pleased to be reunited with his son just a little while ago."

"Orlando's back?"

"Oh, yes, there was a little misunderstanding about a credit card, but all seems to be forgiven. He's spoken with the police and, as it turns out, after I chased him and Zoe out of the *limonaia* he skulked back to his mother's apartment in town and spent the rest of the night there. So you see, he couldn't have had anything to do with poor Mara's slip down the steps."

"But that's impossible. I saw him in the garden just before we found Mara."

"Really? I think you're mistaken, Rose. Were you, perhaps, drinking Cyril's absinthe last night? You know that stuff can make you see things."

"But you can't just let Orlando back here. He was harassing Zoe Demarchis earlier at the English Cemetery."

Mark raises an eyebrow at me. He looks as if I've lost my senses. "I just told Zoe that he's back in the play tonight and she didn't seem at all upset about it. And she has a big scene with him. He plays the friar."

CHAPTER
TWENTY-FOUR

HEN I LEAVE MARK, I CROSS THE HALL TO MY ROOM, BUT ONCE THERE I stand by the window, looking out at the garden, irresolute. What now? Everyone's made some peace with the situation except me. Claudia and Orlando have their settlement, Bruno has Orlando back, Mark has his villa for Hudson, Zoe has her part in tonight's play, Cyril has his "legacy" for posterity, Leo Balthasar will have his film, and even poor drunk and grieving Gene still has his producer's credit and one percent of the revenue. I feel like the bad fairy who hasn't been invited to the party—only I don't have any power to cast a vindictive spell over the festivities.

And would I really want to? The sound of laughter from outside draws me out onto the balcony. The simmering heat has dissolved into the cool of evening. The roses and lemon trees are releasing their scent into the air like a secret they've been holding to themselves all day. The only jarring note in the scene is the police tape around the top of the stairs to the sunken rose garden. I look away from that reminder of Mara's fall, toward the *teatrino,* where I can see stagehands assembling a makeshift balcony for tonight's dress rehearsal. A few of the students and teachers have already laid out blankets on the terraced slope above the grassy stage. Frieda and Lydia are there with a group of students picnicking on the grass, passing around loaves of bread and salami and cheeses and bottles of wine and mineral water. Laughter rises from the grassy bowl, as effervescent as the scent of flowers and the delicate shade of lavender in the sky. Who am I to disrupt this scene? Why shouldn't I be a part of it? Why can't I take my piece of this happiness? I go back inside and open my drawers to pick out something to wear, but the clothes remind me of Mara. Besides, I realize closing the drawer, I'm too sweaty to get dressed. I decide to take a bath first.

I run a hot bath and pour some of the *aqua di rosa* into the water before sinking into it. I rest my head on the cool rim of the tub and close my eyes. Immediately I hear Mark's mocking question: *Do you really think Brunelli is going to divorce Claudia* now? I slide farther down until the water covers my head and drowns out every sound, but it can't drown out the memory of my own answer to Mark. *What happens between me and Bruno now isn't important.* Had I really meant that? Wasn't I playing as much of a part as everyone else here at La Civetta? When it came down to it, I was as willing as the rest of them to take my "settlement" in exchange for keeping quiet about Robin's and Mara's deaths. All I really want—all I *ever* wanted—from coming here is Bruno.

I stay in the tub until the water grows cold and longer, not caring that my skin shrivels and puckers and that the dinner hour comes and passes. As soon as I get out of this tub I'll have to dress and decide what I'm going to do. If I go to Bruno, how can I not tell him what I know about Orlando? But if I tell him, I know that he'll never forgive me for being the one to tell him the truth about his son. Our last chance to be together will be lost.

If I were a girl in a myth, I'd melt into this water and slip down the

pipes. I'd become a spirit made of vapor, haunting the ancient plumbing and circling the drains of La Civetta. But since I'm not a girl in a
myth, I eventually get out of the tub and towel myself off. I get dressed
in the black dress I wore the first night, its long, straight lines seeming
appropriately penitential now. I walk out onto my balcony and see that
there are lights on in the *teatrino.* The grassy arena is full—everyone
must be there. I could, I realize, pack my bags and walk down the *viale*
to the gates, and no one would see me go. I could call a cab from the
tabaccheria and go to the airport and wait for the next available flight. I
could run away; it's what I did last time.

So deeply immersed am I in this picture of leave-taking that when I
hear a voice rising out of the garden say, "Wilt thou be gone?" I half
think it is talking to me. But then I recognize it as Zoe Demarchis's
voice and the lines are Juliet's reluctant farewell to Romeo after their
wedding night.

> *Wilt thou be gone? It is not yet near day:*
> *It was the nightingale, and not the lark,*
> *That pierced the fearful hollow of thine ear;*
> *Nightly she sings on yond pomegranate tree.*
> *Believe me, love, it was the nightingale.*

I'm impressed with how Zoe's pulled herself together since I saw her in
the archives, but I'm even more surprised when I hear Romeo reply in
Ned's surprisingly strong contralto.

> *It was the lark, the herald of the morn,*
> *No nightingale. Look, love, what envious streaks*
> *Do lace the severing clouds in yonder east.*
> *Night's candles are burnt out, and jocund day*
> *Stands tiptoe on the misty mountain tops.*
> *I must be gone and live, or stay and die.*

His voice has none of his usual hesitant and apologetic air. Somehow he
has taken his grief over his mother's death and harnessed it into an in-

strument of great power. When Juliet answers him she sounds as if she knows that her pleas will be ineffective.

> *Yond light is not daylight. I know it, I.*
> *It is some meteor that the sun exhales*
> *To be to thee this night a torch-bearer*
> *And light thee on thy way to Mantua.*
> *Therefore stay yet. Thou needst not to be gone.*

I can just make out the figures of Ned and Zoe on the makeshift balcony. Ned is perched on its very edge, one leg thrown over the railing but still clinging to Zoe, torn by the need to be gone and his desire to stay. I can't help thinking about the last scene I saw played out on a balcony and it's hard not to think about Robin as Ned says his next lines.

> *Let me be ta'en; let me be put to death;*
> *I am content, so thou wilt have it so.*
> *I'll say yon gray is not the morning's eye;*
> *'Tis but the pale reflex of Cynthia's brow.*
> *Nor that is not the lark whose notes do beat*
> *The vaulty heaven so high above our heads.*
> *I have more care to stay than will to go.*
> *Come, death, and welcome! Juliet wills it so.*

I imagine that everyone in the audience is thinking of Robin—at least those who still think he killed himself—but the line that has spoken to me is "I have more care to stay than will to go." I can't possibly leave La Civetta without seeing Bruno first—even if it means that by telling him the truth about Orlando I'll lose him forever. I hurry down the stairs of the rotunda, through the library—empty but for the reek of bitter wormwood and the painted yellow eyes of the owl on the ceiling—and across the *pomerino*, out onto the lemon walk. I can see the lit stage of the *teatrino* from here and the groups of teachers and students sitting on the lawn watching Zoe and Ned finish their scene. I scan the audience for Bruno, but I don't see him anywhere. Then I look up and see a light on in his apartment above the *limonaia*. I wonder why he wouldn't be at the rehearsal to watch Orlando perform. Has he gotten a hint of something wrong with Orlando's story?

As I arrive at the door to Bruno's apartment, I hear Juliet's premonition of Romeo's death—

O God! I have an ill-divining soul!
Methinks I see thee, now thou art so low,
As one dead in the bottom of a tomb.
Either my eyesight fails or thou look'st pale.

And then the door opens and Bruno is there. Although our positions are the reverse of the actors' on the stage—he is above me and I am below—I hear Juliet's fateful premonition echoing in my ears. I feel as if Bruno is already a long way off from me and that I am looking at him for the last time. My expression must give away what I'm thinking, because he says, "Rose why do you look at me like that? You look—what is that quaint English saying? You look as if you've seen a ghost."

"Bruno, there's something I have to tell you—"

"Come in," he says, pulling me in through the doorway. "Why, you're cold—and on such a warm night!"

It's true, I'm shaking. He leads me upstairs and gets a bottle of brandy and two glasses from his kitchen. He pours some in each glass and sits down next to me on the couch. I take a small sip of the brandy and look around me, stunned at how little the apartment has changed in twenty years. The same terra-cotta floors and faded rugs and couches, the same view of the hills of Valdarno, over which the moon is just beginning to rise.

"I hear Orlando came back," I say, trying to think of a way to begin.

"Yes, I was very relieved," he says, taking a long sip of the brandy. I notice that he won't look at me.

"And I heard that Claudia said he was with her in town last night."

"Yes, that's what they've told the police, and the police seem inclined to believe them." He gets up and goes in the kitchen and comes back with a bottle of mineral water. He adds some to his brandy and asks whether I'd like some in mine, but I grab his arm until he puts the bottle down and looks at me.

"You know it's not true, don't you?" I ask. "Orlando wasn't with Claudia last night."

He sighs and sits back down on the couch beside me and bows his head. I move closer and snake my hand behind his neck, massaging the tight muscles there.

"You knew, didn't you? You found something at the top of the stairs last night."

He lifts his head and looks at me, then caresses the side of my face with the back of his hand—a gesture so familiar I feel an ache deep inside me, as if he'd touched a spot that had been numb for so long that when the nerves reawaken they sting. I reach up and grab his hand and allow myself to hope. If Bruno's figured it out on his own, then I won't have to be the one to ruin his world. All I have to do is ask him what he thinks the right thing to do is.

He brings my hand to his lips and kisses it. "You always see everything, don't you, Rose?"

"Well, not everything," I say, and then instantly regret it because I'm referring to the past—to me not knowing that he was sleeping with Claudia all along. But Bruno doesn't seem to notice. He gets up and brings back a box from a side table and puts it down between us. It's a little wooden chest, painted blue with gilt fleurs-de-lis, that I instantly recognize as the one I bought for him on the Ponte Vecchio for Christmas the year I was here. I remember realizing on my way back to the villa what a silly gift it was, that it was the sort of souvenir of Florence that tourists bought to bring home, not something a native Florentine would keep. I'm touched to see that he *has* kept it.

He opens the box. On top of a stack of letters is a gold necklace. He lifts it up so I can see the medallion dangling from its broken chain. It's a medal of Saint Catherine—the same one that Claudia has always worn.

"This is what I found at the top of the stairs last night. I was afraid immediately that Claudia had something to do with poor Mrs. Silverman's fall. She's very protective of Orlando."

"Enough to kill Mara?" I ask, incredulous. Bruno doesn't realize, though, that I'm shocked because I believe it was Orlando, not Claudia, who killed Mara.

"There's something else going on, I think. Claudia's been hard at work making some kind of deal with your President Abrams to settle the lawsuit out of court, and something Mrs. Silverman knew was threatening that. At any rate, I don't believe Claudia set out to deliberately kill the woman, but that they fought and they must have struggled—why else would the necklace break?—and then Mrs. Silverman fell down the steps. Claudia must have left the villa immediately so she could say that she was in town, and then she made Orlando say he was with her. I'm afraid that Orlando would do anything she asked. . . . He always has."

Bruno lets the necklace drop into the box, and then he closes the lid. I've been trying to imagine the scene that Bruno's described, and I find that I can—only too well. Mara and Claudia were both emotional women, fiercely devoted to their sons. And I know one thing that Bruno doesn't—that Mara might have told Claudia that she was going to openly accuse Orlando of killing Robin.

, "You have to tell the police," I say.

Bruno sighs. "*Cara,* I've already promised I won't. I've made my own little deal—"

No!" I say, louder than I'd meant to, "no more deals! Can't you see? All the secrets just add up to more deaths. Mara might not have been the nicest woman in the world—she might have seemed like a silly woman—but she didn't deserve to die." In my anger I ball my hands into fists and pound my legs with them. Bruno grabs both my hands and holds them in his. I feel myself weakening at his touch, but I look at him and ask, "What could she possibly give you that's worth lying for?"

"She's agreed to give me a divorce," he says, "finally, after all these years."

I don't say anything for a moment. In the silence Zoe's voice from the *teatrino*—proclaims, "Love give me strength, and strength shall help afford." "Oh, Bruno," I say, "I think that's what she was planning all along. Mark Abrams says she's settled the lawsuit out of court for a lot of money—"

"I know all that," he says, pulling me closer to him, drawing his arms around my shoulders. "It doesn't matter. All that matters is we can be together finally. Don't you think we've had to wait long enough?"

It's the one question he's asked that I know the answer to. I answer it by pressing my mouth against his and then pressing my whole body against his. He responds just as eagerly, pushing me back on the couch until I'm stretched out beneath him and I can feel every inch of his body along mine, can feel his knee slip in between my legs and nudge them open and feel him press himself against me until I think I'll faint with wanting him. Then he lifts himself up and kneels between my legs, and I sit up, wrapping my legs around his waist and arching my hips up even as I unbutton his shirt and unhook his slacks. I'm afraid of losing contact with him for one second. Afraid that if we move ten inches apart to take our clothes off, one of us will say something that will break the spell of this moment. Above the sound of our breathing I catch a single line from the *teatrino* uttered in Zoe Demarchis's piercingly clear voice—"Farewell! God knows when we shall meet again"—and it only fuels my urgency.

Bruno peels my dress off and I'm half afraid that in the split second of darkness as it passes over my head I'll lose him—that he'll realize that this frenzy to have him inside me comes not just from all the years we've been apart but from all the years apart I know may still lie ahead of us. Because I know, even as I slip down beneath him again and allow myself one long lingering stroke of the smooth dark hairs on his chest (some of those dark hairs going gray now!) before I arch up to meet his own eager thrusts, that this could be our only time together. I can keep the voices in my head—the knowledge of what I'll have to do—at bay only so long, but I silence them now. I enter the rhythm of his body, the steady measure of his hips moving against mine—a meter that will come, like the fourteen lines of the sonnet, to its resolution all too soon, but that also, like a sonnet, feels like it contains something of eternity within it. I can see it in his eyes, in the way he holds my gaze as we both come, that he's seeing the same thing. *All any lovers have is this,* he told me in the garden the first day we kissed. *This moment.* And for this moment, it feels like enough.

Our moment of eternity together has lasted only as long as it's taken Juliet to deliver her soliloquy over the bottle of sleeping potion given her by Friar Lawrence. I hear, as Bruno shifts his weight to lie beside me, her plaintive cry. "Romeo, Romeo, Romeo! Here's drink—I drink to thee."

Bruno strokes my damp hair out of my face and blows on my collarbone to cool the sweat that's pooled there. I touch the furrow that time has carved between his eyebrows and brush my fingertips along his brow. I wish at this moment that we could both swallow Friar Lawrence's magic sleeping draught and sleep here, our naked limbs entwined together on the couch, forever. At least, I think, I can wait until the morning before telling him why Claudia might have murdered Mara. Who could begrudge me one night?

But I'm not to have it. He notices first that the commotion rising from the *teatrino* is not according to script.

"Something's happened," he says, sitting up and reaching for his shirt.

"Come on, Zoe!" I hear someone shout. "That's enough." And another voice, shrill and hysterical: "She's not breathing—someone call an ambulance!"

Bruno's already in his slacks and I'm struggling to get my damp dress over my head. "She has allergies," I say. "Do you have a first aid kit? Something with epinephrine in it?"

He rushes to the kitchen and I hear a clatter of metal pans. "I keep something for scorpion bites . . . yes, here." And then he's running across the room and down the stairs. I follow, barefoot. The gravel of the lemon walk bites into my feet, but then I'm on the soft grass running full tilt down the slope where a circle of actors and spectators has closed around Zoe. For a moment I feel as if I'm flying directly above the scene, suspended in time as well as space. I even have time to notice how beautifully *blocked* the scene is, the actresses with their Renaissance gowns spread out around them as they kneel beside Zoe, and the eighteenth-century statues of Shakespearian heroines in an outer ring behind them, like pale ghosts of the characters onstage. It all feels too quiet as I burst onto the stage—Fortinbras arrived at the Danish castle only to find the kingdom peopled by corpses.

There's only one corpse, though, a Juliet who's died before the fifth act, the only color in her face a strand of bright pink hair that's escaped from her headdress.

CHAPTER
TWENTY-FIVE

I 'M SO SURE THAT ZOE IS DEAD THAT I'M SURPRISED TO SEE BRUNO INJECTING the epinephrine into her arm and Daisy Wallace administering CPR. I'm amazed, too, at the strength with which frail, thin Daisy pummels Zoe's chest—and the ardor. I have the ungenerous thought that she is thinking of lawsuits, but when Zoe stirs and Daisy bursts into tears I rebuke myself for ever disliking the lawyer.

Bruno carries Zoe up to the villa to await the paramedics, and Daisy and I follow. By the time Bruno settles Zoe on the love seat in the library, Zoe has latched onto Bruno like a baby chick imprinted on the first face it sees upon hatching. When the paramedics arrive, she begs him to go with her to the hospital. He glances at me and I nod my agreement. Someone trustworthy has to stay with her, I think. At least neither Orlando nor Claudia would be able to do anything to her with Bruno there.

The thought of someone trying to hurt Zoe reminds me of the vial that was used to hold the sleeping potion in the play. Someone must have put something in it—with Zoe's allergies, all it would have taken was some ground-up peanuts or peanut oil. When Bruno and Zoe have left for the hospital, I go back down to the *teatrino* and look for the vial on the grassy stage, but there's nothing there. I ask some of the stage-hands who are dismantling Juliet's balcony whether they've seen it, but they tell me they haven't. "Usually the props manager collects all that stuff at the end of the play," a girl with flame-red pigtails and a tattoo of a fork on her bicep tells me, "but who knows if she did with all the chaos. Is Zoe going to be okay?"

"I think so. Do you know who handled the vial before the play?"

"We keep the props in a shed behind the greenhouse," she says, pointing toward the *limonaia,* "which is used for costume changes, too. But no one watches that stuff. Cindy—that's the props manager—is probably there now."

I thank the redhead and before I go I give in to an idle urge and ask, "Why a fork?"

She shrugs. "I just like forks," she tells me. "I collect them."

"Oh, okay." I'm halfway up the hill before I think of a more perti-nent question. "Why are you taking down the balcony? Isn't the perfor-mance tomorrow?"

"It's supposed to rain," she says, "or at least President Abrams said it's going to, so we're having the performance in the chapel at the little villa. It's not as cool as being outdoors like this, but it's kind of moody. It will be great for the final tomb scene. I only hope Zoe's well enough to be in it. She's a great Juliet. When she drank the potion she looked like she really thought it might kill her—who knew it almost would?"

I shiver, thinking I may never be able to watch the final acts of *Romeo and Juliet* again. I find Cindy—a bleached blonde with a nose ring—in the garden shed counting swords and stacking lanterns on a shelf above a row of the huge Impruneta earthenware pots used for the lemon trees. I wonder whether this is where Orlando hid as a child. I ask Cindy whether she had the vial before the rehearsal.

"I had it with me until act four, scene one, when I gave it to Friar Lawrence," she tells me.

"Who was played by Orlando," I say.

"Yeah. I had filled it with water myself before the play—bottled water. I can't imagine how anything could have gotten into it that Zoe was allergic to."

"And you don't know where the vial is now?"

She shakes her head. "No, I remember Zoe dropped it to the ground after she drank. That's why we used a silver vial, so it wouldn't break. I didn't see it on the ground after everyone cleared the stage."

I thank her and start back to the villa, crossing through the *pomerino* and to the library. I can't resist, though, a wistful backward glance at Bruno's apartment, but the window is dark now. I turn away from it, remembering how it had been the lit window that had earlier drawn me to Bruno's apartment . . . and then I turn back. The light *had* been on earlier, and we hadn't at any point turned it off. Certainly Bruno hadn't had time to turn it off when we heard Zoe's screams, and he'd left directly from the library to take Zoe to the hospital. Someone else must be in the apartment.

Twenty years ago, Bruno had always kept a spare key under a flowerpot by his door—a practice that even I, a suburban Long Islander, had found overly trusting. Apparently he's still as trusting. I find the key there and let myself in. I come up the stairs as quietly as I can, but I needn't be so careful. The sound of my approach is easily disguised by the sound of running water in the kitchen. Even when I stand in the kitchen door Orlando doesn't hear me, he's so engrossed in scrubbing the silver vial with steaming hot water and a toothbrush. The scene—lit only by moonlight—reminds me eerily of Lady Macbeth trying to clean the blood off her hands.

"Wouldn't it have been better to leave it?" I say, startling him so badly he splashes water in a wide soapy arc when he wheels around to face me. "I mean, everyone will know it must have had something with nuts in it and that you had handled it. What were you planning to do with it after you cleaned it?"

Orlando stares at me with such wild, haunted eyes—the same un-bridled look I'd seen on his face when he rushed from the party after Robin's death—that I almost feel sorry for him Then he looks down at the vial in his red, puckered hands and bursts into tears.

"You're right," he says, hurling the vial against the wall. "I have no idea what I'm doing. I'm no good at this at all. Go to the police. Tell them that I poisoned Zoe Demarchis."

"With what?" I ask.

"With some amaretto," he says with a little laugh. "She was always making such a big deal over not drinking it. She made it quite easy."

"And why?"

"Because she was ruining my chance at inheriting my share of the villa," he says. "Because she took Robin away from me . . . because . . . Oh, what does it really matter? You've caught me." He holds his hands up over his head in a gesture I'm sure he learned from watching Ameri-can TV—which is what tips me off to the fact that it's all an act.

"Not because she knew you pushed Robin off the balcony?" I ask.

The mask slips from his face and he looks genuinely shocked. "Pushed Robin? But I loved Robin—"

"And he left you for Zoe, which must have made you very angry, and he'd stolen the poems you were both going to turn into a screen-play."

"No, you have it all wrong. I'll confess to poisoning Zoe Demarchis. What more do you want?"

"For you to tell the truth. It wasn't you who put the amaretto in the vial—it was your mother, wasn't it? That's why you've washed it, so no one would find her fingerprints. And it was your mother who pushed Mara down the steps last night."

Orlando shakes his head. With his dark curls and his eyes gleaming in the moonlight, he looks suddenly very young, like that boy who had hidden in the lemontree pot, afraid of incurring his grandmother's wrath. "No," he says, "you have it all wrong. You Americans always think you know everything, but you don't understand *anything*. You accuse my mother of these crimes so that you can get my father to yourself, but do you really think he'll stay with you when he knows what you've accused me of?"

He must see that he's hit a nerve, because he smiles. "That's why you haven't told him what you think already, isn't it?" He shakes his head. "And to think Robin admired you so much! You're just as willing as the rest of them to shield his murderer to get what you want. Go ahead, then"—he wipes his damp hands on the rough brown cloth of his friar's robe and then, noticing that he's still in costume, peels the heavy robe over his head. He's wearing jeans and a tight, damp T-shirt underneath—"tell everyone what you think happened on that balcony in New York. See how far it gets you."

He leaves then, stomping loudly down the steps and slamming the door. When I try to follow him, I trip over his discarded friar's robe and come down hard on the tile floor. The shock of the impact brings tears to my eyes, the minor physical pain unleashing the dawning sorrow that things can't last between me and Bruno. I angrily bundle the robe into a ball to toss it out of my way, but instead of relieving my pain I find another. Something sharp inside the fabric sinks deep into my palm. A safety pin to hold the robe closed, I think, withdrawing the pin from my hand, but then I notice that something's attached to the pin. I hold it up into a shaft of moonlight and see a brass button threaded onto the pin. When I turn it around, two eyes stare out at me beneath a crown of coiled snakes.

For a moment, sitting on the tile floor in the moonlight, I feel as frozen as if I had looked into a real Medusa's eyes. But that's only because I recognize where I've seen this button before—on Robin's vintage Versace jacket, which he wore like a good luck charm nearly every day after he returned from Florence last winter. I can picture him in it, the collar turned up against the early spring evening chill as we walked across Washington Square Park, the sun glinting off the brass Medusa head buttons as we stood outside the Graham townhouse and he asked me to come to his rescue at the film show. I'm nearly positive that all the buttons were there. Only someone who had grappled with him in the last minutes of his life would have this button. And only someone who loved Robin would have kept such an incriminating piece of evidence. It makes me almost want to spare Orlando, but then I remember Saul Weiss.

I attach the safety pin back onto the robe and bundle it up, holding it close to my body because I still feel cold. As I'm getting up, I notice something glinting in the moonlight: the silver vial. I slip it into my pocket and then I leave Bruno's apartment for what I'm pretty sure will be the last time.

Back at the villa, I stop at Daisy Wallace's room to see whether she's heard anything from the hospital. Yes, she tells me, Zoe was expected to make a full recovery. Luckily she'd taken a big dose of Benadryl just before the performance, so the allergic reaction was lessened. She should be able to come back to La Civetta tonight. "She begged to come back because she said she hates hospitals. Professor Mainbocher and Professor Brunelli are going to ride back in a taxi with her, but I don't think she should stay in the dorm. I was just going to ask Claudia Brunelli if she could get a room ready for her—"

"You know, that's not necessary," I say quickly. "I've got that extra room attached to mine. Why don't we put Zoe in there? That way if she needs anything in the night I'll be able to hear her."

"Well, if you're sure you don't mind . . ."

"Not at all. I'll go make sure it's ready, but I think the bed's all made up."

Before I go to the little convent room, though, I stop in mine and deposit Orlando's robe into the *cassone* and lock it. Then I go into the other room and turn down the bedcovers and lock the window. When I go down to the *ingresso* to see whether Bruno and Zoe have returned yet, I run into Daisy, Frieda Mainbocher, and Zoe on the steps coming up. "Professor Brunelli stayed in town because he had something he had to do at his wife's apartment," Frieda explains when I ask where Bruno is. "So I brought Zoe back in the cab. Oh, and what an adventure we had! The driver went the wrong way and drove us up and down the hills. We saw some beautiful old convents in the moonlight, didn't we, Zoe?"

"Yes," Zoe answers with what looks like genuine interest despite the exhaustion in her face. "Professor Mainbocher's going to take me to see one in a few days when I'm feeling better. After working with the nuns' chronicles in the archives, I'd like to see where the nuns actually lived."

"There's a beautiful cloister just outside the city . . ." Frieda and Zoe happily chat about convents all the way up the stairs and down the hall to Zoe's new room, Daisy joining in to say she's always been fascinated with convents, too. By the time we get Zoe settled in the little room ("Why, it looks just like a convent room," Zoe chirps, "and look at the view!") the three women have made plans for a dozen excursions to convents, monasteries, and abbeys in Florence and the surrounding Tuscan countryside.

"I had no idea you were so interested in convents," I say to Zoe after Frieda and Daisy have left and I'm making sure that the door to the hall is locked.

"Well, it's not like I want to be a nun." Zoe says, giggling. It's good to see her laugh and to see color back in her cheeks. "But, you know, our dorm used to be a convent and I'd like to see what one looks like that's still got nuns in it—like the one where the nuns who lived here moved to. There was a field trip there last year. I missed it because I was sick, but Robin came back from it all excited, and then he read me one of Ginevra's poems, which was so beautiful and sad—"

"So he *did* show you the poems?" I say, sitting down on the side of her bed. I've tried to say it as gently as possible so she won't think I'm accusing her, but she still colors deeply.

"I didn't mean to lie to President Abrams, honest. When Robin read me the poem I thought it was one he made up. He'd printed it up on the Web site he made for the film—"

"Web site?"

"Yeah, I don't know if it's still up. He'd gotten some computer major to design it and paid for a few months' maintenance. He thought it would generate interest in the film. Do you have a computer?"

I go into my room and retrieve my laptop and hand it to Zoe. I watch over her shoulder as she types in GinevradeLaura.com. The screen turns deep lilac—the color of the evening skies the last two nights—and then a rosebud unfurls on the screen. To the strains of Elizabethan lute music the rosebud opens, blooms, and fades, and then, one by one, the petals fall off the stem.

"You click on one of the petals and . . . ta-da!"

The screen fades and resolves into a schematic rendition of an ornately furnished Renaissance bedroom. "It's my room," I say, amazed at the detail of the drawing. There's the *cassone* and the wall paintings and the tapestry. The only difference between this rendition and the room next door is that the carpet's been removed in the virtual room. Instead the floor is covered by the *pietre dure* rose pattern.

"It's not finished," Zoe says, clicking on the bed and tapestry and getting a window that reads "Site Under Construction." "His idea was to have a poem connected to each object in the room and then if you clicked on the window you'd go outside and find poems in the gardens. Only Robin ran out of money. Here, I think there's a poem in one of these petals on the floor."

Zoe drags the cursor over the rose petals on the floor until it turns into a hand, and then she clicks. The room fades and a page opens that's the color and texture of old parchment. The poem is written in flowing script, which I follow as a voice—Robin's, I realize with a pang—reads aloud.

> Be not dismayed at winter's icy breath,
> At jagged winds that tear and whirl fresh snow,
> Revealing rock as chill and still as death,
> Since balm of rose awaits thee soon below.
> The very wind whose frigid hands thou feelst,
> Those daggered enemies of flesh and bone,
> Transforms to sweetness, hands that soothe and healst,
> When thou descends into the southern sun.
> Here other hands await, mine dewed with love
> As roses are asplash in April's rays,

Their petals plucked by breezes on the move
From icy Alps to open-windowed days.
Our bed awaits thee, strewn with wisps of rose,
My longing more than any the wind knows.

"Those last two lines are inscribed on the fountain in the garden, so it really is by Ginevra de Laura, but where did he find them?"

"Honestly, I don't know. Not in the archives—I told President Abrams that—because I had the key and he was only in there when I was in there, but I do have an idea."

"Yes?"

Zoe blushes again and tilts her chin toward the door to my room. "In there. We sneaked in there a few times—only I didn't like those creepy pictures, so I refused to go there anymore. Robin kept going there, though, and I think he'd gone there with Orlando, so maybe that's where—" Zoe interrupts herself by yawning and I feel instantly guilty that I've kept her up.

"You need to get some rest now," I say, taking my laptop and closing it on Robin's clever Web site. "I'll leave my door open. Don't be afraid to call me if you wake up and need anything."

"S'okay," Zoe slurs, her eyes already closed. "I feel safe here," she says, and then her mouth falls slack and her breathing deepens.

I turn off her light and close the door partially so that the light from my room won't disturb her. I plan to keep my lights on for a while so that I can thoroughly search the room.

First, though, I reopen Robin's Web site and search the virtual room, making a note of every place that's been marked to hold a poem. I end up with a list that includes almost every object in the room: the *cassone,* the bed, each of the wall paintings, the tapestry, the window, the dressing table (although in the picture the place taken up by Lucy Graham's art deco table is filled with a Renaissance curio cabinet— itself decorated with *pietre dure* panels, each one of which hides a window where Robin planned to include a poem), and many of the scattered petals on the floor. When I've completed my search of the virtual room, I start looking through the real one.

I start with the *cassone,* removing Orlando's robe and feeling along the bottom, sides, and top, wincing at the feel of Ginevra's nail marks and the sight of the dark stains on the bottom while I search for a secret compartment. But there doesn't seem to be anyplace to hide anything. After I've put back the robe and closed the *cassone,* I roll back the carpet and creep over the bare floor on my hands and knees (my knees still tender from my fall in Bruno's apartment), feeling for loose stones in the floor pattern. I even crawl under the bed, stifling the feeling I have of being entombed while I'm under there. Then I search the walls, starting on the right side of the bed and going over every inch of painted wall, looking for a hidden compartment. When I get to the tapestry of the two courtly lovers, I lift it and stare at the disgusting picture underneath, forcing myself to inspect it closely for cracks or openings. I find nothing. None of the furniture in the room except for the *cassone* dates from the Renaissance, but still I search the bed frame and the bottoms of the chairs and go through the bureau drawers. In the dressing table I find a drawer filled with letters, but they all date from the 1940s and '50s and comprise the correspondence of Lucy Wallace Graham. I flip through this depressing compendium of the life of a bored socialite: invitations to teas and dinners, responses from garden societies in England concerning Lucy's attempt to get a rose named after herself, and Lucy's own letters to Cyril at boarding school, which she must have collected back from her son. There's nothing in any of these even remotely about love or poetry. The only person I can imagine being interested in them is Daisy Wallace, and so I put them all in an Hermès shopping bag and write her name on it to give to her tomorrow. By the time I've searched the entire room, the sky outside is getting light and I suddenly realize how exhausted I am.

Before going to bed, though, I check on Zoe one more time (I've peeked into her room several times over the night), unable to banish the idea that she's in danger. In the pearl light of dawn she looks very young and innocent—not so different from the young novices who once lived in the convents she's suddenly so interested in visiting, although I doubt any of them ever had Zoe's exact shade of hair. Nor do I imagine that Zoe's fascination with convents would last more than a couple of nights in a real one (although the idea of locking her away in one, out of harm's way, doesn't seem so bad right now).

I go back to my room and crawl into bed, my head a jumble of impressions from the day: the tall gloomy cypresses of the English Cemetery, the red roofs around Santa Croce, Ginevra trapped inside the *cassone* at the foot of my bed, Zoe's pale face when I thought she was dead . . . and running through all of these images are flashes of the moments I spent with Bruno on the couch in his apartment, each of those brief moments seeming to swell over the other events of the day. Each time I remember a touch, a sigh, a glance, I feel him near me.

Just before I fall asleep, though, I recall what Zoe said about missing the field trip to Santa Catalina last year. Robin had come back from the trip "all excited," and soon after that he had read one of Ginevra's poems to Zoe. I'd been more interested in Zoe's inadvertent confession to seeing the poems then, but now I think about that trip to the convent. Had he found the poems there? Is that why no one's found them here—because they're at the convent in the Valdarno? I remember taking a field trip there myself twenty years ago. It was a long trip, but doable in one day and worth the journey. I remember the convent as pretty and peaceful. I close my eyes, imagining an old stone building by a river in the undulating hills of the Valdarno, and for the first time in three nights I fall into a dreamless sleep.

CHAPTER
TWENTY-SIX

I WAKE UP EARLY THE NEXT MORNING FEELING ODDLY ALERT AND CERTAIN OF what I should do, as if a veil that had been hanging over my eyes had finally been torn away—or maybe it's just that my jet lag has finally vanished. When I check in on Zoe, I see that she's still sleeping, but her breathing is regular and more color has returned to her face. I consider waking her to ask whether she'd like to come to the Valdarno with me, but then I realize that it would be too draining a trip for her after what she'd been through last night. Still, I don't feel easy leaving her alone. When I've finished dressing in hiking shorts and a T-shirt, I take the robe from the *cassone* and bundle it into the Hermès shopping bag. Then I go down the hall to the west wing.

Daisy Wallace, wrapped as tight as a mummy in a pale blue cashmere robe, opens her door gingerly as if afraid to let in drafts. "Is anything wrong?" she asks, gripping a fold of her robe to her throat. "Is Zoe okay?"

"She's fine," I say, "but I have to go away today, and I think some-one should keep an eye on her."

"I don't understand," Daisy says. "Why would anyone want to hurt Zoe Demarchis?"

I look anxiously down the hall to indicate that I'm worried about being overheard—I know that Mark's room is in this wing—but Daisy doesn't take my hint and invite me into her room. She does lower her voice to a whisper, though. "Does this have anything to do with what happened on the balcony in New York?"

"I think so," I say, relieved that she's anticipated my fears. "I'm afraid that Zoe maybe saw something." I reach into the shopping bag and pull out Orlando's robe, holding up the piece pinned with Robin's button. "I found this"—I'm about to say "in Bruno's apartment" but change my mind—"in the props room. The button pinned to it be-longed to Robin Weiss—I'm sure of it. If you check with the police in New York, I'll bet they'll have in their report that Robin was missing a button from his jacket."

I look up to see whether Daisy's following all this. Her eyes are as round as the button, but she nods when she sees that I'm staring at her. "So, you're saying it was Orlando who pushed Robin?"

"Yes, I'm afraid so—and he must think Zoe saw him do it. There's also this." I hold up the vial that poisoned Zoe. "It was with the robe." True enough, I think; I found the vial close to where Orlando had tossed the robe.

"You mean he also poisoned Zoe Demarchis?"

"Either him or his mother, Claudia," I say, wishing I could at least spare Orlando the onus of one crime, but there's probably no point—Orlando will try to protect his mother anyway. "So, you see," I tell Daisy, "you have to make sure that neither Orlando nor Claudia gets anywhere near Zoe today."

"But where are you going?"

"I have an idea how Robin found the poems, but I can't go without knowing that you'll make sure she's safe."

"Don't worry," Daisy says, "I won't let her out of my sight—but you can't expect me to keep quiet. I have to take this to the police and I'll have to say you gave it to me.'

I nod, unable to think of an argument against this course of action. It is the best way of keeping Zoe safe, but it also means that Bruno will know that I've accused his son and wife of murder. That I didn't have the guts to do it in person will only make it worse. I don't expect that he'll want to have anything more to do with me by the time I get back here tonight.

It takes two buses to reach the train station near Santa Maria Novella, where I switch to another bus that takes me south into the Valdarno, the valley from whence both the Arno and the Tiber spring, following the river past Incisa Valdarno, where Petrarch was born, and San Giovanni Valdarno, where Masaccio was born and where, in the basilica, is a fresco I remember from a school field trip of a local miracle—a grandmother able to give milk to her starving grandchild. From San Giovanni I take another bus west through the forested mountains of Pratomagno and get off at the little village of Santa Catalina Valdarno, the closest town to the convent. Since it's a three-mile walk to the convent and it's already noon, I buy cheese, bread, olives, and a bottle of mineral water—stuffing them all into the deep pockets of my hiking shorts— before setting out.

The day is warm and my legs are still sore from hiking up the hill to the villa yesterday, but it feels good to be in the countryside. For the first time since I've arrived in Italy I feel peaceful and I wonder whether Ginevra de Laura felt this when she left La Civetta and came to this valley.

In less than an hour I see the convent below me—a collection of low gray-stone (*pietre serena,* I remember that kind of stone is called) buildings with red-tile roofs sheltered in a curve of the river. The buildings are surrounded by olive groves and a grassy pasture sloping up from the river where sheep graze. The convent still produces its own wool for the tapestries it makes, I remember as I walk down through the grove. I pass several nuns in gray habits picking black olives from the trees and dropping them into rough hemp bags that hang around their necks. I notice that each nun has a wooden spindle tucked into the rope belt tied around her waist. I say hello, but they only smile and nod at me. I wonder whether they've taken vows of silence. After the loquacious and literary Sister Clarissa, I'd been expecting a nun conversant with the history of the convent. Now I hope I at least get one who talks.

On the front door of the convent is a sign in Italian that says that the convent is open for visitors from one thirty to four. It's ten after one now, so I walk to an olive tree on a bank above the river and sit beneath it to eat my lunch. The warm trunk feels good against my back and the silvery green light is so peaceful, I soon feel my eyes closing. I think about Ginevra de Laura spending her last years here. It had always sounded like a sentence to me, a harsh exile to cold convent life, but there's nothing cold here. The sound of the river is hypnotic and I find myself drifting into a light sleep. When I wake up, someone is blocking the sun.

"Did you want to see the tapestry works?" the woman asks in an Australian accent. "We're only open for visitors for another half hour."

I look at my watch and see I've slept more than two hours. I should feel achy and miserable from sleeping on the ground, but instead I feel oddly refreshed.

"Yes," I say, "that's what I came for. Thank you for waking me. I had no idea I was asleep for so long."

"You must have needed it," the nun says soothingly. It's what my mother always said when I slept late or fell asleep during the day. It was the one indulgence she allowed me, refusing to wake me up for school if I overslept. It made me cross when I was a teenager, but I feel grateful now for having my afternoon nap sanctioned.

"Yes, I guess I did," I say. "It was just what I needed."

The Australian nun (Sister Kate, she tells me) leads me inside the convent. She shows me the shearing rooms and the great vats where the wool is washed and dyed. "We spin by hand, so the sisters usually spin in their own rooms," she tells me. "And then the wool is woven into tapestries in here." She takes me into a long, cavernous room where a dozen nuns sit at looms. Light comes through wide arched windows glazed with old mottled glass, turning the colored wool on the looms into gleaming streams. The colors of the wool threads remind me of the clear colors of the stones at the Opificio delle Pietre Dure. Ginevra would have been at home here, weaving patterns out of the radiant colors instead of chipping away at hard stone. Between the arched windows hang tapestries produced by the convent—copies, Sister Kate tells me, of designs originally made in the fourteenth century. It's a series of scenes involving a pair of lovers. I recognize two of the designs from the Villa La Civetta: the boy snaring a bird and the young man offering a rose to his lover.

"I think the originals of these two are hanging in the Villa La Civetta," I tell Sister Kate.

"Yes, the convent used to be on the grounds of the villa and the nuns produced many tapestries for the Barbagianni family. After the convent was moved here, the Barbagiannis still sent the tapestries here to be repaired."

"Really? Are there records of the repairs?"

Sister Kate smiles. "Yes. Most of the books were removed to La Civetta after the flood in 1966, but the reverend mother kept the convent record books. Was there anything you were particularly interested in?"

"There was a woman who came here in the late sixteenth century," I say. I notice that I avoid calling Ginevra a nun. "Her name was Ginevra de Laura."

"Of course, the poet. Would you like to see her cell?"

I don't answer right away. I find that although I've traveled all this way to find out what I can about Ginevra, I'm reluctant to look at the confined space where she lived out her final years. Sister Kate, though, doesn't wait for my answer. "Come," she says, "it's on the way to the records room."

She takes me down a long hallway that is, although narrow, amply lit by high clerestory windows along one side. "No one lives in it anymore because of the frescoes," she says. "The reverend mother says they should be available for everybody to see and enjoy." She opens a door at the end of the hall and stands aside to let me enter first. I step into the room expecting a narrow claustrophobic cell, but instead it's as if I've stepped into a garden in the middle of summer.

Every inch of wall space is covered with delicately painted flowers like the millefiori design on a tapestry. At first I think that the flowers are painted onto marble, but when I look more closely I see that the background has only been painted to resemble marble and that each flower, each petal and stem, also has the texture and markings of stone. Ginevra painted the walls of her convent cell to resemble the *pietre dure* she had grown up carving in her father's workshop.

There's no bed in the room, only two chairs in the middle of the floor, one of which Sister Kate sits down in, motioning for me to take the other. "I like to come sit here when I need to find peace," she says as I sit down in the other chair. "It makes me feel as if I'm inside a waterfall."

I look up at the walls and see what she means. The flowers seem to be cascading down from the ceiling, floating toward the floor, as though borne on a current of water. In among the whole flowers are hundreds of rose petals, drifting free. It's hard to define why, but the overall impression is immensely peaceful.

We sit quietly in the room for perhaps a quarter of an hour, and then Sister Kate gets up and, without a word, walks out the door. I follow her to the end of the hallway and then up a flight of stairs. Only when we've come to a paneled room filled with mostly empty shelves does she talk again. "The reverend mother moved the library upstairs after the flood in 1966 and had these shelves built. We're still waiting for the collection to be restored."

"I think it's unconscionable that the collection is still at La Civetta," I say, "but if the villa becomes the property of Hudson College, I'm sure they'll return the books to you."

"That would be wonderful. All we have are some old record books—mostly to do with the weaving and repair of tapestries. They were in the weaving room when the river flooded and so escaped the deluge. They're important, I'm sure, but rather dry reading. I'm afraid there won't be anything here about Ginevra. The work on the tapestries was anonymous." She deftly thumbs through a dozen books and re-trieves one that she opens for me. It's a record of repairs to tapestries in the first decades of the seventeenth century. "But I've always thought that this nun, the one with the beautiful handwriting, might be Ginevra."

I look down at the entries and nearly gasp. The handwriting in the record book is identical to the handwriting of the poems I've found. "I think you're right," I say, surprised to hear that my voice is trembling. I'd like to ask to borrow the record book, but I can't possibly expect the convent to trust anyone from La Civetta with their books again. As if reading my mind, Sister Kate offers to make a photocopy of the page. "We have a brand new Canon copier in the office," she says proudly.

I start to laugh at the incongruity of such a modern convenience in this medieval setting, but my eye is caught by an entry at the bottom of the page I'm holding. I lift it closer to make out the faded ink and the antiquated Italian. It's dated June 5, 1613.

"A new backing of crimson silk sewn for the Barbagianni family," it reads, "for a tapestry of a courtier handing his lady a rose, to be hung in the *camera nuziale* for Fideo Barbagianni's new bride. May the sins of the father not be visited upon the son."

"Oh, yes," Sister Kate says when she sees what entry I'm reading, "I've noticed that one. It's an odd little editorial comment, isn't it?"

I nod, unable to speak.

"You know what I think?" Sister Kate asks, a conspiratorial glint lighting up her eyes. "I think Fideo was her son. She was sewing the decorations for her own son's wedding chamber. I imagine she sewed all her love for him into that tapestry."

"Yes, I think you may be right," I say, handing the record book into Sister Kate's capable hands. I don't add that I think Ginevra may have sewn something else into that tapestry.

All the way back on the long bus ride into Florence, I think about the tapestry Ginevra repaired for Fideo's wedding in 1613. She hadn't seen the boy since she had been banished from the villa when his father died, tossed aside like a piece of outdated furniture. This in itself didn't surprise me. Even if she had been Barbagianni's lawful wife instead of his mistress, she would have had to leave. Widows reverted to the property of their father's households when their husbands died, leaving their children behind in *their* fathers' households. Ginevra's father was dead by 1613. The only other option for a widow was the convent.

So even if Fideo *were* her son, her fate would have been the same. And yet I can't help but think that it changes everything. That it makes her banishment from La Civetta that much crueler and the fact that she repaired the tapestry for his wedding night that much more poignant. Could he have been her son? He was eleven when Barbagianni died in 1593. His mother, whom Barbagianni married shortly after Ginevra disappeared from Florence in 1581, supposedly died during childbirth in February of 1582. According to the version of the story I had heard, Ginevra de Laura became Barbagianni's mistress soon after. Although it would have been common for a man of Barbagianni's wealth and position to have a mistress, it was considered unseemly to install one in his deceased wife's place so soon after her death. But what if Cecelia Cecchi's baby had died in childbirth? If Ginevra had conceived a child when Barbagianni raped her in May of 1581, then she would have had a child a month before Cecelia Cecchi died in childbirth. Perhaps Pietro de Laura contacted Barbagianni to tell him that his daughter had borne him an illegitimate son—or perhaps Pietro heard somehow that Cecelia Cecchi's child had died.

I imagine a deal being struck between Barbagianni and Pietro de Laura. When Pietro discovered that his daughter was carrying Barbagianni's child, he wrote to Barbagianni offering to drop the suit against him if he would adopt the child and take Ginevra as his mistress. She'd live in luxury and she would be close to her son. What other options did she have? Even if she had fallen in love with a young poet in England, she couldn't have married him, especially if she was carrying another man's child. So she returned to Florence and gave her child to the man who had raped her. Then, eleven years later, when Barbagianni died, she wrote to her English lover and begged him to come see her. She was free, but not for long. She knew she would have to leave La Civetta, leave her only child. Did she think her English lover would come and take her away? Did he come at all?

He must not have, I think, as the bus arrives at the terminal across from the church of Santa Maria Novella. The trip back has flown by, so caught up have I been in trying to piece together these bits of Ginevra's life, like trying to untangle the thousand threads of a tapestry. Still, when I check my watch I see that it's after five o'clock and, looking up at the clouds massing over Santa Maria Novella, I see, too, that the day has turned from clear to overcast without my noticing it. Since the next bus isn't scheduled to leave for twenty minutes—and I'm afraid I might get caught in the rain—I wander into the church, remembering that it had been my favorite when I was here before.

Many people consider its late-Gothic interior the most beautiful in the city. Walking down the central nave, beneath the green-and-white striped vaults, I feel the effect of the church's well-ordered proportions. I remember learning that the pillars become narrower as they lead up to the choir to emphasize the length of the nave. The effect is a sense of balance and harmony that imparts a feeling of peace. Like listening to classical music or reading a sonnet. Chaotic emotion distilled into a rhythmic pattern that feels as if it's been going on forever and will continue into eternity.

As I walk back to the bus stop I can feel the tangled skeins of threads rearranging themselves into the pattern of a tapestry. Ginevra would have recognized at once the tapestry that hung in the *camera nuziale* and known it was for Fideo's marriage. Like Griselda, she was reduced to the place of servant preparing for her own child's wedding, only here there would be no last-minute reprieve, no welcome back into the home she had been forced out of. I don't think she would have wanted to return to La Civetta, but I imagine she would have wanted to make the repaired tapestry a wedding gift to her son. What could she have given but the only experience she had of love—the poems she exchanged with her English lover. So she sewed them into the silk lining on the back of the tapestry, where they would lie between the tapestry and the painting beneath it. A barrier between an ideal of courtly love and its desecration.

The bus lumbers toward the Piazza San Marco, where I have to wait again for the bus that will take me to the villa. I should feel impatient to see whether my guess is right, but I don't. I feel as if I'm carrying the peace of the Convent of Santa Catalina with me, like a round weathered stone in my pocket that I only have to stroke to feel sure and calm. When we pass the Casino di San Marco I imagine Ginevra's youth there, working in her father's workshop, chipping stones into patterns of flowers and fruit for wealthy clients. I think of her commissioning the floor for the *camera nuziale* that would always remind her—and Barbagianni—of his violation of her and the blood she shed. Although she was constrained in the choices she could make, she was able to turn her pain into things of beauty: blood drops transformed into rose petals, her lost love affair into sonnets, the walls of her convent cell into a screen of roses, an old tapestry into a reliquary for her poems.

I only wish that I could make the torn threads of my own life into something half as lovely, but as the bus climbs the hill to the villa and my thoughts turn from Ginevra's story to my own, I can't imagine that anything good will come of what I've done. If Daisy has told my story to the police—and I don't see her procrastinating—Orlando and Claudia will already have been taken into custody and Bruno will know it's my doing. That I've proved that Robin didn't kill himself, as I set out to do, gives me curiously little satisfaction. Instead, the burden of my actions feels as heavy and oppressive as the rain clouds I glimpse over the villa's gate as I get off the bus.

As I make my way down the *viale,* there's still a sliver of sun beneath a layer of blue-green clouds that turns the silver leaves of the olive trees in the groves below golden. A stiff wind stirs the cypresses, turning them into writhing flames. Behind me the little villa, the original Convent of Santa Catalina, is alive with light and noise. I remember that tonight's performance is in the old chapel. Everyone must already be there, gone early to beat the approaching storm. The main villa, on the other hand, looks sadly deserted. When I open the front door I stand in the *ingresso* for a moment, listening. The rotunda appears to be empty, as hollow as the shell it's always reminded me of, but when I start up the stairs I'm arrested by the sound of my own name.

I turn around and see Bruno standing at the entrance to the library. When I arrived here three days ago, Bruno had looked much as I remembered him from twenty years ago, but now he seems to have aged a decade for each of the days I've been here. The fact that it only makes me love him more does nothing to relieve my guilt at what I've done to him. I can't even wish these last three days undone, because I can't, in truth, unwish last night.

"So, you're back from the convent," he says with a ghastly smile. "Find anything interesting? I'd hate to think you came to Italy for nothing—"

"Bruno—"

"—nothing but the purpose of destroying my son."

"It's the last thing I wanted to do," I say, "but I didn't have a choice."

"Didn't you? Did you have to sneak back into my apartment to spy on my son? Did you have to steal his costume? As if his having a button that belonged to his dead lover means he killed him! But you must have known that he'd break down at the sight of it. That cold-blooded lawyer had Orlando hauled out of here before lunchtime. When I asked her where you'd gone, she told me you were off hunting for your precious poems. You didn't even have the decency to stay and watch my son be dragged out of the house by the police." His voice, angrier than I've ever heard it, echoes in the rotunda. If I'd needed any further proof that the house was empty, I'd know it from the fact that no one appears to watch this scene. It's no solace, though, that there are no witnesses. The reproach in Bruno's eyes is worse than a hundred judges pronouncing sentence.

"You're right," I say. "It was cowardly not to be here and cowardly not to tell you myself. I tried—"

"Oh, really? I don't recall you trying so hard last night when you came to my apartment. Did you want to make sure you got in a little vacation fling before I found out that you were turning in my son to the police, or did you just want to make your boyfriend jealous?"

"Bruno, you know it wasn't like that—"

"I don't know anything where you are concerned, Dr. Asher. I don't believe I ever really knew you at all." Having uttered these words as coldly as he can, he starts to turn back into the library.

"Wait—" I cry, and then, when he turns back to me, I try desperately to think of anything to keep him from going, not with those as his last words to me ever. But there's nothing I can say that can make up for what I've done to him, and by the time the echo of my "wait" has faded from the rotunda, he's gone.

I feel as though I barely have the strength to make it to the top of the long, winding staircase. My legs feel as heavy as marble, like they may buckle under me at any moment. I imagine myself sprawled out on the steps, flattened by despair, becoming part of the *pietre dure* pattern in the marble. Somehow, though, I make it to my room. When I open the door, the figures in the paintings all seem to be smirking at me. *Didn't we explain the price of forsaking true love?* I imagine them saying. *You think having to disembowel your beloved over and over again is bad, wait. . . . You're going to feel like your own insides have been scooped out of you for the rest of your life.*

The yellow eyes of the owls on the east wall seem to follow me as I approach the tapestry beside the bed. The certainty I'd felt riding the bus back from the Valdarno has evaporated. What's worse, I think, is if I was right and the poems were there but aren't anymore. I stand frozen in front of the tapestry, staring at the figures on it—the young man holding a rose out, the lady's fingers extended to take it but still inches away. The red flower seems to tremble in the air between them, frozen in the moment, like the moment just before a first kiss. I touch my hand to the weave and notice for the first time that someone has embroidered two intertwined initials around the rose. The stitches are so fine, they're hard to make out, but then I recognize a *G* and a *W.*

There could be many, many people with those initials, I remind my-self as I slide my hand around behind the back of the tapestry, my heart pounding. The silk backing is heavy and so old that it crinkles under my touch. Unless it's the paper underneath that makes it crinkle. I run my hands all along the edges looking for an opening in the stitching, barely restraining the urge to rip the fabric backing off. When I can't find an opening, I lift the whole tapestry off the wall and lay it facedown on the bed.

I turn around for a second because I feel as though someone is watching me, but it's only the leer of Nastagio degli Onesti and the pleading eyes of his fiancée that meet my gaze. I retrieve a nail scissors from my toiletry case and begin carefully pulling out the thread around the edge of the tapestry. When I've loosened six or seven inches, I slide my hand in and my fingers touch paper. Then I make myself undo the entire backing. I'm afraid that if I try pulling the sheets out I might damage one. When I've loosened three sides, though, I realize I can turn the backing over like the cover of a book, and so I do, lifting it from the tapestry gently.

At first I don't see anything but red silk, but then I realize that there are two layers sewn together, stitched into a grid like a quilt. Each square is a pocket that holds a sheet of paper. Some hold two or three.

A rose-scented breeze comes up from the garden that stirs the poems in their silk pockets, and they rustle like butterflies trying to break out of their chrysalises. I take them out, making a stack of them in my hands as if I'm afraid they'll escape if I don't hold on to them, as if the wind in the rose garden were calling to them to take flight. Before they can fly away I pick up the poem on top of the stack and read:

The death of hope afflicts thee, my great love,
For love's a flower, come and gone by fall;
But rose aroma lingers, essence of
Our passion which for me still conquers all.
Thy Will's assaulted by the scythe of time,
And bleeding, thou must cling to memory;

But let my heart secrete its healing balm,
To make thee whole and transport thee to me.
Yes flowers die; sad winter's bare; and spring,
Though lush with color, resurrecteth not,
For scarlet petals that green breezes bring
are new as dawn; their predecessors rot.
But our love's never did, and so I plead,
Do hurry to me at wind's flashing speed.

The use of flowers distilled into perfume as a metaphor for immortality is familiar, of course. It's a sentiment expressed in Shakespeare's sonnet number 5, not printed in England until 1609. Ginevra's poem is dated 1593. She might well have come up with the image herself . . . or perhaps she had read Shakespeare's sonnet in private distribution . . . or her lover—the "Will" mentioned in the poem—borrowed the image from her. But did he heed her poems? Did he cross the mountains or turn back? And if he came, what happened? Were they able to renew their love, to forgive old betrayals—or did they let their last chance at love slip through their fingers as I have done? The answer may be in these poems, but I realize I can't stay here to read them. I'll go across the hall to the archive room and scan them into my laptop. I'll leave the originals for Bruno—a parting gift—and then I'll leave La Civetta—this time forever.

Another breeze comes in through the open window, and the pages flutter in my hands like the wings of a trapped moth beating against a lamp. One page, lighter in weight than the others, escapes. It flutters to the ground, skitters across the floor toward the window, and flattens itself on the shutter. I chase after it, and when I've caught it I see that it's a sheet of airmail stationery—the same kind that Robin used to write his note to me in New York. It's not in Robin's handwriting, though.

"My dearest Benedetta," it reads,

I would like you to have this poem written by a woman who lived here at La Civetta hundreds of years ago. I found her poems not long after I took possession of the villa and read them all—at first with great excitement and then with growing sadness. What a tragic love affair between Ginevra and her English lover! It seemed a bad omen for our own love affair. I decided then to leave the poems where I had found them and tell no one about them—except for you, my beloved Benedetta, who has truly been a blessing to me. Over the years you have refused what little gifts I've tried to give to you, but now I want to give you a gift which I hope and pray you will accept—if not for your sake then for the sake of our son, Bruno.

What is this gift? Read the poem. Ginevra wished to give her lover everything she had—the whole of La Civetta—and that's what I would like to give to you and Bruno. Or at least, your share of it with Cyril, who will benefit, I believe, by sharing his responsibilities with his half brother. If you do not want this gift in your lifetime then I beg you to give this letter to Bruno so that he may know that I loved him and wanted him always to enjoy his birthright and make his home here at La Civetta.
With all my love,
Lionel

This then is the letter that Sir Lionel gave to Benedetta Brunelli with the *limonaia* poem—only she had given it back to Lucy Graham in exchange for her agreement that Bruno always have a home here at La Civetta. That's the only part of Sir Lionel's gift she wanted to keep. But if Claudia knew about the existence of the letter—if Robin found it and showed it to Orlando and Orlando told his mother . . . No wonder Claudia sent Orlando to New York to get back the letter. If only she had known it had never left the villa, Robin and Mara would still be alive.

For a second I have an urge to destroy the letter—because of how much trouble it has already caused—but then I decide that I don't have the right to do that. Bruno deserves to see it—to hear the proof of his father's love. I'll leave it for him with the poems. One more parting gift.

CHAPTER
TWENTY-SEVEN

EFORE I GO TO THE ARCHIVE ROOM TO SCAN THE POEMS, I PACK MY BAGS. I'M afraid that if I don't do it now I'll lose courage and not be able to leave later. I also check train timetables and reserve a seat on a morning train to London on my laptop. Then I e-mail Chihiro and ask whether she could put me up for a few days and tell her what time I'll be arriving at the station in Lancaster.

Then I cross the hall to the archive room. I clear space to work on the table beneath the window, stacking the poems next to the scanner. I leave Sir Lionel's letter to the left of the stack, weighted down with a fleur-de-lis-handled letter opener, because I don't need a copy of the letter. From the window I have a good view of the little villa and the *viale,* so I'll have ample warning when the play is done and the guests start back to the villa. No one will be venturing out too soon, I think, noticing the ominous clouds in the northern sky above the villa gates.

Although it hasn't started to rain yet, it's only a matter of minutes now. I can hear the low rumble of thunder, and judging from the strange green tint in the sky I would guess it will be a quite a downpour. Smart of Mark to move the performance to the chapel and convenient for me. I'm glad to have the villa to myself to scan the poems. It's not a job I can do quickly. Each page is fragile, and it's hard to resist glancing at the poems as I place them on the glass plate and watch them appear on my laptop screen.

When I'm finished, though, I feel like something's missing. I look through the stack of poems, reading just the first lines, and realize what's bothering me. The poem that I read last night on Robin's Web site isn't here. Perhaps it was one of the originals that he brought to New York along with the *limonaia* poem, but, then, where is it now? Did he still have it on him when he fell from the balcony?

The image of what would have then become of that poem appears all too vividly in my mind. I can see the sidewalk outside the auditorium splattered with Robin's blood, white petals drifting across the pavement. I remember how just before the film show I'd seen Robin, alive and happy, crossing the park with Zoe, walking through those white drifts as through a foamy surf. He had stooped to pick up a handful of petals to throw at Zoe, and then Orlando had kneeled on that same spot and slipped some of the petals into his pocket. . . . No. I replay the memory in my head like a reel of film and recall something glinting in the sun. Not petals. He had knelt to pick up a button that had come loose from Robin's jacket when Zoe pulled at it. Then, as if someone had left the film running, I see Orlando approaching Mark.

And then the reel stops. I'd gone into the auditorium, confident that Mark would take care of everything. What had Orlando told Mark? That Robin had stolen the poems? Or that he'd stolen a letter that proved that he, Orlando Brunelli, was the rightful heir to La Civetta?

I slide Lionel's letter to Benedetta out from under the letter opener and read it again. What would Mark have thought of Orlando's claim? Would he have realized that everything he had worked for since he became president of Hudson College would evaporate once this boy proved that La Civetta belonged to him? He'd have wanted to see the letter, but surely he wouldn't have deliberately hurt Robin to get a hold of it . . . But if he'd tried to take it from him on the balcony . . . ?

The terrible thought forms in my head with the same vivid clarity with which Robin's blood on the pavement had appeared to me a moment ago. I try to shake it away—to replace it with the scenario I've so carefully built up of Orlando pushing Robin to his death—but instead I see Mark following Orlando out onto the balcony. The door closes in front of my vision, but in my imagination I open it and see Orlando rush toward Robin on the balcony with Mark close behind him—because he wants to get that letter first. If it had been Mark who tried to get the letter from Robin . . .

A crack of lightning makes me jump, and the letter opener clatters to the floor. I stoop to pick it up and slip it into my pocket. When I stand up I see that a curtain of rain has fallen over the view of the little villa. No one will be venturing out of there too soon.

If Mark believed Robin had the letter on him, he might have grabbed something else from him . . . one of Ginevra's poems maybe. If so, he might still have it in his room. And if I want to look in Mark's room, now would be the time to do it.

I gather the poems and bring them back to my room, placing them in my book bag. The letter from Lionel Graham, though, I put in the pocket of my hiking shorts. Then I make my way down the hall toward Mark's room. I'm not sure what I think I'll find there, but I do have an idea of how to get in. When I was here twenty years ago, I learned that these old locks were easy to pick. Fortunately, Claudia's home improvements haven't extended to changing the locks. The sharp point of the letter opener does the trick in minutes.

Mark's room is surprisingly messy and, even more out of character, he's left the bedside light on. His office and apartment in New York are always scrupulously neat, and he's a stickler for turning off lights. He must be under a tremendous amount of pressure to have left such a mess and to forget about the villa's electric bill. His desk is strewn with papers, which, I see when I go through them all have to do with the lawsuit. I find here the agreement he's drawn up with Claudia in which she relinquishes her claim to La Civetta for three hundred thousand euros. It's a lot, but not as much as she'd get if the lawsuit went her way. Was she willing to settle for so much less than her stake in the villa because it had been Orlando who pushed Robin? Or was Mark paying her to keep Orlando quiet? But Orlando loved Robin. If he saw Mark push him, would any amount of money keep him quiet?

No, I must have it wrong. Mark couldn't have pushed Robin. Still, having gotten Orlando arrested I feel I owe it to him—and to Bruno—to do a thorough search. I open the closet and find Mark's locked briefcase. That's where he would keep anything really important. Fortunately, he once needed me to stop at his apartment to pick up some papers for him and he'd given me the combination.

I revolve the well-oiled brass cogs and flip open the locks. Here, at least, Mark's usual fastidiousness still reigns. The matching Dunhill diary and notepad I gave him for Christmas last year are neatly strapped into the top compartment. There's only one piece of stray paper lying across the bottom. I pick it up and shiver at the leathery touch of parchment that's been crumpled like a discarded glove. It's hard to make out the faint ink on the wrinkled page, so I sit down on the bed under the bedside lamp and read the first line.

Be not dismayed at winter's icy breath.

It's as if an icy breath has brushed across the back of my neck. There could be several explanations for what Mark is doing with one of Ginevra's poems, but I'm suddenly sure there's only one. He took it from Robin before he died, thinking it was the letter from Lionel Graham. He must have been awfully disappointed when he found out he had a four-hundred-year-old poem instead. Mark didn't even like poetry.

Another wave of cold air chills the back of my neck, but this time I recognize its source. The door to the bedroom has opened, letting in a cold draft. I lift my gaze to the window in front of me and see, reflected in it, Mark's familiar broad-shouldered silhouette.

"So you've found at least one of the poems," he says as he approaches me. "Let me guess; you've found the others, too? And Sir Lionel's letter? You must have found that or you would never have broken into my room."

He sits down on the side of the bed next to me and reaches out his hand. I'm afraid he's going to touch me, but instead he reaches into the pocket of my shorts and retrieves the folded letter. I slip my hand into my other pocket and grasp the handle of the letter opener.

"Aha!" he says, proud of himself. But it's me he commends. "I knew you'd find it, Rose. You're a marvelous scholar."

"How did you know about the letter?" I ask.

"Well, I really have you to thank for that, Rose. Don't you remember? You sent Orlando to me outside the theater. He was only too eager to appeal to me as an authority figure to make Robin give him back the letter that proved he was entitled to his share of La Civetta. I told him that I'd have a nice long chat with Robin about that letter—and I would have, but your little friend was really very uncooperative. When I suggested on the balcony that we discuss the situation later, he started shouting that he could not be bought for a pound of flesh. He was sitting on that balcony and he took a piece of paper out of his pocket. So of course I thought it was the letter. I merely took advantage of the opportunity."

"But Orlando must have seen you—"

"Of course he did, but who would have believed his word against mine? He was afraid I'd accuse him of pushing Robin . . . which is exactly what I told Claudia I *would* do if Orlando accused me of pushing Robin. She convinced Orlando to be quiet and tried to bribe me to settle the lawsuit out of court. She thought I had the letter because Orlando had seen me take the paper from Robin."

The thunder cracks again, so loudly this time that I jump and the lights flicker for an instant. Looking out the window, Mark smiles. "Good thing I made them switch the performance to the chapel, eh? I don't think anyone will be making their way back here too soon in *this*."

The menace in his voice makes my skin prickle, but when I stand up he doesn't try to stop me. "Well, now you have it," I say. "No more lawsuit. I suppose that even if Orlando accuses you of pushing Robin, no one will believe him."

"Of course not," Mark says, standing, too. "He's been telling that story all day, but thanks to the evidence you provided, no one's inclined to believe him, especially since he didn't come forward sooner."

"And you got Gene to keep your secret by threatening his job?" I ask as I take a step toward the door. Instead of trying to stop me, Mark takes my elbow and steers me in that direction, falling into step beside me. In the hallway he turns me toward the rotunda. "But Leo. Why didn't Leo say anything . . . ?"

"Leo just wanted to go ahead with his film, and for that he needed my permission to use the villa and the poems," Mark says. "They're in your bedroom, yes? I'm sure he'll be happy to see them. Shall we get them together?"

Is that why he hasn't tried to hurt me yet? Unlike the rest of the people we've just mentioned, he must know that there's nothing he can offer to keep me quiet. But how will he do it? He's taken advantage of every opportunity so far or arranged for someone else to look like the guilty party.

"You told Claudia that Mara was going to break her side of the deal, didn't you? So *she* pushed Mara down the stairs. But what about Zoe—what possible harm could poor Zoe do?"

"She saw the letter from Sir Lionel," Mark says, pausing at the top of the stairs. "She doesn't understand its significance yet, but I'm afraid that if she ever talks to Bruno, he'll know what she's talking about. Luckily, with her allergies . . ."

The oculus above us flares hot white. I look up and see a web spreading across the black-green sky—like veins in a giant eye—and I can taste metal at the back of my throat. I feel Mark's grip tighten on my elbow, and suddenly I'm looking down the steep marble stairs, the splotches of red marble gleaming in the metallic glow of the next light-ning flash. I pull the letter opener from my pocket and drive it into

Mark's thigh. His scream is even louder than the thunder. *Please, God,* I think as I run down the hall, *let someone hear that.*

The hall is pitch black, but a faint light is coming through the open door to my room. I run in there and lock the door—remembering only at that moment that Mark has the key.

I hear a bloodcurdling yowl, which I guess is him pulling the letter opener out of his leg, and I run onto the balcony. The terrace below looks far away. If only this were a play there'd be a convenient trellis or vine to climb down, but it's not a play and the fall looks like it would at least twist my ankle—and then how quickly could I get away? He'd have me in the deserted, rain-soaked garden, close to the crumbling— and now slippery—steps that Mara broke her neck on. No—I don't want to go this way, but I do want him to *think* I went this way.

I slip the hem of my T-shirt over the railing and pull until it tears away, making sure the fabric snags on the metal. Then I go back into my room, glancing back to see the piece of white cotton waving in the wind like a white flag. I hear a key slip into the lock.

When the next thunder rumbles overhead, I open the lid of the *cassone* and climb inside, closing the lid quickly so that the thunder will cover the creak of its hinges. Then I lie in the darkness and wait. I try to listen for Mark's footsteps, but the wood is too thick for me to hear anything that's outside of the narrow casket (it looked so much bigger from outside!). Even the thunder is a low rumble from in here. I suppose these wedding chests were made solid and sturdy to protect the bride's valuable clothing from dampness and vermin, the joints smoothly planed and fitted together so snugly that no air will get in. What was I thinking when I climbed in here? Mark won't have to throw me down a flight of stairs—he'll only have to wait until I suffocate to death. Perhaps even now he's figured out where I am and is sitting on top of the chest to make sure I can't escape.

The thought that the lid—only inches from my face—is pinned down is so excruciating that it's all I can do to keep myself from testing it. I run my fingers lightly over the inside of the lid and feel the crescent indentations of Ginevra's fingernails embedded in the wood. What had she said in her deposition? *I was there so long, screaming and trying to claw my way out, that I thought it would be my coffin.* How long, I wonder? How long before she would have run out of air? Or gone insane—another option that occurs to me. That's one of Juliet's fears when she drinks Friar Lawrence's potion—that waking up in her ancestors' tomb she'll "madly play with my forefathers' joints." At least there are no bones here in this coffin . . . only . . .

My hand roving over the lid has lit on something stuck in one of the crescents. It comes loose and falls on my face, and I have to bite my lip to keep from screaming. I pick it off my face and feel its ragged contours—a centuries-old fingernail, relic of my rediscovered poet.

I am half ready to take my chances with Mark when I hear a loud creak—like wood on old hinges. It sounds so much like what the *cassone* would sound like being opened up that I put my hand over my face to protect myself from the attack I think is coming, but when the lid remains closed I come up with another theory. It's the shutter to the balcony. Mark's gone out and found the scrap of my shirt on the railing. Will he believe I've gone into the garden?

Something bumps into the *cassone* and then I hear another creak—this time I'm sure it must be the bedroom door. He's gone downstairs—no need for him to risk the jump from the balcony—and from there he'll go out into the garden to find me. Now all I have to do is get out of this damn box and run toward the *limonaia*. Bruno will be there; he wouldn't have gone to the performance with Orlando in jail.

The thought of Bruno—so close—gives me the strength to open the lid of the *cassone* and pull myself out, gasping in the warm muggy air as though it were an Alpine elixir. Before leaving the room I take the Maglite from my night table and then steal out into the blackness of the hall. I don't turn the light on, though, because I'm afraid that it will draw Mark's attention if he's still in the villa, but I grip it in my hand, ready to strike. I could go through the archive room and down the spiral stairs, but I don't want to risk those twanging steps. So I start down the hall toward the rotunda, following—I can't help but think—the path Ginevra took fleeing from the scene of her rape.

When I come into the rotunda it is empty and dark. No light shines through the oculus. I feel my way along the landing banister, toward the stairs, making myself go slow enough not to trip. I've reached the first step—I can feel the edge of it with my bare toes—when something hard rams into my back. I keep from going over the stairs only by gripping the banister. I can hear the flashlight fall to the marble floor below and crack when it lands. Then I feel my neck wrench as Mark hauls me to my feet by the roots of my hair. He bends me over the banister on the landing and I can feel the cold marble pressing into the small of my back. I feel the hand he has in my hair snake onto my shoulder, shoving me back, while his other hand slides down my leg, behind my thigh, and starts to lift me up—

Another crack of lightning splits the blackness, lighting up Mark's face. He looks—surprised. I feel his hand on my thigh lose its grip, but the one on my shoulder clutches at my flesh as he falls heavily onto me. His weight is pushing us both backward. Beneath us yawns the empty space of the rotunda—not the abysses of the Alps or even the ten stories Robin fell, but enough of a fall to break both our necks. Then something pulls us both back from the edge. Mark slides onto the floor, clutching his shoulder, and at that moment the lights come on.

Cyril is standing above Mark with a small silver pistol in his hand, his face pursed in disapproval—but whether it's because Mark had been about to kill me or because Mark's blood is dripping down the marble steps, I'm not sure. He shakes his head as if he were thinking of how hard it will be to scrub the bloodstain off the marble. I can't think of anything better to say than, "Why aren't you at the play?" to which he answers, "Oh, my dear, when you get to my age you really have had enough of tragic endings."

CHAPTER TWENTY-EIGHT

I THINK YOU'D BETTER GO CALL THE POLICE," CYRIL SAYS TO ME, "AND AN ambulance."

"It's just a flesh wound," Mark says, drawing his lips back in pain. "You could dress it yourself . . . No need to call the po- lice . . . I won't press charges . . ."

Cyril starts to laugh. "Do you hear that, Rose? He won't press charges. I don't suppose you feel the same."

"Certainly not. He was trying to kill me—and he did kill Robin."

"You can't prove that," Mark says. His breath is getting ragged. He really could bleed to death, and though a moment ago he was about to kill me, I find myself not wanting him to die—not out of any sympathy for him but because I want to watch him confess his misdeeds. I would like, ultimately, for Saul Weiss to see him convicted in a court of law for Robin's murder.

"There were other witnesses," I say. "Gene Silverman and Leo Balthasar. I think when they realize how far you went to protect your secret they'll testify against you."

"Yes," Cyril says, "you have no power over them any longer. I certainly won't be leaving my villa to your college with you as president, nor will I allow Balthasar to film on the premises if he persists in backing you up—"

"It won't be *your* villa much longer once the Brunellis get a hold of this." He reaches into his pocket with his good hand and gingerly retrieves the folded letter.

"You'd better take it from him, Rose," Cyril says. "I don't like to let him get too close to the gun."

I take the letter from Mark, but instead of handing it to Cyril I read it aloud. I don't intend to let anyone take it from me again. Cyril is silent after I finish reading it. Mark starts to say something, but Cyril waves the gun at him to be silent. When he finally speaks I'm surprised to hear that his voice—perfectly controlled after shooting Mark—is quivering. "What an old romantic fool—" Cyril begins.

"Let me go and we can destroy the letter. It will only be her word—"

"Which is worth a million times more than any you've ever uttered," Cyril says sharply. "Do you honestly think I'd stoop to such base tactics to avoid sharing my home with my half brother—a brother who's never asked a thing of me? Or that I would condone the murder of an innocent young boy for the sake of property? No, Mr. Abrams, I don't believe you would have ever made a proper steward for La Civetta."

"And you think Claudia Brunelli will make a better one?"

"I don't believe Claudia will have anything more to say about the matter."

"She murdered Mara," I say, "and poisoned Zoe."

"Yes, yes," Cyril says, clucking his tongue, "all terrible things and all for nothing. She and her son have no claim on La Civetta at all. They never have."

"But the letter—" I say.

"Only proves that Bruno has a claim," Cyril says. "As for Orlando, well, the thing is, he's not Bruno's son."

Before I have a chance to say anything, I notice that Mark's eyes are fluttering and he slumps to the floor. "You'd better go call that ambulance," Cyril says. "I'd hate to have his death on my hands."

The arrival of the ambulance, blaring all the way up the *viale,* alerts the audience of *Romeo and Juliet* to the drama going on in the main villa. They flock down the muddy road, the actors still in their costumes, just in time to see Mark loaded into the ambulance. I find Frieda Mainbocher and tell her to get the students back to the dorm, and then I ask Daisy Wallace to bring Gene Silverman and Leo Balthasar into the library. It takes me a few more minutes to get back there myself because Zoe Demarchis corners me and I feel she's owed an explanation of what's happened.

When I tell her that Mark pushed Robin off the balcony she starts to cry. "I should never have believed he killed himself," she says. "I should have known President Abrams was lying."

"You couldn't help that," I say. "Mark took advantage of all our weaknesses. Orlando was too afraid that he'd be accused of killing Robin to come forward with what he saw, and Claudia was only too willing to trade her son's silence for money. He used Leo Balthasar's greed and Gene Silverman's desperation to break into film to buy their silence. Mara was willing to do whatever Gene told her to do if it meant a more comfortable lifestyle. He knew I'd feel guilty if I believed Robin killed himself and he thought I'd be too paralyzed by that guilt to do anything . . . and he would have been right if I hadn't gotten that note from Robin and started to think that Orlando killed him. And once Mark realized I thought that Orlando killed Robin, he thought I'd be too afraid of losing Bruno to tell the truth. He was almost right about that, too. Your only crime was believing what a responsible adult told you to believe. We're all more culpable than you."

She nods, but she doesn't look as if she's ready to forgive herself. I imagine it will take a while. She leaves with Ned and a few others, but I still put off going into the library. In all the crowd there's only one person missing—Bruno. Surely he would have heard the commotion from the *limonaia*—but then Daisy pops her head out of the library and waves me to come in.

Cyril is sitting in his favorite club chair; Leo and Gene are crammed together on the little love seat looking like boys called into the principal's office; and Daisy is standing between them with her blue portfolio balanced on one arm, ticking off points on a hastily scribbled list, pausing only to speak into the phone headset attached to her right ear. In the ten minutes I've lingered in the rotunda she's cowed Leo and Gene into testifying against Mark and formed a plan to minimize damage to the college.

"Rose," she says to me, "the police will want to speak to you first. I've asked them to interview you in the dining room, but they may want you to walk them through the house to show them where Mark attacked you and where he was shot. I will accompany Mr. Balthasar and Mr. Silverman to the police headquarters, where they will be giving their statements, and Mr. Graham . . ."

"Call me Cyril, darling; we are, after all, cousins."

"Cyril will be talking to the police in here." By the time the police have arrived, Daisy has marshaled us into our separate rooms. "Just tell them exactly what happened," she says. "Don't be afraid; you did nothing wrong." Then she closes the door.

Despite Daisy Wallace's unexpected reassurance, I can't help feeling nervous waiting for the police. The formality of the room doesn't help. I look up at the fat cupids on the ceiling and miss the monkeys from the New York version of this room, and I miss having Chihiro by my side. How long ago that last meeting at the Graham townhouse seems! And the night of the film show seems like it happened in another lifetime.

I close my eyes and see an image of Robin Weiss standing at the end of the lemon walk, the same image I'd seen in my mind when Mark asked us to observe a moment of silence for Robin, but then I had imagined Robin looking away and despairing that he'd lost a part of himself—the best part of himself—at La Civetta. I'd let myself believe Mark when he told me that Robin killed himself, but now the Robin in my head turns to face me. He's smiling into the camera, the Tuscan hills behind him, the future in front of him. I open my eyes. When Mark lied, when he told me that Robin killed himself, he'd been protecting himself, but he could have said that it was an accident. There was no reason to claim that Robin had killed himself except that he knew how much it would hurt me and how much I would blame myself. How well he had understood me, I think, beginning to cry for the first time tonight. Even when I started to suspect that Orlando had killed Robin—even when I decided to come here to find out the truth of Robin's death—a part of me had been afraid that I was only trying to avoid the guilt of letting Robin down. Mark knew that and used it. He counted on my guilt to keep me quiet.

I hear voices at the door and steel myself to face the police. I look down at the *pietre dure* pattern on the floor and remind myself that if Ginevra de Laura could face Barbagianni in court and tell her story, so can I.

By the time I have finished with the police, it's after four a.m. They had wanted me to show them Mark's room, where I had found the letter, and then where I'd hidden after I ran from him. The worst moment was when one of the officers had lifted the lid of the *cassone* and noticed the nail marks in the lid.

"Did you do this?" he asked, and for a moment I couldn't remember whether or not I had. For a moment I wondered how I could have lain in that box and not gone mad and tried to scratch myself free.

Before they left me in my room, I asked whether I had to stay in the country. They told me that before Mark could be extradited to America he'd have to face charges for my assault and for the part he played in the death of Mara Silverman. I would no doubt be called as a witness, but there was no legal reason that I couldn't leave until then. Did I have a contact number where I could be reached? I gave them Chihiro's address and phone number in England, and then, as soon as they left, I gathered the poems together and put them in an envelope, which I stuck into my laptop case. Then I picked up my suitcase and headed downstairs.

The truth was, I'd wanted the police to tell me that I wasn't allowed to leave the country. I'd wanted an excuse to see Bruno before I left, to apologize for ever thinking that Orlando had killed Robin, even though I know there's no point. I remember Bruno's last words to me and the way he looked at me. There's no chance he'll ever forgive me. There's no reason for me to stay.

The lights are off in the rotunda as I make my way down the stairs, but now that the storm has passed, moonlight pours in through the oculus and falls on the marble rose petals that trail down the steps and swirl in a circular pattern on the floor at the bottom. The light does not make them look like blood, though, as in the legend, but rather like scarlet leaves swept by the the last winds of autumn. "That time of year thou mayst in me behold, / When yellow leaves, or none, or few do hang / Upon those boughs which shake against the cold, / Bare ruined choirs where late the sweet birds sang." That's what the rotunda feels like to me now—a bare ruined choir. Staring at the pattern as I come down the stairs, I notice for the first time that the marble petals seem to form letters. I put my suitcase down at the bottom of the stairs and turn to look at the floor from another angle.

"I've always thought it looks like a *G* and a *W,*" a voice says from behind me, "but part of the floor was destroyed when the rotunda was enclosed in the eighteenth century. Do you think those poems you found will tell us the answer?"

I turn to see Cyril seated in his armchair, a glass of cloudy liquid in his hand. The green glass shade of the lamp by his side casts a glaucous glaze over his face and the drink.

I remove a thick envelope from my book bag. "I don't know," I say. "I haven't had a chance to read them. Here"—I hand him the envelope—"would you do me one favor?"

"Anything for you, Rose."

"Would you show them to Bruno and tell him I wanted him to read them first?"

"Are you sure you don't want to wait until morning and tell him that yourself?"

I shake my head. "I think it's better this way. He'll never forgive me for being willing to sacrifice his son . . . even if . . ."

"Even if Orlando isn't his son," Cyril finishes for me.

"That's what you meant the other night about sacrificing a young life for the sake of La Civetta, isn't it? I thought you meant Robin, but you were thinking of what it would do to Orlando when he found out that Bruno wasn't his father. . . . How did you find out? Did you perform a covert DNA test on them while they were sleeping?"

I'm only half kidding, but Cyril chuckles. "Well, not quite, but they both had blood drawn last month for a new insurance policy, and I was able to bribe the doctor. I'd always had my suspicions."

"Does Bruno know?"

"I thought it only fair to tell him, but it turned out he had always known that Orlando couldn't be his son."

"But how?"

Cyril raises an eyebrow and waits for me to put it together.

"You mean, he had no reason to think Orlando was his?"

Cyril nods.

"But then why . . . ?" I sink down onto the love seat and Cyril pours me a glass of the absinthe, which I wave away. The last thing I need is to make the situation any more cloudy.

"That's what I asked him. He told me that the man who'd gotten Claudia pregnant was married to someone else and he wasn't interested in having anything to do with the child. Claudia was still his wife and so he felt he couldn't abandon her—or the child. He begged me not to tell Orlando the truth. He said he'd always regarded him as his son."

"And did you ask him why he let me think Orlando was his child?"

"I didn't have to. Isn't it obvious? He thought it would be easier for you if you hated him. That you'd get over him more quickly. A noble idea, I suppose, but he was wrong, wasn't he?"

I nod my head, unable to speak.

"As wrong as it is for you to leave now, Rose."

I look up at Cyril's face and see that it's suddenly illuminated, as if the truth of what he's saying was lighting up his face, but then I realize it's just the headlights of the cab I've called coming up the *viale*. I stand up and bend down and kiss Cyril's cheek, which is surprisingly soft and, even more surprisingly, damp.

"Ah," Cyril murmurs, " 'I crave the grace thy kisses can bestow / Upon my fallen self's scarred flesh and bone.' "

"That's the poem I found the first night. . . . *You* left it for me . . . but how?"

"Robin sent it to me last year with that ominous little note—as if I didn't know what stains this house bears! He wanted me to know he'd found the poems so that I'd back the movie, but the little imp wouldn't tell me where he'd found them. I spent the winter looking for them and then I thought I'd let you have a go. And see? I was right; you found them. You're meant to stay here, Rose; you're meant to be with Bruno. I'm sure of it."

"You've inherited your father's romanticism, Cyril." I straighten up and the headlights from the cab strafe the room and catch a glitter on his cheek; then as they swerve—the cab coming around the circular drive—and leave his face in shadow, the tear vanishes. "But you're wrong about me and Bruno. Don't you see? He was willing to give me up for Orlando before Orlando was even born. Why would he place me first now?"

I turn away then and hurry into the rotunda. As I bend down to retrieve my bag I hear Cyril answer my question, "Maybe because he's acquired a modicum of sense in the last twenty years." But I walk out through the *ingresso* without letting him know I heard him.

"*Andiamo?*" the cab driver asks when I get into the back of the taxi.

"*Sì,*" I say. "*Andiamo.*"

As soon as I settle into my seat on the train I fall asleep. I only awaken when the Swiss customs officials board the train to check passports. For a moment I think that the Florentine police have changed their minds and decided that I'm not allowed to leave the country after all, but after a cursory look at my passport they let me go.

The sun is coming up as the train starts up again. I notice a sudden ordering of white stones along the roadsides and the absence of laundry hanging from clotheslines as we pass over the Swiss border and feel a pang for the mess and drama of Italy. I know I won't be able to go back to sleep again, so I take out my laptop and begin to read Ginevra's sonnets. By the time I've reached Paris I've read all the poems—sixty-six of them—at least twice. Some I've read three or four times, a few so many times that their words have begun to swirl in my head and the rhythm of the train has acquired the meter of a sonnet. In Paris I switch trains in a fog and fall asleep again as soon as I'm settled in my seat, lulled by the beat of Ginevra's poems as I cross the English Channel.

In London I have to switch stations—from Waterloo to Euston—to catch a train to Lancaster. Crossing the Thames in a taxi I glimpse the enormous Ferris wheel, the London Eye, that strange new addition to the London cityscape. I haven't been in London in a decade—not since I attended a conference on Elizabethan poetics—and it occurs to me now that I might have planned this trip a little better to take advantage of passing through. But then I'm not in the mood for sightseeing, nor do I have the money to pay for a London hotel room now that I don't have that consulting check from Lemon House Films to look forward to. I'm not even sure that I'll want to continue teaching at Hudson in the fall. As the taxi makes its way through the London streets, I ponder my economic straits and find myself curiously unrattled by them. I've lived modestly over the years and, thanks to Aunt Roz's rent-controlled apartment, managed to put away a fair amount of savings. The cabin in Woodstock is paid off. I could sell it if I needed to—or I could sublet the MacDougal Street apartment and live in Woodstock until I got another job. I could take time to finish my book on the sonnet—or I could take the year to write a book about Ginevra de Laura. The story that is emerging in her poems has seized me in a way that I would have thought impossible when I left La Civetta this morning. Perhaps it's because her own ruined love affair is even sadder than mine. It may be meager comfort, but by the time I've reached Euston Station I no longer feel like the only person in the world whose heart has been broken. Still, I don't want to spend an hour sitting in the station watching young lovers saying tearful good-byes or springing into each other's arms in gleeful reunion. I decide to roll my suitcase over to the British Library instead.

The new library was built since my last trip to England, but I know that the things I'm looking for, which were at the British Museum the last time I was in London, are in the John Ritblat Gallery now. I look at the Blackfriars mortgage deed with Shakespeare's signature, at the Booke of Sir Thomas Moore, which many scholars think is written in Shakespeare's handwriting, and at the portrait of Shakespeare by Martin Droeshout on the title page of the First Folio. I find myself looking at the portrait as if sizing him up as Ginevra's English lover, but then shake myself. There's been nothing in the poems that proves Ginevra's English lover was William Shakespeare. I check my watch and see that I should start walking back to the station, but before I go my attention is drawn to the 1609 edition of Shakespeare's sonnets. It's opened to sonnet number 116.

> *Let me not to the marriage of true minds*
> *Admit impediments. Love is not love*
> *Which alters when it alteration finds*
> *Or bends with the remover to remove.*
> *O, no, it is an ever-fixed mark*
> *That looks on tempests and is never shaken:*
> *It is the star to every wand'ring bark,*
> *Whose worth's unknown, although his height be taken.*
> *Love's not Time's fool, though rosy lips and cheeks*
> *Within his bending sickle's compass come;*
> *Love alters not with his brief hours and weeks,*

But bears it out even to the edge of doom.
If this be error, and upon me proved,
I never writ, nor no man ever loved.

Turning away from the display case and making my way through the crowded lobby of the library, I find, to my embarrassment, that I'm crying. I cry all the way back to Euston Station, through the rain that has begun to fall—a sudden, violent shower that recalls the tempests that aren't supposed to shake true lovers. It's ridiculous, I tell myself when I've boarded the train to Lancaster. No lover ever lived up to the ideal that Shakespeare proposes. *Of course* love changes when the object of that love changes. I can't expect Bruno to still love me after he realized that I'd turned his own son in to the police. Just as he didn't expect me to keep loving him when I believed that he'd been sleeping with Claudia. If I had clung the longest to love even after I believed myself betrayed, that didn't mean I'd been the truer lover. It just meant that nothing had come along to replace that first love.

Ginevra had no better luck. I reread the poems again and at last I see her story clearly. She'd written the *limonaia* poems—and all the others urging her lover to come to Italy—not only to gain her lover back but also to make herself believe that their love was so strong that it could weather betrayal and the lapse of time. But she had been wrong. There'd been no reconciliation, no last-minute reprieve. In the end she'd gone alone to the Convent of Santa Catalina to live out the rest of her life.

By the time I arrive in Lancaster I feel like I've not only traveled halfway across and off the Continent but also across four centuries. And yet, as I catch sight of Chihiro on the platform—attired in a sort of neo-hiking–cum–Mary Poppins get-up of neoprene climbing tights tucked into green thigh-high Wellies under a Harris tweed capelet— I feel that while I've come to the end of the story of my love affair, I haven't come to the end of the story of Ginevra de Laura and her English lover. I suspect, actually, that I've come to where their story began.

CHAPTER
TWENTY-NINE

I T RAINS EACH MORNING MY FIRST WEEK IN THE LAKE DISTRICT, WHICH SUITS my mood just fine. I leave my light Italian silks packed in my suitcase and purchase waterproof hiking boots and a waxed Barbour rain jacket. I consider buying a cheaper jacket but then hear, as clearly as if she were standing next to me, Mara telling me that the classic Barbour is really an *investment*. Each morning I print out a few of Ginevra's poems and toss them into my book bag along with water, a chunk of cheddar cheese, and a package of McVitie's Hob Nobs. (Chihiro's pantry, which in New York held little else but ramen noodles, is here stacked with such British delicacies as PG Tips tea, McVitie's digestive biscuits, Cadbury chocolate, and Marmite.)

I spend each morning and afternoon hiking through a light but drenching drizzle, climbing toward mist-enshrouded views. I don't really care how far I can see when I get to the top of another peak, though; I care only that the walk has some goal—a crest or lake view, a ruined tower, a literary marker where Wordsworth stopped and wrote a poem—because otherwise I wouldn't know when to stop. When I reach my goal, I eat my spare lunch and read a few poems. Sometimes I read them aloud, a practice that would be considered eccentric any other place on the planet but here in the Lake District, where declaiming metered verse is fairly common behavior. The only thing that distinguishes me from my fellow Barbour-clad tourists is that I'm not reciting Wordsworth or Coleridge; I'm reading the lines of an unknown Italian poetess who lived four hundred years ago.

In the evenings Chihiro comes back from her research at the library at Dove Cottage and we share a dinner of shepherd's pie and Guinness drafts at the local pub. It takes five or six nights just to catch her up on the events of my short stay at La Civetta and then another night to read and dissect a long e-mail from Daisy Wallace.

"She says that when Saul Weiss heard that Mark is being charged with Robin's murder he decided to come to Italy to attend Mark's trial in Florence."

"Really? Why not just wait until he's extradited to America?"

"Daisy says he 'wants to keep an eye on President Abrams and remind the Italian court that he's awaiting more serious charges in the States . . .' I imagine he needs to feel like he's doing something. Cyril's given him a room at the villa for the summer and Daisy says that Frieda Mainbocher has taken him under her wing."

Chihiro nearly spills her Guiness. "God help the poor man—he could be smothered!"

I laugh, but then I shake my head. "You know, actually, I can see them getting along. Apparently they're going through the villa's accounting books together—"

"Asher, are you 'shipping' Frieda and Saul?"

I take a sip of my ale to hide my smile. "Well . . . they both do have an interest in double-entry bookkeeping . . ."

Chihiro squints her eyes as if examining an image of the accountant and the social historian together and then nods her head up and down. "Okay . . . yeah . . . maybe. . . . Now what about Claudia? Has she been brought up on charges yet?"

"Daisy says that Claudia is being charged with the Italian equivalent of manslaughter for Mara's death," I tell Chihiro. "She claims that Mara thought Orlando was trying to seduce Ned and when Claudia laughed at her she became hysterical and attacked her. She said she slipped down the stairs in the struggle."

"Hm," Chihiro says, blowing at the foam on her Guinness, "do we believe that? Mara *was* high strung . . ."

"It could have happened that way," I admit. "Daisy says that either way Claudia's bound to end up in jail for years. When Mark's extradited she'll face charges as an accessory after the fact for Robin's murder because she didn't come forward with what Orlando told her. Gene Silverman and Leo Balthasar will also be charged as accessories."

"And Orlando, too?"

"Yes, but Daisy's hopeful that he'll get a lenient sentence. While Gene and Balthasar stayed quiet for reasons of personal profit, Orlando was afraid he'd be accused of murder. He claims he didn't know his mother was trying to bribe Mark to settle the lawsuit—only that she begged him to stay quiet so he wouldn't be accused of murder himself. Combined with his youth, Daisy thinks he shouldn't have to serve any time at all."

"So there's no reason for Bruno to be angry with you anymore, right? Certainly he can't blame you for mistakenly thinking Orlando was Robin's murderer when so many people were conspiring to make it look like that—and if you hadn't stopped Mark, he'd be facing murder charges."

I shrug and take a long sip of the sour warm beer.

"Have you heard from him?"

"No," I say. "And I don't expect to. I accused his son of murder. I don't think he's going to forgive me for that." I finish my lager and put the mug down on the table harder than I meant to, upsetting Chihiro's full mug and spilling some of the creamy white foam on top. I take my time coming back from the bar with paper napkins to clean up the mess, but Chihiro still isn't willing to let the subject drop. "Have you heard anything else about Bruno?"

I tell her that Frieda Mainbocher e-mailed to say that Bruno had given a small informal lecture on the poems of Ginevra de Laura. "Zoe IM'd me to say it was the most romantic love story she'd ever heard. 'Better than the Brownings!'"

"See?" Chihiro says. "He wouldn't even have the poems if not for you! Maybe he's changed his mind about you after reading their story."

I shake my head. "You don't know the story," I say.

"That's because you haven't let me see the poems yet. You must have figured out the story by now."

She's right; I've read the poems so many times that I know most of them by heart. "I'll tell you what," I say. "I'll tell you their story tomorrow night. Then you can judge whether it's the kind of story that's likely to renew your faith in love or not."

"Fair," Chihiro says. "But I've got a bottle of Laphroaig that says your story won't change my mind about you and Bruno."

"Okay," I tell her, "as long as we open the bottle *while* I tell the story?"

So the next night we settle down in front of the electric heater with the single malt scotch and Ginevra's poems, which I've divided into three stacks. "The first group of poems starts in June 1581, when she and her father left Italy and came to England."

"Which is the same time Shakespeare disappears from Stratford for two years," Chihiro points out.

"Right, Shakespeare would have been seventeen—just three years older than Ginevra. Stephen Greenblatt and E.A.J. Honigmann believe that Shakespeare came north to work as a tutor in the household of Alexander Hoghton—"

"Because of Hoghton's will, right?" Chihiro asks, topping off my glass of scotch. It occurs to me that if Chihiro probes each detail of the story this thoroughly, we'll both be unconscious by the time I reach the end of it.

"Yes," I say, checking my notes, "Alexander Hoghton's will, dated

August third, 1581, requests that Sir Thomas Hesketh 'be friendly unto Fulk Gyllome and William Shakeshafte now dwelling with me and either to take them unto his service or else to help them to some good master, as my trust is he will.' "

"And both Hoghton and Hesketh lived in Lancashire—not so far from here. Is there anything in Ginevra's poems that indicate where in England she went or where her English lover came from?"

"I haven't found any location clues yet—at least none that I've recognized—but it does seem likely that her lover was a tutor or teacher of some sort. She writes in a sonnet called 'The English Lesson' that 'I cater to vocabulary's Will; / When studying with thee I will not rush, / And gladly linger over final points, / That dazzle like the brightest, nearest stars.' "

"Vocabulary's *Will*? Do you think it's a pun on the name Will?"

"Possibly. Shakespeare certainly punned on his own name often enough, and she does it in another poem—'Thy Will's assaulted by the scythe of time,' for instance, and in the last poem she wrote before leaving England, 'This child might be the Will of crime and sin.' "

"*That* was her parting note?"

"Well, yeah, she tells her lover that she's pregnant with another man's child and her father demands that she go back to Italy and live as her rapist's mistress and 'pledge my unborn child / To custody of that unhuman man.' "

"Wow, that's some Dear John letter! You know, if she were really Shakespeare's Dark Lady, that send-off alone would explain why he was so harsh to her in the sonnets."

"I've thought about that," I say. "Shakespeare falls in love with this beautiful young Italian girl—he's only seventeen himself, so she'd probably be his first love—whom he thinks is innocent, and then he finds out she was pregnant with another man's child all along." I pause to take a sip of the Laphroaig, thinking, not for the first time, of the parallels to my own story. How devastated I'd been to learn not just that Bruno had been unfaithful to me, but that he was going to have a child with someone else. "And then she deserts him to become that man's mistress."

"Ouch," Chihiro says. "You know, Shakespeare wrote twenty-eight Dark Lady sonnets. Some critics think the number was deliberately chosen to represent his disgust with women's menstrual cycles."

"Well, there's no doubt that Ginevra's lover was angry with her. All the poems Ginevra wrote in 1593"—I point to the second stack of poems—"refer to this great betrayal in their past. She begs him to forgive her and come to Italy. I guess she hoped he would be more liberal in the warmer, more relaxed atmosphere of La Civetta. You can't really blame her," I say, shivering and helping myself to another glass of the scotch. Although the climate in the Lake District suits my mood, I can't help pining for the warmth I've left behind, especially at night with the wind rattling the windowpanes in Chihiro's cottage when I remember the lilac skies from my balcony at La Civetta.

"The saddest poem in this period is the one in which she tells him that her sacrifice has been twofold. She not only sacrificed him for her child, but she was also forced to sacrifice her role as mother. Her child was given to Barbagianni to replace the stillborn child of his lawful wife. She was allowed to stay in the house as Barbagianni's mistress, but was never acknowledged as the child's real mother. Then when Barbagianni died she had to leave the house that now belonged to Lorenzo Barbagianni's brother and her own son. She pleaded with the poet to come to see her one last time before she consigned herself to the convent."

"And he did?"

"According to her poems—yes. The last three poems written in 1592 recount his brief stay. One begins with the announcement of his arrival—'How wonderful, to once again embrace, / and sample the sweet treasure of your lips.' The next celebrates the renewal of their love. Everything sounds hunky-dory, but then there's this one. Listen:

> *I understand thy angry, scathing flight*
> *Behind an oaken screen engraved in rose,*
> *Just like a player's changing out of sight,*
> *Between the scenes, as any actor knows*
> *To do; and thy hath done, so many times.*
> *Yet now it is no play, but warring hearts*

That we perform, and I record in rhymes;
If only mercy softened anger's art!
Let thee be moved to one more role, the kind,
Forgiving lover whose sweetness defies
Betrayal, shame, the wounds of words designed
To scathe and scorch; all bitter, venomed lies.
Let our love's petals shimmer, scent the breeze
that blows so softly through our memories."

"It doesn't sound like things went so well," Chihiro concedes. "What do you think she told him? I mean, he knew already that she left England pregnant with Barbagianni's child. What else was there to reveal?"

"I think she told him that Fideo was his son," I say.

Chihiro's eyes widen, but then she nods eagerly, "Yeah—how did that other line go: 'The child must be the *Will* of crime and sin.' "

"Exactly. And years later, in the poems she wrote in the convent, she writes to Fideo:

These words of loving kindness I bestowst
On thee are thy mother's and not her ghost's,
As well come from a man whose eloquence
Takes pride in you, despite your ignorance
Of an unhappy birth's true circumstance."

"But if Ginevra wrote the poems, why do the words come from someone else?"

"Because her English lover taught her to love poetry and to write it. In a poem called 'The Sonnet Lover,' she writes, 'Since thou became my sonnet lover I / Have danced with iambs, kissed pentameter.' It was the language of their love affair, and when the affair was over it was all she had left of him. So when she writes her sonnets she feels as if her words are his words, too—after all, she chose to continue writing in English even when she was no longer sending the poems to him."

"So it's the English lover who will be proud of Fideo even though—"

"He was originally ignorant of Fideo's birth's true circumstance, namely, that Fideo was his son. I've checked the dates and it makes sense. Ginevra was raped by Barbagianni on May first, 1581; she had left Florence by June first; and she wrote her first poem to her English lover on June seventeenth, 1581. Cecelia Cecchi died in childbirth in February of 1582 and Ginevra leaves England that same month. I think that when Pietro de Laura heard that Barbagianni's wife had died in childbirth and lost the child, he wrote and told Barbagianni that Ginevra had given birth to a son. I think Ginevra was pregnant, but that she hadn't had the baby yet, because it was her English lover's son. The trip back to Italy could take months during the winter when the Alps were impassable. They could have stopped somewhere on the way for her to give birth and then continued on their way. Barbagianni wouldn't have been able to tell if the child was a few months older or younger."

"Wow," Chihiro says, "Pietro had chutzpah. What if the baby was a girl—or died along the way?"

"If it had been a girl I'm afraid it *would* have died along the way. Imagine how frightened Ginevra must have been waiting to give birth."

"And so," Chihiro says. "years later, after Barbagianni is dead, she decided to tell her English lover that Fideo is his son. And when she did—"

"He didn't take it so well that she had stolen his son away. He retreats 'Behind an oaken screen engraved in rose, / Just like a player's changing out of sight.' "

"Jerk," Chihiro says, swilling the last of her scotch. "What other choice did she have?"

"Still, you can't blame him for being angry. She betrayed him. She stole away his son—"

"This is how you think Bruno feels, isn't it? Because Ginevra's lover wouldn't forgive her for stealing his son, you think Bruno will never forgive you for turning in Orlando."

"You have to admit," I say, holding up my now-empty glass, "there's an eerie similarity. I can't believe Bruno hasn't noticed it—"

"Which doesn't mean he'd feel obliged to act like Ginevra's lover did. Maybe he'll realize by reading the poems that it was foolish of Sonnet Guy to refuse to forgive Ginevra, and that it's just as foolish for him not to forgive you."

"Well, then, I'd have heard from him, right? So," I say, getting up to go to bed and weaving a bit as I start up the stairs, "do I owe you a bottle of Laphroaig?"

When there's no answer, I stop halfway up the stairs. Truthfully, this isn't a bet I want to win. Although I've given up on Bruno, I'd hate to think that Chihiro, who's always right, has. But when I turn around I see that the only reason she hasn't answered is that she's succumbed to the Laphroaig and fallen dead asleep.

The next morning I sleep late, and when I get up Chihiro's already gone. In the kitchen I find Ginevra's poems stacked under the empty bottle of Laphroaig. They're not in the same order as I left them last night and I wonder whether Chihiro woke up later and reread them. I notice that the poem she's left on top is the "Screen" poem. She's underlined the lines "I understand thy angry, scathing flight / Behind an oaken screen engraved in rose" and penciled a note to me in the margin. "Asher, see page 38 Honigmann."

My copy of *Shakespeare: The 'Lost Years'* by E.A.J. Honigmann is lying on the table next to a package of Hob Nobs. I put on the kettle for tea and then turn to page 38 and read, while chewing a dry mouthful of oatcake, the paragraph that Chihiro has underlined.

"The Great Hall will particularly interest students of 'Shakeshafte,' since Sir Thomas Hesketh's 'players' must have performed in it. While not as large as the great Banqueting Hall at Houghton Tower, which is lengthened by its minstrels' gallery, its magnificently carved screen and other woodwork make it a most beautiful and impressive room."

I go on to read that the moveable screen at Rufford Old Hall (Sir

Thomas Hesketh's ancestral estate) is seven feet wide, paneled on each side, and elaborately carved with quatrefoils in circles and "other late Gothic ornaments." Might one of those ornaments be the roses mentioned in Ginevra's poem?

The kettle whistles and I make myself a cup of PG Tips—tea so strong it cuts through the fog of my Laphroaig hangover. Or maybe it's the direction my thoughts are taking that's scoured clean my brain. If I can connect an image from Ginevra's poem to a physical detail in the Lancashire house where Shakespeare is believed to have performed, then I may be on the road to proving that Ginevra de Laura *is* Shakespeare's Dark Lady. I look up from the Honigmann book and out the kitchen window. For a change it's not raining. The sky is a deep Alpine blue, dappled with clouds, as Shakespeare himself would say, *as white as the driven snow.* When I look back down I see that Chihiro has left the keys to her Range Rover and a map of Lancashire. My exhilaration is tempered for a moment by the thought that Chihiro is only trying to distract me from my broken heart.

On the road to Lancashire I admit to myself that I have, all this last week, allowed myself to believe what I scoffed at Chihiro for suggesting last night. How had she put it? That Bruno would realize by reading the poems that it was foolish of "Sonnet Guy" to refuse to forgive Ginevra . . . and that it was just as foolish for him not to forgive me. Ever since I started reading Ginevra's poems on the train, I've been imagining Bruno reading the same poems and putting together the same story that I have been. Some days while I read one of Ginevra's poems perched on a rock above a waterfall or by the side of a gloomy northern lake, I can almost feel Bruno's presence. I would look up from Ginevra's words and for a moment imagine him standing there—his dark hair beaded with the rain, his haunted eyes as gloomy as the deep mountain lakes. And even though I know he'll never appear like that, the thought of him has driven me to keep reading the poems and spinning Ginevra's story—this sense that it's a story we are telling together.

And so I imagine him in the passenger seat of the Range Rover as I drive to Rufford Old Hall—I can hear his voice giving me the directions and admiring the scenery. I imagine him commenting on the Tudor half-timbered façade of the sixteenth-century hall as I pull up in front of it and noticing the hammer-beam roof. He'd know that the gardens we passed walking to the house are late Victorian, not Elizabethan. He might compare the topiary to the clipped hedges at La Civetta. While he paid our admission he'd tell me to look through the brochures on the rack by the entrance and pick out a place for us to have a picnic later. Since I can't be two people, though, I pay my single admission fee to an elderly woman in a gray cardigan who looks like she could easily play Miss Marple, and leave the brochures alone. Then I ask for directions to the Great Hall.

I see the screen as soon as I enter the hall. "Movable" is perhaps a misnomer; it looks as though it weighs several hundred pounds at least, but I can imagine how it would be useful in a performance. As I walk across the hall, the sound of my footsteps on the stone floor echoing in the vaulted space, I seem to hear the echoes of those long-ago theatricals. What kind of plays would a man like Thomas Hesketh have commissioned his players to perform? Farces by Terence and Plautus, perhaps? Did a young Will Shakespeare dart behind this screen to change roles? Did a young Ginevra de Laura, visiting from a nearby house where she and her father were working on a *pietre dure* floor, watch from the audience and await his return? When he turned his face away from her forever, did she remember this screen and imagine that she could call him back onto the stage of her life?

When I reach the screen I see that it is indeed carved with roses. I touch one of the carved roses and remind myself how common an image it is. This doesn't prove anything—and yet I feel sure that Ginevra stood here and watched a young William Shakespeare step behind this screen to assume a new role and that years later when he turned away from her in anger she hoped he might turn back again, his anger transformed into love—just as I continue to foolishly conjure Bruno out of these cold northern mists.

I turn and leave the Great Hall and find my way to the exit. Of course I'll have to do a thorough search on movable screens to find out how often roses appear on them, but I feel sure already that I'm on the right track, that in the end I'll hunt down Ginevra's English lover—her Sonnet Lover—until he turns his face to me and reveals the features of Will Shakespeare. I know, too, that it will be the making of me academically. I won't have to worry about tenure. I won't have to worry about getting a new job. I can see the path ahead of me, and it should make me happy, but instead it just looks like a long and lonely road.

As I'm going out I notice that a stack of the brochures has slid out of its plastic sleeve and fallen facedown to the floor. As I kneel down to pick them up, I hear "Miss Marple" say, "Could you straighten those out for me, love? I've been meaning to since the visitor before you knocked them all over, but I didn't want to leave my station."

Since the hall is deserted, it's hard to imagine why she was afraid of leaving her desk, but when I straighten up and look at her I notice the cane leaning against the old woman's chair and realize she probably can't get to the floor too easily. "I'll put them back," I tell her, turning the stack over. It's then that I see what they're for. I nearly drop them myself, but manage to put all but one away neatly in their slot. Then, clutching the brochure open to the directions page in my shaking hands, I hurry back to the Range Rover.

The house—another sixteenth-century Tudor hall—is only ten kilometers from Rufford Old Hall. I grip the brochure to the steering wheel to follow the directions and nearly drive into a hedgerow, trying to steal glances at the description of the house and gardens. "Built in 1549 . . . attractive landscaped gardens . . . panoramic views over the Mersey Basin toward Wales . . . intriguing period interior with secret priest's hole . . . marble inlaid floor with floral pattern . . ."

When I pull up in front of the timber-framed wattle-and-daub manor house, I have to peel the brochure off the palm of my hand, leaving flakes of text and color photography on my sweaty skin. I notice that there's one other car parked in the lot—a Mini with a rental plate. I sit, staring at the "panoramic view over the Mersey Basin," for several minutes before I can will my legs to move; then I get out of my car and follow the rose-lined path to the front door.

"The hall most likely takes its name from the rose gardens," the brochure, whose text I seem to have absorbed through my pores, says. "Although another local legend claims that the name dates from the installation of the unique marble floor in the Great Hall . . ."

I see a sign with the words "Visitor's Center, Pay Admission Before Entering" pointing to a path that winds around the side of the house and another sign that reads "Great Hall" pointing to a heavy oak door. I go toward the door. It opens directly into a large vaulted hall. I look down and my throat closes with disappointment. The floor is dull gray stone with irregular splotches where water has dripped on it for centuries. "The floor is in need of restoration," the brochure had read, but surely this can't be . . .

Then a swath of light filters through the clouded lead-glass windows at the end of the hall and falls on the stone at my feet. I kneel down to meet the light as it reaches me and touch an inlaid marble petal. I rub the stone until the original pink color emerges from the grime, then I follow the pattern until I reach a rosette at the center of the floor. The pattern is the same as the one in the rotunda of La Civetta, but where there the pattern is cut off by the eighteenth-century restoration, here the pattern is complete. I trace the initials with my hands, following the pale pink marble shapes that turn a darker red as my tears dampen them. When I've traced the final loop of the G where it intersects with the W, I sit back on my heels and see that I'm not alone in the hall. The room begins to spin and I feel myself sway.

"*Cara,*" he says, striding over the scattered marble roses to reach me, "you're not going to faint, are you?"

I start to get up, but first I touch one of the rose petals and silently ask the two poets whose initials are carved in the floor for the right words to say. But when I go to him I find there is no need of words.

ABOUT THE AUTHOR

CARCL GOODMAN is the author of *The Lake of Dead Languages, The Seduction of Water, The Drowning Tree,* and *The Ghost Orchid. The Seduction of Water* won the 2003 Hammett Prize, and her other novels have been nominated for the Dublin/IMPAC Award and the Simon & Schuster Mary Higgins Clark Award. Her fiction has been translated into eight languages. She teaches writing at the New School University in New York City.

ABOUT THE TYPE

This book was set in Garamond, a typeface originally designed by the Parisian type cutter Claude Garamond (1480–1561). This version of Garamond was modeled on a 1592 specimen sheet from the Egenolff-Berner foundry, which was produced from types assumed to have been brought to Frankfurt by the punch cutter Jacques Sabon (d. 1580).

Claude Garamond's distinguished romans and italics first appeared in *Opera Ciceronis* in 1543–44. The Garamond types are clear, open, and elegant.